Harry Perry Robinson

Men Born Equal

A Novel

Harry Perry Robinson

Men Born Equal
A Novel

ISBN/EAN: 9783337032777

Printed in Europe, USA, Canada, Australia, Japan

Cover: Foto ©Andreas Hilbeck / pixelio.de

More available books at **www.hansebooks.com**

MEN BORN EQUAL

A Novel

BY

HARRY PERRY ROBINSON

" When none was for a Party
But all were for the State
And the Rich man helped the Poor
And the Poor man loved the Great"
MACAULAY

NEW YORK
HARPER & BROTHERS PUBLISHERS
1895

IN

GRATITUDE TO, AND REVERENCE FOR

THE MEMORY OF

JAMES H. HOWE

THAN WHOM THIS COUNTRY HAS LOST

NO BETTER CITIZEN, OR NOBLER, GENTLER MAN

CONTENTS

CHAPTER		PAGE
I.	AN AFTERNOON CALL	1
II.	FRIENDS AND ACQUAINTANCES	13
III.	THE HOUSE IN FOURTH STREET	28
IV.	OVER THE DINNER-TABLE	39
V.	BEHIND THE SCENES	55
VI.	TWICE TWO AND ONE OVER	66
VII.	A MAN OF AFFAIRS	81
VIII.	THE APOSTLE AND THE MULTITUDE	91
IX.	LOOKING INTO THE GULF	101
X.	THE POWER OF THE PRESS	117
XI.	AT CROSS-PURPOSES	129
XII.	THE BEGINNING OF THE STRIKE	142
XIII.	MY SISTER'S KEEPER	154
XIV.	AN EVIL GOD	169
XV.	THE GATHERING OF THE STORM	185
XVI.	A TALK AT THE CLUB	198
XVII.	BETWEEN THE CUP AND THE LIP	211
XVIII.	THE FOUNDLING	225
XIX.	A HOME-COMING	238
XX.	ON THE VIADUCT	254
XXI.	IN THE VALLEY OF SHADOW	265
XXII.	THE INQUEST	274
XXIII.	HORACE PUTS HIMSELF ON RECORD	287
XXIV.	THE WHIRLIGIG OF TIME	304
XXV.	A TRIP TO THE CEMETERY	321
XXVI.	MY FRIENDS THE ENEMY	332
XXVII.	UNSTABLE AS WATER	345
XXVIII.	REAPING THE WHIRLWIND	360
XXIX.	ON THE SLEEPING-CAR	368

MEN BORN EQUAL

I

"It is not worthy of you," she said, petulantly. "I am sure that it is not; and you ought to know it!"

She was standing just inside the large bow-window, the lace curtains (not white, but écru) hanging on either side of her. Facing the window, she drummed impatiently on the glass with her fingers as she spoke. The man whom she addressed without looking at him stood some two yards behind her, near the middle of the room, half leaning on the back of a large rug-covered arm-chair.

"I think," he said, quietly, "that there are a good many things in politics that you do not understand."

"Of course there are," she retorted, "a great many things. But there are also a good many that I *know*" (and she rapped the window sharply to emphasize the word) "without having to understand them."

"I can believe that," he laughed; "but what is it in this case that is so poor as to be unworthy of me?"

"What? Why, all of it! The cause (as you call it)—the party—the men whom you associate with—their whole behavior—everything—nothing!" She had turned to face him, and spoke vehemently, throwing out her right hand nervously as she enunciated each successive count in the comprehensive if disjointed indictment.

His quietness of voice and manner was in sharp contrast to

1

her warmth. By the half-amused, half-admiring look on his face it might have been conjectured that instead of continuing the discussion he would have preferred to tell her how charming she looked, as she stood, flushed and alert, framed in the draperies and the sunlight. But what he said was :

"Well, as to the cause, you flatter me, of course, in thinking that I am too good for any cause; but this cause is the cause of the people, and I cannot imagine that that is unworthy of anybody. As to the party and the men—I confess that 'sometimes their conduck isn't all as fancy paints;' but the best and noblest cause accumulates all sorts of followers. We would rather have all the good men; but if the bad ones come too, how can we say them 'nay'? The cause itself in some measure dignifies them. Besides," he added, "the bad man's vote counts, too."

"But why have you *all* the bad men and none of the good?" she broke in. "Why is everybody whom we know against you? There is papa and Judge Jessel and Mr. Carrington and Major Bartop and—"

"Major Bartop," he said, "is a Democrat. I can hardly say that he is with us now, because since the fusion he has taken no active part in politics. He has been very active in the past, however—was in Congress and ran for governor once, and was generally conspicuous as a partisan. Now, it is true, he holds aloof."

"Of course he does! How could he help it? Don't you think that the withdrawal of a man like that, whose traditions are on your side, is an even stronger condemnation than if he had been always opposed to you? Why don't you hold aloof, as you call it, too?"

"The case is different," he said. "Major Bartop has won his spurs. He is twenty years older than I, and his record and his place are assured. I have still to win mine. It would be more fair if you should

> "'. . . with Fortune chide
> The guilty Goddess of my harmful deeds,
> That did not better for my life provide
> Than public means, which public manners breed.'"

"I don't know who your poet is—"

"It is Shakespeare."

"Well, I don't care! It does not sound like him, and you have probably twisted him from his context."

"I confess that it is reasonable to believe that Shakespeare was not alluding to American politics ; but, as Henry James would say, the 'immitigability of our moral predicament' is about the same in all ages, and Shakespeare's dilemma still fits me. He took to deer-stealing and a disreputable life about London playhouses. I have to wallow in politics."

"That is not true," she said, earnestly. "You do not mean what you say, and are doing yourself an injustice. You are not in politics for the sake of making a livelihood. That is the wretched and, at the same time, the absurd part of it. You have taken up the line that you have because you believe it to be your duty. If you were only a dilettante—an idler who was playing at politics to pass the time—then it would not matter. Neither I nor anybody would care. But you are not. You have entered into it with your heart and soul, and you have entered on the wrong side. This is the misery of it!"

Horace Marsh dropped his jesting tone. He moved away from the arm-chair and stood with his hands clasped behind him, and looked, not at his interlocutrix, but over her head and beyond into the sunlight and the blue sky.

"Yes, you are right," he said. "I was not speaking seriously, and I am in politics because I believe it to be my duty. It is not a merely local question—not a question of Major Bartop—of your father—of me, Miss Holt. It is not confined to this city—to this State—to this country. Nor is it of this century only. It is the old, eternal conflict which has torn all communities and all peoples since man had the lust of power and the lust of life." He spoke slowly, pausing once in a while to choose a word, and solemnly, as one conscious of a responsibility resting upon his words. "It was the cause of those who were in bondage in Egypt, and it was the cause of the black man in the South. It is the cause of the voiceless millions all over the world and of every age —or if not voiceless, they might as well be so, for they are

spent with labor and weak with lack of food, and their voices
reach only to ears that are deaf, on which they beat in vain.
They are the millions of the cities and of the farms—the
granger and the yokel, the ryot and the fellah—by whatever
name those may be known who water the furrows with the
sweat of their faces; the starving 'submerged tenth,' the
canaille, the dock-laborer of London and the mechanic out of
work—all they who crowd the alleys and the tenements and
the poor-houses of great cities. Beneath the crust of every
civilization since the world began there has been the same
teeming, reeking misery. Sometimes it bubbles to the surface, in bubbles which burst in dynamite and blood. Sometimes the whole body of it rises in upheaval and shatters the
crust, so that the barricaded streets run red and palaces go
down in flames. Sometimes leaders arise who are able by
the more peaceful process of the ballot to make some fissure
in the crust—an air space, through which breath and sunlight
come for a while to the mass below. But the struggle and
the seething poverty never end. It seems as if now, for a
decade or two past, the terrible forces beneath the surface
have been working towards revolution—not here only, but
in all countries of the world together—as they have never
worked before. It may be that the end is coming—the last
great battle of the North—and that society will reconstitute
itself upon some larger plan which lies even now laid out in
the eye of God. But whether it be the end or only one more
boiling over, to be followed by another subsidence, I think
the change will be mightier and more far-reaching than any
which has been wrought before. I think, too, that, though
the struggle is world-wide, it is here in these United States
that the real battle will be fought and the real victory won.
As we threw off monarchy and stamped out slavery, so, it
seems to me, destiny will have it that here shall be the
scene of the final triumph over wretchedness and want. We
have built the two sides of the arch, and it needs only the
key-stone. . . . I may be dreaming," he went on—" it may be
but young enthusiasm ; but I think not. The thing will come,
and left to itself it will come by brute force. This country
is within a measurable distance of anarchy to-day. In the

last resort of violence the physical superiority is necessarily with the many; and if we leave the lines to be drawn again as they have been drawn always before, though all the brains and refinement and learning of the world are on one side, they will be no match for the muscle which is on the other. In the older countries now the revolution is on the road to working itself out with the bomb and the firebrand and the knife. Surely we, in this country of freedom, can find a better way! We have scorned before the precedents of the ages, and we can once more. It is only lack of such leaders as might win the victory by peaceful means that throws the multitude back on its ultimate and one certain resource of violence. The change will come as surely as justice is enthroned in the mind of the Almighty, and if not led otherwise, it will come by blood. But it *can* be led otherwise, and in the new groupings of parties now in progress in these United States it seems—not alone to me, but to many others —that there has arrived at last the opportunity for which mankind has waited through the centuries. And in proportion to the opportunity is the peril, if the opportunity be neglected."

As he spoke, with the September sunlight on his lifted face, there had been an earnestness and an exaltation in his features which appealed immediately and irresistibly to all that was feminine in his hearer. She, uplifted with him, stood with her eyes fixed on his, her lips parted and face flushed, and her fingers clasped nervously before her. But now his manner changed, and something of the former tone of banter came back to his voice.

"Of course, in such a cause, we cannot pick our fellow-workers. It is difficult to fight the cause of the people without having some considerable part of the people on your side, and some of them are not very refined nor very intellectual. They would be ill at ease, perhaps, in this room—and that is the shame of it. In another generation the people may all be at ease together. The best people, as the world understands it, are seldom on the right side; and least of all in this one eternal controversy. The best people—the counterparts of your father and Judge Jessel and the rest—were not on the side of our Saviour and his apostles."

As he had changed his tone and dropped to his every-day level again, the spell passed away from her, and the last sentence threw her sharply back into her old attitude of antagonism.

"That is not fair," she said, quickly. "An argument from Scripture can never be fair. It does not appeal to reason only, and we cannot meet it as we do an argument based on other authority."

"That is true," he said, smiling, "and I withdraw it. Let us say, instead, that the best people were not on the side of the revolutionists in France."

"And what analogy is there between our attitude to-day—the attitude of papa or myself—towards the working-classes and the attitude of the nobility towards the French peasantry? I suppose you compare me to the Countess of What's-her-name who wondered why the starving poor of Paris were clamoring so foolishly for bread when they could buy such nice *brioches* for a sou. You represent me to your own mind, I presume, as soon to be confronting a red-capped mob armed with pikes and pitchforks, with the house in flames around me."

"Now, Miss Holt, you are more unfair than I. The personal argument is less permissible than the scriptural, especially from a woman, in proportion as the extraneous disabilities which it imposes are worse. But," he added, "I can imagine no one who would confront a mob—or do anything else—more superbly."

She gave the words a half-contemptuous acknowledgment, and was about to speak again when the butler entered and announced "Mrs. Tisserton."

Mrs. Tisserton was exceedingly blonde — a blonde of the "negative type," but to such an extreme that the mere negation of color became positive. Small, regular features, fluffy flaxen hair, and pale blue eyes, combined with a trick which she had of keeping her lips slightly parted as if in perpetual interrogation, gave her a curiously childish face. Without being beautiful, she was a woman who could not but attract attention (especially of men) in whatever company she found herself. The extreme blonde—probably in virtue of a certain suggestion of potential frailty which her appearance conveys to the masculine mind—is ever more stared at in the street or in a car or in any place where people are gathered together than a handsomer brunette. Mrs. Tisserton's appearance did her an injustice. The ordinary woman of the day, with the usual social prejudices and predilections, if thrown into casual contact with Mrs. Tisserton — say, on an ocean steamer — would have looked upon her with suspicion, and have accepted her as an acquaintance only tentatively and with much caution. Yet here in the community where she had dwelt, as girl and matron, for twenty years, no woman was more universally accepted, had lived more completely beyond reproach, or was more sincerely respected by those who knew her best. Mrs. Tisserton had herself come to be thoroughly aware of the equivocal attractiveness of her appearance, and had not infrequently confided to her husband her determination some day to dye her hair and live the rest of her life a brunette and in peace.

" I never meet a new man," she said, " who seems to take any sort of pleasure in my company " (a thing which men, new or old, might very reasonably do) " without being conscious that every woman in the room, except half a dozen who know me too well, is regarding me as a dangerous, designing, and, probably, disreputable person. Nature ought either to have made me as bad as I look or else have made me look as good as I am."

On this occasion as she entered the room and saw the only two occupants (of whom she was probably already aware that at least one had something more than an inclination for the other's company) standing and talking with greater warmth than usually characterizes the casual chat at an afternoon call, she stopped for a moment, as if apologetically, just inside the door. Miss Holt, however, advanced with a certain quick and almost impulsive cordiality which was characteristic of her.

" How do you do, my dear ? I am extremely glad to see you," she said. " We were talking politics, and Mr. Marsh was comparing himself to the apostles, and saying that I ought to be treated like one of the French duchesses and things who were impaled by the mob and carried round in pieces."

"How excessively disagreeable of him," murmured Mrs. Tisserton, as, after shaking hands with the accused, she sank into a comfortable chair. "I am not as sorry that I interrupted you as I thought I was. Why is Mr. Marsh like an apostle?" she asked. She had a curiously deliberate and even way of speaking, with an equal accent on every syllable, which gave strangers the impression that she was affected. "It sounds like a riddle, doesn't it? And I give it up. It cannot be anything in his personal appearance."

"No; it is his zeal," said Miss Holt. "I may be misrepresenting him, but I understood him to say that it was his zeal for the voiceless millions. He is to be a sort of mouth-piece for the misery of the centuries, and he thinks that you and I and all of us frivolous social beings are heartless. Which way do you propose to level, Mr. Marsh—up or down?"

"Neither," said Horace. "There is no talk of levelling. Rich and poor there must always be; but there need not be hatred between them."

"And has he been trying to convert you?" asked Mrs. Tisserton. "To make you a sort of Séverine or Louise Michel? I saw that Louise Michel, in a French paper the other day, said that her profession was that of a promulgator of revolutions. Fancy making a profession of promulgating revolutions, especially a woman!"

"It would be rather hopeless," said Marsh, "to endeavor to make Miss Holt resemble Louise Michel. I went to hear her in London once. She is such a deplorably unattractive person and looks so harmless! The man who was with me said that she reminded him of a 'mother-in-law who had seen better days.'"

"I think that is wicked!" said Mrs. Tisserton. "Why do people make fun of mother-in-laws? They are other people's mothers, and it is awfully bad mannered. Look at Jack's mother—was there ever a dearer old lady?" (Jack, it is needless to say, was Mr. Tisserton.) "But I wish I could remember in time when I am speaking whether they ought to be called mother-in-laws or mothers-in-law."

" I know," said Marsh; " it is like majors-general and aides-de-camp."

"Or those abominable French participles," suggested Miss Holt, " which always ' agree ' with the other thing, and become feminine and plural when you do not expect them to."

" I am so glad that Ada Cambridge had the courage to call her book *The Three Miss Kings*," said Mrs. Tisserton ; " *The Three Misses King* would have been insufferable."

At this point the party became aware that a new caller had arrived at the front door, and Marsh rose to take his leave.

" However," he said, " I did not come to talk politics or grammar, but " (addressing Miss Holt) " only to say that I was extremely sorry that I should not meet you at the theatre on Wednesday. You know that I am sorry ; but it is my first important speech out of my own bailiwick, and I must be on hand."

" I think it is mean," said Miss Holt ; " the Braces are giving a theatre-party, and Mr. Marsh was to dine with us here first. And now the apostle has to address the multitude on that same evening."

" Jack heard you speak the other night somewhere in ' your own bailiwick,' I suppose, and he was very complimentary— for Jack, that is," said Mrs. Tisserton, " for Jack is not effusive. But you really ought to be flattered, because I know he did not agree with you, and Jack is not a bit like an apostle, you know."

Marsh had doubts as to the degree of the compliment conveyed by " Jack's " admiration. Tisserton was not an intellectual critic ; but a speaker who hit his level would probably strike a fair proportion of a mixed audience. Marsh was spared the necessity of expressing his sense of appreciation of Mrs. Tisserton's husband's encomiums, however, by the entrance of a new-comer, whom the butler announced as " Mrs. Flail," and who was already responding to Miss Holt's greeting in a loud and self-assertive voice.

Mrs. Flail was obviously a personage of local importance. Her appearance acknowledged it ; her voice and manner proclaimed it. The widow of a banker who had died some ten

years before, leaving her in more than comfortable circumstances, but childless, she had since then devoted much of her
means and nearly all of her time and energy (which latter
was extraordinary) to the management and support of those
multitudinous feminine organizations which seem necessary
to the social life of any self-respecting community, especially
if that community be located in the Western States of America, in these last days of the nineteenth century. It was she
who had invented Egyptian Lunches—the mysterious functions at which a select circle of erudite ladies assembled
every alternate Tuesday throughout a winter, and one of the
party having first read an essay, by way of grace, on some recent phase of Egyptian discovery, the coterie sat down to
lunch and discussed chicken-salad and cuneiform inscriptions
together, and digested views on *cartouches* while nibbling
salted almonds. They were an immense success.

It was always, as a matter of course, in Mrs. Flail's draw-
ing-rooms that the lion of the day, whether an African ex-
plorer, a Russian princess, or a new pianist, was first exhibited to the élite of the city. The lion's managers counted
upon this private exhibition, in making their dates for the
tour, as an eminently advantageous business detail. They
would no more have permitted the lion to decline Mrs.
Flail's invitation than they would have neglected to advertise
in the local papers. All of which (though Mrs. Flail was
doubtless ignorant of some of it) was evidence of that lady's
importance. The number of "classes" which she had organized in the course of ten years was almost incalculable—
classes in every European language and almost all branches
of history, in china-painting and water-colors, in photogra-
phy and palmistry, in æsthetics according to Delsarte, and
mnemonics according to Loisette, in Buddhism and cookery.
But though she was most conspicuous in organizations of an
intellectual sort, her labors in the cause of charity were
scarcely less exacting. It was with difficulty that she prevented her sewing-circle at times from colliding with the date
for a class on Moorish architecture, and it sometimes taxed
both her ingenuity and the speed of her horses to wedge in
the meeting of the managers of the *crèche* between a class on

Confucianism and a French *conversazione* on the women of the Second Empire.

She rustled into the room now with a nimbleness which was hardly to have been looked for in a person of her ample proportions. She talked rapidly and with an enthusiasm singularly unlike the even flow of Mrs. Tisserton's placid voice. There could hardly, indeed, have been a stronger contrast than was presented by these two women — one blonde and rather frail, almost infantile of face, very gentle of manner, dressed in a perfectly fitting tailor-made costume of dark green, and charmingly gloved and booted—the other florid and largely built, black-browed, and with massive, square-cut features, full of energy and self-assertion, shod in square-toed walking-shoes, wearing a black glove on one hand only and a carelessly put on and apparently home-made black cashmere gown, which hung in superfluous folds about even her ample form. When Mrs. Flail sat down it was cornerwise, and on the very edge of the large chair on which Marsh had formerly been leaning. Sitting, with this good lady, was not a means of rest, but rather the taking up of a strategical position—the *en garde* of a fencer bracing himself for encounter with an antagonist.

" What!" she said, somewhat out of breath, as she saw that Marsh was taking his leave, " am I driving you away? I have been trying to find time for ever so long to get to your office to call on both you and General Harter to wheedle you into subscribing to our new kindergarten. What is a good time to find you?"

" Well," replied the other, smiling, " we are nearly always to be found there, one or other of us, and shall always be delighted to see you, whether we feel able to subscribe or not. The children at the kindergarten do not vote, do they? If you could manage it so that a subscription might justifiably be regarded as a campaign expense, you will probably, in these piping times, find the General easier prey. The exigencies of politics leave him little margin, I fear, for charitable purposes."

" The children's parents vote," said Mrs. Flail. " But I decline to degrade the kindergarten to the level of politics—at

least, until it becomes necessary to interest the school-board
in taking it into the public-school system. However, you will
see me—be sure of that."

Miss Holt walked as far as the door of the room with
Marsh, and stood for a minute holding the portière back
with one hand as she gave him the other. He held it while
they exchanged the last sentences.

"We see you at dinner on Monday, remember," she said,
"if we are to be disappointed later."

"I am not likely to forget it."

She was looking at him very frankly, and, it seemed to
him, something more than kindly, out of her large brown
eyes. But was it anything more than kindness? Was there
anything else there than the universal good-fellowship which
she felt for everybody whom she liked? How often had
he asked himself this same question on parting from her!

II

FRIENDS AND ACQUAINTANCES

As Horace Marsh left what the local papers were pleased to refer to as "the Holt mansion," he stood for a while on the broad steps, buttoning his gloves, and trying to read in retrospect the riddle of the eyes which had been looking so straightly into his.

Of his own love for her, he had no doubt, and had had none for some months past. Thoughts of her were always with him in his sub-consciousness as a background to whatever he might be doing or saying; as Goethe wrote to Charlotte Von Stein, "Among people I name thy name to myself silently." His actions and ambitions he immediately and almost involuntarily referred to the standard of her approval, constituting her the innocent censor of all his thoughts and deeds, and doing nothing without asking first in his heart, "What will she think of it?"

In spite of this, he was allowing himself to follow a political course which was essentially distasteful to her. Conscious of the paradox, he was yet satisfied with the motives which impelled him to go as he did.

In the first place, as he had told her, there were "a good many things which she did not understand" in politics; and in the second place, after she should come to understand them, he believed that she would say that he had done well. Thanks to a certain clean sense of self-respect which was in him and a deep-rooted desire to live rightly, the result partly of inheritance and early training, and partly of the conviction to which his own observation had led him, that honesty of purpose and strength of principle form the only sure foundations of any manner of real success in this life, he had believed it better to hold to the course which conscience pointed out to him, confident in his own ability to make something of his career, and believing that, as she saw him succeeding, he would in the long-run be more sure of her esteem than if he were now at the outset to give up his principles for her sake, and espouse at her bidding a cause which he believed in his heart to be bad.

Women, he knew, loved strength in men. The majority of them love, first, physical strength, and for the sake of it will forgive almost any coarseness or brutality. They will even love brutality, mistaking it for strength. But women like Miss Holt, Horace said, are ultimately to be bound and held only by force of character and principle. No good woman ever yet failed to love a man more when she found that even she herself could not turn him from the course which he knew to be right. To the credit both of himself and of his estimate of Miss Holt, be it said that Marsh had never once seriously considered yielding to her in this. He thought that he would give almost anything in the world to make things otherwise—either that she might see things in the same proportions as he saw them, or that the conditions of society might be so changed that there would be no room for this gulf between them. But he had not entertained the idea of abandoning his course.

As he walked, still pondering, down the steps and along the white-flagged pathway to the sidewalk, he was emphatically a good-looking fellow. Those who came to know his face well said that he was handsome, but " good-looking " was a title which no one would deny him. His was an easily recognizable type, and it is one of the two best types of our young American manhood. About thirty years of age, with good blood in him, cleanly brought up and college-bred, he was now confronting life soberly with a reasonably correct estimate of its requirements and responsibilities. Born in Massachusetts, the son of a clergyman and a scholar, he had gone through Harvard creditably, and, after a post-graduate legal course, spent two years in Europe. On his return to America he had migrated to this Western city to enter the office of an old friend of his father, a lawyer favorably known beyond the limits of the local bar, but who had died a year later. Thrown on his own resources, the young attorney had for a while possessed a modest office and a still more modest practice of his own, until, taking an interest in local politics and so coming into contact with "General" (otherwise known as "Judge" and also as "Governor") Harter, he had been invited by that distinguished and versatile gentleman to fill the place of a partner who had recently moved out of the State. The firm of Harter & Marsh had been in existence now for some two years.

It was a perfect afternoon; one of those exhilarating days of Indian summer, of which nature usually vouchsafes some six weeks or two months throughout the Western States in the autumn. Then, under the pale-blue sky, there is a quality in the thin sunlit air perhaps more delightful than anything to be met with in any part of Europe, and which goes some way to make amends for the malevolence and treachery of the climate for most of the remaining months. It would have been difficult not to feel "glad of the joy of living" on such a day; and, on the whole, Marsh was contented with himself and with the world.

The street along which he was walking citywards was what the real-estate advertisements termed "the most desir-. able residence portion of the city." On this bright day the succession of obviously well-to-do houses, each standing back from the roadway with a well-kept lawn in front, looked attractive enough. The buildings themselves exhibited all the amazing variety of which Western architecture has shown itself capable. A heavy, jail-like establishment of rough-hewn red stone, with narrow windows, stood next to a square-set, comfortable colonial house of yellow brick with white trimmings and broad windows set in the smooth walls, next to which flaunted itself a large wooden villa, with innumerable piazzas, above which rose a riot of shingled gables and obtrusively ornamental chimneys, the whole culminating in an abomination of a cupola (they called it "cupelo" here) capped with a pretentious weather-vane. The entire structure, a mere heaping together and conglomeration of "features" with not so much as a hand's-breadth of unadorned space on which to rest the eye, was painted reddish-brown, save where the pillars of the piazzas were picked out in yellow and white.

As Marsh arrived at this particular house, a carriage with two showy sorrels came down the driveway, driven by a coachman in gaudy livery. Our friend, standing to let the carriage pass in front of him across the sidewalk, was rewarded by being made the recipient of an effusive bow and smile from the pretty but unnecessarily youthful matron who was within—Mrs. Carrington. This was the Carrington residence, and one of the Misses Carrington, as tall as her mother and looking nearly as old, still stood under the *porte cochère* watching the carriage drive away. Marsh smiled in ungrateful cynicism as the showy turnout clattered into the roadway.

At the next corner he was arrested by hearing his name called, and, turning, saw approaching along the cross-street a man, at sight of whom his face brightened.

"Hallo, Charlie!" he called, as the other came within speaking distance; "where have you been hiding yourself?"

"Well," said Charlie, shaking hands cordially, "I've been pretty busy up at the works. They're increasing their electrical plant—putting in a lot of new machinery and things—and have had a hard time about it, too. Some of it has not been the result of accident, either."

"How do you mean?"

"Oh, little things have been going wrong in a way in which things don't usually go wrong of themselves. You know, of course, that there has been talk of trouble for some time, and the men are feeling pretty wicked. There'll be a strike before long, all right."

"Do you mean that the men have been tampering with the machinery?"

"I don't think the climate does it," said Charlie.

It was hazarded that Marsh belonged to "one of the two best types of our young American manhood." If so, then Charlie Harrington was a specimen of the other. He also looked what he was—a mechanic who was also a gentleman. He and Marsh came from the same town in Massachusetts, and had been good friends as boys together till each had started out on the path in life for which he considered himself best equipped. Harrington had taken to mechanics because he loved them—because Nature had seen fit to implant in him, as she sometimes does, an instinctive understanding of mechanical laws, just as she makes other men—men of ability, after their kind—who can be in contact with machinery for years without even coming to understand what it is that makes an engine "go." After distinguishing himself not a little in his course at the Institute of Technology, he had spent two and a half years in the Pennsylvania Railroad shops at Altoona. During those years his spare time was devoted to the study of electricity, and when he left the railroad company's employ it was to enter the service of a large corporation which built and handled electrical plants and supplies. This connection it was which brought him in contact once more with Marsh, when he was sent out by his company, only a few months after his old friend's removal to the West, to superintend the installing of a lighting plant in the large iron and steel works which were the chief industrial establishment of the city. When the task was completed, Mr. Holt (his daughter Jessie we have already met), who was the president of the iron and steel company, and had seen something of Harrington during the work of installation, invited him to stay and take permanent charge of the electrical plant at the works, in addition to acting as consulting engineer to the street railway company of which Mr. Holt was also president and general manager. Harrington had accepted the position, and had remained in it ever since.

The two friends saw less of each other than either wished, but when they met the old footing of boyish familiarity was resumed. Walking together now, they chatted interestedly of each other's affairs. Harrington told of his recent experiments and his present ambitions, and of the labor troubles which were threatening at the steel works. He told also of the progress of his love affair. He had, as Marsh knew, been engaged to be married for some time, and now formally bespoke Marsh's services as best man at the wedding, which was to occur early in the following January.

Drifting back to the labor question, Marsh had asked his friend how the strike, if it came, would affect him.

"That's the worst of it," Harrington replied. "I don't think any of the officers of the company suspect it, and I may be wrong myself, but I have an idea that personal dislike for me has a good deal to do with these present troubles. If there happened to be a man in my place who was what is called a 'friend of labor,' I think they would leave the electrical apparatus alone."

"What have they against you?" asked Marsh, in some surprise.

"I never had much of a labor record," said Harrington. "Of course, in my present position, I could not be expected to belong to an organization; but I didn't when I was with the railroad. Not only that, but I talked on the subject pretty freely at times. If I had been a little older, probably I would not have done it. Those things follow a man; and though I have said nothing much here, the men know how I feel. And then there's another reason."

Marsh waited for him to explain himself, which he presently did.

"This man Wollmer," he said, "who pretty well runs labor matters to suit himself in these parts, boards with Mrs. Masson. He started to make love to Jennie, and not unnaturally blames me because she will have nothing to say to him. If he saw his chance, I guess he 'ld do anything he could to hurt me. That's what makes me have to be pretty careful up at the works. It wouldn't be difficult, for a man who knew how, to fix those wires so that some day when I was going about my business I'd be dead before I knew it. . . . The old lady," he added, after a pause, "would rather Jennie took him than me. She don't like me a little bit."

They walked on in silence for a while, when Harrington suddenly called his friend's attention to a man who was advancing to meet them.

"Do you know him at all?" asked Harrington.

"Marshal Blakely? Oh yes," replied his friend.

"Know him well?" Harrington asked again. Before answering, Marsh waited until the subject of their conversation had passed them, the two men saluting each other with their canes as they met.

" No," he said, " not exactly well. I see him around the club a good deal and—elsewhere."

By " elsewhere " he meant chiefly in Miss Holt's company, but he did not care to be specific.

" Handsome chap, isn't he?" asked Harrington again.

" Infernally handsome!" Marsh responded, with considerable emphasis, and added, under his breath :

> " ' The sort of beauty that's called human
> In hell.' " . . .

" What the novelists call 'distinguished looking,' " volunteered the electrician. " But what kind of a fellow is he?" he pursued. " Is he a man that it is likely to do a girl any good to know?"

Marsh was so startled by the question that he asked, sharply :

" Why? What makes you ask that?"

" He's been hanging around Jennie's sister, Annie, a good deal" (Jennie Masson was his *fiancée*), "and in a sort of underhanded way that I don't like. The old lady does not know it, and I guess he thinks that nobody knows it; but Jennie told me, and I saw them together myself a few evenings ago. I was just leaving the house, about ten o'clock, and passed them as they were saying good-night rather confidentially at the corner."

The information interested Marsh considerably.

" No, I don't think it is likely to do her any good," he said ; " not that I know anything definite against the man. But—well, perhaps it is only his confounded good looks. It is impossible not to feel suspicious of a fellow with a face like that. He is what the careful European mother would call a typical 'detrimental.' Besides—"

But he broke off, for what he wanted to say was that the young lady's social position was not exactly that which a man of Blakely's stamp would probably require in the woman to whom he paid serious attention. But it was difficult to say this of the sister of his friend's future wife.

At the next corner the two men separated, Harrington being on his way to call on Miss Masson, and Marsh strolled on towards his office. There was no need of haste, for it was Saturday afternoon, and returning to his office at all was little more than a formality, "to see if anything had come in." As he walked he thought of Marshal Blakely and of what he had just heard about him.

Marsh hated Blakely cordially. Probably he would have done so under any circumstances, for the two had little in common; but what might have been only a negative antipathy was aggravated into intense dislike by the fact of the undeniable friendliness which seemed to have developed between Blakely and Miss Holt. It was easy for Marsh to tell himself that she was not the girl to be seriously attracted to a man like Blakely. The fact remained that she did appear to like him, and, as Marsh had lately said, he was indubitably "infernally handsome." Blakely was the only man in whose presence it had seemed to him that Miss Holt showed the least embarrassment of manner. At first Marsh had striven to believe that it was only his own jealous imagination; but the day came when he knew that it was not.

It was in a ball-room, and he was standing talking to Miss Holt when Blakely entered the room (he had a habit of arriving at dances an hour or two later than anybody else), and as he did so Marsh saw her manner change. They were separated by nearly half the length of a good-sized ball-room from the door at which Blakely entered, but Marsh caught the one quick glance with which she recognized him almost before he was inside the door. It was as if she must have been watching the doorway for his arrival. Marsh saw also that Blakely's eyes rested on her as he looked round the room. Instantly a restraint and self-consciousness had come into Miss Holt's manner. She was nervous and distraite, playing alternately with her programme and her fan, and only by an evident effort succeeding in keeping up a lifeless and desultory conversation. Meanwhile Blakely was moving up the other side of the room, stopping for a minute to talk to one woman, to bargain with another laughingly for a dance, then leaning over to speak to a chaperon seated on a chair against the ball-room wall, or moving aside to let a promenading couple pass; and he did it all with an air for which Marsh cursed him in his heart. During this time Miss Holt's back had been turned to the new arrival, and certainly her eyes had not rested upon him since that first minute when he was at the doorway. None the less, Marsh could see that she was acutely conscious of the other's progress up the room, in the course of which he had now passed the point opposite to where the two were standing. Miss Holt, as if by accident, shifted her position, so that by turning her head very slightly to the right she could look directly at Blakely where he now was. At the instant that she did so, as if there had been some sympathetic communication between them, Blakely also turned towards her, and their eyes met. This time both bowed across the room. Blakely did not, as Marsh had expected, come over to speak to her, but went deliberately on his way, while Miss Holt turned quickly back to her companion, with a higher color in her cheeks and a confusion in her manner as she said, all in one sentence:

" I beg your pardon— I'm afraid I was not attending to what you said— How warm this room is !— Let us go and sit on the stairs— Shall we ?"

Marsh could not reply for the wrath and the turmoil which was in him. Bowing his acquiescence and offering her his arm, he walked in rigid silence with her from the room, feeling the blood buzzing in his temples. They found a place at the foot of the stairs and sat down ; but though the silence was torture to Marsh, he found it impossible to speak. In a few minutes Blakely came strolling in seeming aimlessness out of the ball-room. He glanced carelessly over the various groups scattered through the hall, and made his way slowly to where Miss Holt was seated on the stairs. Her self-possession had returned to her now, and it was with perfect freedom that she shook hands and commented laughingly on the lateness of his arrival.

"And is there any use in my asking for a dance at this period of the evening ?" he had asked.

" I am not sure," she replied, although Marsh was aware that she had refused half a dozen applicants in the last fifteen minutes.

"Yes," she added, after pondering over her programme for

a while, " you can have that one—No. 16. There is somebody's name there, but he has another dance and I will excuse myself."

" It is very good of you, and more than I deserve," said
Blakely, gratefully, a sentiment with which Marsh most thoroughly agreed. A moment later the music began again, and
Miss Holt's partner for the next dance appeared, and led her
away with an air of smirking and apologetic triumph.

Marsh thought that he had never felt quite so miserable in
all his life as he did that night and for days after. Miss Holt,
he knew, had only met Blakely once or twice before, and
Marsh tried to assure himself by explaining to his own heart
twenty times a day that it was nothing more than the natural
curiosity of a woman to see something more of a handsome
stranger whom she had necessarily heard a good deal talked
about. Since that evening (which was two months ago) he
had seen no recurrence of embarrassment in Miss Holt's manner in Blakely's presence, and had gradually acquired something like confidence in his theory of woman's natural curiosity. He had a younger sister, married now, acquaintance
with whom had taught him how large a space the youth of
the other sex occupies in the thoughts of even the best and
purest girls of the present day. The lover's natural conceit
also came to his aid and helped to allay his uneasiness. The
more he saw of her the more he was convinced that there was
no danger of her being seriously and permanently attracted
to such a man as Blakely. None the less, he hated Blakely,
and was wretched when they were together. This afternoon
he had an unreasonable suspicion that Blakely was on his way
to call on Miss Holt when they had met, and wished with all
his heart that he could find some decent excuse for returning
to the house himself.

But this was obviously out of the question. So he walked
moodily to the building in which his office was located. In
the firm's outer room a belated typewriter was still at work,
hammering spitefully on the keys, as if resentful of being
detained so long after business hours. Under ordinary circumstances Marsh would have spoken to her kindly in apol-
ogy for her detention, for he knew that she was working on

a brief for him. But he only wondered to himself whether she, too, would neglect a good, sterling fellow for the sake of a flashy, dissipated scoundrel, with a heavy cavalry mustache and a pair of black eyes.

Passing into his private room, he picked up two letters which were lying on the top of his desk, and looked indifferently at the addresses. The handwriting did not interest him—bills probably ; so he threw the two envelopes discontentedly aside, and sat down to sway himself moodily from side to side in his revolving-chair. As he did so he became aware that the door from his room to that of his partner was ajar, and from within came the sound of men's voices, raised as if in heated discussion.

" It's dom ticklish work, I'm tellin' ye," said a loud voice, with a strong Irish brogue, which Marsh recognized as belonging to one of the Democratic city officials. " That road passes mighty near to the State's Prison, that's what it does." There was a pause, and then the same voice resumed : " It isn't for now, I'm manin', for the boys would all be in it togither. But suppose by any dom slip the election was to go the wrong way, and the Republicans got possession of the books and begun to make investigations ?"

" They're more likely to get possession of the books if you don't do it than if you do," said another voice, which Marsh also thought he recognized. " But you can fix it—charge it up to street-cleaning or police or something. If the men strike there will be need of extra expenditure for police, and don't you forget it."

" I'm thinkin' it would be more sagacious to assess the boys openly," answered the Irishman ; but Marsh was alarmed at what he had already heard and was anxious to hear no more. He opened his desk noisily, and swung the rolling top back with a crash, while he shifted his chair, making as much noise as possible, and coughed ostentatiously. The voices in the other room sank so that they reached him but as an indistinguishable murmur. A few minutes later Marsh heard a footstep cross the adjoining room, the door was pushed open from the other side, and General Harter's imposing figure stood in the doorway.

"Hallo, Marsh!" he said, with well-assumed heartiness; "did not know you were here. Come inside! We are holding an informal council of war."

"I only got in a few minutes ago," said Marsh, as he followed his partner into the other room.

It was a large, well-lighted apartment, indicative of the politician rather than the lawyer. The long, heavy mahogany table, covered with blue baize, with a clump of inkstands and pens and blotting-paper in the centre, was more suggestive of meetings of a campaign committee than of confidential interviews between attorney and client. At present the only occupants of the room were the two whose voices Marsh had already recognized. Timothy Sullivan, the big Irish politician, was sitting in an arm-chair, with his silk hat tilted forward on his forehead and his long legs stretched out on the carpet in front of him, his toes in the air. The other man, who stood looking out of a window, turned as the two lawyers entered, and showed, as Marsh expected, the reddish-bearded face of August Wollmer, the labor-leader.

"Come in, me boy!" the Irishman called, in his loud, thick voice, "we was just after talkin' about yersilf. When the Gineral here thought he heard you outside there I was just sayin' that it was a dom fool piece of business the way your dates were set for the campaign. Holy Moses! we want you to speak in every ward in the city, and as many of the large towns outside as you can make before election. It's the big audiences that you ought to have, instead of squanderin' yer talents on a lot of Jim Crow, cross-roads places that don't poll enough votes among 'em to elect a scrub-woman. What's the use of havin' good speakers if you don't use 'em? I'm goin' to give the committee some straight talk on the subject, an' don't you forget it." And he snorted contemptuously at the outrage which was being perpetrated.

Marsh knew that the whole thing was a lie, born of the impulse of the moment; but before he could reply Wollmer spoke.

"That's so," he said. "I want to have you come out to the works and talk to the men there. I haven't heard you speak myself, but those who have say you are the best man we've got."

"Oh, I guess they've given me all I deserve," said Marsh. "I am down for Jackson on Thursday and Olympia the following week."

"That's all right!" broke in the Irishman, impetuously. "I haven't nothin' to say against Olympia nor yet Jackson. They're good towns enough. But do ye look at some of the speakers that are booked for all the big places—umbrageous idiots, who can't hold a candle to yersilf." He spoke with intense indignation, and shook the square forefinger of his fat right hand at Marsh as if he were inculcating at once all the three hundred and sixty-five virtues of Abracax.

Marsh was still too young not to feel pleased, in spite of himself, by the flattery which was thus thrust upon him, and he could not but admire the readiness with which the gross Irishman had brought his batteries to bear.

But the subject was not at the heart of any one of the party. Marsh showed no enthusiasm, and the General did not speak at all, so the conversation soon flickered out in a few desultory oaths and objurgations from the big Irishman. In a short time the two visitors took themselves away, and Marsh, after some commonplace remarks on affairs of the office, returned to his desk, leaving the General alone.

It was drawing towards evening, and the typewriter had gone, leaving the completed brief on Marsh's desk. He took it up, but did not read it. The times were out of joint. Blakely, he supposed, was still with Miss Holt, and he fumed inwardly at the thought. And then there was this crass Irishman and the oily Teutonic agitator! ... "It is not worthy of you," she had said. "The cause—the party—the men whom you associate with!"

Horace Marsh had thrown himself into politics with all the single-hearted zeal of the young reformer. From his boyhood he had taken an interest in social questions, and in his travels in Europe had investigated not a little for himself the condition of affairs in France, England, and Germany. He saw how selfish and mercenary the majority of the "champions of the people" in all countries were, and how vicious was nine-tenths of the doctrine that was preached from the platform and the press to the working-classes of the world.

But he had become convinced also that mighty forces were
at work beneath the surface—forces which could not be
checked, and which were in terrible danger of being turned
into channels which would bring horror to mankind. In
America it seemed to him that the peril was even nearer than
in any country of the Old World. There was less individual
anarchism of the violent sort—less talk of bombs and bloodshed. But though the current here ran silently, was it not
deeper? In the movement towards industrial revolution in
America there was less outward threat of force. It masked
itself with the semblance of lawfulness and constitution-
ality; for the laws and the Constitution of the United States
give a more generous shelter to treason than those of any
other nation. And was not the danger, therefore, greater?

When Marsh returned to this country and took up life in
earnest the Third Party movement was about beginning to
assume something like national importance. He saw how
grossly the party in some localities—in this State and in that
—was being misled and put to most pitiful uses; but in
it also it seemed to him that he saw a force rising which
was as yet measurably free from the dangerous teachings of
the European socialists, and which, with no evil traditions
behind it, might be guided into paths which would lead it to
greater good than the world had seen. If only the conscience of the people could be aroused! Then the American nation would sweep away the wire-pullers and the ward
politicians, and march on, guiding itself temperately and
purely.

When he spoke from the platform it was on a lofty level
and with a high enthusiasm of conviction which never failed
to carry an audience with him. When confronted with the
tricks and meannesses of the politicians of the day they revolted him. What need had the sacred cause of them?

Of all the professional politicians whom he had met, General
Harter had inspired him with most confidence. He had believed in him thoroughly—believed that he was possessed of
the same high ideals as himself. He believed in him still.
It was true that in some few small things it had not seemed
to him that his senior partner was as—well, as rigidly scru-

pulous in his moral sense as he had thought. But they had been small things only. The conversation of which he caught the scraps that day gave him a deeper uneasiness than anything that had yet occurred. And he sat at his desk, pondering moodily until the room darkened into twilight and grew chill.

THE HOUSE IN FOURTH STREET

THE lower end of Fourth Street, where Mrs. Masson and her daughters lived, had once been the fashionable part of town, but in the rapid growth of a Western community business of a petty retail kind was already encroaching upon it. At one corner of the square on which the Massons lived stood a small "fruit and confectionery" store, nailed to the doorposts of which hung recent copies of the cheaper illustrated weekly papers. Immediately opposite a photographer's studio bore the name "Eldred, Artistic Photographer," in large gold letters of flowing script on a black sign reaching the full width of the second story of the building. At No. 319 — the next door to the house where lived the object of Harrington's devotion — a large white card-board sign announced that there was the place of business of "Madame Starret, Parisian Dressmaker. Dressmaking taught in all its branches." Nearly every other house on both sides of the street bore cards in the lower windows or pendent from the door-handles, informing passers-by that there were rooms to rent within, or that boarders were taken by the day or week.

The house in which we are chiefly interested was one of a row of some six or seven three-storied brick buildings, uniform in size, and very plain and bare of ornamentation. Once white, the paint had become blotched and discolored, especially where the rain-water leaking from the rusty pipes had stained the walls into irregular, map-like patterns of yellow and gray. The front door of each house, some four feet above the level of the sidewalk, was reached by a short, steep flight of artificial stone steps, with an iron hand-railing on either side.

As Harrington approached No. 317 another man came out of the doorway. Seeing the electrician advancing, he waited on the bottom step, and, while the two were yet some paces apart, called out to him without formal greeting:

"You are luckier than I to-day, Charlie!"

"That so? Why, what's up, Tom?"

"Annie's sick," said Tom, dolorously. "Miss Jennie says she does not know what's the matter; but she's in bed, and I can't see her."

"I'm sorry, Tom," said Harrington. "I hope it's nothing serious."

"Oh, I guess not. Miss Jennie says not."

Tom Weatherfield was, besides being very much in love with Jennie Masson's younger sister Annie, a printer. A sober, industrious fellow — unusually sober and industrious for a member of that ordinarily rather dissipated and sportively inclined fraternity—he had accumulated means enough (or, as he would have said himself, "got enough ahead") to launch out in a small job-printing office of his own. Having thus worked out his independence, he now felt justified in undertaking to support a wife—which wife he proposed should be Annie Masson. There had been no definite announcement of an engagement, for Annie—a fair-haired, pink-cheeked girl of a rather shallow prettiness — was inclined, while accepting Weatherfield's attentions publicly enough, to be secretive as to the progress of their relations. Her sister asked no questions, and those which Mrs. Masson ventured upon received but unsatisfactory answers.

Harrington liked Tom Weatherfield. He pitied him, of course, for the absurdity of his being in love with Annie Masson. Not that Annie was not a good girl enough. Harrington always said that she was "one of the dearest girls in the world;" but for some time he had persisted in regarding Tom's unconcealed admiration for her as a Machiavellian ruse, under cover of which the villain hoped to worm his way into the elder sister's heart. Weatherfield, however, was not a man whom it was possible to suspect for long, and Harrington had gradually thawed towards the young printer until an entirely cordial friendship had grown up between them.

Harrington now began to ascend the steps, while Weatherfield, a picture of desolation, moved up the street. After going a few paces he turned.

"By-the-bye," he called back, "did you hear that there was to be a joint meeting of the steel-works men and street-railway hands on Monday night at the new Labor Temple?"

"I didn't know the temple was ready."

"It isn't," replied Weatherfield; "but it is near enough to it to hold a meeting in."

"What will they do?" Harrington asked.

"Vote to go out together, probably," said Weatherfield, who, as a member of the Typographical Union, was better informed on local labor matters than was the electrician. "If they don't, then the mill men will go out alone, in the hope of the other fellows following later."

Harrington made no comment on this information, but turned to go into the house, ringing the bell shortly, and passing on into the hall without waiting for an answer. As he entered Jennie Masson came out of a side-room to meet him.

"I thought I heard your voice," she said, as she held up her lips to be kissed.

Hers was, perhaps, not a pretty face; but it was a face that Andrea del Sarto would have loved. Her features were regular and clearly cut, with a singularly restful expression, and the soft brown hair, parted smoothly back on either side of an unusually white forehead, gave her an air of curious and Evangeline-like purity. The gray woollen gown was almost concealed under a large white apron which reached from her bosom nearly to her feet, and which was streaked here and there with patches of color and stains of many indistinguishable hues. The apron—as well as the stains upon it—needed no explanation, for she had come to greet her lover without laying aside a small plate which she held in her left hand, while in her right she carried a little implement with a crooked onyx tip, known to china-painters as a "burnisher."

"That's pretty!" he said, approvingly, as, after kissing her, he took her by the wrist and raised her hand holding the plate, so that he could look at it. "How well the two golds come out!"

"Yes, I think they do," she said, putting her head on one side and looking at her work critically. "I should like to do a set like this in pink, but it is impossible to get the right pink. I wish I could go to the Crown Derby works and steal some of their color. They are the only people who can really get the proper shade. A miserable woman sent me a sample of a new color the other day which she guaranteed to be the real Du Barry. I knew it would not be before I tried it; and it came out of the kiln a horrid magenta—just as they all do."

He had slipped his arm around her waist, and they walked side by side through the front room, from which she had issued (and which was the family parlor), to the dining-room, which opened off it to the rear, and which also served as her studio. The dining-table was pushed to one side, while beyond, close under the window, stood a smaller table of plain deal covered with a newspaper, on which were strewn in confusion half a dozen plates, a cup or two, bottles of turpentine and gold, a ragged and paint-stained silk handkerchief, two old knives with blades thick with pigment, and a dozen or more of brushes, pencils, burnishers, etc.—all the working outfit of the china-decorator. Some deep shelves set into a recess in the wall supported a medley of china plates and cups and saucers, vases of all imaginable shapes, small pitchers, and odds and ends of queer pots and things intended for toilet articles. Most of these were still white; others had been experimented on and abandoned; others again were waiting to be fired, and still others had apparently been given up as failures after firing—a pathetic accumulation, which Harrington had christened "the poor-house," made up as it was of the incompetent and the broken-down, those who had started in life radically incapable, and had never been put to any use, and those who had been given their chance, and passed through the furnace and gone wrong.

"I hear that Annie's not well," he said, as she took her accustomed seat at the work-table.

"No, poor girl! I suppose Tom told you?" He nodded.

"We do not know what is the matter—nothing definite, I think. She is just run down, and does not want to see anybody—not even a doctor; so I have persuaded mother to get her out of town for a few weeks, and she is going to Aunt Susan's, in Indiana, where she can have as much fresh air and as little company as she pleases. Mother and Aunt Susan do not speak, so I had to write myself and make arrangements."

At this moment a sharply nasal voice was heard calling from above—one of those voices which Dr. Holmes hated so cordially. In the West the responsibility for this quality of voice is thrown upon New England (for which, perhaps, Dr. Holmes himself is largely to blame), but it must be confessed that long sojourn in the Western climate, and even distillation to a second and Western-born generation, does not render it materially more dulcet.

"Jennie! Jennie!" called the voice.

Jennie laid down the plate and burnisher, and went into the hall.

"Yes, mother!"

"Is that Harrington fellow down there?" Mrs. Masson asked, loudly enough (and with obvious intention) for Harrington to hear.

"Yes, mother!"

"How long is he going to stay?"

"I don't know, mother; I haven't asked him," replied the girl.

"Well, don't he know Annie's sick?"

"Yes, mother!"

The person up-stairs could be heard moving away, grumbling incoherently to herself, having, she conjectured, attained her object of making the man below sufficiently uncomfortable. Indeed, as the girl returned to the room she found Harrington (although he was not unused to these encouraging receptions from the lady of the house) looking very miserable.

"I am awfully sorry, Jen girl!" he exclaimed, ruefully.

"Why, dear? It isn't your fault," she said, as she returned to her seat with a slightly heightened color in her clear cheeks and recommenced rubbing the plate vigorously, almost viciously, with the little burnisher. "Besides," she added, after a pause, and looking up smilingly, "I like you well enough for two."

"I believe you do, sweetheart!" And he slipped from his chair on to his knees, putting his arms around her waist and looking up into her face. "I know you do, Jen; but I am almost afraid to say it. It seems so presumptuous and impossible."

She had laid down the plate and the burnisher, and stroked his hair back caressingly from his forehead.

"I don't only like you, Charlie," she said, softly, "I love you. I believe you are just as good and true as a man can be."

"I would have to be, darling, to be good enough for you."

Their lips met, and Harrington returned to his seat. Some minutes of silence followed, in which both were very happy. The chill of the icy blast from above-stairs had vanished under the warmth of the one kiss.

Mrs. Masson, it should be said, was not Jennie's own mother. She was Masson's second wife, and when he married her Jennie was already ten, and her sister seven years of age. The girls had never liked their step-mother, and since their father's death, four years before, had known little of the comfort of home-life. Jennie was patient towards the older woman— more patient than her impetuous sister—and never failed to show her the respect, even if she could not feel the love, which was due to a mother.

For a while nothing was to be heard in the room but the peculiar tinkle of the onyx point on the china, and Harrington sat and watched the rapidity with which she handled the little tool. She had unusually white and shapely hands, almost ideally perfect hands, in spite of the constant contact with turpentine to which they were subjected, and Harrington liked to look at them.

At last she broke the silence.

"Tom was telling me that the trouble with the men up at the works is coming to a head."

"Yes, I'm afraid it's so," said Harrington. "It's an idiotic

3

thing, I think, and our friend Wollmer is more to blame
for it than any one else. The company is losing money; it must be at present prices. All the higher salaries
have been cut, but none of us has thought of grumbling.
We can't expect the company to go on in times like these,
when it is running behind right along, to pay us as much as
it does when it is making money. It can't do it. Moreover,
it will not hurt the company to shut down—that is to say,
that of course it hurts any company to go out of business for
a while, and with a large plant like ours there is considerable
actual expense and danger in shutting down and opening up
again, apart from the loss of business. But the loss would
not be as great as it would be from running three months
with the present pay-rolls and business as it is to-day. A
company hates to shut down if it can avoid it. It probably
could avoid it—anyway, it is willing to try—if the men would
consent to the reduction. If they won't consent, the works
will shut down, that is all. The men have the chance of working at about eighty per cent. of their present pay or not
working at all. They cannot possibly compel the company
to go on at the old scale; that would simply mean insolvency;
and it is better to shut down and wait for better times than
it is to fail."

"Then why don't the men see it in that way?" she asked.

"Because they are fools, most of them. Because they
choose to believe what Wollmer and the rest tell them, instead of looking at the facts and facing the situation squarely. They are just like any other lot of men. A few loud-
mouthed, restless, pernicious fellows among them do all the
talking. Two-thirds of the rest never think for themselves,
and believe whatever the leaders tell them. The other third
sit back and say nothing, either because they know it is useless or because they are afraid of the union."

"But I can't understand how men can be so silly," she
said. "Why does not somebody tell them the truth?"

"Tell them, darling! Who can? They won't listen to anybody. The press sometimes does, but it is the papers which
they don't read. The papers which they do read cater to
them and encourage them. If a sensible man gets up in

meeting and tries to speak, he is cried down and ridiculed; and more than that, he is treated as a spy and a 'scab' ever afterwards. Nobody can tell them anything except these same loud-mouthed ones and the union leaders, who have no ends to serve but their own aggrandizement, and haven't done a stroke of work for years except with their mouths."

"But Mr. Wollmer talks here about the tyranny of the corporations, and says that the company is trampling the life out of the laboring men."

"Of course he does," said Harrington, hotly. "Trampling the life, indeed, when it furnishes them their bread and butter! When the works were started it was not, of course, as a charitable institution. It was not with the direct intention of furnishing work and a living to so many men and their families. But the result has been the same. The stockholders who have put their money into it have not so far received a penny in return. The first year the works about paid expenses. The second year they made a profit, but instead of declaring a dividend it was decided to increase the plant, and that increase is only just completed. About the time they began to put in the new machinery the financial panic struck the country, and since then business has been at a stand-still. Not only has the company not made any money, but it must have had to borrow heavily. The men who invested about two million dollars in the thing have so far not received a cent's return. More than that, they have lost about half a million or three-quarters of a million of their money. So much has just gone out of sight. There has been the depreciation in value by wear and tear in three years' run, and then in addition to that all property has gone off from twenty to thirty per cent. in value during the panic. Up to date the men who created the mills have lost somewhere from half a million dollars upwards. Meanwhile they have paid for labor some five or six million dollars, first and last. Every penny there has been in it the men have got, and half a million or so to boot. They have taken no chances, and have had to stand no loss. Everything they have done they have been paid for in cash on the 10th of every month—and paid in good wages, too. Some of those men get six and seven dollars a day. Now, because the company cannot stand it any longer—after it has lost money and borrowed and run behind—and has to ask the men to help it through by taking a cut in wages, they talk about tyranny and trampling the life out of them. Oh," he added, in a tone of deep disgust, "it makes me tired!"

"What will happen if they do strike?" she asked, anxiously.

"They will be beaten," he replied. "They have not a ghost of a chance of success. They cannot possibly compel the company to do the impossible. They may come to time quickly, or they may stay out and make trouble—hang around and talk anarchism and drink while their wives and children are hungry at home. They may grow violent, and riot and destroy property. Then they will end by 'compromising,' which is the phrase the labor leader uses for backing down when he has been beaten — the same sort of a compromise as Lee made at Appomattox."

"No; but what I meant was, how will it affect you?" she asked.

"Oh, I may be out of a job for a while, but most probably the company would keep me in some way. If there is any need of men—either as watchmen or special police or deputy-sheriffs—in case of trouble, I should offer my services. I can be of a good deal more use than strangers who don't know the works."

"But you will not put yourself in any danger, will you?" and she laid her hand tenderly on his knee.

"Not unless I have to," he said, laughingly, and taking her hand in his, "you may be sure of that. I have too good a thing waiting for me next January—a thing with brown hair and the sweetest gray eyes in the world." He pressed her soft, white hand caressingly to his lips and cheek, and then continued, lightly: "But all this is a long way ahead. The men have not struck yet. There are too many 'ifs' in the way before I can do anything very desperate for us to worry about it now."

Once more the voice of Mrs. Masson was heard calling—if possible, a shade more sharply than before.

"Yes, mother," said the daughter, hurrying into the hall and speaking from the foot of the stairs.

"Is that man there yet?"

"Yes, mother."

"Well, ain't it nearly supper-time?"

"It must be within an hour of it, mother."

And the old lady was heard retreating again, with Parthian murmurings of discontent, into her room above.

Harrington was only amused this time as he came forward to meet his sweetheart.

"Well, Jen," he said, "I guess I had better be going, any-way."

They stood inside the room while they bade each other a lovers' farewell, and walked out hand in hand into the hall. As they opened the front door Wollmer was ascending the steps.

"Good-evening, Miss Masson," he said, raising his hat, and without recognizing Harrington. "How is your sister this evening?"

"She is doing nicely, thank you," she replied, standing aside to let him pass into the house, where, as Harrington had told Marsh, he was now boarding. The others made no comment on the meeting, but their eyes met laughingly.

"Good-bye, Jen," said Harrington, tenderly, taking her hand, and, after a stealthy glance up and down the street, raising it hastily to his lips.

"Good-bye," she said, as he ran lightly down the steps. After a couple of paces he turned and lifted his hat to her, while she laid the tip of a white forefinger on her lips and tossed him the most fairy-like of kisses.

How quiet the street was on a Saturday afternoon! She thought so as she stood for a moment and watched his retreating figure, then turned and looked the other way, where no moving thing was in sight but one stray dog, sniffing aimlessly along the gutter. He thought so, too, as he walked briskly northward, and turned the corner where the newspapers fixed to the door-post of the little fruit-store flapped drearily in the slight breeze that was blowing. And neither he nor she had the gift of second-sight to enable them to see that street but a few short weeks in the future.

Have you ever noticed how a house which has become suddenly notorious as the scene of some awful deed of violence, or because a great criminal has lived within its walls, changes its aspect from that day? You may have passed the house in your daily walks for years, till every window and chimney, every shrub and tree about it, is familiar. It was nothing more than a commonplace homestead enough—no more than one grain of corn in a bushel-measure full. Suddenly the day comes when crowds flock to stand and gaze upon it, and you stand with them. And now for the first time it comes to you that this house stands apart from every other house. It bears the impress of crime on every face of it. How forbidding is that low doorway!—and the rear window (the very kitchen, doubtless, where the deed was done), set back in the angle of the abutting wall! How did you fail to notice it before? The very hasp on the front gateway has a sinister look, as if it were put there that it might lift noiselessly to the midnight criminal.

Is there no science, no architectural phrenology or palmistry, by aid of which we can tell these houses in advance—divine which building is destined to be the abode of virtue and peace, and which to live to be pointed at with shuddering, and "bear the rust of murder on its walls"? It needs no science after the event.

IV

MONDAY evening, which was the date set, it will be remembered, for the joint meeting of the mill hands and street-railway men, was also the time at which Miss Holt had told Horace Marsh that she and her father counted upon seeing him at dinner.

In former days the comfortable yellow stone house had been the scene of frequent entertainments on a generous scale. Since Mrs. Holt's death, however, three years before, Mr. Holt and his daughter had not found the heart to undertake any functions of hospitality more formidable than an occasional dinner-party, except when, once or twice, the house had been thrown open for a concert or a reading in aid of charity.

Within a few weeks after the loss of his wife, Mr. Holt, finding life insupportable in the old home, haunted by the memories of twenty years of her presence, had taken his daughter to Europe. Returning himself a few months later, to take up his quarters in a hotel, he had left her in Paris with some friends, in whose company she had spent a year and a half in England and on the Continent. The house, which had been in the care of servants during these two years, had been reopened on Miss Holt's return to America, and for the past twelve months the father and daughter had lived there, not reconciled to their bereavement, but growing by degrees less acutely and constantly conscious of it, and coming gradually to reassume the family's former position in the social life of the community.

Miss Holt made a sweetly gracious hostess, and Horace thought that she had never looked more charmingly than when she greeted him that evening. She was dressed in a gown of

black and pale violet, cut moderately low, in an almost straight
line from shoulder to shoulder, and showing to advantage a
neck which, she was perhaps not unconscious, was good to be
seen. A deep bertha of black lace fell over the violet waist, and
a drapery of the same material, with one broad satin band half-
way down, veiled the violet satin skirt. The large black satin
sleeves, puffed very full, ended just above the elbow, showed a
well-formed and very white arm below. Her only jewel was
a large and quaintly-set amethyst ring on her left hand—a ring
which had belonged to her mother and grandmother before her.

Mr. Holt was a spare man of less than medium height; indeed, Horace noticed now, as they were side by side, that he
was only almost imperceptibly taller than his daughter. White-
headed, gentle of manner and low-voiced, he had the air of the
scholar and recluse rather than of the man of affairs; yet in
all the State there was no one whose voice and example were
so powerful in financial and commercial matters as Lawrence
Holt's. In conversation he had a trick of keeping his eyes on
the ground, as if listening with attention to all that was said,
then raising them suddenly to his interlocutor's face, when
their blackness and brilliancy were not a little startling to
those unaccustomed to it. It was probably this trick that was
responsible for his reputation of being a difficult man for a
stranger to talk to, although no one of his varied interests and
the many demands upon his time could have been more unaf-
fectedly easy of access to all comers.

The dinner being given as an informal welcome to Judge
Jessel and his wife on their return after spending the summer
abroad, the judge, a massive, square-cut man, with a clean-
shaven and ideally-judicial face, was seated at the table on Miss
Holt's right hand and Mrs. Jessel in the same relation to the
host. Mrs. Jessel, scarcely less massive than her spouse,
though shorter, was a dear motherly soul whom everybody
loved. There are people of whom we say that they are "good-
hearted," and it is intended and accepted as the poorest and
most negative compliment—a last resort of politeness towards
one of whom we would not speak ill. There are others in
whom good-heartedness is so pronounced and positive a quality that it transcends all others, and we speak of it without a

thought as to whether they have all or no other virtues behind it. Everybody loved Mrs. Jessel, without stopping to question if she were intellectual. Nor would any one have thought of suggesting that she was not the best of company, although in parties of more than two her contribution to the conversation would often be confined for half an hour together to the constant flicker of a kindly smile and an occasional nod of sympathy and encouragement.

Seated at the table, Horace found himself with Grace Willerby—a school-day friend of Miss Holt, who was now staying in the house on a visit which promised to last some weeks— (who was to Judge Jessel's right) on one side, and Mrs. Bartop, the wife of Major Bartop, in regard to whose politics Horace had found it necessary to enlighten Miss Holt, on the other. Beyond Mrs. Bartop sat Mr. "Jack" Tisserton; then Mrs. Flail, who occupied the seat on the left hand of the host. Facing our friend sat Arthur Pryce, a long-limbed Englishman, with Mrs. Tisserton, who had Major Bartop on her right, between her and Miss Holt, on one side, and a Miss Caley on the other.

As soon as the party was seated the deep voice of Judge Jessel made itself heard.

"What a comfort it is to be back in the civilized West again," he said, in the tone of a man who settles comfortably in an easy-chair from a hard day in the saddle, "after months of the crude and barbarous East. In Europe there is more luxury and less comfort—at least, for the stranger—than I had conceived possible."

"You probably saw England only from the hotel point of view," suggested the Englishman, "and not from private houses. Englishmen themselves never live in their own hotels, you know."

"There is something in that, I suspect," said the judge— "like the Arabs who, for fear of the tax-gatherers, preserve an outward appearance of abject poverty, and keep their luxury for the private recesses of their own dwellings. But it is not hospitable. Strangers may be pardoned for wishing that they would turn things inside out once in a while. However, we did spend a week or two in the house of some friends in

Kensington Gate, in London, and it was the most amazingly
well-ordered establishment that I ever saw. I will always believe that there must have been a huge Corliss engine somewhere down in the cellar, pounding silently along, whose revolutions governed all the movements of the house. Mrs. Jessel
would not let me go down at night to see, lest I should catch
cold. But such unfailing punctuality and regularity of movement are not in the nature of human beings. There were times
when it was oppressive. I wanted to stand up and shout."

During this conversation Marsh had felt Mrs. Bartop, on his
right, growing more and more uneasy. Mrs. Bartop had no
sympathy with the West. After a continued residence in one
locality of some twenty-five years, she still persisted in regarding it only as a temporary exile. She would have her friends
believe that this quarter of a century was no more than a mere
way-side stoppage in her life's journey—but the alighting of a
bird on a bough in mid-flight. "As soon as Bartop's business
will permit," she would say, "we intend to go back. All my
family are in the East, you know." Meanwhile Bartop's business had not permitted for twenty-five years, and showed no
signs of being less exacting in the future. With all its absurdity, there was something of pathos in the uncompromising
hopefulness of the woman—the hopefulness of Dickens's pris-
oners in the Fleet. In appearance and disposition Mrs. Bartop was considerably more of a grenadier than her kindly husband, who, nevertheless, had the record of a dashing cavalry
officer on the Confederate side in the Civil War.

"You remind me, judge," she broke in at last, in a rather
hard voice, "of the Chicagoan who did not like Switzerland
because it was too hilly. 'Give him,' he said, 'Illinois.' I
cannot imagine how anybody can really like the West, with the
bad service and the dirty streets and the newness of everything. It is so impossible to *get anything* here," she added,
comprehensively, "or to know what anybody is doing."

"Oh, I am not speaking of the Eastern States," said the
judge, good-humoredly, "but of Europe." But Mrs. Bartop,
who had never been abroad, recognized no difference between
New York and Boston and London and Paris. The civilized
world was divided into two geographical entities, the "East,"

comprising all Europe, Asia, and Africa, and the Eastern States of America, and the "West," consisting of that part of the United States west of the Alleghanies; and she had her doubts as to whether this latter half was part of the civilized world.

"It does not seem to me," said the musically placid voice of Mrs. Tisserton, "that there is much West any longer. I have looked for the typically Western town so far in vain. When I was in Minnesota I thought that surely that would be Western enough, but the people of Minneapolis pride themselves on being not at all Western. And they are not. They are in the first generation as yet out there, and the people all came from the East—chiefly from Maine apparently, except those who are Scandinavians, and I don't know but that some of them came from Maine too. In Helena, Montana, it was the same. Society there is composed entirely, we are told, of members of the best Eastern families. This summer I was in Colorado Springs for a while, and one of the first things I learned was that I should find the place 'just a little bit of the East planted in the middle of the West.' Is there any West any more?"

"Not this side of Buffalo and Pittsburg," said the judge, laughingly. "That is where the West used to be. Now the East has just flooded over and beyond that, and has left the West stagnating behind it."

"Who is it," asked Miss Holt, "who calls Dakota a 'wilderness lighted by electricity'?"

"When I was in Dakota—" began the Englishman, sententiously addressing Miss Caley, who sat beside him, in evident preparation for an anecdote of some length. Mr. Pryce's anecdotes were notorious. He was reputed the dullest story-teller in the Western States, and when he commenced with "that reminds me" his friends fled. His turning to Miss Caley was a signal for the breaking up of the general conversation. Mrs. Flail at once attacked the judge for information as to whether, as he had mentioned Kensington Gate, he gave much time to the study of the antiquities in the Kensington Museum; Tisserton engaged Mrs. Bartop with: "I was talking to your husband the other day;" while Miss Holt leaned over to the major with a malicious glance at Horace, which the latter caught, and said:

"I did not know till the other day that you were a Democrat, major."

"What enemy has done this thing?" asked the major, playfully. "Who has been seeking to prejudice you against me?"

"No one; it was said in self-excuse. A friend of mine, who is also a Democrat, quoted your example at me as a proof of his own respectability."

"Oh!" and the major also threw a glance of intelligence in the direction of Marsh. "Well, as I have company in my shame, I do not mind confessing. It was born in me, I am afraid, Miss Holt—a sort of hereditary taint."

"My friend also said that you took no active part in politics now—which is the reason, I suppose, that your other friends are in doubt which side you belong to. Have you retired from the lists, or are you only waiting, like Le Noir Fainéant, to see which is the weaker side, then to plunge in and give your help to those who need it?"

"Nothing so chivalric as that, I'm afraid," replied the major. "I suppose I have retired from the lists. The fact simply is that though I am a Democrat, I am not a Populist. As I say, I am a Democrat from heredity and from conviction. I could not have inherited Populism because it did not exist when I was born, and as for conviction—the Populists haven't any; only theories."

"So, since the two have united, you have no party to which you can belong. Poor man!"

"It is a pitiful spectacle, is it not?" he asked. "Mrs. Bartop advances it as another argument why we should go back East. To think of living in a country where you cannot even get politics (let alone bonnets and dresses) to match your complexion! I ought to say, however, that if there were more Populists of the stripe of your friend there, it would not be so difficult to work with them. I admire him."

"Do you hear that, Mr. Marsh?" asked Miss Holt, raising her voice and addressing Horace. Of course he had heard. Though endeavoring to maintain an animated conversation with Miss Willerby, he had not lost a word of what was being said at the foot of the table.

"I beg your pardon?" he asked, looking innocently at his

questioner. Miss Holt, with a movement of her hand, waived the responsibility of explanation on to her neighbor.

"We were talking politics," said the major, and by this time the whole company was listening, "and I was explaining why, though I was a Democrat by inheritance, I was not a Populist."

"He was also saying," added Miss Holt, "that if there were more fusionists like Mr. Horace Marsh it would be less difficult to work with them."

Horace bowed his acknowledgments. "And if," he said, "there were more men like Major Bartop with us, ours would be easier work. We need you badly, major," addressing him directly. "The sons of Zeruiah," indicating the other end of the table with a motion of his head, "are in danger of being too hard for us."

"It is not so much Mr. Holt and the judge and the other disreputable Republicans that you have to fear," said the major; "it is your own ragged regiment that is likely to make the trouble."

"All the more reason then, surely," said Horace, "that such men as you—men who are honored by the rank and file, and who have won their confidence by gallant leadership in former fights, often very hopeless ones, should not fail them now. How can you expect a party to go right if you leave them to the leadership of the wrong men? If you would talk to them you could do more in a week than I could hope to do in two years."

"The political party does not commonly care to listen to anybody who does not happen to tell it just what it wants to hear. I have 'been there,' as they say," and the major smiled cynically in remembrance of former defections from his standard when he strove to lead his party by paths which it liked not.

"But this party has as yet no preference as to what it hears—within certain limits," continued Horace. "It is waiting with its ear to the ground to catch the voice of its king. It can be led."

"My sympathies," broke in Judge Jessel, "are with Mr. Marsh, I confess, although I am a disreputable Republican. Looking, that is to say, at the Populist cause as a national

movement, it is leaderless. It might be moulded. The hour
has arrived, but the man is yet to seek. Perhaps we have no
statesman in this country to-day who is equal to the task; if
there were such a man—a man whose voice the nation was already accustomed to listen to, whose principles were beyond
reproach, and his public career unstained even by a suspicion—
he might place himself at the head of the movement, and make
it, perhaps, as noble in its ends as any party that the world has
seen. But when we come to look at the Populists locally, the
case is different. The party is not lovely, viewed piecemeal,
and it is becoming worse daily. I fear that it is not through
Populism that the salvation of the country is to come. It is
more likely to be through the reaction against Populism. The
decent people of all classes may be forced to band themselves
together to crush the third party, and out of that union may
grow the force which the country needs."

"But how, in default of a national leader, can we do otherwise," asked Horace, "than work each in one locality with such
material as comes to hand? I know no other way that we can
bring reform on a national scale except by doing that which is
laid before us and within our reach."

"And what"—it was Mr. Holt who spoke now—"what is
the reform that you expect to reach? Is it the overthrow of
what some of your friends call the 'conspiracy of Wall and
Lombard streets?' Is proprietorship theft? Will you redis-
tribute property and all start equal again?"

"No, not that, of course," said Horace, smiling, and speaking, as he continued, carefully. "It is not so much the reform
we hope to make as the revolution we hope to prevent. There
is nothing wrong with any individual holding of property,
however great; nor with all the individual holdings in the
mass—with what is called the existence of the moneyed class.
The individual ownerships all over the country, whether small
or great (except in so far as they may have been acquired by
fraud and in violation of law), are justly held. They were
either 'occupied' by the present owners, in virtue of their
superior moral force or business talents, or they were inherited
from those who had 'occupied' them legally before. The
titles are good and in accordance with the law. The law itself

is good and in accordance with the eternal principles of right.
But through the progress of generations, concurrently with
the building of the law, there has crystallized round the mass of
individual ownerships cohering together a sentiment which is
fundamentally bad. I do not know what to call it, except the
idea of wealth; and this idea has altogether too much influence
in the disposition of the affairs of the nation. It is not that
any individual millionaire or any corporation has too much influence at Washington. It is not even that any group or class
of individuals has too much influence. It would be difficult—
but less difficult than invidious—to go to Washington and lay
one's finger on specific instances; instances of what in its gross-
est form is flat bribery, and in its mildest form is the swaying
of the Chief Executive by considerations of family and of con-
nections in the appointment of a justice of the supreme bench,
an appointment which in itself may be admirable. It is not, as
I say, however, any question of individuals or of a class. If it
were, the matter would soon remedy itself by the constant accessions to and defections from the moneyed classes in this
country, though I take it that the infusion of new blood in the
House of Lords in England every decade is scarcely less than
that into our aristocracy of wealth here. Yet no matter how
the component atoms of the class shift or rearrange themselves,
there is the all-pervading idea of nobility over there, with its
thousand ramifications and associations accumulated through
the centuries, and there is the idea of wealth, of more recent
growth but scarcely less all-permeating, here. It may be that
neither Congress as a mass, nor any individual Congressman,
nor any officer of the government will have been consciously
subjected to an undue influence during a whole session. Every
man connected with the affairs of state may be guided by his
conscience only, and honestly believe himself to be beyond reproach, yet at the end of a session this idea will be found to
have been all-pervading, to have governed in the distribution
of appointments and pensions, in appropriations and charters
and tariff schedules. It has not been more powerful nor less
present with one party than another, or one administration
than another. It rather accumulates strength and becomes
more firmly seated with each succeeding government. And

there lies the danger." He paused for a moment before concluding. "It is no change in the law that we need, it seems to me; still less any disturbance of existing rights and interests. It is a sweetening of our national sentiment, a depolarizing of our ideas. And I know not how that is to be reached except through the medium of a new party and new men. And it must be reached somehow, or the outlook is terrible. There will be revolution."

The young lawyer had been listened to with attention; but though he directed his remarks chiefly towards Mr. Holt, he was conscious of only one auditor, and of her he was acutely conscious. For her part, Miss Holt had been absorbed in what he was saying, and had paused with her fork half-uplifted in her hand, and the same expression on her face as had been there two days before, when Marsh had talked of his ambitions to her alone. When he ceased Judge Jessel spoke.

"I confess again that I go a long way with Mr. Marsh. There is danger, and there is need of sweetening—'oh, for some civet!'—and it is difficult to see how either of the great parties is to be the purifying instrument. One yields the reins to the other, and the taint is equally in both. If both together—that small circle of both parties which really guides the nation—were to step aside, there is nobody yet for them to hand the administration to—nobody but the mob, which is far more reckless and impure than either. It is the great neutral mass of right-thinking American citizens who need to be aroused and to act unitedly."

"Which," said Major Bartop, "I take it, is flat mugwumpery."

"And which is why," Marsh interjected, laughingly, "I appeal to Major Bartop to come back and lead us."

Major Bartop remained silent. Mr. Holt brought the subject back to lower and more commonplace grounds by saying:

"The trouble with the third party in this locality is that it shows no inclination to seek new leaders or to be held to any principles at all. It has simply been an accession to the ranks of the Democracy in exchange for a forfeiture of much of its respectability. So far as the guidance and mechanism of politics go, they are in the hands of the usual municipal ring of worthless 'ward heelers'—an Irishman to poll the Irish vote, and a German for the German vote, and a Scandinavian for the Scandinavian vote, and their Irish and German and Scandinavian friends. And just now it seems as if the labor tail was wagging the whole aggregation."

"By-the-bye," said the judge, "there is a labor meeting to-night, is there not, in which you are somewhat interested?"

"Yes," Mr. Holt replied, "at the new Labor Temple."

"Oh," remarked Judge Jessel, "the Labor Temple is completed, is it? They were struggling with it when I went away. Didn't you tell me that you helped them out?"

"A little," said Mr. Holt, drily. "I gave them a thousand dollars in behalf of the street-railway company, and another thousand in behalf of the iron-and-steel company. Then when they were in difficulties about getting the roof on the building, I gave my personal check for five hundred more."

"H'm! and the first use they put it to is to holding a meeting for the purpose of striking against you and the mill company and the street-railway company together. Verily the 'whirligig of time' does 'bring in its revenges.'"

"I think the Labor Temple is so good, architecturally," remarked Mrs. Flail, with the feminine preference for form over matter. The best of women, in keeping her household accounts, is more interested in the neatness of her book-keeping than in economy in results. A blot of ink on one of the columns is a calamity far outweighing a failure to find a balance.

"Don't you like it?" she said, addressing Mr. Tisserton. "I think it is so symbolical."

"Symbolical of what?" asked that gentleman.

"Oh, of the idea, you know," said the lady, somewhat vaguely. "It is a compromise between severity and vulgarity —an engrafting upon classical models of the modern utilitarian ideas. It is what it is meant to be—a temple, but a temple to the nineteenth century working-man. I took a good deal of interest in it when the movement was started."

Jack Tisserton felt that this conversation was beyond his depth. As he said himself, he "left all that kind of thing to his wife." He took refuge in appealing to Mr. Holt.

4

"What is the particular trouble with the men now?" he asked.

"The old trouble," the host replied; "the same trouble as is being felt all over the country. The absolute inability on the part of manufacturing or industrial enterprises either to earn or to borrow money to cover their expenses, and a simultaneous determination on the part of the men to be paid money, whether we can get it or not. I wish they would tell us how to get the money. We will do it gladly enough."

"It seems so hard," said Miss Holt, wistfully, in the silence which followed. "These men must know that papa would do anything in the world for them individually—in fact, we do a good deal for their wives and children when they are sick, and so on. We are not monsters. Yet now they simply won't believe what papa tells them. What can we do?" she asked, despairingly. As she looked round the table for an answer her eye fell upon the Englishman, who felt himself in some way compelled to reply.

"You cannot do a thing," said he, "except fight them. They'll learn in time. You are going through the same thing here as we have had to meet in England, you know."

There appeared here to Mrs. Flail an opportunity to obtain instruction. Assuming the air of a counsel cross-questioning a not too notoriously trustworthy witness, she said:

"What is your impression, Mr. Pryce, of our social system in America? Do you like the equality of the classes?"

Mr. Price smiled languidly.

"Whenever I am asked that question," he said, "I always quote a friend of mine—a young Englishman with whom I first came over. We had been in New York about a week, I fancy, when an American, with whom we had got into accidental conversation at the hotel, began to ask us a whole lot of questions, you know, and finally he asked us what you did just now—what we thought of the equality of the classes. 'Oh, I don't know,' replied Birchall (that's my friend, you know), 'I don't mind the equality of the classes.' He was thinking of the chaps on the elevated railroads, and the waiters and janitors and elevator boys, and all those sort of people, you understand. 'I don't mind their equality,' he said, 'but what I do hate is their damned superiority!'"

The general laugh which followed, Mrs. Flail felt to be in some measure at her expense, and she hastened to cover her discomfiture by asking another question.

"And what do you think of our country as a whole, Mr. Pryce?"

The tone in which this question was put said plainly enough, "Answer me that, if you can," and the fixity of gaze with which she held her victim while awaiting his response conveyed an evident intimation that he was expected to equivocate and have recourse to subterfuge, but that no shuffling would be permitted. The Englishman, however, was equal to the emergency.

"I don't think of it," he said; "it is altogether too big. No one mind can think of the whole of it at once. If you divided up the task, you know—let the contract by sections, as it were—to some six or seven minds at once, they might be able to evolve a simultaneous thought on the whole country. One mind can't do it."

Miss Holt thought it well to interrupt the cross-examination, and having caught Mrs. Jessel's eye and received a sympathetic nod from that good lady, signifying that she was ready, the hostess rose and, followed by the other women, left the room. The men soon followed, and found Mrs. Flail entertaining—or, at least, occupying the attention of—the company with a description of a new violinist who had that day arrived in town, and was to perform in concert on the following evening. As the men entered they caught Miss Caley's voice interrupting the elder woman's narrative with the question:

"What colored eyes has he?"

"My dear child, don't ask me," said Mrs. Flail. In which response she showed very clearly how widely she differed from the majority of her sex; for whereas a man, in describing another, will sum him up in general terms by saying that he is tall or short, dark or light, and "a pretty good-looking fellow," a "rather colorless, unprepossessing kind of a chap"—or some such characterization, looking rather to the quality of the man than the details of his physiognomy—a woman, in similar case,

will give " the inventory of his features," with the color of his
eyes, the shape of his nose, the nature of his mustache, and
(especially) the quality of his teeth.   And what man ever
thought it worth mentioning that another had good teeth ?

During the evening Miss Caley played on the piano, first a
sonata of Beethoven and then the inevitable bit of Grieg.   The
Englishman also obliged the company with the " Arab's Love
Song " and " London Bridge," which he sang with a rich bary-
tone voice, which, his friends said, " was worth the other six
feet of him."

Horace, after much manœuvring, had succeeded in placing
himself on a sofa by Jessie's side.

" I like to hear you talk as you did to-night," she said,
frankly, as soon as he was seated, " and I am not sure that I
wasn't wrong the other day when I told you to emulate Major
Bartop and hold aloof.   It may be better to work earnestly,
even if your friends think you are mistaken, than to sit still
because the work isn't all that you might wish."

Horace could have grovelled upon the Turkish rug and
kissed her feet for this.   Under more favorable circumstances
it is difficult to say to what length his adoration might not
have carried him that evening; but, as hostess, Miss Holt was
compelled to give more than half her attention to the other
members of the party, rising to thank one of the performers
or to plead with another, and to execute those innumerable little offices which are incumbent on a hostess if an evening is
to " go right."   But Horace was blissfully happy.   He barely
refrained from telling her incoherently in words, and he did
all he could to tell her with his eyes and the pressure of her
hand at parting.   When he left the house he sprang down the
steps at one stride, and could have shrieked aloud to the night
air in very joyousness.

When the last guest had left, Mr. Holt hastened to the library, where the butler had told him that James Darron, the
manager of the steel company, was already awaiting him, together with Superintendent Boon of the street railway.

" Well ?" asked Mr. Holt, as he entered the room.

" Well," said Darron, " they decided to wait for a while."

An evident look of relief came into Mr. Holt's face as he seated himself at the table, motioning the others to do the same.

"Tell me about it," he said.

"There was a big meeting," Darron began, "and it all went one way. There was the usual talk, and the more extravagant the speakers were the more they were applauded. Some of them were pretty bitter—especially Wollmer and Henderson and Riley and Craft. Up to the last minute it looked as if there could be only one conclusion—they would all go out at noon to-morrow. Suddenly Wollmer came forward and said that General Harter, the candidate for Governor of the State on the Democratic ticket, was present, and would like to speak. Wollmer asked them to give full weight to what the General said. Harter then came out (he was enthusiastically applauded) and spoke in his usual pompous way. But it was a mighty good talk. He counselled them to moderation, and implored them not, by any hasty action, to bring distress to the city or discredit to the fair name of the dear State, to the highest office in which he had the honor now to be an aspirant. You ought to have heard them cheer! He asked them to wait. Appealed to them not to dedicate the new and glorious edifice in which they were assembled by any headlong action which they might regret. He offered his services as arbitrator—either alone or in company with the mayor of the city and the Republican candidate for Governor. 'Anyway,' he said, 'wait until you have exhausted every resource, when the crime of what may follow will be on the heads of those who refuse to meet you.' When he got through, as soon as he could be heard through the applause, Wollmer besought the meeting to take the advice of the honored statesman who had just sat down. He said Harter was right, and they had better wait. There was some more talk, and then a joint committee was appointed to confer with the management of the two companies and report at another meeting to be called by the committee when it saw fit."

Mr. Holt made no comment on this narrative.

"I think," said Boon, "that it was a put-up job from first to last."

"Of course it was," said Mr. Holt—"of course it was. And a clever job, too."

As he said good-bye to the two men at his front door a few minutes later he murmured to himself again, "A very clever piece of work—confoundedly clever!"

V

It was clever. That was evident from the tone of the local press on the following day.

Horace, stopping at the club on his way home from the dinner, had heard there the result of the meeting, in much the same words as it had been given to Mr. Holt in the library, and in his condition of semi-intoxication it had been another cause of rejoicing. At breakfast the next morning he read the account of the affair in the newspapers with eagerness.

First he looked at the organ of the local Democracy, the *World*. The account of the meeting, several columns long, was headed in the approved alliterative journalistic style of the day: " Hearkened to Harter!—The Democratic Champion Saves the City !—He Pours the Oil of Reason on Labor's Troubled Tide !—The Strike Postponed, as Violence Hides Its Head before His Cogent Counselling !"

On the editorial page the same journal devoted a column, in all the dignity of " double leads " and much confusion of metaphor, to the praise of the " gallant General." " Seldom, or never, perhaps," so it was asserted, " had it fallen to the lot of any man in public life at one single stroke of statesmanship to render so signal service to his party, the people, and his State. At the last moment, when all seemed lost, and when the ardent but not unjustifiable language of their proper leaders had already swayed the seething meeting to the point where all stood waiting only to cast the last irrevocable lot; when it seemed that no human voice could stay the tide of indignation and of wrath—at this moment there leaped Curtius-like into the gulf our honored candidate for

Governor of this noble State, and by one act of self-devotion
he saved the city from the red peril which threatened it.
Never before has the gallant General shown so conspicuously
his courage, his statesmanship, and his power over the people, who are determined to have no other man for their next
Governor."

Even the papers of the opposition were compelled to give
the Democratic candidate some credit for his action. They
did it sneeringly, however. The *Republican* spoke of the
scene as "dramatic in the extreme; perhaps too dramatic to
have been given unrehearsed." The opportunity to do the
right thing was so obvious that little credit could be claimed
for having seized it. It would have been a disgrace to any
man not to have done so. "Those who understand 'General'
Harter have long ceased to be surprised at, however much
they may regret, the air of trickery and charlatanism with
which he succeeds in investing his every public act."

On the whole, the episode had been a distinct triumph of
Democracy, and still more a personal triumph of the senior
member of the firm of Harter & Marsh. So it was in the
best of spirits that Horace took his way to the office, his
light-heartedness finding vent *en route* in the purchase of
three dozen roses, which he ordered to be sent to Miss Holt.
He nodded gleefully to such acquaintances as he met on the
street, and all the way to the Metropolitan Block (where his
office was situated), and even going up in the elevator he was
humming to music of his own making the lines:

> "'For each red rose the secret deep
>   In its sad, happy heart encloses
> Of kisses, making love's heart leap;
>   And every summer wind that blows is
> A prayer that maidens be less coy
>   Of kisses ere brief life be sped.
> Heaven taught the earth a fair employ
>   When Venus kissed white roses red.'"

When he arrived he found that his partner had been at the
office early, and was already receiving visitors and congratulations. The first caller of the day had been Sullivan, the big
Irish politician. He strode into the General's inner office un-

announced, and slapped his hat and cane down noisily on the baize-covered table. Then thrusting his hands into his pockets and standing with legs wide apart, he shook his head admiringly at the General, who smilingly awaited a greeting.

"Oh, it was slick!" broke out the Irishman, at last—"it was dom slick! It was just a Napoleonic stroke of genius, that's what it was! I had me doubts, when we wer' talkin' it over in the office here, whether the thing could be done. But done it was—done to the queen's taste, bad cess to her! Tim Sullivan was wrong for once—and oh, it was slick! Holy Moses, it was slick! Have ye seen the papers?" he asked, banging his huge hand down on the table.

The General had. In fact (though this did not appear), he had read the proof of what the *World* was to say on the subject the night before. He accepted the Irishman's enthusiasm now with becoming modesty. Presently Wollmer entered—a very different entry to that which the Irishman had made. He came in noiselessly, almost stealthily, but the oleaginous smile of satisfaction on his features was scarcely less expressive than the other's boisterous hilarity.

"And now here's the pair of ye," said the Irishman, as he looked them over from head to foot. "Oh, but it's two Machiavelis ye are! Cæsar and Pompey and Pompey and Cæsar—an' ye could have given the both of them points! There was never a mother's son of a Greek of them all could have held a candle to ye!"

Timothy Sullivan was never notoriously accurate in his classical or literary allusions. The opposition papers seldom failed to recur when possible to a meeting some years before, at which the Irishman had referred to German as one of the "dead languages," and it was he of whom the story was told that, after a certain election in which his party had been defeated chiefly, as it was understood, by the Scandinavian vote, he had expressed a fervent wish that "every dom Swede of them was back in Switzerland."

When Marsh arrived there were already some half a dozen of the leaders of the local Democracy assembled in the room, and among them pranced Sullivan in ecstasy, calling upon each new-comer to witness to "the slickness of it." In the presence of the later arrivals, however, a critical observer might have noticed that no further reference was made to the *coup* having been prepared in advance. With all his apparent impulsiveness the Irishman never made mistakes of that kind. Marsh was barely inside the door before he was seized by the lapel of his coat and led up to where the General was standing.

"Let me introjuce ye," said the Irishman, "to Mr. Aristides Gambetta Cavour, yer partner in business, ye lucky spalpeen, who is otherwise known as the Moses and Aaron combined, or the Siamese Savior of the Dimicratic party."

While Horace was congratulating his partner the Irishman put on his hat.

"I'll be back after a while," he said to the party, "but meantime I'm thinkin' that there are some boys as 'll be wantin' drinks, and there is never a Dimicrat in all the Fourth Ward—man, woman, or child in arms—that can ask a drink of Tim Sullivan this day and be refused. This is no day for a man who votes the ticket to go dry! 'Twould be a shame to the party, it would; a dirty shame."

An hour or so later, as Marsh was sitting in his office, Charlie Harrington walked in. He had come down-town—an unusual thing for him in the forenoon—to assist at the departure of his *fiancée's* sister for Indiana.

"Is that the sister you said you had seen with Blakely?" asked Marsh.

"The same; Jennie only has one sister."

"Well, it may not do her any harm to be away from him. You told me that she was engaged to somebody, didn't you?"

"We don't know whether they are engaged or not. They act like it—anyway, Tom does," Harrington said. "We have our hopes, Jennie and I, that the wedding in January may be a double event. Nothing definite has been said on behalf of the other couple, however. It will be pretty hard on the old lady," he added, thoughtfully, "if both the girls leave together."

Presently the conversation drifted to the meeting of the

night before. Harrington did not appear to be much impressed with the behavior of the gallant General, a fact which Marsh set down chiefly to his friend's Republicanism.

"It was a cheap trick at best," said Harrington, "and if the men weren't fools they would have seen it. To be led by the nose and played upon and worked up to excitement, and then—presto! Wollmer pulls a string, and they are all put to bed again and tucked in, like good little children. I don't want a strike, but I almost wish that some hot-headed man had got up and told the meeting how it was being fooled, and spoiled the game."

"Why, do you think it had been planned in advance?" asked Marsh, with a remembrance of the hints of the Republican paper.

"Of course it had," said the other.

"I think not," Marsh replied, quietly. "I have not asked the General, but I think not."

Harrington made no reply, but after a short silence he said:

"I should think you would be afraid of being drawn too far into this labor business. Of course, you know what you are about; but don't you find Wollmer and his crowd a little difficult to stomach as collaborators?"

"They are not my collaborators," said Marsh, with some warmth. "We mark out the policy of the party, and if Wollmer or any one else chooses to follow us he can. Of course, the more who follow the better. But they must follow on our terms, and if the labor element or any one else think they can dictate to us, they will find themselves mistaken."

"To a man up a tree," said Harrington, "it looks a good deal as if the labor element was dictating now. I wonder if you know, Horace," he added, after a pause, "what a thoroughly brutal set these labor leaders are."

"In what way brutal?"

"Well, I was only in contact with it for a couple of years," Harrington said, "and it did not matter with me. I did not go into the railroad service to make that my career, and so far as I was concerned it was only a certain amount of discomfort for those two years, and a constant necessity to look out for myself.   To be sure," he added, "It has followed me here, as I was telling you the other day, and I still have to be pretty careful lest an accident should happen.   But with young fellows who go into railroading for their life's work it is different, and it is not as bad in the shops as it is in some other departments.   It used to be the case that any clean, industrious, and reasonably intelligent young fellow who went into railroading at the bottom and attended to his business was sure of promotion.   A pretty large percentage of the presidents and general managers to-day worked up that way.   But the brotherhoods have changed all that.   A young fellow goes in now full of ambition and determined to carve out his own salvation.   He has not been in the service long before the brotherhood is after him, and he has to make his choice between an honorable career and loyalty to his company or submission to the brotherhood.   If he chooses the latter, there is an end.   He can rise so high, but he will never be fit to become an official.   If he is a self-respecting fellow with nerve he will choose the other course, and then the trouble begins.   It is not long before he finds that he is unpopular with the other men.   His work is made just as hard for him as it can be, and life gets pretty near being a burden.   If he holds out, there are lots of ways of discrediting him.   An accident happens, and he is to blame.   He knows better, but there are plenty of witnesses against him, and the management has no choice but to let him out.   And when a man is once let out in that way he can hunt for another job at railroading until he dies in the poor-house.   He has to choose another career if he wants to make a living.   If that does not work, it is not difficult to get a man killed or maimed for life in the train and yard service.   Again there will be no lack of witnesses to prove that it was his own fault.   If somebody else is shown to be partly to blame, the only difference is that the railway company has to pay damages, and then the brotherhood has the laugh on the two enemies at once—the man whom they killed or crippled, and the company as well.   I tell you," he added, bitterly, "it is just as impossible for a clean, self-respecting, honest young fellow nowadays to go into railroading, beginning at the bottom of the ladder and

working up to the top, as they used to do fifteen or twenty
years ago, as it is for him to walk across the Atlantic! Even
in my own short time in the shops I saw something, and heard
a good deal more."

"You know more about these things, probably, than I do,"
said Marsh. "But if what you say is true, that only makes
one more abuse that we have to reform."

"And you can't be too quick about it," replied the other.
"But the way things are going now it looks to an outsider
more as if labor was going to run the party than as if the
party was going to reform labor. However," and he got up
from his chair, "I didn't come in to talk politics or to argue
—only to shake hands and see how you were."

Marsh rose also, and the two stood chatting laughingly for
a few minutes on the old footing of boyish good-fellowship
before Harrington went away.

Left to himself, Horace felt the first serious misgivings as
to his political career which had beset him since he threw
himself into public life. His ideals were unshaken. The
belief in the country's needs, the conviction as to where his
own duty lay, the visions which he had of the nation's future
—these were beyond the reach of doubt. But these men
with whom he was working, whom he believed to be informed
with the same inspiration as himself, was it possible that they
were other than he had supposed? He had indignantly repu-
diated the idea that Wollmer was his collaborator. But the
General? Could he have stooped to so tawdry a trick on the
preceding night as Harrington had implied? He shrank, too,
as he remembered those words he had overheard three days
before: "Mighty near to the State's Prison," the Irishman
had said. "Charge it up to street cleaning or to the police."
And Marsh seemed to hear again the echo of the accents in
which Wollmer had spoken. The General had not taken
part in the conversation; but he was there in the room undoubtedly, a party to all that was going on. Bah! it could
not be. It was something else they were talking of, something in itself harmless. He would not believe it otherwise.
He would ask the General frankly for himself, and knew that
it would be explained. And he thrust the thoughts from

him, and plunged into the work which lay before him on his
desk.

It was well—or was it ill?—that Horace could not hear another conversation which went on shortly afterwards in the
same adjoining room. The participants, as before, were the
General, Wollmer, and the Irishman.

The last named had returned from his errand of mercy,
which had evidently not been in vain.

"Holy Moses!" he exclaimed as he came into the room,
using his favorite form of invocation; "but it's nothing
more than one colossal sponge, is the City Hall. The whole
gang has its mouth wide open, like so many birdies all agape
in their nest waiting for their mother. Ye might parade the
entire street-sprinkling force of the city round the hall till
sundown, every cart of them squirting whiskey, and ye would
be no nearer the bottom of their appetites than when ye
started. Talk of the thirst of the Sahara and India's coral
strand! Why, it's milk and honey beside the capacity of this
self-same Dimocracy when treats are free!" And he wiped
his broad face with a large handkerchief, perspiring at the
very thought of the scenes that he had been through. He
himself had doubtless taken his share of the refreshments in
honor of the previous evening's triumph, but whiskey had
little effect on his huge frame. His voice, perhaps, was a
trifle louder, and his movements somewhat more emphatic
than usual, but where there was so much volume and emphasis already a little additional of either made no material difference.

The triumvirate had been in consultation for perhaps an
hour, and apparently things did not go smoothly. The General
sat with his chair tilted back, a look of annoyance on his face,
and drummed nervously on the table with his fingers. The
Irishman's hands were thrust nearly to the elbows into his
capacious pockets, and beneath his hat, balanced on the very
back of his head, his face was flushed and thunderous. Wollmer leaned serenely on the table, making figures with a stubby
pencil on a sheet of paper.

"It seems to me," said the General, "that two months

before election is too soon. It will be difficult to keep them quiet so long, and if there is serious disturbance it may do more harm than good. The public sympathy is always with the strikers at first, but violence soon wears out the public's patience."

"An' if the cost is to be anywheres near what you say," said the Irishman, addressing Wollmer, "there isn't a city in America, barrin' the New Jerusalem with its golden streets, whose treasury could stand it. Eight weeks of such pipin' as that—it would beggar the Rothschilds themselves to pay the bill. Four hundred thousand! Holy Moses!"

"I see no alternative," said the General; "you must manage somehow to hold them for a while yet."

"I have held them pretty well," snarled Wollmer, "already. I worked it last night for you. But let the men once get an idea that I'm fooling them, and the whole crowd of us can go to blazes."

"What is the longest that the committee can now defer calling the next meeting?" asked the General again.

"Well, we may be able to wait a week—then three days more before the day of the meeting—then two days more. We may stretch it to two weeks altogether."

"That makes six weeks to election after they've struck," said the Irishman. "Three hundred thousand! And how much will you get out of that yourself?" he asked suddenly, looking straight at Wollmer.

"I do not know what business that is of yours," replied Wollmer, with confident impudence. "The situation is this: The General here has to be elected Governor, and the city Democratic ticket must go through. Well, the General's business is to go on as he has been going and run his campaign. When he and the party are elected, you will have the city patronage and the rest, and that is good enough for you. To do this you need the labor vote. I can give it to you, but I propose that I shall name the price and not anybody else. And there is not going to be any auditing of my accounts, either. I have to turn over the vote—that is my business. You can furnish the funds to buy it with—that is your business. There are three thousand men in all, and, at ten dollars a week, that is thirty thousand dollars. Add all the expenses that will come up, and it makes fifty thousand dollars. Six weeks at that is three hundred thousand. You can take it at that price or leave it, just as you please."

"That's about one hundred thousand for Mr. Wollmer," said the Irishman, quietly. The other made no reply, but confined himself to scribbling on his scrap of paper. Suddenly Sullivan threw his head back and burst into a deep-chested guffaw.

"An' to think of us settin' here," he said, "an' hagglin' like so many fish-wives, when it's closer together we are than Fidus an' Achates, an' there's just as much chance of our failing to come to terms as there is of the crown of my hat quarrelin' with the brim. So far as I'm concerned, it's just this: it isn't Tim Sullivan that proposes to put himself in the penitentiary at this point in his glorious career. Nor is it that same Tim Sullivan who proposes to lose this election. Sure, haven't we two weeks to work in yet? Let yer committee go ahead and dally along just as much as ye can, an' by the time that ye can't do nothing any longer I'll know just what the resources of the city can surrender."

He was the same genial Irishman once more, and all trace of menace or of wrath had passed from his face. But Wollmer was not easily taken in.

"Well, as you please," he said, indifferently; "I just wanted to have an understanding. You know now what it will cost, and there is no chance, either one week or two weeks hence, of its being any less."

It was difficult to find any satisfactory answer to this, so the Irishman contented himself with stretching himself till his huge joints cracked and yawning cavernously, while the General coughed.

"By-the-bye," said Sullivan, suddenly changing the subject, "how much does the boy there know of things?" and he nodded towards Marsh's room.

"I never talk to him of campaign matters," said the General, uneasily, "except as concerns his own speeches."

As a matter of fact, the General had of late begun to feel ashamed in the presence of his young partner. He knew that

Marsh believed in him thoroughly, and he dreaded, when they were together, lest the young man should lead the conversation to the level of the ideal politics in which he lived. Perhaps the General had some echo of a remembrance of high ambitions which had inflamed him at Horace's age. At least, he guessed vaguely how abhorrent much of his present work would be to the younger one, and he shrank from converse with him on political affairs, lest by some chance word or false ring in his voice the other's suspicions should be awakened.

"It is a purty boy," said the Irishman, with a nod of intelligence. "As I was tellin' him the other day, the party will be wantin' United States Senators some day soon of just such stuff as he. But he'll have to leave his campaign in the hands of his friends, for Tim Sullivan's much mistaken in the lad if he'll ever take kindly to politics outside o' the public speakin'. He does that to suit Demosthenes himself, for it's a spark of the sacred fire itself that's in him. But it isn't the sacred fire that wins elections in these degenerate days. It's great stuff to set the meetin' cheerin', but when it comes to castin' votes it's other things entirely that counts. But it's a good lad," the Irishman continued, "an' we must keep him with the party, an' I'm thinkin' the best way to do that is to let him know as little as may be of what the party's doin'. When ye're breakin' a pup there is such a thing as scarin' the beast at the outset, and never a cent of good he'll be to ye thereafter."

The big Irishman, accustomed to handle men, spoke of the young lawyer as of a child—a child to be petted and pleased with fairy tales and promises of toys, while his mind is shielded from knowledge of the wickedness of the world.

VI

TWICE TWO AND ONE OVER

THE next day, being Wednesday, was Miss Holt's day "at home." On this particular Wednesday she was assisted in the reception of her callers by her two friends, Grace Willerby and Mary Caley. From the middle of the afternoon until six o'clock there was a constant coming and going amid the flutter of skirts and ripple of laughter, while the reception-rooms were clamorous with the twitter as of an aviary and the tinkling of teacups.

Horace had intended to call that evening. He had work, however, to get out of the way before he left town on the following day for his speech at Jackson, which compelled him to stay at the office until late. It was eight o'clock before he reached his club for dinner, and after half-past nine before he found himself on the Holts' door-step. The first thing that he was conscious of on entering the dimly lighted room was that Marshal Blakely was talking to Miss Holt.

Blakely was comparatively a new-comer in the city, having arrived only some two years before, when Miss Holt was in Europe. In a Western town of only moderate size (less than two hundred thousand inhabitants) "society," though including usually some amazingly incongruous and even unpromising elements, is necessarily small; the smallness being the result, however, less of a premeditated exclusiveness than of lack of proper material. In fact, the "scarcity of men" or of "girls," as the case may be, furnishes each season a never-failing topic of conversation among hostesses and mothers, and as a subject for lamentation offers a pleasing alternative to the perennial grievance of the poverty and crudity of the available supply of domestic help. Society, therefore, welcomes with cordiality any reasonably presentable accession to its ranks arriving with even moderate credentials from other cities. The number of these accessions will rarely exceed one or two in any given season, and in the case of a man it is only necessary for a new arrival to show some aptitude to the usages of society, and to avoid making any very serious blunder, to find himself, soon after his introduction, not only universally invited, but even recognized, in a rather tepid way, as the "rage" of the day. It is surprising to see over what indifferent material, of the youthful male sort, Western society can become mildly enthusiastic.

In Blakely's case the enthusiasm had amounted to something more than tepidity. His remarkably good looks and air of a man of the world were in themselves sufficient to excite at least a languid interest in the women accustomed to the rather monotonous and, it must be confessed, mostly somewhat commonplace men who constituted local society. Moreover, whether from policy or inclination, he had not shown conspicuous anxiety to be "taken up," but had refrained from cheapening his company or making his presence common at all those miscellaneous festivities of a lesser sort in which Western society disports itself. Given these factors, the result was a mathematical certainty. He came to be an invariable topic of conversation at feminine lunches and five o'clock teas. It was generally surmised that there had been some tremendous romance in his past, many versions of which, ranging all the way from the accidental suicide of his beloved to tales of Corsican vendetta, gained considerable currency. Hostesses were most gracious to him. Girls fluttered at his approach. Even men who were not naturally drawn to him, from hearing him so much discussed by the women, came to regard him as in some way a person of more than ordinary importance, and treated him with cordiality and even deference at the clubs and in business.

Letters from her friends had given Miss Holt, while in Europe, more than one description of him. Mrs. Tisserton had written that he was like "some sort of an evil god," and added that she "pitied the girl who found herself in his power, as probably many had done in the past, and doubtless more would do in the future." It is not in feminine nature not to feel some curiosity to meet an evil god, especially when the owner of that nature is twenty-three years of age and the god some half a decade older. But some months had passed after Miss Holt's return home before she met Blakely. She had heard much of him. "Oh, but you *must* meet him," her friends said, and more than once she was told how much he wished to be introduced to her. But at first Miss Holt had not been "going out," and then came Lent. Finally, when she did see him, it was at the theatre.

She was in a box on a level with the stage, but removed some distance from it. Shortly before the curtain rose she became aware of a man in evening dress (which was not the invariable costume of men attending the theatre there alone), who was taking his seat in the parquet, some three or four rows farther to the rear of the house, and perhaps six chairs distant from the line of the box. Her glance had only fallen on him for an instant, but she knew at once that it was he, and she was further conscious that his eyes were fixed on her. One of her companions leaned over and whispered hurriedly that there was Mr. Blakely. The thing annoyed her. The information was superfluous, and, moreover, had been so clumsily imparted that she was well aware that he had seen the movement and understood it. Miss Holt, therefore, kept her eyes obstinately on the drop-curtain, refusing to turn her face by the smallest inclination in his direction. But she knew that he still looked at her, and under his gaze she felt her pose growing stiff and awkward, and herself becoming, an unusual thing for her, embarrassed and self-conscious.

All through the evening she felt that his eyes were on her much more than on the stage. Twice during the progress of the play the restraint became intolerable, and she had suffered her glance, as if carelessly, to wander over the house and fall on him in passing. Each time his eyes had shifted away, so that without their glances meeting she could not help knowing that his had but just left her face. Moreover, she knew that he meant her to know it. She was constrained and uncomfortable throughout the evening. It made her angry— firstly, because there was no reason for embarrassment, and, secondly, because she knew that he must notice that it existed, and could scarcely fail to understand its cause.

As the curtain fell on the last act and she rose from her seat, her face turned involuntarily full towards him. He was looking at her, and for a moment their eyes met steadily. Then hers fell, and she turned confusedly to the man who was holding her wrap for her. She was painfully conscious that she flushed as she did so, and her spirit chafed under the unreasonableness of the whole thing. All the way home in the carriage her face burned, and long after she should have been asleep she tossed uneasily, full of wrath and mortification, and haunted the while by that scene in Tolstoï's *War and Peace*, wherein Natacha surrenders herself to Anatole in one meeting of their eyes in the opera-house.

For some time she had rather avoided meeting him, and had endeavored to turn the conversation into other channels whenever his name came up. When they did meet and were introduced, he had been singularly silent and deferentially reserved. No reference was made on either side to the evening at the theatre, and he had compelled her to bear the larger share of the conversation, while he listened with downcast eyes and an attitude of extreme humility. There was nothing of the air of the conqueror about him, nothing to imply the existence of any previous relations between them, except, perhaps, even in his humility, the slightest smile about his lips, and sometimes an inscrutable light of something between amusement and self-confidence in the recesses of the eyes which he raised once and again to hers, which seemed to tell her, so that her whole being revolted against it, that his air of deference was but to humor her, and that their positions to each other might be otherwise if he pleased it. His quietness and submissiveness were so different from his ordinary manner towards women that she could not fail to be aware of them, or to know that he intended she should be aware of them, and that they were meant to convey to her an intimation that she stood apart from all other women in his regard. He could not have adopted an attitude more surely calculated to pique her pride or to make her more acutely conscious of the influence which he had already established over her.

Never before had any man succeeded in placing her in a similar, and what was so essentially a false, position towards

him. She told herself that he was insolent; but that he had
not been. She said that his behavior was unwarrantable; but
what had he done that was tangible at which offence could be
taken? She assured herself that she hated him; nevertheless,
she was conscious of a persistent and unreasonable desire to
see him, and when driving in the street her eyes would continually single out from among the throng on the sidewalk
men whose figures from a distance resembled his. But though
she seemed to meet Horace Marsh frequently when down-town,
and other acquaintances from time to time, she had never yet
seen him.

Then came the evening at which Horace had been so miserably aware of her constraint at Blakely's presence. Since then
they had met several times, and, as Horace had seen, she had not
again betrayed any embarrassment in his company. She told
herself that there was no longer danger of her feeling any—
that the effect of his fixed gaze that evening at the theatre
had been no more than she would have felt at being similarly
stared at by any other man whom she had not met, but whom
she had heard much talked of. She even affected to be more
at ease in his company than in that of any other man of her
acquaintance, adopting with him a tone of light-heartedness
and nonsensical raillery which was new in her. But at the
bottom of her heart she knew that she was acting, that the
gayety was assumed only because she feared to give him an
opportunity of being serious. So far he had maintained his
first attitude of deference. She was safe at present within the
defences of forced mirthfulness which she had erected around
her; but he had made no attempt to break these defences
down. Should he attempt it, how strong would they prove?
She scarcely dared to think, but once and again a certain tone
in his voice, or a new light in his eye, had made her heart
throb so that she nearly choked, and made her tremble in her
intrenchments.

To-night, for the first time, he seemed to have made up
his mind to abandon in part, but in part only, his attitude
of humility. There was something more of confidence in
his manner at meeting, something—not quite a pressure of
her hand, but the holding of it prisoner for an instant—

which awoke her alarm. Then he had referred to their first meeting.

"I have not seen you at the theatre for a long time," he had said.

"No, I have not been there at all this fall—not since last spring," she replied.

"I have only seen you there once," he said, with his eyes downcast.

She strove to make her voice sound careless and indifferent as she asked in reply :

"When was that?"

But the tone sounded false to herself, and he had not answered. Only he raised his eyes to hers, and his gaze said plainly enough: "There is no need for me to tell you; we both remember." He quickly dropped his eyes again, and both sat silent for a space. It was at this moment that Horace entered the room. There were half a dozen others there, but he was conscious, acutely conscious, only of those two, and he knew that there was silence between them, and that something was passing—if not a crisis, at least something which marked an epoch in the relations between this man whom he hated so and the woman whom he loved.

She rose to meet him quickly, and as if she were very glad— as indeed she was—to escape from the strained silence which seemed to be stifling her. Horace saw that she was glad, but he was too near guessing the reason of it to take much comfort in her friendliness.

"I am so much obliged to you for the flowers," she said, nodding her head towards a side-table whereon his roses stood, massed in a deep-toned Rookwood vase. "There was no card with them, but I know they came from you—did they not?"

"There was no need of a card," he said, half-jestingly, "for 'each red rose,' you know, has a capacity for speaking which other flowers have not."

"Is that so?" she replied, indifferently. "Anyway, I adore American Beauties; they are so full of sunlight, and their perfume intoxicates me. I want to crush them, or bury myself in them, or roll over them, like a cat, or something. Sniffing is so inadequate!" And she walked over to them now

and thrust her face into the blossoms, and found their dewy
scented coolness inexpressibly refreshing.

Horace passed on to shake hands with the other women, and
to exchange words of greeting with the men in the room. He
was still standing up engaged in this when he saw that Blakely
was saying "Good-night" to Miss Holt.

"Must you be going?" he had heard her voice say, and the
tone sounded conventional enough. She alone knew that for
the first time in her life she wished for a man to stay even
while she feared lest he should. "Or does he know it, too?"
she asked herself, with trembling. There was a quiet, authorita-
tive look of understanding in his eyes, and a pressure of her
hand—a definite pressure this time, which could not be mistaken—which she fancied told her that he read her heart.

Others left soon after. At nearly ten o'clock it was probably
too late to expect more callers, and there remained with the
three women only Marsh and Barry, Marsh's chum, who would
presumably wait that they might go home together.

"I know that I arrived most unorthodoxly late," said Marsh,
as the five were seated in an irregular semicircle round the
open fire, "but I had a lot of work to do which kept me at the
office, and I am to be out of town for a couple of days. I had
to come to-night, or I should not have had the distinguished
pleasure of seeing you ladies again until Saturday, which would
have been intolerable. And now that I am here I know that I
ought to be going again. But that looks equally intolerable—
especially as I have Barry to keep me in countenance."

"To-morrow," said Jessie, "is the day when the apostle ex-
horts the multitudes, is it not?"

"To-morrow," said Horace, briefly; "and the apostle hates it."

"What, the multitude?" asked she. "Bad apostle!"

"No, the job," Marsh replied, "if the apostolic calling can
be said to resolve itself into jobs. I wonder," he added, medi-
tatively, "whether the real apostles ever hated to talk—whether
there were times when they were not in the mood for it, and
whether they were nervous beforehand. One cannot imagine
it, but I suppose they did."

"Is it not recorded," asked Barry, "that on one occasion at
least Peter stood up and was bold?"

"Yes," Marsh replied; "but that was before a comparatively small audience. Besides, the mere fact that it was worth recording then would seem to imply that he was not always so."

"But on this occasion," interjected Miss Holt, "I thought the apostle was eager for the fray. He spoke as if he were a few days ago."

"In some ways he is," Marsh said, slowly. "He wants to make the exhortation well enough. But to-morrow he would rather be elsewhere. I should like to have been a member of the theatre-party."

"Who is going?" asked Miss Caley.

Horace had been longing to ask that question, but did not dare.

"I do not know them all," said Miss Holt. "I understand there are to be three boxes. The Tissertons are going, I know, and we three, and—and Mr. Blakely." There was an almost imperceptible change of tone as she mentioned the last name, but a change which at least one of the auditors caught. "Are you going, Mr. Barry?" she asked, quietly, turning to that person.

"No, I am not bidden," he replied. "Mrs. Brace does not like me."

"Impossible!" exclaimed Miss Willerby, with exaggerated incredulity.

"But a fact, just the same; and I have been overwhelmingly sweet to her," Barry complained. "It was not my fault in the first instance, anyway. I accidentally overheard her lecturing Brace one day—oh, years ago. It was at the Carringtons', at a dance, and I was hunting for my partner round those interminable verandas. Before I knew it I had heard two or three sentences, and before I could escape she had discovered me. Jingo! she was giving it to him, too!"

"What a shame," said Miss Holt, languidly. "He is such a dear, inoffensive, gentle creature."

"You cannot imagine his not behaving like a perfect lady under any circumstances," Miss Willerby remarked.

A certain proneness to sarcasm was that young woman's chief fault. A striking, even a handsome girl, tall and slender, blonde, but with dark eyebrows, had she been born to wealth she would have been the pet and leader of any society in which she might have been thrown. As it was, she had been familiar from a child with all the shifts and inconveniences of a household in straitened circumstances. At first she had rebelled bitterly against her inability to have as many dresses and hats, as many ornaments and pleasures, as other girls of her age. Gradually, however, she had learned to keep her resentment to herself, and by the use of her deft needle to repair as far as possible the deficiencies of her wardrobe. She was never richly, but always becomingly dressed. As soon as her education was completed she had been compelled to take a place as teacher in the public schools, and the days which her friends spent in pleasure and flirtation and thinking of their dresses had been occupied for her with work, and work of a hard and harassing kind. Reading much by herself in the long evenings, she had acquired a certain independence of thought, as she had early learned to rely upon her own resources for her gowns. She was not cynical; the natural fulness and sweetness of her nature forbade that—only a somewhat reserved girl accustomed to think and act for herself, reconciled to the fact that one of her moderate means could in her position in society expect few lovers. In return she was inclined to be regardless of what the world, from which she received so little, thought of her. Her pupils loved her, and her friends of both sexes said: "What a pity she does not marry; she would make such a splendid wife!" When any suggestion of the kind was made to her she laughed a little bitterly, saying that she would always be an old maid; she could not afford a husband. For the rest, she kept her own counsel, did with even good-nature her day's work as it was allotted to her, and was the strength and comfort of a somewhat sordid and cheerless home. It was not surprising if, in her broodings, and feeling herself, as she did, so much apart from the world to which she was so near, she had acquired a trick of sarcasm of speech which was really without malice or uncharitableness. In speaking of her to Horace, Miss Holt had said more than once that there was the making of a heroine in the girl—if she was not one already.

As she sat now in the centre of the circle about the fireplace she was conscious, but not resentfully, of being the odd member of the party—the puss without a corner. A stranger coming in would probably have said that she was the handsomest and most interesting person in the room. But on her left sat Miss Holt with Horace on the other side of her, and Miss Willerby did not need to be told how little Horace cared whether any other person was present or not. On her right Barry's body was inclined at as sharp an angle as possible towards Miss Caley, to whom, from time to time, he addressed trivial asides in a subdued tone of infinite tenderness.

Barry was always in love with somebody. He never denied it, but justified himself by quoting Sterne: "I have been in love with one princess or another all my life, and hope I shall go on so till I die, being firmly persuaded that if ever I do a mean action, it must be in some interval betwixt one passion and another."

Marsh, some time back, had been immoderately delighted by accidentally coming across, in Longfellow's "Spanish Student," the lines:

> . . . "That heart of thine
> Is like a scene in the old play; the curtain
> Rises to solemn music, and lo! enter
> The eleven thousand virgins of Cologne!"

He had gleefully given the quotation to Barry to read, and since then, whenever the latter embarked on confidences in relation to his latest flame, it was only necessary, to close the conversation, for Marsh to say, in a tone of affected carelessness:

"By-the-bye, Barry, have you ever read 'The Spanish Student'?"

In Miss Caley it seemed as if Victorian had met his match. It is Howells who has made one of his characters say that "What's passing in every girl's mind when she's thinking" is "processions of young men so long that they are an hour getting by a given point." Miss Caley was a soft, kitten-like young person, undoubtedly pretty, but possessed of an incurable habit of flirtation. Neither age nor condition of servitude appeared to make material difference in the other party, provided only that the other party was of the male sex. She had a preference for youth — anywhere from fifteen to thirty-five years of age—and a decided preference for dark eyes and a curly mustache. But in default of these desirable accessories, almost anything male would suffice. Let it be the aged minister, come to make a pastoral call, or a messenger-boy arriving with an accidental *billet-doux*, it was beyond the power of Mary Caley to prevent her eyes from saying to them, as plainly as eyes could speak : "Do fall in love with me! Please fall in love with me!" It was not her fault, she honestly believed. Those incorrigible eyes, with their long brown lashes, were simply beyond her control. Their appeal, moreover, was not often resisted. Even the minister pronounced her a "decidedly prepossessing child," while the messenger-boy dreamed for nights afterwards of rescuing her from Indians, and longed for the day when another message would take him to her house. For the others, those with the eyes and mustaches, they often took it seriously—for several days at a time. During those days she went in ecstasy, moving joyously through the house spilling snatches of song, and always on the lookout for callers or messages or presents of flowers and bonbons—of which she received amazing quantities in the course of a year. She said it was all "such fun," and would confide to other members of her family in occasional bursts of hysterical confidence, mingled with laughter, during which she would hide her face and her blushes in the sofa cushions, what he (the "he" of the time being) had said to her; to all of which the members of the family would listen, too much amused to be seriously shocked, for they knew that it would not last, and that admonition would be wasted. Then "he" would grow jealous; there would be a stormy scene of recrimination and tears, and all would be over —forever. A day or two days, or sometimes a whole week, would pass, during which she hated mankind, and revolved fearsome thoughts of prussic acid and pistols. This was only the overture, however, to the next act. The curtain rose with a new leading gentleman.

Just now her eyes talked to William Barry. The fitful firelight helped them, so that they were astonishingly eloquent. Nor was Barry likely to steel himself against them.

And all this Miss Willerby understood as she sat and looked into the fire.

For Horace, he only knew that Blakely was to take his place at the theatre next evening, and that she was sitting by his side now, and that his heart was breaking. She was dressed in a simple, half-evening costume of the soft material known to dress-makers as "Henrietta," of the same shade of violet as she had worn at the dinner—her favorite color, apart from the fact that she was not yet fully out of mourning. It was cut round at the neck (in what is called the Gretchen style), and as she lay back in her voluminous chair the firelight lit up the fulness of her throat and the soft curves of her cheek, once and again touching the white forehead, from which her dark hair was drawn in rippling waves upward and backward. Her beauty was of a high, serene type which would stand this mode of coiffure, ruinous to a merely pretty face which relies on piquancy for its charm. As she reclined now, in an attitude of complete relaxation, her hands resting on the broad arms of the chair and her head thrown back, the eyes almost closed as she looked at the fire, so that the dark lashes nearly rested on the cheek, with the whiteness of the throat and forehead, she seemed to Horace beyond expression beautiful with a beauty that was queenly and most pure. He longed to lean over and put his lips on hers; and he clinched his hands till the nails almost dug into the flesh as he said again and again to himself that he must win her. Surely it must be so! Why else had he thus been thrown near her, and why was this love, on which all the hopes and ambitions of his life depended, given to him if it were to be futile? And he sickened and burned at the thought that any other man—and, most of all, Blakely—could ever possess her.

The conversation was desultory and lifeless, as it could not help but be when more than half the company were so busy with their own thoughts and emotions.

"But there must be some men, *surely*," said Miss Caley, plaintively. "Mr. Blakely is going to be of no use to *us*," indicating Miss Willerby by a glance.

Miss Holt made no sign that there was any significance in the speech, and there was silence.

"I wish I were going," said Barry to Miss Caley, in an undertone full of meaning.

"I wish you were," said that young lady, casting her eyes down with the air of one from whom a reluctant confession is wrung.

Then they drifted back to the subject of Horace's impending speech. Miss Caley thought it must be just sweet to be able to sway masses. Didn't Mr. Barry think so? He did, and was deliciously conscious of being swayed himself.

"Are you ever nervous?" asked Miss Willerby.

"Horribly!" Marsh replied. "I am uneasy for a day before, and the last half-hour is agony. When I am being introduced to the audience I am going through the very valley of the shadow. I run cold up the back, and my mouth is sticky. By the time the applause has died away the faces before me begin slowly to individualize themselves, instead of being merely a sea of white discs. But the silence when the applause stops and the audience comes to attention is awful. It is a frightful effort to break it, and when I do so my voice sounds cracked even to myself. After a few words it begins to steady down, quite of its own accord and without volition on my part, and adjusts itself to the room. Once it has fairly found its gait, as it were, I like it, especially if the audience is responsive, and answers promptly when I call upon it."

"It must be splendid!" said Miss Caley, with enthusiasm. "Is your eloquence turbid, Mr. Marsh?"

"Sometimes my thoughts are," he laughed.

There was a moment's pause, and then Miss Willerby spoke.

"'Twixt banks intent the turbid river rolls,'" she said, musingly, to the fire. "Nobody can tell me where that quotation comes from."

"Shelley," suggested Miss Caley.

Even to Barry there was a certain ineptitude in this, and he said, humbly:

"I don't think it can be Shelley. It doesn't sound like him."

"Don't you think so? I love Shelley, don't you?" she asked, confidentially. He did, of course, as was his duty.

"What is it?" she asked, feeling her way to a quotation:

> "'The fountains mingle with the rivers,
> The rivers kiss the sea.' ...

I think he is sweet!"

" Was the quotation from Willerby ?" asked Miss Holt.

" No; it was the first line of a poem that I saw published
the other day in an educational paper—an original poem by a
young Hindu student in some college in India. I think it is
immense."

" What does he mean by 'intent' ?" asked Horace.

" I don't know: I don't think he did. He used all sorts of
queer words later on—like a negro, without any apparent recognition of their sense. But if some great poet had written
that, we should all say it was splendid—' 'Twixt banks intent.' "

And silence fell again.

" I didn't know that Indians spoke English," said Miss
Caley, presently. " I thought they spoke Indian. Didn't
you ?" turning to Barry.

" Well—er—" and he hesitated—"they do, you know, naturally—Hindustani, that is. But they are taught English."

" Oh ! by the missionaries and things."

Barry nodded, without committing himself in words.

" I should love to be a missionary—it must be so noble !"
she said; " wouldn't you ?"

" If you were a missionary I would rather be a savage," he
said, softly. " Would you teach me ?"

" If you'd promise not to eat me," she laughed.

" I don't know whether I would or not;" and he looked at
her carnivorously.

Meanwhile the clock on the mantel showed that it was nearly eleven o'clock, and Horace knew that they must be going;
so he rose reluctantly. The others did the same.

" It is awfully hard to go," he said, " and plunge into the
outer darkness."

" Don't call it that !" said Miss Caley; " the outer darkness
is where devils and things are thrown."

" And don't you consider us as two poor devils ?" asked
Marsh. And there was real misery in his eyes—misery mingled with reproach,— as he took Miss Holt's hand to say
" Good-night." She gave it, and smiled very sweetly and tenderly in reply, as if she would like to comfort him and make
amends.

When the men had bowed themselves out and the front door was shut behind them, the three girls stood for a minute musingly. Miss Caley sat down at the open piano and ran her right hand lightly over the treble. Then she jumped up again.

"What eyes Mr. Blakely has!" she said.

There was no reply for a minute; then Miss Willerby, standing with one foot on the fender, said, with apparent irrelevance but in a tone of conviction:

"The tip of Mr. Marsh's little finger is worth the whole of Mr. Blakely, body and soul together, with all his cousins and aunts and parents and grandparents and remote ancestors thrown in."

"Don't talk of remote ancestors just before going to bed!" exclaimed Miss Caley. "I know I shall see ghosts if you do."

Miss Holt had not seemed to hear this conversation, but had touched the button of an electric bell, in response to which the butler now entered the room.

"Is Mr. Holt still in the library, Thomas?" asked his mistress.

"Yes, miss."

"Will you girls have anything to eat or drink before going to bed—lemonade or anything?"

"Gracious, no, dear!" said Miss Willerby; "we have been eating and drinking all day!"

"Well, let us go and say good-night to papa. You can turn out the lights here, Thomas. Come on, girls! Good-night, Thomas."

"Good-night, miss;" and the butler moved silently over to the piano-lamp and, stooping under the shade, felt for the knob by which to turn it down; while the three left the room, Miss Holt leading and the others following, Miss Caley with her arm caressingly round Miss Willerby's waist.

VII

A MAN OF AFFAIRS

BARRY, in addition to his extraordinary susceptibility to the charms of the fair sex, was a person of some originality in other ways. His father had been one of the "early settlers" when the now flourishing city was no more than a trading-post in the wilderness, and the son had lived here, except for occasional absences of a few months at a time, all his life. Having been at school with more than half of the women and men of his age in town, he called them by their Christian names, and they in turn, men and women alike, called him "Will." He had led more cotillons and acted as best man at more weddings than any other three men in the place, and had danced and fallen in love, for he was now thirty-six and had begun to dance at eighteen, with more than a dozen successive "crops" (as he called them) of girls. His partners of to-day had sat upon his knees years ago when he called to make love to their aunts and elder sisters, and his partners of the old days had daughters to whom Barry found it necessary now to take off his hat in the street. It would not be many years before he was dancing with them, he said. He himself had scarcely aged in the last eighteen years. In appearance he was tall and loose-jointed, slightly round-shouldered, with lightish brown hair and mustache, the former dry and unruly, especially one lock which insisted on falling over his forehead almost to his eyes, so that, as he hurried about a ball-room, he was forever smoothing it with his hand or throwing it back with a colt-like toss of the head.

His business capacity had not so far given evidence of being remarkable. For a time he had studied law, and had been admitted to the bar. The window of his office bore the sign in

6

gold letters "William Barry, Attorney-at-Law—Real Estate and Loans." As a matter of fact, he did almost anything now except practice law, interesting himself in whatever came his way, especially in the organization of companies (which were never fully organized) for the exploitation of impracticable patents. He was not known to have made money in anything; but was constantly losing small amounts in almost everything. However, though his father had been of a thriftless turn in his later years, there still remained enough of the original homestead claim, now valuable city property, to make the son something more than well-to-do, and to place him, barring some exceptional recklessness, beyond the danger of financial discomfort to the end of his days. Business, with him, was not a means of making money, but a method of passing the time. He supported his office much as another man might support a stable or a conservatory. He used to say himself that it was fortunate that he was not of a naturally industrious disposition; it would soon ruin him. At present he only worked half the time — dabbled in business as one might dabble in horse-racing—and the expenditure came comfortably within the limits of his income. If he were to work all the time, he would assuredly live beyond his means.

It was in this same paradoxical spirit that he approached the details of his work. It was not the commercial value of a scheme that interested him so much as its artistic merits. Thus he had a few days before unfolded to Marsh the outline of a project for a new company to which he was just then devoting his time. It was to be called the National Monumental Association, and was in the nature of an insurance company; but instead of paying a sum of money to the heirs at death, the association would erect a monument to the deceased in some conspicuous location in the city. The plan contemplated, in the first place, the securing from the city of an exclusive franchise for the erection of monuments in the parks and public squares, the association agreeing, in exchange for the franchise, to erect at least one monument every year in commemoration of some distinguished fellow-townsman. The designs for the monuments would be subject to the approval of the City Council. A list of some two hundred or two hundred and fifty "prominent citizens" was drawn up, and these were to be approached and solicited to subscribe. A payment of two hundred dollars a year, during life, would secure at death a life-size marble statue of the deceased, to be erected on a site selected at the time of payment of the first premium. Two hundred and fifty dollars a year would secure an heroic figure with a base ten feet in height. Five hundred dollars a year would suffice for a granite plinth twenty-five feet high and a colossal figure on the top. Special rates were to be provided for equestrian statues, memorial arches, and fountains, and for statues approached by flights of steps and supported by symbolical groups, while scales of payment were further graded in accordance with the desirability of the site selected.

"It isn't in human nature," he said, enthusiastically, "that any of these men will refuse to come in. Ninety per cent. of them will subscribe, anyway. There will be money in it, and, moreover, the association will be a public benefactor. In twenty-five years the city will be better supplied with statues than any town of its size in the country."

Whether he was really in earnest in the scheme or not it was difficult to say, but at least he was devoting his time to its development with considerable ardor. He had drawn up the articles of association and a draft of a franchise to be submitted to the council, and was at work on the prospectus, in which the advantages to subscribers were set forth in alluring and picturesque phraseology. He had had maps of the city prepared, on which all possible monumental sites were marked with a red star, and each was numbered. These were to be classified according to their desirability and their suitability for special types of monuments. Draughtsmen were at work designing statues of a variety of types which were to be used by the canvassers of the association in soliciting patronage, and full instructions were to be drawn up for the guidance of the canvassers in approaching every individual on the list—with hints as to his character and means, and the class of statue which each was most likely to be disposed to invest in.

This preliminary work on his schemes Barry never failed to elaborate on the minutest scale. Usually the scheme ended with this preliminary work, and Marsh did not anticipate that the National Monumental Association would ever advance beyond the stage at which his other projects had been dropped—as, for instance, his Ladies' Clearing - house and Five o'Clock Tea Parlors, on which he had been so busy a few weeks ago. This plan contemplated the establishment somewhere downtown, in one of the large office buildings, of a suite of rooms to be furnished as luxuriously as possible, with heavy draperies, deep chairs, and mellow lights, at which women would drop in and chat during the afternoon, and where men, leaving their offices for twenty minutes in the middle of the hurry of business, could refresh themselves with a cup of tea amid these sumptuous surroundings, and with the added distraction of women's society. He was sure that both men and women would patronize the parlors largely—especially in view of the clearing-house feature of the scheme. Women would not only meet here and exchange calls, but they would leave at the office blocks of their cards—two hundred, say, at a time—together with lists of those for whom they were intended. The lists thus left would be checked off against each other, and the cards "cleared," as checks are through a regular clearing-house, once a week, or as often as might appear desirable. It would relieve women of all the drudgery of the social "calling" of to-day.

Barry had spent considerable time in what he called "missionary work" among the women of his acquaintance in behalf of this enterprise. He had obtained the refusal of a long-term lease on a desirable suite of offices suitable for the purpose; had made elaborate calculations of income and expense; had received estimates and competitive designs for the decoration and furnishing of the rooms from all over the country. Then the thing had been shelved — only for a while, Barry said, because he was busy with other things.

The number of schemes of this kind which he evolved was almost endless. One was for an International Matrimonial Bureau, a regularly incorporated company, which was to place the existing system of international marriages of American heiresses to European noblemen, where Barry asserted it rightfully belonged, on a frank and open commercial basis. Wealthy fathers of marriageable daughters in this country were to be invited to subscribe in annual payments to a common fund,

which fund was to be used for purchasing the outfits and paying the travelling expenses of eligible noblemen in Europe, who
would be consigned to this country with letters of introduction
only to the subscribers to the fund.

Another plan contemplated the contracting for advertising
rights in all the elevators in office buildings in large cities, the
space to be sublet to advertisers, as is done now in street-cars, .
etc. Yet another had in view the establishment of what Barry
called a Card School, whereat, in apartments similar to those
of the Social Clearing-house and Five o'Clock Tea Company,
ladies were to be given lessons in whist, écarté, euchre, piquet,
Boston, cribbage, bezique, hearts, and whatever else might be
the fashionable card games of the day.

In all of Barry's schemes there was sufficient commercial
plausibility to forbid their unqualified condemnation without
trial; but they possessed also a certain twist and eccentricity
which prevented their being a tempting field for the invest-
ment of capital. The only company which he was known to
have ever fully organized was one for the refining of sugar by
the use of an electric current, based on patents which had sub-
sequently been proved to be worthless. For the rest, they
never advanced beyond the preliminary stages, but sufficed
meanwhile to keep their originator pleasantly and not too ex-
pensively occupied, as well as affording endless entertainment
to his friends.

Barry's mother had died when he was a child, and his father
had followed her when the son was sixteen years of age. He
had no brothers or sisters. Marsh liked him, as did everybody
else, and for nearly two years the pair had shared the suite of
bachelor apartments which they now occupied—two sitting-
rooms, two bedrooms, a bath-room, etc. The rooms were situated well down-town, and on this Wednesday night the two
walked the mile and a half which lay between the "Holt mansion" and their quarters almost in silence. It was a beautiful
night, crisp and cold, without moonlight, but the sky luminous,
and every star brilliantly distinct. The paved sidewalks lay
glistening white before them, and on either side the outlines of
the houses and trees stood out in clear-cut silhouette against
the steely background. They walked briskly, each occupied

with his own thoughts, their arms swinging, and their foot-steps, as their heels struck the stones in unison, echoing in the silent night air. Scarcely a word had been exchanged when they reached their quarters.

The gas having been turned up, each disappeared to his own room, but presently reappeared, patent-leather shoes having been exchanged for slippers, and dress-coats for, in Marsh's case, a gray sack-coat, and, in Barry's, for a gorgeous scarlet smoking-jacket, faced with quilted blue silk. The room was large and comfortably furnished, the big centre-table littered with books, magazines, and writing-materials. Three of the walls were almost covered to a height of some five feet from the floor with book-shelves, well filled with the united libraries of the two men. Above the book-shelves hung a number of engravings and etchings, all good and some of considerable value, sprinkled between trophies of fencing masks and foils, tennis-racquets, boxing-gloves, guns, rods, riding-whips, and the like. Over the entrance was a large elk's head with branching antlers. Along the fourth side of the room, on either hand of the fireplace, ran a deep wall-seat, comfortably upholstered and strewn with many cushions. On this, after the two had filled and lighted their pipes (for both were, in the privacy of their chambers, pipe smokers), Barry threw himself at full length, while Marsh sank back into the recesses of a vast arm-chair. The latter smoked a short English brier, while his companion flaunted one of those impossible German mon-strosities with a portentously long and flexible stem and a painted porcelain bowl, with which Barry was always in diffi-culties, and constantly spilling the lighted tobacco in small heaps on the floor, which smoked like altar fires until he rolled off the lounge to stamp them out with his foot.

For some minutes they puffed in silence, which was at last broken by Marsh.

" What's a man to do when a scoundrel comes across his path and gets in his way ?" he asked.

" What kind of a scoundrel ?" queried the other. " One that the police are after, or just an every-day, evening-dress, snake-in-the-bosom, husband's-best-friend kind ?"

" Well, the police would be no use in this case."

"Oh!" said Barry, sententiously, "then the best thing to do is to let him alone."

"But if he is in love with the girl you are in love with?" Marsh suggested.

"The man who is in love with your girl is always a scoundrel," remarked the dogmatic Barry.

"Well, but what would you do?"

"What *would* I do?" snorted Barry, contemptuously. "What *do* I do, you mean. Why, go in and cut him out and get the girl. Sometimes," he added, philosophically, "the other fellow goes in first, however, and then he gets the girl."

"Generally, I should say," Marsh remarked, "judging from results. You don't seem to have hung on to many of the girls that you have got."

"That's a fact," Barry exclaimed, briskly, and with a certain bird-like air of surprise, as if some entirely new and interesting fact had been brought to his attention. "I haven't, have I? Not one! Nary girl."

Then silence intervened again. Presently Barry continued:

"He is a scoundrel, though. I'm with you there."

"Who?" asked Marsh, in surprise.

"Why, Blakely," replied the other. Marsh made no comment, but he had not intended that the personal application of his inquiries would be so readily grasped and so bluntly put into words. They puffed on again for a while, and then Barry broke out:

"It's an amazing thing," he said, "how good girls insist on falling in love with worthless men. The better the girl, in fact, the worse the man whom she seems to prefer. Given a good girl with a good brother, and she will always fall in love with a man whom he won't ask to his house."

"It really seems," Marsh assented, gloomily, "as if the average woman liked wickedness in men."

"Like it!" broke in Barry, "she adores it! It is just the kind of wickedness that she ought most of all to abominate that she adores most. A clean fellow, with honest ambitions and made of the right stuff, has no manner of show compared to a dashing, dissipated rake, who makes a business of making fools of women. If getting a wife was the only end of existence, we should have to turn our code of morals upside-down, and blackguardism would be a leading virtue."

"I wonder, however," suggested Marsh, "if men are not equally fascinated with bad women."

"Bad men are," said Barry—"and the majority of men are bad.   Scott! what a beastly thing the average man of the day is!   And, therefore, in a casually assorted hundred men, the fast, flashy woman will find more admirers than the sweet, modest girl.   But the best men want their women good—especially for marrying.   But the trouble is that it is the best women who want the bad men.   They take them like people in England eat that fruit—what is it called?—medlars!—just rotten!   And they marry them, too."

"'Here continueth to rot the body Sir Somebody Something,'" Marsh quoted from the famous epitaph.   "But there is one thing to be said: women don't know what a bad man means."

"Not until they marry him," said Barry, "and then they find out.   It's terrible.   And what is to be done?   Tell them everything?   Nobody can do that except the girls' mothers, and it must be pretty hard for a mother to put those kind of things into a pure girl's mind.   And do we—the other men, I mean—want girls to know everything?"

"There is no way to help it except by men being better," said Marsh.   "The average man—take the average man in the average ball-room—isn't fit to touch the average girl that he dances with."

"Of course he isn't.   But you may as well talk of making the earth roll backward as of making men better.   So long as society is anything like what it is, and human nature is human nature, men are going to be beasts and women are going to love them for it."

"I am not so sure of that," said Marsh, thoughtfully. "One thing, I think, is certain, and that is, that in the last hundred years, whether men have grown to be any better in regard to women or not, they have grown to seem better. The tone of conversation among gentlemen has immeasurably improved.   There weren't any gentlemen in those days, according to our ideas, or mighty few.   Men bragged about

things then that they keep to themselves to-day, and from
boasting of a thing to being ashamed of it is a good long
step towards reform. It is quite true that we still regard as
venial offences lots of things which ought to be treated as
deadly sins. But they are offences now. They were not in
the last century; and I think we are on the upward road the
whole time. I believe in human nature—in social as well as
political ethics. It is Emerson, isn't it, who says that it is
only by strength of its silent virtue that mankind continues
to exist—or words to that effect? In this and in other things
I think men are getting better, and will get better."

"Maybe; but not fast enough to do much good in our
generation. It may come in time to save our granddaughters,
but I doubt it. No wonder they draw Cupid as blind! And
yet they say that the unknown is always terrible. Not for
women it isn't. I suppose the time is coming when we shall
be ashamed to lie and steal from the custom-house and the
government in matters of taxes, and so forth. But we are a
good long way from it yet."

There was a silence of some minutes, during which the
thoughts of each wandered after their own bent. At last Barry
spoke again.

"Look at Effie Marston, who married that Braisted fellow,"
he said. "She was one of the sweetest girls in town, and
there was not a decent man here who would have put him up
at a club or asked him to dinner. I saw her a year afterwards
in New York. What a wreck she was! I hardly knew her."

"Then that Hardy girl—Nellie—" said Marsh, "throwing
herself away on King!"

"Yes; there's another case. Why, I was in love with
Nellie Hardy myself once. Not sure that I wasn't in love
with Effie Marston, too, for that matter."

Marsh's pipe was out, and he rose and knocked the ashes out
and hung it on a rack beside the mantel.

"Speaking of girls," began Barry, in a new tone, "did you
notice Miss Caley much? I think she's about as fascinating a
thing as I have ever seen—"

"Have you," said Marsh, as he stretched himself drowsily,
"ever read Longfellow's ' Spanish Student' ?"

"Oh, *shut* up!" exclaimed Barry, as he rolled off the lounge, upsetting in the process his ashes on the floor. "Damn Long-fellow's 'Spanish Student'!"

And he, too, put away his pipe, and stretched himself.

VIII

Long after Barry was asleep Marsh lay tormented with thoughts of Blakely and Miss Holt as they would be at the theatre the next evening. When he slept it was to dream confused dreams of Miss Holt, dressed in the garb of an apostle, on trial for misappropriating municipal funds, and pleading in excuse that she did not know that Blakely was rotten. Before his usual hour for rising in the morning he found himself suddenly wide awake, his mind picking up the dismal thread of his thoughts where he had dropped it the night before. In the cold, new light the situation showed even more cheerless than it had overnight. In desperation he threw himself out of bed and dressed with superfluous energy, splashing much in his bath, and brushing his hair with ferocity. But do what he would, forever was there drumming in the back of his head the thought that they would be together that evening. At breakfast he pretended to read the paper, but what he read was meaningless. He saw what purported to be a "special telegram" from Jackson, saying:

"The largest rally of the season is expected at Jason Hall to-morrow, when the Hon. Horace Marsh is to speak on the principles of the new Democracy. The distinguished young orator will arrive in Jackson in the afternoon, and will be met by a deputation of leading Democrats, who will escort him to the Boston House, where a suite of rooms has been reserved for him during his brief stay in the city."

He smiled to himself at the "Hon." before his name, and wondered what the deputation of leading Democrats would do if he failed to appear on the appointed train, but stayed behind to attend a theatre-party. The morning was cold and raw, and Marsh's temper did not improve as he walked through the chilly air to his office. He opened his mail and found it uninteresting. A letter from a client making polite suggestions as to the line of defence in a certain suit only made him wish that there was some legal method of proceeding against Blakely—an injunction to stop the theatre-party, or something of the sort. The regular monthly statement from the livery-stable at which he kept his saddle-horse conjured up the vision of those two riding side by side, "Mr. and Mrs. Marshal Blakely"—and how superb she was on horseback! And he rode well, too, confound him!

Then his partner came in, rubbing his hands cheerfully and asking him when his train left.

"In about three-quarters of an hour," said Marsh, in a tone of discontent; "it leaves at ten ten."

"Well, you haven't much time, have you? How are you feeling to-day? We want a rattling speech to-night."

Marsh grumbled something about feeling well enough, and the General retired to his own room, unpleasantly conscious that his young colleague was not in a kindly mood.

"Get me a messenger-boy, will you, Franklin," Marsh called to one of the clerks in the outer office, and he heard the " whir-r-r-r" of the mechanical call that was affixed to the wall as Franklin turned the handle. The boy came, chewing gum, and lolled against Marsh's desk, letting his eyes wander superciliously round the office as Marsh gave him his instructions to go to his rooms, get his valise, take it to the station, and wait there for him. The boy fumbled tediously over his book of charges.

"Thirty-five," he said. Marsh gave him the money and fifteen cents for himself. The boy turned the coins over in his hand, but made no remark either of thanks or complaint.

"Sign that," he said, laying a crumpled ticket on Marsh's desk. Marsh did so, and the boy lounged out of the office whistling, and hitting the chairs as he passed them with a stick which he had in his hand.

Twenty minutes later Horace had said good-bye to the General, and was buttoning up his overcoat on the point of leaving the office when Sullivan came in.

"Marrchin' order, is it, me boy?" he rolled out, laying a heavy hand on Marsh's shoulder. "The young Hannibal in the act o' starrtin' to cross the Alps and invade the innemy's counthry. But it isn't vinegar at all that he'll be usin' to soften the rocks, but just honey and molasses and sweet blarney. Well, give it to 'em, me lad! There's a score or so o' benighted Republicans too many in Jackson that's needin' convartin' badly—not to mention certain self-glorified Dimicrats that thinks they own the party."

At length Marsh reached the station, and found the messenger-boy, the valise on the platform beside him, engrossed in the titles of the paper-covered novels at the news-stand. Marsh relieved him of his charge and signed the crumpled ticket once more, and the boy lounged away again without having said a word. It was a local train, consisting of only one day-coach and a smoking-car. The coach was stiflingly hot, and the red plush seat which Marsh selected looked very dusty. There were about a dozen other people in the car, including the inevitable baby. It seemed to Marsh as if the train were an unconscionably long time in starting, and then it ran slowly and stopped at every station. At each stop the agent came out with a scrap of paper in his hand, and a row of men in dusty brown clothes, their trousers tucked into their boots, and broad-brimmed slouch-hats on their heads, leaned against the wooden depot-building, and looked moodily at the train as it pulled in and out. As it started the brakeman came into the car, banging the door behind him, and set himself to work clatteringly at the stove, with no other apparent purpose than to make a noise. Marsh tried to force himself to think of what he was to say that evening, but all the while the wheels pounded over the rail joints with a "clickety! clickety! Marshal! Blakely! clickety! clickety! curse him! curse him!" and it grew hotter and hotter in the coach, and the baby cried, and Marsh wondered why on earth he had ever gone into politics.

About one o'clock he ate a sandwich—an intolerable deal of bread and not one ha'pennyworth of ham — at a small way-station, and drank two mouthfuls of gritty coffee. Returning to the train, he entered the smoking-car for a cigar after his meal, but the place smelled foully, and the floor was littered with tobacco-juice and orange-peel. Horace threw away his cigar before it was half smoked, and returned to his place in the day-coach.

About three o'clock they reached Jackson, and Marsh, stepping from the car, was met by the deputation of leading Democrats, three in number, each wearing a silk hat and a flower in his button-hole. The spokesman introduced himself and then his fellows, and insisted on taking Marsh's valise from his reluctant fingers. The party entered a large open hack, which was waiting for them, while the driver, having alighted from his box, but holding the reins in his hands, held the door open and swore at the horses, which showed signs of fidgeting. It was only two squares to the Boston House, a low, two-story, wooden building, where Marsh registered and shook hands with the proprietor, who said that he was glad to meet him. The "lobby" of the Boston House was a big bare room, with an uneven plank floor still wet with washing, studded with large leather cuspidors and with a huge iron stove in the centre, around which were seated a dozen men, who looked in seemingly contemptuous curiosity at the party as it entered. In one corner was a cigar and news stand, and in another the hotel office. The walls were hung with flaming advertisements of railways and framed pictures of blonde young women in excessively low evening dress, who sipped in simpering delight champagne of various brands.

Would Mr. Marsh like to drive around town, or was he tired after his journey, and would he prefer to go to his room and rest? He would much rather go to his room, if the gentlemen did not mind. On the contrary, the gentlemen were evidently relieved. It would be necessary, they explained, to leave the hotel at about half-past seven, when the same deputation would have the pleasure of escorting Mr. Marsh to the hall, and if Mr. Marsh would not object to taking his supper rather early—say, at half-past five—they would have an informal levee in the hotel lobby for an hour or so, in order that the local Democracy might meet and be individually presented to the distinguished guest. Mr. Marsh signified his modest acquiescence in this arrangement, and was shown to his "suite of rooms."

The suite consisted of the ordinary Western hotel bedroom, and a small and uninviting bath-room opening therefrom. The bedroom exhibited the usual poverty of furnishing. A large double bed; a chest of drawers surmounted by a mirror; a small, oblong deal-table, covered with a white table-cover, in the centre of the room; one rocking-chair; two cane chairs; a white ice-water pitcher, and a corrugated china match-safe on the mantel completed the equipment, except that on one wall hung an engraving—an excellent impression of Girardet's reproduction of Jules Romain's "Triomphe de Vespasien et de Titus," and Marsh wondered how in the world such a thing came to be in such a place. He looked at it for a while, and thought what a dreadfully jolty and uncomfortable vehicle the triumphal car must have been, and what ridiculously small heads the horses had for their fat and well-fed bodies. He gazed aimlessly out of the window, and read the advertisements on a hoarding opposite. Then he shook himself, and set resolutely to work to rehearse his speech for the evening. But it was useless. The words would not come, and the only thing that he could think of was the theatre-party. So he let his thoughts have their way, and somehow the hours dragged along.

At the appointed time he went to supper, and wrestled for a while in the mournful silence of the bare dining-room with a piece of impossible steak. Reaching the lobby of the hotel, he found his three friends of the afternoon already awaiting him, and the tedious process of introduction began. For over an hour he stood there, and shook hands with an immense number of uninteresting people—mostly colonels and judges and majors—who seemed to have nothing to say beyond that they were pleased to meet him. He did his best to find some remark to make to everybody, and to keep up between times a fragmentary conversation with the body-guard that had grouped itself around him. Gradually the room filled up, and the air was thick with tobacco-smoke.

"I haven't seen so many people in this room," said the spokesman of the deputation at his elbow, "since Voorhees was here two years ago." The spokesman was a red-faced, plethoric gentleman, who somehow conveyed by his manner the impression that whatever he said was of great moment.

Marsh endeavored to look properly flattered. But all the while he was sickeningly conscious that the whole thing was a ridiculous farce. He felt, as he had never felt on any former occasion, that he and these men had little in common, that he was not of their kind, and that they were not the material of which the ideal party for the redemption of the country could be formed. The announcement that it was "nearly time to be moving" came as an immense relief, and he escaped again to his room, to spend as much time as possible in washing his hands and face, arranging his necktie, and putting on his overcoat.

On the way to the hall he could think of nothing except that elsewhere others were on their way to the theatre, and as he stood among the side-scenes on the stage he had a curious feeling that he was not really there. The voices of the members of the body-guard which had again accumulated around him came from far away, and their demonstrative enthusiasm as one after another peeped out to see how the hall was filling up appeared absurdly trivial. Then the moment came when the body-guard filed on the stage, and took their seats, among much shuffling of feet, on the chairs which were arranged in a semicircle facing the audience. Only the spokesman of the deputation, who was also to be chairman of the meeting, stayed with him. The short burst of perfunctory applause which had greeted the appearance of the body-guard died away, and silence settled on the house, broken only by an occasional cough or the movement of feet in the rear. Then the chairman signalled to him, and the two stepped out. This time the applause was more in earnest, and Marsh found himself bowing in the glare of the foot-lights, with no thought except of the ridiculousness of his being here when the whole happiness of his life was at stake in a game which was being played that night a hundred miles away.

The formal introduction was soon over, and as the chairman retired to his seat the applause broke out anew. Horace stepped forward mechanically, and squared his shoulders as if to begin to speak. He let his eyes wander over the sea of faces before him, and the big audience was still as if it were

frozen. Seconds passed, and he did not speak. The silence
became oppressive, and an uneasy shuffling of feet broke out
here and there in the hall. Suddenly Horace's voice came
forth in spite of himself. He knew the first few sentences
of his speech by heart, and, as it seemed to him, without any
volition on his part, the voice spoke them. He was afraid—
so this voice which issued from him said—that the audience
might be disappointed in what he had to tell them, being misled by the advertised title of his address. If under the name
of the principles of Democracy they expected him to elucidate
the motives of the Democratic party of the past, if they expected any fiery arraignment of the members or the actions
of the Republican party, they would be disappointed. The
principles of the Democracy, the principles which he trusted underlay and would always inspire the united party to
which they all belonged, were simply the principles of honor
and truth which underlay and inspired all right government
in all ages and all nations. "It is necessary" (so the voice
continued) "that we—you and I—should understand these
principles and lay them to our hearts ; for this government is
a government by the people, and it is we—you and I—who
are of the party of the people, and" (and he raised his right
hand involuntarily to emphasize what he was saying) "we—
must—govern !"

There was a moment of silence as he paused, with his
hand uplifted. Then in a sudden crash came the applause.
Thenceforward it was easy. The audience proved itself quick
and responsive, and he played with it. He talked to them
and they listened. He dropped his voice to a conversational
tone to tell an anecdote, and they laughed. He rose to a
higher level and spoke of the eternal principles of government,
and they seemed to hold their breath. He drove home a
maxim of political morality, or flung at them some high aphorism of one or other of our country's great men of the past,
and the thunder came in reply.

For an hour and a half he spoke, with no thought now
save of the cause of which he was speaking. He led his
audience with him out of the valley and low ground of partisan politics, up to the foot-hills, and then to the mountain-

7

tops; and he held them there. There was no abuse of individual leaders of the other side, nor of the Republican party itself. In much the same language of abstraction and generality as he had used at the Holt dinner-table, he told his hearers that it was not by arraigning individuals or inviting recrimination that the ends of the nation could be served or the ends of right. Let the dead past bury its dead. There had been errors made and wrongs done; but it was idle to throw all blame for those errors and those wrongs on one party or one set of men. "Let us rather rejoice," he said, "that Providence in its mercy has seen that with only men to govern—men with all humanity's natural proneness to err and to be unjust—the history of our country holds so much that is high and noble. Let us rejoice rather in our common heritage of honor, seeking not to pull down but to build up, not striving to distinguish between this good thing which is ours and that doubtful act which is theirs, but holding intact as on one glorious scroll all the noble traditions of our country's past. We are not the heirs to the estate of any party, but to all our nation's history. Let us remember the wrongs done only as warnings to us in the future; let us cherish whatever is good for an example for our guidance. We can take no backward step. All the glory that is gone, though living with us yet, is but a preparation for the greater glory yet to come. It is into our hands—the hands of you and me—that the destiny of the nation that we love so well is to be given—given only in trust for the generations that come after. It is for us to see that in our hands the nation passes only from greatness to greatness, and this cannot be except we place our trust in God, and recognize that only by truth and justice can any government prosper."

He had spoken throughout not only with spirit and enthusiasm, but with a tone of conviction in the future of the cause which gave a singular weight and air of truth to whatever he said. The speech was hardly what his audience was accustomed to listen to or to look for in party oratory. There were some who felt at times a certain thrill which somehow reminded them of long-forgotten sensations which had come to them as children when in church. But though most

of what they had heard was unexpected and strange, they
could not but feel that it was good and impassioned and pure.
They had listened breathlessly to every word, and at the end
they were conscious that their faces were flushed with a certain triumphant exaltation of spirit. The applause as the
young orator closed was deafening, and he was compelled
again and again to come forward and bow repeated recog-
nitions long after he had stepped back and his place had
been taken by the chairman of the meeting, who stood smilingly waiting in silence before he could ask for the usual vote
of thanks.

In doing so he also took occasion to "make a few remarks." They were brief, but they jarred on Marsh's senses
horribly. He, in speaking of the party's mission, had necessarily referred to "those influences of wealth and position and personality which are supposed to have more weight
in our government than is consistent with the principles on
which our Constitution is founded." He had spoken only in
the broadest terms fitted to the high ideals which he preached.
To his amazement, however, the chairman selected this one
passage of his speech for special comment, and he gave to it
a local significance which was not only far from Horace's intention, but which revolted him. The words to which they
had just listened, said the chairman, on the subject of the in-
equality of the distribution of wealth and the tyranny of the
corporations, and those millionaires whose fortunes and power
were based upon the iniquities of the Republican party's system of government for the benefit of the few would, the
chairman was sure, have more than common weight, inasmuch as their distinguished guest resided in, and had only
that morning left, their sister city, which, as his hearers
knew, was about to be convulsed by a Titanic struggle between the forces of outraged labor and tyrannical capital.
As the speaker had so eloquently said, it was one of the
proudest boasts of the Democracy that it was the friend of
labor, and the entire party in the State would sympathize with
the working-men in the noble conflict in which they were
embarking.

For a moment Horace had a wild idea of protesting against

assigning to him any such sentiments as the chairman credited him with. But that was obviously useless. He was already bowing in acknowledgment of the applause with which the thanks of the meeting had been voted to him, and from all parts of the house, amid much trampling of feet and scraping of chairs, a movement had set in towards the stage. Then came more handshaking, and Horace was compelled to smile his thanks to endless meaningless compliments; but through it all he could only wonder dully what had happened at the theatre.

At length he was alone in his room at the hotel once more, and almost as soon as he was in bed he fell asleep from mere physical exhaustion.

He returned to town by a train leaving in the middle of the forenoon, being escorted to the station by the deputation of the preceding day. Half-way on his journey he obtained at a way-station his customary morning paper. His speech he found reported at considerable length, filling over a column of "special telegram," and he read it with the usual annoyance at printers' errors and reporters' ineptitude. When he came to the last paragraph, however, his face lowered. The chairman's closing remarks were also reproduced in full, and, turning to the editorial page of the paper, he found there a long article, very laudatory of himself, in which all that the chairman had said was imputed to him, and he was represented as having made a stirring speech in behalf of the cause of labor and in bitter arraignment of the two companies of which Mr. Holt was president.

Had he been more experienced in the intricacies of practical politics, he would doubtless have understood that the word had gone out from headquarters that the strike was to be an issue in the campaign, and that the cause of the strikers was to be the cause of the party. As it was, he only cursed the clumsiness of newspaper writers in his heart, and thought with agony of what Miss Holt would think if she should see that paper. There was little chance of that, however, he guessed; for it was not probable that the Democratic party organ furnished the regular morning reading in the Holt household.

IX

LOOKING INTO THE GULF

NOVELISTS have much to say about the slender thread upon which the fortunes of our lives are strung—the trifling accidents and chance meetings by which our destinies are swayed; but we hear little of the narrow escapes—the propinquities which just miss being meetings—the coincidences which barely fail to coincide. If once in a while we find ourselves confronted by a well-known face in a foreign land, we think it a marvellous thing, smacking almost of the supernatural. But how often do we escape these collisions only by a hair's-breadth? We enter the very car, perhaps, from which our friend alighted at the last station; we tread in his footsteps, where he has been but a minute before; he passes by the door of the house wherein we are hidden. So in dreams ten thousand things may come to us—things clothed in verisimilitude, and which might just as well happen; but they do not. And they pass and are forgotten. At last comes one dream which impinges, be it never so slightly, on the happenings of the next day or the next month, and we cry, "A miracle!" We store it in our memory, and tell it again and again in after-years, as in some sort reflecting credit on ourselves, testifying to our possession of a measure of a second-sight.

There was a moment when Horace was on his way to take the train to Jackson when, had he but turned his head, he might have seen Miss Holt. She, indeed, saw him, and leaned forward in her brougham, wishing that he would turn, and ready on the moment to tell her coachman to stop. Without any close analysis of her feelings, she felt that she had caused him to suffer, and was eager to make amends by wishing him at least good-speed on his day's errand. But there was no good fairy to touch him on the shoulder—no magnetism in her thoughts to make him turn. So he passed on, brooding with downcast eyes, missing the smile and the touch of the hand and the kind words which were awaiting him, and which would have gone so far to alleviate the discomforts of the trip—to have made the hot and dusty car clean and comfortable, to have rendered the sandwich palatable, and given the coffee flavor. So largely subjective are the impressions which we receive from external things.

Miss Holt, at the time, was on her way to her father's office, to discuss with him some questions of domestic expenditure. She had arisen that morning with a light heart, and Miss Willerby had not failed to notice the joyousness with which she presided at the breakfast-table. Arriving at her father's office, and learning from the obsequious clerks without that he was disengaged, she passed in unannounced. He was always glad to see her, for they were good friends. As they talked now she stood by his side, with her arm caressingly on his shoulder. She had about concluded the mission on which she had come when a clerk announced that the committee was there.

" I said that I would meet them at a quarter-past ten this morning," Mr. Holt said to his daughter, "and it is five-and-twenty minutes past now. Show them in !" addressing the clerk. And then to his daughter again, " Would you like to hear what they have to say ? If so, go in there," pointing to the door of another room, "and leave the door ajar. The other door into the hall is open, and you can step out whenever you are tired."

She kissed him hurriedly, and without a word went into the room which he had indicated. She had hardly pulled the door to behind her, leaving it an inch or two open, when the committee entered, seven in number. They came in, treading on each other's heels, and with a curious mixture of bashfulness and defiance in their manner.

" Come in, gentlemen," said Mr. Holt, advancing and shaking hands with each, " and be seated, please."

Chairs enough had been placed in the room in anticipation of their coming, and they had soon arranged themselves, each sitting stiffly, holding his hat in his lap. A stenographer also entered, and took his seat at a table in one corner of the room.

"Now, gentlemen," Mr. Holt began, "before we proceed to business, let me know exactly with whom it is that I am dealing. Whom do you represent?"

It was Wollmer who replied.

"We are a joint committee representing the employés of the Western Iron and Steel Company and the street-railway company—all classes of the employés of both companies."

"And to begin with, Mr. Wollmer," for Mr. Holt knew Wollmer well, "which do you personally represent?"

"I represent both. I am committeeman-at-large."

"But of which company are you an employé?"

"Neither," said Wollmer, uneasily; "I represent the organizations."

"Then I am afraid I must decline to talk with you," said Mr. Holt, firmly, but courteously. "I can recognize nobody in these negotiations but the employés of the companies."

"You decline to recognize the organizations?"

"I do."

"You know that that is one of the questions now at issue, and that the organizations propose to insist on recognition?" asked Wollmer, threateningly.

"I have gathered as much," replied the other. "But I have no intention, on behalf of the companies, of conceding the whole question by recognizing the organizations through you in advance." After a moment's pause, Mr. Holt continued: "I have no objection to your remaining in my office, Mr. Wollmer, if these gentlemen desire it, as a spectator, but I must respectfully decline to allow you to take any part in the negotiations."

"I don't think," said Wollmer, endeavoring to speak calmly, "that you are taking the right course to reach a settlement, Mr. Holt."

"I am sorry," Mr. Holt replied, curtly; "but I am protecting, to the best of my ability, the interests of the companies which I represent. And now, gentlemen," addressing the others

with a business-like air, " I understand that you six are all employés of one or other of the companies. If you will permit
me to suggest it, I think it will be better—indeed, I presume
it is what you would propose—that we should take up the affairs of one company first. If it is agreeable to you, we will
give the iron-and-steel company preference. If you will arrange yourselves, gentlemen, so that the representatives of the
iron-and-steel company sit together, we can confer in regard
to the interests of that company. It may even be better when
that is concluded to postpone the conference with the employés
of the street-railway company until another day, in order that
we may think over the situation carefully."

In accordance with his suggestion there was a shifting of
seats, until Mr. Holt, who knew all the men present by sight
well enough, saw that the three representatives of the iron-and-
steel company—Henderson, Riley, and Smith—were together,
Henderson sitting next to Wollmer, who had retained his place
at one end of the row. It was to Henderson in particular,
though his glance also took in the other two, that Mr. Holt now
addressed himself.

"You have come, I believe, gentlemen, as a properly accred-
ited committee of the employés in the shops of the Western
Iron and Steel Company," he said, "to protest against the new
scale of wages."

Henderson bowed.

"On what grounds do you protest against it?"

"Because the wages proposed are less by about fifteen per
cent. than the union schedules. The agreement under which
we are working now is based upon those schedules—"

"Not ostensibly, I believe," interrupted Mr. Holt. "There
is no reference to the union in the agreement. And I think
you are aware, Mr. Henderson, that the company and myself
have always consistently declined to recognize the union or any
of its rules or schedules in any way."

"We consider that immaterial," replied Henderson, "so far
as the wages are concerned. We do demand recognition of
the union hereafter. There was no reference to the union
schedule in our last agreement, but the wages were based upon
it—"

"They may have coincided with it," suggested Mr. Holt.

"Coincided with it," agreed Henderson; "and, so far as we were concerned, it was the fact that they coincided that caused us to accept them. We decline now individually and collectively to work for less than that schedule." Here Wollmer leaned over and whispered something in Henderson's ear, who, thus prompted, added, "And, for the purpose of preventing any similar attempts in the future on the part of the company to reduce wages below the scale, we demand that the union shall be recognized, and that it be stated in the agreement that our wages are based on the schedule."

"And if the company refuses to accede to these demands?" asked Mr. Holt.

"This committee will have no alternative except to recommend a strike," replied Henderson.

"Let me understand this clearly," said Mr. Holt. "In the written statement of your demands, which I have here, the first three articles are concerned with wages only. No reference to any organization is made in them. The fourth article alone demands the recognition of the union, by itself. Do I understand that that fourth article is an integral and necessary part of your programme?"

"It is."

"That is to say, that it is perfectly useless to endeavor to come to any understanding on the wage question—not that I mean for an instant to suggest that the company could possibly contemplate any other terms than those proposed in the new schedule; yet it would be perfectly useless to endeavor to find any ground of compromise, as, whatever wages we might offer, none would be acceptable unless we recognized your organization?"

"The wages must be based upon the union schedule."

"That is not my question. What I want to know is—do you absolutely insist on a recognition of the union, in so many words, as a necessary concession on our part?"

"We do."

There was a general movement and shuffling of feet among the members of the committee—a movement as of relief when a crisis is reached and tension suddenly removed. In the next room Miss Holt drew a long breath and leaned forward again to listen. Mr. Holt threw himself back in his chair.

"Well, gentlemen," he said, "now I think we understand each other. This is not a question of wages, but of the union. I have here," laying his hand on some papers which lay before him, "a number of extracts from our books, balance-sheets, and summaries of pay-rolls, which I was prepared to go over with you—not so much with expectation of finding any ground for mutual concession, but rather hoping to appeal to your reason by showing you the necessity, the inexorable necessity, of our position. I was prepared to discuss matters with you most fully and frankly. But all this, it appears, is useless. I may say at once, gentlemen, that the Western Iron and Steel Company will never do what you demand. We will shut down rather, and stay shut down until the plant goes to pieces from rust and rot. We have placed no restrictions upon our men joining any labor organization that they pleased; but we insist upon our right to employ whom we please, whether members of any particular organization or not. We will not surrender that right. We will not throw over our non-union men whom we now have with us. We will under no circumstances recognize any union or order or brotherhood or organization or corporation as having any authority over our employés *as* our employés or any right to come between us and them. We are always glad to hear any complaint which our men may have to make; we will meet them in a spirit of fairness, and will endeavor to remove any reasonable grievance which may exist. But we will deal with them directly. We will not recognize the union."

The men received what he had to say in silence. After waiting for them to speak, he continued:

"This seems to me to end our meeting, unless you have some other alternative to suggest."

"I know of nothing more," said Henderson.

"Well, let us have no misunderstanding. There is no question of wages now at issue between us. It is a question of the recognition of the union, pure and simple." He looked at Henderson as if expecting a reply.

"Yes," said that gentleman, reluctantly. Mr. Holt turned to his stenographer.

"Watson, would you mind reading over those last words of
mine to these gentlemen?"   Watson did so.

"You three gentlemen all clearly understand that?"   Each
of the three addressed said that he did.

"Well," continued Mr. Holt, "reporters of the newspapers
will undoubtedly wish to talk to both of us on this subject, and
there is no room now for any divergence in our sentiments.
The question at issue is one of the union only—not one of
wages."   And he arose as if to terminate the interview.

"One thing more," said Henderson, who had been confer-
ring with Wollmer in whispers; "will you submit the matter
to arbitration?"

"To whose arbitration?" asked Mr. Holt, who had been expecting this question before.

"Well, say to General Harter."

"No."

"On what grounds do you refuse?"

"Because I do not think General Harter would be a fit man.
I wish to say nothing disparaging of him, but as candidate for
the governorship on a party ticket he would be incapable of
giving the case a dispassionate hearing.   It is not General
Harter that I object to; it is the Democratic candidate for
governor."

"So you decline to submit to arbitration?" asked Henderson.

"By no means.   If you will select some party who is not a
candidate for office, I will name somebody on my part.   I will
name one now.   I will name Judge Jessel.   Let those two select a third party, and I am willing to leave the question at issue
to them—either the simple question of the recognition of the
union or the entire list of articles in your demands."

"We cannot do that," said Henderson.   "General Harter
has offered his services, and it would be discourteous of us to
refuse to stand by him."

Mr. Holt smiled.   "Or I will consent to abide by the decision of any committee which the Chamber of Commerce may
appoint, or the Board of Trade, or any other association of
business men."

"The business men would side with you," said Henderson.

"I think they would," returned Mr. Holt, dryly.

The men now rose, and as they did so Mr. Holt said again:

"Once more, let there be no misunderstanding between us. I do not decline to submit to arbitration. I only decline to accept as arbiter any man who is a candidate for office on either side in the coming election. I offer to accept arbitration on any other reasonable terms."

The men signified their understanding, and were preparing to leave the room when Mr. Holt turned to the three who represented the street-railway company.

"Gentlemen, you have heard the position which your friends have adopted on behalf of the iron-and-steel company's employés. I suggested at the beginning of the meeting that it might be well for us to postpone our conference until another day. If it is agreeable to you, I shall be pleased to meet you at the same time to-morrow here. Meanwhile, I hope you will think the matter over clearly in your minds. Your demands are much the same as those of the employés of the iron-and-steel company. With you, also, there is a question of wages, and there is a question of recognizing your union. I may say here now that, on the question of the labor organizations, the attitude of the two companies is the same. I want you three, between now and to-morrow, to consider your own interests carefully and those of your families, so that you may not come, if it is possible to avoid it, with the door already shut against any possibility of compromise, as it has been shut to-day."

The men accepted what he said in sullen silence, and turned to leave the room. During the continuance of the conference Wollmer had with difficulty restrained himself on several occasions from breaking in. Now that the formal meeting was over, he could refrain no longer.

"It's all very well for you, Mr. Holt," he said, hotly; "you are rich and powerful, and think you can trample on the laboring man as you please. It is no question of a livelihood with you. With these men—with us—it is; and we may be weak and poor singly, but you may be sorry that you made an enemy of labor yet before you've done. You have everything you want. Your daughter has her carriages, and all the dresses, and—"

"Silence, sir!" broke in Mr. Holt, authoritatively. "I forbid you to say one word about my daughter or my domestic affairs. I am meeting these gentlemen (not you) in behalf of the two companies, and not in my individual capacity. I do not mind telling you that for the two years in which I have been president of one of them, and that for the three years that I have been president of the other, I have received no cent of salary from either. I have large sums of money invested in both, on which as yet I have received no return. If I have an income from other sources, I earned that income myself, and it is a matter which in no way concerns either you or these gentlemen."

Wollmer made no reply, but followed the others out of the room with a swaggering gait. Mr. Holt made a sign to the stenographer that he would not be needed any more. As soon as the door was shut behind them, Jessie came from her hiding-place with blanched face.

"Oh, papa!" she sobbed, falling on her knees at her father's feet, and laying her face in his lap, "can I do anything to help? Is it true that if I didn't have a carriage and so many dresses—"

"Hush, my child! No," said her father, tenderly, patting her on the shoulder; "it makes no kind of difference, and it was only that fellow's insolence."

"Oh! but I spend so much! If I didn't, and we economized on our household expenses—not to interfere with your comfort, you know, papa, but just luxuries—we could save twenty thousand dollars a year so easily!"

"And how would we save it, my darling? We should have to cut off a good many contributions to charity. We should have to discharge two or three house-servants and at least one man from the stable. Would that do any good—throwing them out of work? And all the money that you spend, my child, goes to labor in one way or another. It is not wasted. And if you did save twenty thousand dollars a year? That would be less than fifty cents a month divided equally among all the men. The question of wages is one of three hundred and fifty thousand dollars a year. Twenty thousand dollars are of no use, even if it were possible for me to give my private income to pay the companies' employés. The money is better spent—better so far as the interests of the poor are concerned —as we spend it now than it could be in any other way."

She rose from her knees, and laid her face against his for a minute; then moved to the window, where she stood and wiped away the tears that ran down her cheeks.

Mr. Holt also rose, and, standing beside her, put his arm round her waist.

"They always try to make capital," he said, "by attacking the individual who may be rich, no matter how hardly he earned his money or how he spends it. But it is not a question of individuals; it is not a question of you or of me. It is a question of one-half of mankind against the other half; a question of all countries and all ages."

She remembered how Horace Marsh had said the same thing to her a week ago in almost the same words. She did not reply, but stood silent for a while longer; then, turning to her father, she took his face between her hands.

"And I only make it harder for you, don't I, you dear old papa," she said, "with my tears and silliness? But I don't want to! I am not crying now, and I am going right away, in one of my very most expensive dresses" (it was a charming black tailor suit) "and the carriage waiting for me at the door," and she ran laughingly to the door, and threw him a kiss as she went.

As she appeared on the sidewalk below, the carriage, which had been waiting on the opposite side of the street, crossed over, and she told the coachman to drive her home. Inside the brougham she lifted her veil again and wiped away the later tears, which were still wet upon her cheeks. One of the most tender-hearted of women, she had all her life suffered intensely at the sight or even the thought of the misery of others. No inconsiderable portion of her time as well as of her income was spent in works of charity, and a day rarely passed in which she did not drive to some poor house to relieve distress, knowledge of which had come to her through one channel or another. Of the labor question she had thought but dimly until recently, and then only as some remote and uninteresting abstraction —much as she thought of the Tariff, or the Bering Sea controversy, or the Irish question. Of late, when this remote abstrac-

tion had suddenly seemed to become concrete and near at hand
—so as to be threatening the very peace of her own home—the
aspect of it which chiefly struck and pained her was the apparent unreasonableness of the men. Surely they knew, as she
had said at the dinner-table, that she or her father would do
anything they could to help them! What, then, did they want?
The impossible? It had seemed to her that it must be that they
did not understand. They must be under some absurd misapprehension—a misapprehension which could be reasoned out
of them. Now for the first time some definite recognition
of the immensity and reality of the terrible problem came to
her. It seemed as if a great cloud had settled over the earth,
and beneath it opened an abyss, black and fathomless, full of
writhing, struggling men and women—"one-half of mankind
against the other half."

Heretofore the men at the works and the employés of the
street-railway company had seemed her friends—there were
good men and bad among them, she knew; but she felt kindly
to all, and had assumed it as granted that they felt kindly to her.
Could it be that they were her enemies—that they sneered at
her dresses and her carriage as she passed? And she sank back
into the shadow of the brougham as she thought of it. Could
it be possible that these men hated her? And she remembered
what Horace had said about the French revolution, and shuddered—not with physical fear for herself, but in mere horror at
this new aspect in which the world appeared to her.

She remembered now how as a child the knowledge of death
had first come to her. It was only a dog that died—a poor,
silken-haired, bright-eyed terrier which she had loved very
dearly; for there is a golden age in childhood, when beasts and
men speak one another's language and are of kin. They had
told her that Gyp was dead — dead forever; and this new,
strange word made her heart stand still. She had watched in
tearless silence while they buried the poor thing beneath a lilac-
bush; then she had crept away by herself and cried—cried as
she had never cried before, till her mother came and found her,
her little body convulsed and weak with sobbing. For some
days she crept forlornly about the house—so silent now that
Gyp was gone — and would not play, but only sit and think.

Her father bought another dog; but it was not Gyp. Then
as she sat on the floor by her father's side while he was reading the paper, she had looked up suddenly and asked:

"Haven't you got a papa, papa?"

"Not now, Jess," he replied; "he was your grandpa."

"Where is he now?"

"He is dead."

"Dead" again! So papas died and dogs died and roses
died—died forever! She told her dolls of it, and they cried
over it together. It terrified her to have the gas turned out,
not for fear of the dark, but because the light had "gone
dead;" and she watched the birds as they flew, and feared lest
they should die as she watched.

> . . . "The woful cry
> Of life and all flesh living cometh up
> Into my ears, and all my soul is full
> Of pity for the sickness of this world."

Then she had fallen ill, and lay through the long days and
nights in the hush of the darkened room, her little face hot
and flushed with fever, and had talked incessantly in her
delirium of Gyp and of grandpa and of dead flowers. Her
mother had taken her away "into the country," where slowly
she had grown well again, and her thin arms and wasted body
became plump and firm. But the thought of death stayed
with her. Her parents said that her illness had changed her
wonderfully; that she had become, instead of the bubbling,
prattling child that she had been before, rather melancholy and
reserved. But it seemed to her that the world had changed,
and that sunlight had gone out of it.

The second great disillusion which we must all suffer, the
knowledge of evil in the world, had come to her gradually.
She had pondered over it by herself, and had asked many
questions not a little perplexing to answer. But she had
taken refuge in her faith in God—a faith which she had never
lost—the perfect faith which is given to many women, but to
which few men in these days can attain.

Now, without the physical shattering which the knowledge
of death had brought to her as a child, she seemed to feel the

same dull terror. There was the same darkening of the world.
It was not only death, but "the spirit of murder working in
the very means of life":—

> . . . "So the fair show
> Veiled one vast, savage, grim conspiracy
> Of mutual murder."

When nearing home the carriage met one of the electric
street-cars, and it seemed to her that the engineer (or motor-
neer—she hated the word) eyed the carriage and her askance,
and with a look of suspicion and dislike that she had not seen
before. She turned her face away, and would not look at the
conductor on the rear platform of the car as it passed.

At lunch she was absent-minded and silent, so that Miss Willerby wondered what could have happened since the morning
to change her so, while Miss Caley (who had received an immense box of candies from Barry) prattled and laughed, and
talked childish nonsense.

After lunch the three went for a walk together, and when
they returned Mr. Barry called and hung over the piano while
Miss Caley, after much urging, played to him, and looked un-
utterable things out of her eyes. With the five-o'clock tea
came the evening paper, and Miss Holt read the account of the
morning's conference. It was a Republican paper, and the report of what had occurred was fairly accurate. A strike, so
the paper said, was now inevitable. It would probably be declared early in the following week.

Jessie dressed for dinner listlessly, and with no pleasurable anticipation of the evening's entertainment. She wished that they
were not going. She knew how worried her father must be,
withal that he kept such a brave and smiling face at the dinner-table, and she would much rather have stayed at home that
evening, and tried to pet and comfort him. But she took a
long and very tender farewell of him, and they drove to the
theatre.

In the foyer they were met by Mr. Brace, and found the
rest of the party gathered about the ladies' dressing-room. All
had arrived except Mr. Blakely, who came a minute later, and
then they made their way in single file to the boxes, with much

8

rustling of skirts and the usual difficulty in being allotted to
their respective seats, during which the eyes of the whole house
were fixed upon them.

Miss Holt found that Blakely was assigned to the seat next
to her, at her right shoulder. In front of her sat Miss Willerby, with Pryce, the Englishman, as cavalier. Behind her
was Mrs. Tisserton, with the " dear, inoffensive creature," their
host. They were in the same box that Miss Holt had occupied
on that night when she had first seen *him* here, the other two
boxes between them and the stage being occupied by the rest
of the party, Miss Caley being placed in immediate contiguity
to the footlights, where she sat charmingly conscious that she
was the most conspicuous person in the house.

It seemed to Jessie, with some feeling of wonderment, that
she was very little moved by Blakely's proximity. Even when
he said, meaningly :

" I have seen you in this box before," she had only replied,
with perfect simplicity :

" Yes, I remember."

He, too, was conscious of the change. Somehow, he felt, she
was further away from him ; something had come between
them since last night, and he wondered what it might be.
Could she have heard anything against him? Had Marsh told
her anything after he himself had left? But what had Marsh
to tell? He was very attentive to her, in all those small ways
for which companionship at the theatre gives opportunity.
He had helped her in taking off her wrap, and even ventured
to touch, under pretence of arranging, the light black lace scarf
which she kept over her shoulders. He held her opera-glasses,
ready to offer them whenever a new character came on the
stage. He folded her programme, and was solicitous as to the
position of her chair. There was devotion in his every movement ; but she was unresponsive and inaccessible. So he sat
back and chewed his mustache, and, while watching her out
of the corner of his eye, affected to be engrossed in the music.

At the end of the first act the occupants of the boxes
clapped, and Blakely joined in in a polite, perfunctory way as
he leaned over and made a commonplace remark about the
music. She answered briefly, and turned to look over the au-

dience. A question from Mr. Brace was answered in a mono-syllable, and with a forced smile upon her face. Then she settled in her seat, and gazed absently at the drop-scene. Think-ing it best to let her have her way, he remained silent. Pres-ently she turned to him.

"Do you know much about the labor question, Mr. Blake-ly ?" she asked.

The question startled him.

"I do not know much about anything," he replied, modest-ly ; "but we all have to know something of the labor question. I understand that your father is likely to have a strike on his hands—and an ugly one, I fear. We had a strike once (my father has some cotton-mills back East, you know), and it was not a pleasant experience."

"What did you do ?" she asked.

"Oh, we beat them. They stood out as long as they could, but their wives and families were starving, and the fools had to give in. They did some rioting, threatened my father's life, and destroyed some of his property, and all that. Some of them—six, I think—went to jail for it."

There was a hardness and lack of sympathy in his tone that hurt her. He smiled as he spoke. There was no thought for the misery of the wives and children who had been starving, or for the wives and children of those who went to jail. The wickedness, the inhumanity of it all evidently did not appeal to him. It was a necessary condition of society. These men were enemies, that was all ; and they must be beaten, and starved and jailed.

At this moment Miss Willerby leaned back and said, in a half-whisper :

"Don't you wish you could hear what Mr. Marsh is saying now ?"

It may have been only by accident that the suggestion came at that moment, or it may have been that she had heard Blakely's words, and guessed their effect on his auditress. But however that may be, her words had their effect. Jessie's thoughts turned to Marsh — he, at least, had sympathy with the "voiceless millions " in their misery. To him it was not merely a necessary and inevitable warfare, this between capital and labor. He believed it to be reconcilable, and was devoting his life's work to endeavoring to bring about a reconciliation. Yes, she thought, as the curtain rose again, she would give much to hear what he was saying, and still more, she thought, to have him here by her to talk to him and hear him talk.

After the second act there was a general shifting of places among the men of the party. Blakely's seat was taken by an insipid, fair - haired youth of the name of Baldwin, who displayed a great quantity of white shirt-front, white vest, white collar and cuffs, whom Jessie knew but slightly and was compelled to some extent to entertain. Blakely she could see in the stage-box talking to Miss Caley, who chattered effusively to him with rather exaggerated gestures—for the benefit of the house.

At supper at Mr. Brace's house, after the opera, Miss Holt again found Blakely next to her. The party was a merry one, seated at two round tables, nine to each, between which laughing badinage passed back and forth. She continued to appear light - hearted with the rest, and parried every effort of her neighbor to bring the conversation between them down to a personal footing. She could not but be aware that he was looking unusually handsome even for him, and more than once, on meeting his eyes, she was compelled to avoid their glance with something of the old feeling of fear. On the whole, however, she was conscious of greater security and more self-confidence than she had felt in his company from the time of their first meeting; and it was with a certain placid satisfaction that she noticed his look of disappointment as she replied with genuine indifference to his impressive "Good-night," into which he threw all the depth of meaning of which his voice was capable.

X

As Horace conjectured, there would, under ordinary circumstances, have been little chance that Jessie Holt would see the
morning *World*. But though the Republican journals furnished
the usual reading both of Mr. Holt and his daughter, all the
local daily papers were received at the house. This morning,
with the impression of the events of the preceding day still
upon her, Miss Holt looked eagerly over the columns of the
Republican for a report of Horace's speech, and finally found
a three-line item in an out-of-the-way corner of the paper,
which merely mentioned the fact that he had spoken, and had
" entertained his audience with the usual Democratic sophis-
tries." So she went to her father's library for a copy of the
World, and, finding here the fuller article, settled herself in a
corner to read it.

Lacking the necessary experience to fill out the skeleton of
the reporter's abstract, she could only gather that the speech
had been a dignified appeal in behalf of high principles and
sound morality. The newspaper summary, however, fell far
short of satisfying her, and she wished that she could have
heard him, or that she might inveigle him into going over the
ground again at a private performance for her benefit. She
had stopped reading at the point where Horace had closed
his remarks amid enthusiastic applause. Resuming again, she
went on :

" As soon as Chairman Dallas could make himself heard, he
moved a vote of thanks to the orator of the occasion in a short
speech, in the course of which he said . . ."

She read on unsuspectingly. Then her cheeks began to
burn. When she reached the end of the article she drew a

long breath and sat gazing dazedly before her. She did not
for a moment do Horace the injustice to believe he had said
the things which seemed to be imputed to him. Without stopping to consider how such a misrepresentation could have occurred, her woman's instinct told her that there was an error
somewhere. But he had sat there and heard this other man
speak! He had not protested against it! He had acquiesced
in it!

After a while she began aimlessly to turn over the pages of
the paper in her hands. As she did so her eye again caught
Horace Marsh's name in the middle of one of the editorial columns. She read a few lines, and then went back to the beginning of the article and read it steadily through.

When she had finished reading she was faint and sick at
heart, and, passing her hand over her forehead, found it damp
with a cold moisture. So he *had* said it! He had said it all,
and more! He had "scathingly denounced," so the paper said,
"the arrogance and inhumanity of those who are seeking to
trample on the rights of free men, and degrade them to the
level of the pauper laborers of Europe." That meant her father. Since yesterday afternoon it had seemed to her that
Marsh was the one man whom she longed to talk to, the one
human being who might be able to help her. He understood
these things—not only understood them, but was setting himself resolutely to face them with courage and, what was more,
with hope. It was hope that she needed. If she could only
meet him, she had thought, he would be able to show her
where there was a ray of light in the darkness.

And now! How could he come to their house as he had
done? How could he sit at her father's table? The thought
of it was intolerable. She would say that it was impossible
but that here was the cold, hard type before her eyes. She
read the article once more, and was sitting still staring at the
paper when Thomas, the butler, came to ask for the day's
orders. She would be there in a minute, she said. Then she
rose, and tore the paper, slowly and mechanically, into small
pieces, and threw them into the waste-basket.

It was not until two hours later that Horace read the same

article on the train. He was still chafing at it when he reached his office that afternoon.

"Anything special happened, Franklin, while I have been gone?" he asked of the clerk.

"No, sir, I think not."

Entering his own office, Marsh took off his hat and overcoat, and, after a glance at the envelopes which were awaiting him, went straight into his partner's room, the door of which stood open. The General was sitting at his desk, but rose to greet the young man cordially as he came in.

"Well, I congratulate you," he said; "you must have done well—remarkably well, by all accounts."

"They seemed to like it," Horace replied; "but have you seen that cursed article in the *World?*"

"What article?" asked his partner, uneasily.

Marsh picked up a copy of the paper which was lying on the table—open at the editorial page, curiously enough, and folded so that the very article in question was uppermost.

"This thing," he said, slapping it contemptuously with the back of his hand, and handing it to his partner. That gentleman began in apparent innocence the supererogatory task of reading the article again; for not only had he read it more than once himself, but it had been approvingly discussed in his office by a large number of leading Democrats during the day.

"Oh yes," he said, with an air of sudden recollection, after reading a few lines, "I saw that this morning. These papers are always making clumsy mistakes. Of course, you did not say anything of the kind!"

"Why, I never mentioned labor matters! If I had mentioned them, it would have been in a different strain to this stuff here. In the first place, Mr. Holt is my friend. In the second place, I believe he is right in this matter. He is a gentleman, and a man to be trusted and honored, while Wollmer and his gang—" Horace checked himself before putting his opinion of the parties in question into language which would have been somewhat too forceful to be courteous, considering the General's intimacy with the labor leader.

"It is an unfortunate mistake," said the General, soothingly; "but there is no great harm done, and it can be corrected."

"Yes," Marsh retorted, little mollified, "it can be corrected. I shall write to the *World*, and go and try to see Pawson. If I don't see him, I will see somebody up there."

The General had wit enough not to appear to oppose his young partner's plan directly.

"Well, if you think best. But I would not do anything rash," he said. "You know there has been a second meeting this morning between Holt and the street-railway men. It ended the same way as the one did yesterday, and the strike, on both companies, is now practically a certainty. Do you think that to-morrow would be an opportune time for saying anything on the subject? It seems to me," and he dropped into the pompous senatorial tone in which he loved to deliver anything which sounded like a noble sentiment or a maxim of patriotism, "that in moments of peril such as this, it is the duty—I may say, the bounden duty—of all good citizens to do all in their power to allay public apprehension, and to refrain from doing anything to excite ill-feeling."

"In justice to myself, however, whether I am a good citizen or not, I have got to have this thing straightened out."

Then an idea occurred to the General. With all his six feet of stature and imposing presence, and in spite of his public prominence and conspicuousness as a party leader, General Harter was something of a moral jelly-fish, needing in crises the support of stronger men. Once assured of their backing in private, however, there was no one who could present himself more effectively before the public, or impress the mob more successfully with an idea of his independence of character. At this juncture he needed Sullivan. If any one could smooth the ruffled feathers of his young partner and lure him from the flight which he threatened, it was the big Irishman.

"By-the-bye, speaking of this morning's meeting," he said, "that reminds me that I promised, when the result of the meeting was known, to call up Sullivan, and let him know when I could see him. I am afraid he will be waiting to hear from me."

He pressed a button, and Franklin entered.

"I wish you would telephone to the City Hall," said the General, "and tell Mr. Sullivan that I shall be glad to see him right away at this office."

A minute later Franklin returned, and said that Mr. Sullivan would come at once.

General Harter detained Marsh some time longer, asking him questions about his trip, until he judged that Sullivan might be close at hand, and then let him go. The General's office had two doors. As soon as Marsh closed one behind him, the General opened the other wide, and left it standing so. It led directly into the hall, and the Irishman would pass it on his way from the elevator, and the General did not wish him to come through the outer office, where he must meet Marsh before he had seen him himself.

Sullivan arrived much out of breath with his hurried walk, and breathing stertorously.

"Holy Moses!" he grunted, "it's comin' up in the elevators that tires me so. It's just the idea of climbin' does it. All the way up I am thinkin' of the stairs that I might be walkin' up if the elevator was broken down, and the thinkin' of them is as bad as the walkin'."

He drew a chair up to the General's desk, and the two held a short colloquy in undertones. Then the Irishman rose.

"Sure an' I'll fix the lad!" he said, and walked into Marsh's room, hammering on the door as he did so with the heavy gold-headed walking-stick which he always carried.

"How are ye, me boy?" he cried, heartily. "So the young Hannibal has crossed the Alps and back again without so much as losin' a life or burstin' a button. An' ye struck 'em in fightin' trim, too, I hear?"

"Oh, I got along all right," Marsh replied.

"To be course!" said the Irishman. "To be course ye did. An' have ye read the paper to see what a blatherin' idiot that man Pawson has been makin' of himsilf."

"Yes, I have," Marsh jerked out, discontentedly.

"Well, an' if it isn't just like the man. It isn't only that he never opens his own yawping mouth without puttin' his foot in it, but he won't let another man open his without wantin' to stuff his whole undacent extremities in there too—

an' it's up to the knee they go every time. When I read the
paper myself this mornin'," he continued, unblushingly, "I
says to mesilf, says I, 'He don't know the young Spartacus yet,'
says I, 'an' he couldn't appraciate him if he did'—no more
than a pig can appraciate quails on toast. If it wasn't just at
this time I would advise ye to write to the fool and set him
straight."

"I have intended doing so, anyway," said Marsh.

"Oh, but ye can't now, me lad," and the Irishman shook
his big head gravely. "Ye can never do it in the world.
The town's just bubblin' now, an' for the next week it 'll
be touch an' go betwixt peace and bloodshed. There's only
one man in this whole city that may be able to prevent a
strike, an' that's your own highly respected partner within
there. Ye saw that the other night. The boys trust him—an'
well they may—an' it's just the chance there is of his bein'
able now to stop the trouble. But one word from yersilf on
the other side—bein' as ye are not only the leadin' orator of
the Dimicratic party, but his very partner and colleague—
one word from yersilf, and it's bloody war. It 'ld be settin'
the torch to the capitol—like the geese themselves. It's riotin' there 'ld be inside of a week, an' yerself would be responsible. I'd pity the feelin's of ye when the strike had come,
and there was riotin' and women cryin' and men bein' killed,
an' ye tryin' to slape o' nights with the weight of it all on
your conscience. Let alone that ye 'ld wreck the party and
blast yer own career—the purtiest career, be it said, in these
United States to-day."

"But a lie has been told about me!" Marsh exclaimed, as he
rose and paced the room—"a lie which wrongs me, and must
be set right."

"Oh, pshaw! An' how many lies do ye think have been
tould of Tim Sullivan? There's never a wake but the Republican organs call me a horse-thief, which is a lie an' a foolish
one; for what would I be doin' with a horse, when there's never
a baste that's been built since the days of Troy as could bear
the weight of me? An' the party papers call me a high-minded
gentleman and model citizen — an' that lie's foolisher yet.
They've lied about me both ways for twenty years, an' for all

their lyin' I've never a friend or an innemy more or less than
I've made mesilf.   It was younger than ye are now that I was
when I was on the force, an' the papers accused me o' usin' my
club outrageously on inoffensive citizens, just for all that I'd
hit a man one when he talked back on the strate to me.   It's
simmerin' mad that I was when I come to the station that
mornin' and tould my tale to the captain.   An' the captain, he
just looked me stiddy in the eye, an' 'Go aff to yer bate,' says
he. 'But it's a lie!' says I. 'Let 'em lie,' says he. 'But
what 'll I do?' says I. 'Go aff to yer bate,' says he. 'But
they've lied on me!' says I. 'Let 'em lie,' says he. 'But how
can I stop it?' says I. 'Go aff to yer bate,' says he. 'If ye
think it 'll help ye,' says he, 'ye might soak yer head for a
while.' An' I've never forgotten the lesson. When they lie
on me now, an' I feel the Irish blood of me risin', 'Let 'em
lie, Tim Sullivan,' says I, 'an' go aff to yer bate,' I says."

Marsh laughed in spite of himself, and the Irishman followed up his advantage.

"It's better use yer can make av yer time than stoppin' to
fight with every sort of a fool that lies on ye.   It wasn't the
girl that stooped to pick up apples as won the race in the
Bible. An' as for this particular lie, it's a clumsy one, an'
them as knows ye know it's a lie, and them as don't can think
what they please. If ye have any friends," he added, innocently, "that yer want to set straight, on the quiet like, do it.
Tell them the falseness of it, if ye think there's need. But as
for writin' to the papers an' wreckin' the party an' ruinin' the
General an' settin' the town by the ears, it's not yersilf that
could do it."

Marsh stood with his hands in his pockets, looking out of
the window in evident indecision, and the Irishman knew that
he had gained his point. So he rose to go.

"It needn't occur again," he said. "I'll speak to the blatherin' idiot Pawson mesilf, an' tell him I'll break the pagan head
av him if he fails to have ye correctly reported hereafter. It 'll
be aisy enough whenever ye speak to have it said that, 'in accordance with his custom, the young orator made no reference to
local issues, but confined himself entirely to a brilliant elucida-
tion of the lofty principles which should inspire the party in

its general behavior,' or words to that effect. It won't be two weeks before every man and child in the city knows ye for the only man on either side as never descends to speak on the labor question."

Marsh still gazed from the window without replying, and the Irishman, not even saying good-bye, left him, to re-enter the General's room.

" It's red-hot the lad is," said he, winking at that gentleman, and speaking in tones loud enough for Marsh to hear, " over what the pestiferous lunatic Pawson was after sayin' in the paper to - day. Maybe you didn't notice it! Well, it was outrageously unjust, an' no blame to the boy for bein' hot. It's but for the sake of yersilf an' the party the lad's decided not to write to the papers to-day and vindicate himself from the aspersions on his character."

A minute later Marsh heard the ponderous footstep of the big politician as he went to the elevator. Sullivan whistled quietly to himself as he descended, and by the time that he reached the street the whole affair had gone from his mind. It was only an incident in the day's work.

In accordance with the Irishman's suggestion, Marsh sat down and wrote to Mr. Holt. It was a brief and dignified letter, in which he simply said that he hoped that it was not necessary for him to tell Mr. Holt that he had been entirely misrepresented by the Democratic papers that morning, and that in his remarks at Jackson he had said nothing to give any excuse for the views which had been ascribed to him. He had not referred to labor matters at all, or said anything which could, however remotely, be construed as expressing a sympathy, which he did not feel, with those who were endeavoring to make trouble between the men and Mr. Holt's companies.

Mr. Holt received the letter the next morning and read it through. The explanation was not necessary, for Mr. Holt knew enough of Marsh, and was sufficiently familiar with political trickery, to have already conjectured that the thing was a mistake. Still, he liked Marsh, whom he believed to be a clean and capable young fellow, for having written. Then the incident was forgotten under the pressure of more important affairs.

As General Harter had said, the street-railway employés had chosen to adopt much the same position as had been taken by the men of the iron-and-steel company. The conference with Mr. Holt had been brief and futile, and a strike was now assured. In accordance with his engagement with the Democratic leaders, however, Wollmer was compelled to prevent matters coming to a head for another week, if possible. So he impressed upon the committee the necessity of taking every possible step to avoid appearance of precipitateness, and to surround the strike with all the circumstances of legality. Before calling a general meeting of the men, at which only a quarter or a third could be present, they must "poll" the men individually, and get the formal vote of the majority of all concerned in favor of a strike. This could be done in three or four days. The vote could then be reported to the meeting, and in the eyes of the public there would be every evidence that the committee had acted in the most conservative way, and that the strike was only finally decided upon after every resource had been exhausted, and in obedience to the deliberate decision of an actual majority of the men. Pains were taken that the public should be well informed through the press of the prudent course which the committee were taking, and of their extreme reluctance to force a crisis. So the town knew that there were yet some days of breathing-time.

For the management of the two companies, however, these were busy days. As for the steel works, there was no question as to the course to be pursued. When the strike came the shops would be shut down for an indefinite period. Every precaution would have to be taken to avoid danger to the property at the time when the men quitted work, and to protect it against malicious injury afterwards.

With the street-railway company it was different. It could not shut down and remain idle indefinitely. It must make every effort to maintain its service unimpaired, at whatever cost, and must run cars on all its lines every day under penalty of forfeiture of its franchises. After much consultation, the officers of the company decided that the only course to pursue was to anticipate the strikers by "locking out" as many hours as was necessary before the strike was to occur.

Experience with electric street-railway strikes in other cities had shown that while some men, when the appointed hour arrived, might take their cars back to the barns, the majority would leave them wherever they might happen to be on the route. Before leaving, moreover, not a few would probably disable the car in some way. By waiting for this to occur the company would at the least be put to considerable inconvenience and expense, and might suffer material loss by the damage to its equipment. It was deemed wiser to forestall the men, and to prevent them from taking the cars out at all that day.

But the officers knew that at best they could reckon on the loyalty of only a very small proportion of the employés. It remained to have in readiness such reinforcements as were available. Communication was opened with agents in various cities, who were instructed to engage the best men to be got, and to send them on at once—not in parties, but singly; representatives of the company would meet them at the station, and care for them until the day when they would be needed.

It was on Friday that the fruitless meeting between Mr. Holt and the employés of the street-railway company had been held. By Monday recruits were already arriving, one and two at a time, from Chicago, St. Louis, Kansas City, Omaha, St. Paul, Minneapolis, and other cities. By Tuesday night the company had sixty men in readiness. On Wednesday it was announced by the committee that the poll of the employés was finished, and the joint meeting was called for the following evening. That afternoon one hundred and fifty men had arrived in town or were on their way, due to arrive during the night, in addition to fifty who had been engaged in the city itself, and instructions were sent to all agents that no more were needed.

The meeting was held, and Wollmer presented the report of the committee. A large majority, over seventy per cent., of the street-railway men had voted in favor of a strike, and over ninety per cent. of the iron-and-steel company's employés. The committee, Wollmer said, had exhausted every argument with the management of the companies, but in vain; the gentleman who was president of both companies would listen to no reason. It was only with the greatest reluctance that the committee had finally decided to take the individual votes of all concerned. Those votes were overwhelmingly in favor of an immediate strike on both companies. This, the speaker believed, ended the duties of the committee, who desired to express their appreciation of the obligations that they were under to the Hon. William Harter, the candidate for governor of the State on the Democratic ticket, and begged to be discharged. It rested with the meeting to take such action as it saw fit.

The meeting was not slow in taking that action. A vote of thanks was awarded to the committee, and another to General Harter. The resolution declaring, after much preamble, that it was the duty of the officers of the several organizations to which the employés of the two companies belonged to order a strike in the usual course, and that the officers and members of all such organizations should act together for the best interests of all, was then put and carried amid a tumult of applause. The exact time at which the strike should take effect was left to the officers of the various organizations to decide; but a recommendation was made that it should not, if possible, be deferred beyond forty-eight hours after the time of the adjournment of that meeting.

A few speeches were made, which were for the most part moderate and conservative in tone. Once a speaker arose who commenced with much waving of his arms to advocate the use of dynamite and Winchester rifles; but he was promptly hooted down. Within two hours after coming to order the meeting had adjourned in a dignified manner and without disturbance. Except for a few scattered shouts and cries from different quarters of the large audience, the men filed out of the temple in silence, as if fully conscious of the responsibility of their action, and resolutely prepared to stand by it to the end.

To the public—to one who could not see beneath the surface and understand how the wires, in the fingers of half a dozen men, were pulled so that all the mass of sober, self-respecting citizens were no more than puppets in their hands, and who could not read the motives by which these leaders were prompted—the meeting was an impressive manifestation of the self-control and love of law and order of the American working-man. And it was as such that the papers of all classes spoke of it the next day.

XI

It is a natural infirmity of the human intellect that it should regard as new any fact with which it comes in contact for the first time ; and it seemed to Jessie, not so much that her eyes had been opened, but as if a change had come over the spirit of the world. The illusion in her case was heightened, and in a measure justified, by the fact that some of the phenomena in her own horizon were new and even from day to day in process of generation. The strike itself was a distinct fact which had not previously existed. It was only the gathering into one thunder-cloud at the storm centre of the scattered forces and elements which had hitherto been spread harmlessly all over the skies. But who, though he dreads the storm when it comes, has a thought for the moisture and electricity which may be carried in the air when the heavens are clear ? Moreover, Horace Marsh's disloyalty, as it seemed to her, was a thing of yesterday. It marked an epoch.

In all her acquaintance with Marsh she had rather shrunk from questioning her heart in regard to him, or speculating as to their possible future relations. That he loved her, she was aware—as no woman could have helped being. How seriously he loved her, or how much of his life and hopes were involved in his passion, she had not cared to consider ; chiefly, probably, from the instinctive dread of her gentle nature of the thought of causing suffering to any one. For had she put the question to herself, she knew, without putting it, she must have said that she did not love him. She admired him and liked his companionship. She recognized his intellectual strength and his moral cleanliness. As a figure

9

in a latter-day romance she would have sympathized with
him, and her judgment would have pronounced against any
heroine who rejected him. But neither men nor women
bring to the consideration of the affairs of their own hearts
the same dispassionate reason with which they pass upon the
conduct and analyze the mistakes of others. How many
women have refused to marry men who would have made
them happy, and rejoiced sincerely in the good-fortune of
girls, their friends, when they have accepted these same men
—and then earned the pity of those friends by throwing
themselves away on husbands who were worthless? Any gam-
bler will tell you how much easier it is to play another man's
game than to use judgment when your own money is at stake.

Jessie had never felt in Horace's presence those tender
emotions—those swayings of the inclination "dearer than
can be justified to reason"—which are accepted as the necessary and proper symptoms of love. Only for that one day—
when driving home from her father's office, at the opera,
and during the wakeful night which followed—had she for
the first time experienced any conscious desire for his companionship. Then, indeed, she had turned to him, whether
for his heart's sympathy or for intellectual consolation she
had not considered. Only she longed for him. And with
the very next morning had come the disillusion and the
wreck !

During these days she did not speak of him. Had she
done so, things might have gone differently. There were
times when she wondered that her father had not mentioned
his name, for it seemed to her that the disgrace of his defec-
tion must have touched her father as closely as it had herself ; but the work of preparation for the coming struggle left
Mr. Holt little leisure to think of other things, and Marsh,
with the episode of the speech at Jackson, had been completely forgotten. Jessie even expected that casual visitors
would speak of it; for was not his shame public ? Did not
the whole town know it?

It was well that she was compelled to busy herself with the
affairs of the household and the entertainment of her guests,
as the misery of the time could scarcely have failed to bring

on a second sickness similar to that of her childhood. She
often longed to be alone in the house; but without her being
aware of it, the presence of her two friends and the necessity
of exerting herself in their behalf was the best medicine possible. Once Miss Willerby had asked whether it would not
be better that she should go away—whether she was not
rather in the way in this season of anxiety.

"No, dear," Jessie had said, as she put her arms around
her friend's waist. "We need friends now; we need anybody who will not desert us in the time of trial."

The bitterness with which she spoke surprised the other,
who, however, concluded merely that Jessie's mind must be
filled with something that her father had told her, of some
desertion to the enemy on the part of political or business
friends whom he had trusted. She did not think of Marsh.
She had not seen the paper containing that fatal article, and
knew nothing of the struggle which had been going on in
her friend's heart. That Jessie should be anxious and should
show it in her face and manner was only natural at such a
time. There was no need to look for specific reasons for her
lack of spirits.

As for Miss Caley, she was engrossed in her relations with
Barry, an affair which was rising to its crisis with all the rapidity and certainty of a Greek tragedy. When the protago-
nist was on the stage—that is to say, when she was in Barry's
company—the action moved quickly. In the intervals she
herself played the part of the chorus, with rhythmic confidences about the domestic altar of the Holt household. The
impending strike she accepted with complacency as a fitting
setting for the piece, giving it just the circumstances of
gloom and dignity which were needed. The chorus, perhaps,
was a trifle more personal and frivolously inclined than is
customary; but it possessed compensatory advantages in the
matters of entertainment and transparency of motive and expression. Indeed, her comments upon the plot were *naïveté*
itself.

"He has the most wonderful memory!" she assured her
friends one day, after Barry had gone. "He has been quoting
Shelley to me nearly *all* the afternoon. I happened to say, you

know, that I was fond of Shelley that evening when we were
sitting round the fire, and he has been reading Shelley ever
since! And if you *could* have seen his eyes!" And she
gave a little shiver of ecstatic reminiscence. "And when we
talked about the emotions and how funny it was that we
always knew whether one was going to like a person when
one first saw them. That wasn't the case with Fred Jones
and me, because we hated each other for ever so long at first.
But then we hate each other now again, so it's all right.
That proves the rule, you know. But, anyway, I didn't tell
him anything about Fred (I had two letters from Fred to-day),
and he—Mr. Barry, I mean—said that he had known that he
was going to like me awfully just as soon as he came into the
room. I told him I did too. But that wasn't quite the truth,
you know, because I hardly saw him for *ever* so long. But
what could I say? I couldn't tell him that. But he must
have suspected something, because he said that he had been
awfully jealous of Mr. Blakely that first night. As if Mr.
Blakely gave him any chance of being jealous! Why, he
didn't even *look* at me!"

At other times the strain was stormier, fraught with stress
and woe. On one occasion after Barry had made his exit she
was discovered sitting, as it might have been Ariadne pas-
sioning, looking very small and forlorn on a very large sofa,
with a little much-crumpled handkerchief in her hand, and
evident signs of tears about her cheeks and eyes.

"It is all the horrid strike," she said, sobbing. "Can't the
police or somebody do something to stop it? We have been
talking all about it, and he said if there was a riot and the
company needed men to help it that he would be sworn in
or something, and would go out and fight. And I positively
forbade him to do it. I said if he cared for my wishes a bit
he wouldn't, because he might be killed; and I said if he
didn't promise not to, I would never speak to him again as
long as I lived. And he was just as obstinate! He said
that I wouldn't mean it always, and that I couldn't want him
not to do his duty. Oh, he's awfully high-minded! And
then I got angry. He has been telling me about his business
—about making people pay things, you know, until they died,

and then putting up statues to them (it was just as interesting!), and I asked him whether he would pay, and what kind
of a statue he would put up to himself if he got killed. And
that made him angry. He said that I was heartless and
couldn't really care for him, or I wouldn't talk in that way.
And then he went away—as solemn and cross and dignified
as he could be." And she rubbed her cheeks with the
crumpled pocket-handkerchief, and sat the picture of desolation.

But Jessie, listening, wondered how Barry's "high-minded-
ness" would consort with Marsh's principles. Living together
as they did, how did they agree? What shame it would be
to Horace if the time ever came when Barry did offer his
services!

Meanwhile it was ordained, by that contrariness which
sometimes looks so much like deliberate malice on the part
of fate, that Horace and Jessie should not meet. For the
first day or two after his return he had been restrained from
calling, partly by the necessity of attending to work which
had accumulated in his absence, and still more, perhaps, by a
feeling of bashfulness and uncertainty as to the effect of that
article, supposing it to have been read, and of his note to
Mr. Holt. At length, not having heard in reply to the note,
he had called at the house on Sunday afternoon; but nobody
was at home. It perversely happened also that Mr. Holt, returning before his daughter, had picked up the card which
Marsh left, and, after reading it, thrown it into the bowl which
stood on the hall-table for the reception of the pieces of paste-
board after they had done their duty; and there it was irrev-
ocably lost. Mr. Holt had not thought of the matter again,
and Jessie never knew that Horace had been to the house.
On Monday Marsh had to leave the town for his speech at
Olympia, returning on Tuesday, and leaving again on the following day (which was Miss Holt's day at home) for a trip
to a number of smaller places in the State, which would keep
him away for a week.

His silence Miss Holt of course ascribed to shame. When
on the Wednesday she received some roses from him, sent
just before he left the city, she threw the card, which this

time accompanied the flowers, into the fire, and gave the
roses themselves to the butler with injunctions to take them
out into the kitchen.   But the prudent Thomas took them to
his own bedroom instead, wondering meanwhile who it might
be from whom his mistress did not care to accept flowers.
He hoped it might be that Mr. Blakely.   But, whoever it was,
Thomas was loyally convinced that he deserved it.

Nor did Jessie derive any news of Horace's movements
from the newspapers.   She confined herself now to the reading of the *Republican,* in which no mention was made of
Marsh's doings or sayings, though there was abundant abuse
of the Democratic leaders in general for their demagogic
and hypocritical friendship (so the Republican organ styled
it) for the working-man, and their advocacy of his cause in the
present labor troubles—abuse, however, which was shrewdly
tempered with expressions of Republican sympathy for the
same working-man (whose vote would count on either side),
viewed as an abstraction, although the sympathy was prevented from being actively displayed in his behalf in the immediate and local controversy by what the organ wished to
be regarded as a judicial impartiality, which forbade either it
or the party to assume a hasty attitude on either side in any
personal quarrel without the fullest understanding of all the
arguments of both parties.   In fact, the Republican press
was in a particularly uncomfortable dilemma, of which it was
able to do no more than dally with both horns with the best
grace that it could.

Had Miss Holt chosen to read the Democratic papers she
would have found all Marsh's speeches reported, not, indeed,
at as much length as those of some other speakers who devoted themselves to the discussion of the labor question, but
still with a fulness which showed that the party attached considerable importance to the young lawyer's words and influence.   Sullivan appeared to have kept his promise to interview the editor Pawson—or, at least, some instructions had
gone forth from Democratic headquarters which prevented a
repetition of the misrepresentation to which Marsh had been
subjected in the matter of his speech at Jackson.   More than
once, indeed, in the editorial comment upon his utterances,

Horace recognized an echo of Sullivan's words, when the
Irishman had suggested in the office how the general tenor
of Marsh's oratory might be explained to the public; and, as
a matter of fact, as Sullivan had foretold, those members of
the party who were close students of the internal currents in
public affairs soon came to understand that of all the Democratic speakers Marsh alone was conducting a campaign of
principle, and without reference to local or temporary issues.
The better men admired him for it, but those of the baser
sort decided that he lacked courage, and wondered why any
man should hesitate to come out frankly in favor of the principles of his party. Marsh himself was so engrossed in his
own work and so filled with his own ideals that he was hardly aware how far he had drawn away from the rest of his
party — or the rest of his party from him. He read the
papers, indeed, and noticed regretfully how violently individual speakers expressed themselves on the question of the
strike—a violence, however, which, remembering his own experience, he conjectured to be largely intensified in its filtra-
tion through the editorial mind of the "blathering idiot"
Pawson.

Of her other friends and acquaintances Miss Holt saw even
more than usual. They naturally called to condole with her
on the threatening aspect of the situation (sometimes, it
seemed to her, that they came rather to rejoice in it), and,
moreover, there were callers on Miss Willerby and Miss
Caley as well as on herself.

Mrs. Bartop had held forth at considerable length on the
deplorable condition of a community where such a state of
affairs was possible.

"As I tell Bartop," she said, "it is inconceivable that such
a thing could happen in the East, or in any well-governed
city."

Mrs. Flail had called, even busier than usual; for while she
permitted no interruption of her regular meetings, and the demands on her time made by the various organizations in which
she was interested had to be met, she was further immersed
in preparations for a gigantic soup-kitchen for the comfort of
the families of the men who would be thrown out of work by

the strike. The incongruity in her appealing to Miss Holt for assistance in such a cause did not appear to strike the estimable woman. That evening Miss Holt referred the matter to her father.

"Subscribe, by all means," he said, smilingly.

"I thought you would want me to," the daughter said, "but it seemed better to ask you first."

"Don't do more than other people—so that it will look conspicuous, or as if we were trying to be quixotic. But do what is right. However," he added, after a pause, "I doubt if there will be any need of soup-kitchens. The strikers are not likely to starve, I understand."

"Why not? I hope not, I'm sure."

"Well, there may be nothing in it; but there are ugly stories afloat about an intention to use the city's funds in support of the men. It hardly seems credible, but the City Hall crowd are pretty unscrupulous."

Blakely had called, and shown considerable tact. Having expressed his sympathy with Miss Holt and her father briefly, and in words which sounded earnest, he had devoted himself during the rest of the hour for which he stayed to talking to Miss Willerby, until at parting, when, pressing his hostess's hand, he had said:

"I wish I could do anything, even the least thing, to comfort you and make the worry less," accompanying the words with a look for which Miss Holt was very grateful, and which made her feel that she had done him an injustice in pronouncing him hard and unsympathetic. At least, how much better his course was than that of the other—the other who, alone of all their friends, deserted them now.

Not in the Holt household alone, but all over the city the impending strike was the chief topic of interest. Although the recommendation after the meeting in the Labor Temple had been in favor of declaring the strike effective within forty-eight hours from the adjournment of the meeting— which forty-eight hours would have expired on Saturday night—it was not difficult for Wollmer, who desired to keep to the letter his agreement to delay matters for a full two

weeks, to persuade the labor leaders that Saturday would be
a most injudicious day on which to strike, as it would give
the companies (and the street-railway company especially)
a day and a half, or until Monday morning, in which to collect their forces and prepare for the business of the following week. Eleven o'clock on Monday forenoon was the time
then finally decided upon.

During these days of suspense there was perhaps no house
in the city, outside of that of Mr. Holt, wherein as much
anxiety was felt as in the establishment in Fourth Street,
where Wollmer boarded with Mrs. Masson. With the extra
work and additional precautions which were now necessary,
Harrington could spend but little time in his sweetheart's
company. When he was with her, much of the trouble was
forgotten, for he managed to maintain a show of light-
heartedness, and ridiculed her apprehensions for his safety.
But in his absence, while she sat at her small table and
"dusted" and painted and burnished at her cups and saucers, the clouds gathered again. However brave he might
be, her heart told her that the peril which lay ahead was a
real one; and when they met at the breakfast and supper
table Wollmer spared no pains to increase the uneasiness.
He took malicious pleasure in telling again and again how
confident were the men and how sure of victory; how impossible it was for the street-railway company to hope to operate its cars, when there were not only their own striking
employés to contend with, but the two thousand men from
the steel works as well; how the strikers intended, in the first
place, to bring all their united forces to bear upon the street-
railway company to compel it to come to terms, and, failing
that, how it would be impossible for any leaders to restrain
the men from wrecking the iron-and-steel plant. Arriving
at this point, he never failed to dilate upon the hopeless-
ness of the iron-and-steel company's endeavoring to protect its property against the overwhelming numbers which
would be arrayed against it, and the certain death which
would await any handful of volunteers whom the company
might attempt to install as a garrison at the mills.

In all this he was aided and abetted by Mrs. Masson.

She listened approvingly to Wollmer's doleful vaticinations, and when he finished would seize the opportunity to drive the nail home in her step-daughter's mind by specific inference to "that Harrington fellow" as one who, by his wicked foolishness, was most certain to invite his own destruction.

The effect upon Jennie of these conversations, to which she was treated twice a day with unfailing regularity, can easily be imagined. Moreover, she had other causes of anxiety besides her fear for her lover. She had cause to have serious doubts as to her step-mother's sanity. Not only did that individual appear to grow daily more and more subservient to Wollmer's influence, and more and more vindictive in her hatred of Harrington and all who were opposed to the strikers in the present trouble, but she had taken of late to throwing out, from time to time, mysterious hints of some unknown benefit which was to come to the Masson household in case the Democratic party was victorious at the coming election and General Harter became governor of the State. This windfall, of whatever nature it might be, seemed to depend more on the General's personal success than on the triumph either of the party or the strikers. The hallucination, Jennie conjectured, was the result of some absurd delusion which, to secure his own ends, Wollmer had woven about the old lady's mind; none the less, on more than one occasion, when her step-mother was throwing out these dark allusions from behind the teacups at the table, Jennie thought she caught an expression of curious bewilderment in Wollmer's face, as if he were as much at a loss as herself as to their meaning. Usually Wollmer received these remarks in silence; but once he said:

"Yes, it is going to be a great thing for the cause of labor if the Democrats win, as they're bound to do."

"It ain't so much the party," croaked the old woman, who was singularly yellow and ill-favored; "it's the governor. It's a good deal to be governor of a State like this, even if it ain't quite the same as being president. A governor can do a lot for those as he's bounden to. But as for this other Harrington fellow—"

And there was always in her mind, which seemed to be as wrinkled as her cheeks, this same connection between the General and the " other Harrington fellow." The latter, on being informed of the step-mother's eccentricity, had laughed at it.

"Poor old lady," he said, pityingly, "Wollmer is too much for her. I don't wonder that eternal listening to him is affecting her brain. Perhaps he'll be turning your head next, Jen."

They were standing as they talked in the front parlor of the Masson abode, a cheerless room, in spite of the efforts of the two girls to make it seem home-like and inhabited. A large mirror with a plain gilt frame surmounted the mantel, in the centre of which, among a number of knick-knacks of various sorts, chiefly of Jennie's decoration, stood a photograph of Mrs. Masson, taken some twenty years before, when she was Mrs. Brady, a widow, and which showed her at that time to have been by no means an unprepossessing woman. It was, indeed, the remnant of these good looks which had attracted Mr. Masson a few years later, and it was not until after he had persuaded her to take his name in place of the lamented Brady's that he discovered how thoroughly vicious and shrewish a person he had given to his daughters as a second mother.

"Pretty hard to believe that she ever looked like that, isn't it?" Harrington asked, musingly. "I wonder if you'll ever change so much, Jen? If so, it will be in the other direction and because your halo begins to blossom."

"I guess not, Charlie," she replied, absently. "But what on earth has General Harter to do with us or you?"

"Nothing. Wollmer has just been stuffing her mind full of nonsense, that's all. He has been telling her how much he can do with Harter—and I guess there's something in that—and what influence he is going to have with the administration when Harter's elected ; and she, poor old woman, has got it into her head that in some way she is to share in the good things. Perhaps she's going to marry Wollmer," he added, laughing; " as he can't get the daughter, he'll content himself with the step-mother. How would you like him for a father ?"

Jennie only shook her head and smiled sadly.

Another cause of uneasiness to Jennie Masson was her sister Annie. Annie, it appeared, had never reached her Aunt Susan. The aunt lived at Western, Indiana. By an absurd but intelligible mistake Annie had left the train at Caston, a town forty miles this side of her proper destination, being misled by the similarity of the names as pronounced by the stentorian but not too carefully articulate brakeman. The train had gone when she discovered her mistake. It was slowly growing dark, and the station-agent had told her that there was no other train by which she could reach Western until the same hour on the following day. Understanding her dilemma, the agent had volunteered his services, and had directed her to a house where, with his assistance, she had obtained lodgment for the night. The house, Annie wrote her sister, was so clean and nice, and the people, Mr. and Mrs. Dale, who had the dearest little seven-year-old girl in the world, were so kind to her that she had come to the conclusion that she would be very much more comfortable with them than with her rather imperious-minded aunt at Western. So she had made arrangements to remain where she was indefinitely. The agent had sent for her trunk next day, and as the time passed she had grown altogether delighted that she had made the mistake that she had.

Her sister knew enough of her wayward disposition to deem it better to refrain from expostulations. So she wrote lovingly, saying how glad she was to know that Annie was comfortable, and sent word to Aunt Susan that, owing to a change in plans, Annie would not visit her. The disappointment was softened by the present of a dainty little cup and saucer of Jennie's painting, which were altogether too good for her aunt to appreciate. Indeed, that lady contemptuously pronounced them "finicking."

Altogether, Jennie Masson had worry enough in these days; she saw so little of Charlie now, and had no one else to go to for comfort and courage. Even Tom Weatherfield, who called occasionally, was too dolorously self-centred in his beloved's absence to afford much companionship or consolation. They were gloomy times, Jennie felt, as she sat and worked all day with her sweet, peaceful face bowed over the little bits of china which grew to be so beautiful in her hands.

XII

At the steel works the strike was inaugurated in orderly and peaceful fashion. At one minute before eleven o'clock the full force was at work, each man in every department apparently intent on the task before him. By two minutes after eleven every tool was deserted, every man walking silently to the coat-room, rolling down his shirt-sleeves or wiping the perspiration from his face as he went. Fifteen minutes later the last of the long files of men had issued from the various buildings, and the strike had begun.

The officers of the company made no attempt to interfere or to argue with the men. There was nothing, except the unusual silence of the hands and the absence of the customary horse-play and joking, to distinguish it from the ordinary breaking up, when the great whistle sounded the end of the day's work. Apparently the idea occurred to James Darron, the manager, who stood watching the men moving by.

"No whistle to-day," he remarked to Harrington, who happened to be by his side, "nor for many a month to come, I guess."

In their respective buildings the foremen of the different departments were at work, with the assistance of some two-score of outside men, whose services had been engaged for the day. The great engines were shut down and the fires extinguished; the hand-tools, which had been dropped by the men where they stood, were collected and carried off to the store-room; and on the machinery wipers were at work, cleaning up; men with baskets and brooms went through every shop, gathering up the scraps and sweeping out. By dusk the work was finished. Two watchmen, for no extraordinary precautions were considered necessary, remained on guard, and for the first time since the fires had been started, nearly three years before, the great plant on which ten thousand souls depended for their immediate livelihood, and which indirectly supported twice as many more, was dead, with not so much as a smouldering spark of life in all its huge frame.

Harrington waited only long enough to see that the men left peaceably, and that there was no immediate danger either to the property as a whole, or to the electric plant which was immediately under his care. By half-past eleven he was on his way to the central barns of the street-railway company.

It was with no little anxiety, and a curious feeling of homelessness, that he set his face city-wards. The last news from the street-railway company's offices, received by telephone about an hour ago, was to the effect that there had been no trouble, and that cars were running. The men, this much Harrington knew, had been unprepared for the action of the company. Of all the old employés, only eighty, of whom fifty were conductors and thirty engineers, had been regarded as trustworthy enough to be retained in the service. Of the rest, each had been met at the barns that morning with an envelope containing his pay and a formal notice of discharge. With the two hundred new men and the eighty who were considered loyal the company had been able to put enough cars into operation to fairly accommodate the public.

Beyond this, the brief telephone message already mentioned was all the information that had been received at the steel works. What might have happened in the last hour Harrington could not guess; but he feared the result of the arrival down-town of the hands from the works.

The iron-and-steel company's plant was situated at the north end of the city, while the barns for which Harrington was bound lay about two miles distant to the southwest. The quickest way to go from one point to the other was by means of an electric car on the line which passed within two hundred yards of the mills, changing at a point about half-way down town to a car which ran directly to the barns.

When Harrington reached the tracks no car was in sight in either direction, though the road lay straight and unobstructed as far as the terminus of the line to northward, and for nearly a mile in the direction of the city. This was ominous; and he set himself to walk at a rapid gait towards town, keeping between the rails. The road seemed strangely deserted and silent. It was a clear day, cold enough for his breath, as he walked, to be faintly visible in the atmosphere. The rails in front of him glimmered coldly in the thin and fitful sunlight. The road was dusty, with a white and powdery dust, for there had been no rain now for some three weeks, and very bare in its whiteness, with the wires overhead and the poles at regular intervals on either hand, and not a moving thing in sight, except where some clumps of black figures, presumably the rear-guard of the receding column of strikers, were just disappearing where the street curved in the distance. There were no stores on this first half-mile of the road, nor any buildings—save on one side a small group of cottages, standing well back from the highway, and on the other, still farther off, a clump of farm buildings in the middle of a patch of wind-swept cottonwood-trees, which had been there before the city existed.

Harrington hurried on, walking in the middle of the road, and growing more anxious with every minute as no sign of an approaching car reached him. At length a man appeared coming in the opposite direction, and Harrington hailed him.

"Can you tell me if the cars are running?" he asked.

"I guess so," the stranger replied. "They have been, after a fashion, all mornin'."

"Any trouble down-town, do you know?"

"I don't know. I hain't been down-town to-day."

This was some consolation, but of a slender and negative sort; and Harrington started again to walk rapidly. As he did so he thought that he caught the faintest echo of the peculiar reverberant, humming noise made by an approaching car. The sound grew louder, and as Harrington approached the bend in the road a car came sweeping round the corner. It was empty, but there was an extra man with the engineer, and two others stood one on each side of the conductor—strikers, evidently, endeavoring to persuade the men to join them. Immediately behind this car came two more in quick succession. On each of these also strikers were laboring with both the em-

ployés. In one sat a solitary, venturesome passenger, and of
another Harrington noticed with alarm that one of the windows was broken.

There was no likelihood that the first of these cars would
reach the terminus of the line and return in time to be of any
service to our friend, so he struck off to the sidewalk, for he
was reaching the region of retail stores, and pushed on his way.
At the junction with the line to the barns—what was known as
the Lincoln Street line—a car going in his direction was just
passing, which Harrington boarded. There was no other passenger within, nor was there any one with either the engineer
or conductor.

"Had much trouble?" Harrington asked of the latter, as he
stepped on the platform. The conductor only looked at him
surlily and did not reply.

"I'm an officer of the company; my name's Harrington,"
he exclaimed. "I'm just down from the steel works and on
my way to the barns."

"No; can't say as we've had much trouble," said the conductor thereupon. "It looked ugly a while back; but it ain't
a marker to what's ahead."

"It looks serious, does it?" Harrington asked.

"You bet! If I'd a-realized, I don't know as I'd have come."

"You are one of the new men? Where do you come
from?"

"Cincinnati," replied the conductor. "We had a strike
there a year and a half ago; but gee-whizz! Not but what
we was warned," he added, "for the company did not get us
here under no false representations. They told us all about
the steel works an' everything; but these things sound sort o'
different five hundred miles away to what they does when you
gets in the midst of 'em."

Harrington could not blame the man for his uneasiness, but
it filled him with foreboding. He measured the conductor
with his eye, and saw that he was a strong, well-built fellow,
with a clean-cut face. He had, it appeared, been through a
strike before, and might be accepted as at least a fair sample
of the new men. If, then, he was already showing signs of
weakening so early in the fight, it was a poor outlook for the
10

company. Harrington had taken a seat inside the car, and leaned forward to speak to the conductor again.

"Is this your last trip before dinner?"

"No; I've got to make one more, I guess."

But there was a half-heartedness in his voice which seemed to his hearer to imply an uncertainty as to whether he would ever make that trip.

Nothing more was said, and the electrician turned his attention to the people on the sidewalk. This was a busy part of the city, and as the car passed everybody stopped to look at it, rather as if they expected that it might explode. At each corner stood a knot of idlers, of whom it was difficult to say who were strikers and who were not, but they made no demonstration of hostility. Once a small child, perhaps eight years of age, ran alongside of the car for some distance, crying "Scab! Scab! Scab!" and some loungers at a corner cheered him on with "That's right, sonny!" Harrington glanced at the conductor and saw that he flushed, though he stood with his arms folded, looking straight ahead, affecting not to hear. At another place a large woman, standing bareheaded in a doorway, screamed out something unintelligible and shook her fist at the car. Something in the tone of the voice reminded Harrington of Mrs. Masson.

As they approached the barns the number of idlers on the sidewalk increased, and at one place a man swung himself on the car as it was moving, while two more climbed up beside the engineer. The one who had boarded at the rear began to talk eagerly to the conductor, but in a voice so low that Harrington could not catch what he said. The conductor did not answer, only once shaking his head to reply to a question in the negative, and then moving into the car as if to escape further argument. Harrington knew the other by sight as a former employé of the company, and apparently was recognized in turn, as he judged from the look which the striker gave him as he dropped off the car again, calling to the conductor as he went:

"You're a fool if you don't—and you may be worse."

The last two squares before the barns were reached were crowded. On either side of the street a continuous wall of strikers, in some places two or three deep, lined the road, and a storm of hisses and groans, with shouts of "Scab!" accompanied the car. In the immediate vicinity of the barns the crowd was so dense that there was barely room for the car to pass, and so demonstrative that Harrington thought an attack was about to be made, and he stepped quickly out to help the conductor. Amid the shouts and groans he caught his own name more than once, and the threats of many of the shaken fists, he saw, were intended personally for himself. It was a sea of angry faces and waving arms that he looked down upon, and his blood tingled. Suddenly the car swung round the corner and in another moment was safe under the shadow of the barn, and Harrington was conscious that he drew a deep breath of relief as he stepped to the ground.

No; he certainly did not blame the man from Cincinnati for his uneasiness.

The central barns immediately adjoined the company's main power-house, and here Harrington had work to do which kept him for an hour or more. As he moved about the power-house talking to the men, or sat in the office in conversation with the minor officers of the company, he could hear the shouts from the crowd without rising and falling as one car after another came in or went out, or as some incident arose to enrage or divert the mob. Every one who arrived from down-town brought news that it was at "the loop" that the aspect of affairs was most threatening. Harrington was anxious now to visit the other power-house and the barns upon the South Side. To do this his way lay by the loop in question—a point in the centre of the city where the various lines converged, and, circling around two blocks of buildings, started on their return journeys. Here on ordinary days, when the full service was in force, there was an almost continuous procession of cars.

Boarding the next car that left the barns, Harrington started on his trip down-town. As they swung out into the street there arose the same roar of groans and curses as Harrington had already passed through once, and the same mass of angry faces and waving arms surrounded him. No attempt was made at obstruction, however, and the trip passed without

incident of moment until the beginning of the loop was
reached.   Here, in the space of a few squares, were massed
several thousand people, the strikers being reinforced with all
the idlers and curiosity-seekers who gather on such occasions.   Approaching the loop, Harrington dropped off the
car and made his way to the sidewalk, where, behind those
who stood in their places along the curb, a sluggish stream
of passers in either direction slowly forced its way along.
With this current he moved laboriously to the vicinity of
the corner where the cars were most frequent and the crowd
densest; then edging himself as nearly as possible to the
roadway, he watched over the shoulders of those in front of
him the passage of the cars.

Each as it approached the curve was stopped, and waited
for some seconds before proceeding.   Two or three passed
without mishap; then Harrington saw the engineer on the
next car, as it stopped, raise his fist as if to strike one of the
men who was clinging to the railing and, presumably, abusing
him.   In an instant the line of men on either side broke, and
a dozen at once were swarming round the engineer.   It looked
for a moment as if he would be pulled from his place and
badly handled; but the cries of "Let him go!" "Leave the
scab alone!" and the like, which rose from a hundred throats,
brought the strikers to their senses, and they drew back, one
who had snatched the engineer's cap from his head throwing
it contemptuously into his face, amid the hoots and laughter
of the crowd.

Scarcely had the noise created by this incident subsided,
when the engineer of the next car to arrive at the corner
stopped his car, gave the lever one additional and vicious
jerk, and, throwing his leg over the railing, jumped to the
ground.   There had been desertions before, but this was the
first that Harrington had seen, and his blood boiled as the
throng around him shouted in frantic exuberance of delight.
The deserter was caught up almost as soon as he touched the
ground, and, hoisted shoulder-high, was passed, struggling
and kicking in the air, back to those on the sidewalk, where
he was soon lost to sight.   Turning his attention again to the
car which was standing idle, Harrington felt his heart leap as

he saw the conductor pass quietly through the car, shutting both doors carefully behind him, and take the engineer's place. The air was full of the cries of the strikers, who for a moment did not appear to notice a figure which came from Harrington did not know where, and stepped on to the rear platform of the car. It was Superintendent Boon, of the street-railway company. The self-appointed engineer saw him coming through the car, and waited with his hand on the lever. The superintendent stood by his side and asked him a question or two—presumably as to his ability to handle the car. The other nodded in reply, and as the lever was released and swung round the car moved off.

For some time longer Harrington stood. It was keenly exciting; but, on the whole, the electrician was considerably encouraged, perhaps surprised, to see how little disposition to use violence the strikers showed. They were for the most part good-humored and ready to laugh at any ludicrous turn which affairs might take, and the jeers and abuse were mingled with good-natured chaffing and raillery.

Around this corner were stationed some twenty policemen, who, however, made no effort to interfere with the actions of the crowd. Probably it was well that they did not, for a show of authority on their part might have lessened the good-humor of the men, and the representatives of the law were far from being strong enough to cope with the mob in case of a collision. But Harrington fancied that he saw something more than a prudent neutrality in the attitude of the officers. They seemed to him to have rather the air of sympathizers with the strikers, and to rejoice with them whenever they gained an advantage. The mayor of the city, as Harrington knew, was a demagogue of the shallowest type, a creature of Sullivan's, who had already in semi-public utterances voiced his advocacy of the strikers' cause. It was generally understood among the officers of the two companies that they could expect but little active support from the municipal authorities, except, possibly, in case of extreme riot and disorderliness. At present, at all events, the crowd at the loop showed no signs of awe of the police, nor did they pay any attention to their presence.

Then came another desertion. This time it was a conductor who dropped quietly off the car as it came to a stand-
still, and waved his hand to the crowd. At first the bystand-
ers were uncertain whether or not to interpret his action as
making an accession to their ranks. At this signal, however,
the air was rent with their applause, and the conductor was
picked up and passed along as the engineer before had been.
The engineer of this car had not noticed the departure of his
fellow-employé, and stood for a while with a look of bewildered inquiry on his face at the noise which the crowd
was making, waiting for the conductor's signal to start.
When the signal did not come he turned to look at the conductor, and then for the first time discovered that he was
alone. The crowd, understanding the situation, redoubled
their shouts and laughter, and when a voice from the rear,
rising above the tumult, yelled "Where is my wandering
boy?" even the engineer smiled. Harrington had by this
time forced his way to the front, and, seeing that the car was
one which would carry him to his destination, he stepped on
the rear platform, and gave the starting signal in two quick
jerks of the bell-rope, nodding as he did so to the engineer, who, being an old employé of the company, recognized
him. As the car started a broken orange, thrown somewhere from amid the mass, struck Harrington on the shoulder, spattering his chin and shirt-front with juice and pulp.
The crowd, many of whom knew him by sight, roared
their applause at the accuracy of the aim. Lying on the
seat inside the car, where his predecessor had thrown it
before leaving, Harrington saw the brass conductor's badge,
which he picked up and pinned on the breast of his own
coat.

The run to the South Side barns (in the course of which
Harrington collected fifteen cents for the company in fares)
was made without interruption, and he left the car without
regret. He was glad enough when the badge and the fifteen
cents had been safely surrendered at the superintendent's
office at the barns. Here at the power-house Harrington
found enough to do to keep him busy until late in the afternoon, and his knowledge of the progress of affairs was con-

fined to the intelligence brought by the men as they came in
or which arrived over the telephone.

The day, indeed, passed without any more serious disturbance than Harrington had already seen. The strikers as yet
were evidently disposed to use no other force than that of
moral suasion. There were a few breakages of car windows,
and one engineer who was struck by a stone on the temple
was badly but not fatally cut. Two or three cars were more
or less disabled by accidents arising from the awkwardness of
"green" engineers, and, most serious of all perhaps, several
women and one man were injured in various degrees in the
crowds on the sidewalks. For the rest, the strikers did not
seem to take things very much in earnest on this first day.
By dark the crowds about the loop had materially dimin-
ished. At eight o'clock the company abandoned its service
for the day, and both sides rested on their arms.

Looking over the field, the officers of the company were
fairly satisfied with the result of the day's warfare. Of the
two hundred and eighty men who had started out on the cars
in the morning, forty-three had gone over to the enemy. On
the other hand, nearly a thousand applications for employment had been received at the company's various offices from
men out of work. None had been engaged. Probably seventy or eighty per cent. of the applicants would be unfit for the
positions, either physically or morally. In such cases a great
many men will apply for places out of mere bravado and for
amusement, so that they may say afterwards that they handled a car for a day during the strike. A still larger number,
men to whom honest or continuous work is naturally re-
pugnant, would apply, not for amusement nor with a view to
earning wages, but in order that, by deserting, they might
earn the gratitude of the strikers, and perhaps work their way
into the ranks of those whom the labor organizations supported during the continuance of the strike in more or less afflu-
ent idleness. Some few also might apply with the deliberate
intention of injuring the company by disabling a car when on
the road and then leaving it. Against all these classes of im-
postors it was necessary for the company as far as possible to
protect itself. Every applicant, however, had been instructed

to sign his name on rolls kept for the purpose, and to call again on the following day.

The strikers, on the other hand, proclaimed themselves equally well pleased with the outcome of the day. At a crowded mass-meeting held that evening, which was addressed by Wollmer and the other labor leaders, every speaker congratulated the men on the good-temper and the law-abiding spirit which had been shown. The desertions from the enemy were exaggerated. The company, it was declared, had been making desperate efforts for weeks past to collect men from every city in the country. It had drawn upon every possible source. The men had seen the result. It had started the day with a miserably inadequate service, and the defections since the strike began had reduced the force to a little over one hundred men. All that the men had to do was to continue their efforts to win the employés over one by one, and there could be but one outcome.

As for the employés of the iron-and-steel company, they might have to wait a little longer. They had expected that. Let them now work with the street-railway men to win their fight, and the moral weight of that victory would aid them enormously in their own cause. The iron-and-steel company could perhaps afford to keep the works idle for a while, but the stockholders would not consent to an indefinite prolongation of the shut-down until their property went to pieces from rust and decay. Sooner or later, by early spring at furthest, the company would be compelled to resume operation. When it did so, then would be the time for the men to assert themselves, to insist on re-employment and on the recognition of the union.

The speakers were not only enthusiastic, they were triumphant. The audience responded with prompt and boisterous applause at every opportunity.

During the proceedings Timothy Sullivan sat upon one side of the stage, concealed from the audience, but where he could see and hear the speakers. As the meeting broke up, Wollmer joined him.

" It's Niagara itself ye've let loose," said the Irishman, in a low tone, " an' can ye hould it ? Ye've got it now all right,

but how long will it stay?   So long as she keeps within her
banks 'tis well, but once let her get away from ye an' flood
the country, an' you an' I an' all the Dimicratic party might
as well be swimmin' the Whirlpool Rapids."

"I shall hold them," said Wollmer, complacently.

"Oh, I know ye'll try," sneered Sullivan, "for there's
twenty thousand dollars a week in it for yersilf.   But, by
God, it 'll come dear if they get away from ye!"

XIII

MY SISTER'S KEEPER

THE second day of the strike passed as uneventfully as the first; but when the third day opened the strikers were aware that a large number of new men had been enlisted, and that the company intended to increase its service. Had the news not already leaked out, the perceptible increase in the number of cars and the new faces which appeared on some of them would have soon proclaimed the fact. This action on the part of the enemy was regarded by the strikers as in the nature of a challenge—an invitation to leave their intrenchments and fight in the open. Nor were they slow to respond. There was less laughter now among the crowds around the loop, and more bitterness in the abuse which was directed at the men as they passed on the cars. Stones and other missiles began to be used freely, and on many occasions men, climbing on the front or rear of a car, struck at the engineers and conductors with their fists or with sticks.

Towards the end of the forenoon one of the new hands derailed his car at a switch only a few squares from the loop and in a central part of the city. Whether it was an accident or the result of malicious intent it was difficult to say; but the suspicion of intention was strengthened by the fact that as soon as the car had come to a stand-still, lying diagonally across the roadway, both the engineer and conductor deserted to the strikers. The engineer of the car following chanced also to be a new and inexperienced man. The corner of the derailed vehicle projected very close to the rails on which he had to pass. Believing, however, that there was space enough, and flurried perhaps by the yells of the throng on the sidewalk, he endeavored to go by without slackening speed. He

had miscalculated the distance, and struck the rear of the derailed car with sufficient force to throw it still farther from
the rails, so that it lay almost directly across the road, while
the second car was also thrown from the track on the opposite side.

On the commencement of the strike Mr. Holt had advised
his daughter to avoid driving down-town. On this particular morning, however, news reached Jessie, shortly after
breakfast, of a poor family on the West Side which was in the
extremity of distress—a widowed mother who was ill, while
her children were hungry and in want of the bare necessaries
of life. Jessie had invited Mrs. Tisserton to luncheon that
day, and to reach the part of the city where the poor family
lived and return in time for lunch by any other means than
driving would be impossible. In her father's absence she
sent for Wilson, the coachman, and consulted him as to the
safety of making the trip. Now, Wilson, possessed of a pro-
found contempt for the strikers, individually and collectively,
had grumbled not a little at what he considered Mr. Holt's
superfluous caution.

"As if," Wilson snorted, "either me or the princess" (for
so the servants called her) "was afraid o' this riffraff."

On being summoned to the presence of his young mistress,
he ridiculed the idea of danger.

"I'd show 'em!" he said, truculently. "Savin' yer presence, miss, I'd show 'em!"

The precise nature of the punishment which he proposed
to inflict upon any of the mob who presumed to interfere
with their progress did not appear; and Miss Holt had an
uneasy feeling that his attitude lacked something of being
adequate to the occasion. It was less the voice of the sagacious minister who, after weighing the chances of danger in
a proposed enterprise, had decided that the undertaking was
safe, than of a hot-headed captain, eager only to come face
to face with the foe. But her own anxiety to go on the errand of mercy overcame whatever forebodings she might have
felt, and Wilson received orders to bring the brougham round
at once.

The trip across the city was made without interruption,

and Miss Holt had no difficulty in finding the address to which she had been directed. The destitution of the family had not been exaggerated. They lived in two small rooms on the third floor of a large building—rooms very bare of furniture, and from which Miss Holt's eye, experienced now in the sad significance of the hieroglyphics of poverty, saw at a glance that every article on which money could possibly be obtained had already found its way to the pawnbroker. Here dwelt the mother and her three children, the eldest a girl of eight and the youngest a boy of three and a half years. The sound of crying came to Jessie's ears as she approached the door, and it was not until she had knocked twice that a voice within said "Hush! be still," and the door was cautiously opened a few inches.

"Does Mrs. Silling live here?"

"Yes; do you wish to see her?"

"If I may, please."

"I don't know as you can," replied the girl of eight, who already had the manner of a woman, and whose face was old in the knowledge of sorrow; "I'll ask."

Jessie did not wait for the child's return, but, pushing the door open, stepped into the first of the two rooms. In the middle of the naked floor sat the two younger children, their poor little bodies partly covered with rags which it was absurd to speak of as "clothing." They had between them an old horseshoe and a piece of cotton-cloth twisted to the semblance of a doll for playthings. The thin faces under tousled hair were smudged and wet with tears. As she met their wide eyes, with the expectant awe-stricken look—so unutterably pathetic in the children of the very poor—Jessie's heart ached.

But her immediate business now lay in the farther room, where, in the dim light—for there was no window to the second apartment—stretched on a mattress, on the poorest of broken beds, and covered only by a worn red quilt, lay the mother. Only the thin white face was visible, which hardly turned towards the visitor as the large dark eyes looked up to Jessie. The latter felt a lump rising in her throat as she laid her ungloved hand upon the woman's forehead, and there

was something in the softness and warm tenderness of the
touch which brought tears to the big, sad eyes. Jessie felt her
own tears coming. To conceal them she turned to the eldest
child, who stood silently by the bedside.

"How long has your mother been ill?"

"Been sick? More'n a month now."

"Your father is dead?"

The child nodded.

"Your mother does washing when she's well?"

The child nodded again.

Jessie looked round the room, and saw how forlorn it was.

"It is very cold here," she said.

"It's awful cold nights," said the little girl. "We hain't
had no fire for—oh, for weeks. I tries to sell papers some
evenin's," she added, as if apologizing for not being better
able to support the family, poor, wan little thing! "But it's
hard for me to be away. *They* can't take care o' mother,"
nodding her head in the direction of the smaller children,
who had now crept into the rear room, and stood, hand in
hand, gazing, fingers in mouth, at Jessie. Heavens! what
care could be taken of any one amid such surroundings?

"Could you come away with me now for a few moments
and leave them?" Jessie asked of the eldest girl again.

"I guess so."

Jessie waited an instant in unconscious expectation that
the other would "put on her things." But it soon appeared
that the child was ready to go. There was no need of preparation, for she possessed no other costume. So Jessie
leaned over the bed and stroked the sick woman's forehead,
and stooped and kissed her.

As she went to the door, followed by the girl, she stopped
for a minute by the younger children, and, taking a hand of
each in hers, "You must be very good till we come back,"
she said, "and if you don't cry or make a noise of any kind
I'll bring you something you will like."

"What is your name?" she asked her companion as they
went down the shaky stairs.

"Lizzie."

"Has a doctor seen your mother?"

" No."

Arriving at the street, the child looked in amazement at the brougham which was moving up and down, the horses stamping, and tossing their heads, the object of admiration to, as it seemed to Jessie, an almost incredible number of ragged and dirty little children.

" Is them yours?" asked Lizzie, breathlessly.

" Yes, they are my father's. Now, where can we get wood and coal?"

" Next block, on the other side of the street," said the little girl, pointing in the direction indicated with her thin hand.

" And where is there a drug-store?"

" Round the corner, that way."

" Well, now go to the wood and coal place and give them that." And Jessie put a bill into the girl's hand. " Bring back, yourself, as much wood as you can carry, so that we can start a fire at once, and tell them to send some more, and some coal as soon as possible. Give them all the money, and tell them that you will use it up as you need it. Do you understand?"

The girl nodded.

" Run along, then. I am going to the drug-store and over there," indicating a general store at the corner, " and will be back almost as soon as you."

From the smooth-faced clerk at the drug-store she obtained the address of a Dr. Chinnery, and drove to his house. The doctor was not at home, so Jessie left a message for him, asking him to call on Mrs. Silling as soon as possible, and to take charge of her case, and proceeded to the general store which she had already noticed. After a visit to a dairy, where they also sold bread and other products of the bakery, she returned to the wretched rooms, taking with her an india-rubber cat and a large woolly ball as presents for the children.

Here she found Lizzie on her knees before the stove, in which a fire was already roaring with a blaze of kindling-wood, while the two younger ones stood on either side, and spread their little hands to catch the first rays of warmth.

"That's right," Jessie said, cheerily; "and have you been very good?" she asked the elder of the two little ones. The child looked up shyly and nodded.

"Then," said Jessie, kissing her, "here's what I promised you," and she produced the woolly ball. The smallest child was soon in possession of the cat; and the two, without a word, sat down solemnly on the floor for a deliberate examination of these new and amazing properties.

Jessie walked to where the sick woman lay, who, too weak to speak, raised her left hand feebly from under the quilt, and laid it, palm· upward, on the bedside. Jessie understood, and placed her own left hand in it, while with her right she stroked the white forehead. The thin fingers closed round the soft hand and clung to it tenaciously.

In a few minutes the articles which Jessie had ordered arrived. Some milk was soon warmed, and the two younger children sat themselves on the floor, with their backs against the wall, each with a cupful of milk, into which they dipped lumps of the bread and ate it—a proceeding to which they sat themselves with such voracity that Jessie was compelled to tell them that they must eat more slowly, or she would have to take the good things away again. Lizzie also had her cup of milk and her bread, but she set it on the floor in a corner while she watched Miss Holt pouring some of the warm liquid from a teaspoon between the sick woman's lips. Without the doctor's approval, Jessie did not dare to allow the invalid to take too much. A little hot milk could do no harm, but beyond that she was afraid to venture.

"I am not going to give you anything more to eat now," she said to Mrs. Silling, "because the doctor is coming soon, after I have gone — Dr. Chinnery." The woman smiled faintly and nodded. "He will know what you ought to have and what ought to be done for you. You are to do just what he says, and Lizzie can get anything you want from the drug-store round the corner." Jessie kissed the woman's forehead again, adding, "Now be brave until he comes, and we will soon have you well again."

Taking Lizzie into the other room, she asked her if her mother belonged to any church.

"She used to go to the 'Piscopal church on Sixteenth Street, but that was long ago."

"Has the minister ever been here?"

The child shook her head. "I guess he hasn't any use for poor folks. We can't give nothin' to the church."

How had she come to think these things? Probably she had heard her mother talking, and it was not the first time that Jessie had caught from the mouths of little children of the very poor fragments of wisdom, showing a bitter and cynical knowledge of the world, which Jessie herself could scarcely appreciate.

"Your things are at the pawnshop?" she asked; for she knew that these matters are talked of with a directness and absence of shame among the destitute to which she had had some difficulty at first in accustoming herself.

The child nodded and glanced round the empty rooms.

"How much do they amount to altogether?"

"Eighteen dollars and thirty cents," said the child, promptly. "The last thirty cents was for Nellie's shoes."

"Will they deliver them here, or do you have to fetch them?"

"Have to fetch them."

"Well, here are twenty dollars, and five dollars more in case you need anything that has to be paid for," and as she gave the child the money she had no misgivings that it would not be properly spent. "Indeed, there are some things that I want you to get. You must go and buy a broom and a scrubbing-brush and some soap to scrub the floor — you know the kind of brush I mean?" The child nodded again. "And have you a pail?"

"We've got that one," said the child, pointing to one which stood in a corner.

"Will it hold water?"

"If you don't fill it too high up."

"Well, it will do, I dare say. Now, when the doctor comes I want you to ask him whether it is safe to scrub the rooms, or whether the damp would be bad for your mother. Do you understand? If he says it would be bad, then just sweep them out; but if he will let you, give the floors and wood-work a good scrubbing with soap and hot water. Do that before you get the things from the pawnshop. I would not give the children " (and there was no sense of incongruity in speaking to this little thing of eight years as to a grown-up woman of the "children ") "anything more to eat yet. Wait until the doctor comes, and tell him what they have had; show him the things there, and ask him if you had not better cook a piece of the steak for their dinner. But, child, you have not had anything to eat yourself yet!" Jessie suddenly remembered.

"That's all right," said the girl; but she cast an almost wolfish glance into the corner where her cup stood on the floor, with the big slice of bread on the top of it.

"You are a brave little thing," and Jessie laid her hand on the rough, brown head. But the child only looked up at her with surprise in her eyes.

Jessie went back to the inner room, Lizzie following silently, and pressed the sick woman's hand.

"I will be back to-morrow, and meanwhile Lizzie and the doctor will take care of you." And the thin lips moved in what Jessie knew was meant for a blessing.

"Good-bye!" she said to Lizzie, stroking the child's head.

"Good-bye!" replied the other, simply, and Jessie knew there was no need for the child to put her gratitude into words. But the second girl, Nellie, came running up, and, clutching Jessie's dress with both her hands, put up a wet and crumby mouth to be kissed. Jessie caught her up and kissed her, and saw that she left a tear on the dirty little cheek as she did so. The smallest, a mere fragment of humanity in the middle of the bare floor, only sat and pinched the india-rubber cat.

Sinking back into a corner of the brougham as she started home, Jessie ran over in her mind the things, in the way of bedding and clothes for the children, that she would bring from the house or buy before her visit on the following day. Occupied with these thoughts, and full of the pathos of the scene which she had just left, she scarcely noticed which way the carriage was going. For the time the strike was forgotten, until suddenly there broke upon her ears the roar of

11

voices, heard from a few squares away, as the crowd gathered
by the loop greeted some incident of the conflict. Jessie now
became aware that Wilson, in bravado, had taken in returning
a route which led more nearly through the centre of town
than that which he had followed earlier in the day. Through
the glass in front of her Jessie could see that there was a considerable crowd assembled at the next corner, and a minute
later the carriage was swinging round the same corner, with a
wall of men on either side.

As soon as Wilson had turned the corner he found himself
confronted by the two cars which had been derailed some fifteen minutes before. The horses had grown accustomed to
the electric cars when moving peaceably on the tracks; but
two cars thrown sideways across the road were a new thing
to them, and, as their driver tried to slow them down, they
showed evident signs of alarm at the obstacle in front. Taking in the situation rapidly, Wilson had concluded that there
was room enough to pass on the right side of the street between the front platform of the foremost car and the sidewalk, and determined to put the horses through there—at
least, the strikers should not see him turn round. If there had
been no other element to be taken into account but the obstacle of the cars themselves, he would probably have succeeded in holding the horses while he steered them past. But
at this moment the crowd recognized the carriage, and immediately a roar arose from both sides of the street which, added to the unknown danger of the obstruction in front of
them, so terrified the horses that they commenced plunging.
At the same time two missiles were thrown from somewhere
in the crowd—one an apple, which struck the wood-work of
the carriage so close to the window that the pane was spat-
tered with juice, and the other a stone which, as Jessie could
see, came perilously near to hitting Wilson as he sat on the
box.

The situation was critical. The horses continued to plunge
and rear, while Wilson, with his voice and occasional light
touches of the whip, strove to bring them to their senses. It
seemed to Jessie as if every moment would be the last—as if
in the next instant the horses would surely break from all re-

straint and dash either into the yelling crowd upon the sidewalk or against the barricade in front.   But as high-bred
horses will (for horses differ in their reasoning power in moments of danger almost as men do, and it is in crises that
both show the blood that is in them), even in their terror, the
beasts recognized the familiar voice of authority.   They
plunged and reared, now jerking the brougham violently forward for a few feet and then almost as suddenly backing.   At
the end of some minutes, while the mob shrieked itself hoarse,
the carriage had scarcely moved from its original position,
except that it had worked a few feet, perhaps, nearer to the
right side of the road, on which lay the only chance of passing the obstacle ahead.

Suddenly a figure, different in dress and manner from the
mass of the strikers, pushed through from the sidewalk to
the roadway and advanced towards the carriage.   It was
Blakely.   Keeping an eye on the horses, he opened the carriage door.

"Be perfectly cool," he said ; " but you had better get out.
Wait till the horses back again.   Give me you left hand, and
step out quickly, when I say so, on your right foot—mind,
your right foot."

She leaned forward and gave him her left hand, which he
took in his, as she was bidden.   A moment later the horses
backed again.

" Now !" said he, sharply.   She jumped lightly out, while
he slipped his right arm round her waist to steady her, and
drew her away from the carriage door, which, still holding her
left hand in his, he then reached out to and shut.   It was only
just in time ; or perhaps the click of the closing door was the
last straw which broke the self-restraint of the frightened animals.   They plunged wildly forward.

" Oh, he'll be killed !" screamed Miss Holt, as Wilson
threw his whole weight on to the right rein.

There was a sudden sway of the carriage and a breaking of
the front ranks of the crowd as the horses dashed almost on
to the sidewalk ; a sharp, resonant crash as the axle of the left
front wheel struck the corner of the car.   The jar made the
carriage rock till it seemed as if the coachman must lose his

seat, but he did not. An instant later he was as firm and square-shouldered as ever, talking soothingly to the horses, which were plunging again in the open roadway beyond the barricade. It was admirably done, and the yells of the crowd sounded more like a cheer as, with the whole space of the road ahead of him, Wilson quickly brought the spirited animals under control.

"He's all right," said Blakely. And Miss Holt drew a long breath of relief. Then she realized the conspicuousness of her position, standing, Blakely holding her hand, in the middle of the road, with the eyes of all the crowd on either side fixed upon them. But her companion drew her arm deliberately under his, and walked to the sidewalk, while the men in front fell sheepishly to either side, and made way for the pair.

"I am almost mean enough," he said, in a low voice, as they pushed through the throng, "to wish that the carriage *had* been smashed—not so as to hurt Wilson, of course, but so that if there had been anybody inside, *they* would have been hurt. Then I should have the credit of having saved you from something."

"But you did," she replied; "the danger was just as great, even if it ended all right. I am as grateful as if you had saved my life."

"And there is only one thing in all this world which I should prize more than your gratitude," he said, speaking still more low.

She did not reply, and he thought it best to change the subject.

"You will walk home, will you not? Please," he pleaded, "let me have the pleasure of escorting you. It might be unsafe to get into the carriage again. The horses are frightened, and we do not know how much the carriage is hurt."

"I suppose I had better walk," she said, doubtfully.

"Let me leave you in here a minute," as he stopped before the open door of a store, "until I go and tell him that you will walk."

She stepped up obediently on the step of the store in ques-

tion, while he released her arm and left her, to push his way
to the street again. Wilson had turned the horses, and was
walking them quietly back, looking for his mistress in the
crowd. As she stepped up into the doorway he saw her, and
drew up to the curb just as Blakely emerged from the throng.

"That was splendidly done," said the latter, cordially, and
Wilson touched his hat modestly in acknowledgment of the
compliment. "But Miss Holt thinks she would rather walk
home, and asked me to tell you to drive on."

"It's all right, Mr. Blakely," said Wilson, who was reluctant to give the strikers the comfort even of the knowledge
that they had interfered with the drive; "she may just as
well let me take her as not."

"She's a little frightened," Blakely replied, "and it is better that she should walk a bit."

He stooped over to look at the axle.

"The carriage isn't hurt, is it?"

"Oh no, sir!" said Wilson, in a tone of contempt, scarcely
deigning even to lean over on his box enough to look down
at the wheel which had suffered the collision; "just a little
paint, that is all, sir."

That appeared to be the case.

"Pretty well built," remarked Blakely, and, nodding to Wilson, he returned to Miss Holt, who, from her position on the
door-step, waved her hand to the coachman as he whipped up the
horses and swung them round with rather unnecessary dash, to
show the onlookers that neither he nor the horses had suffered.

It was impossible that Jessie should not tell herself how
handsome Blakely was as he turned his laughing face up to
her again, and how enormously to advantage he appeared in
contrast with the men around him. He had borne himself,
too, admirably, with just that self-possession in the moment
of danger which appeals most directly to a woman's admiration. She thought of him as he had been in the theatre on
that first evening, and it was with a return of the old embarrassed feeling of subjection that she placed her hand again
on his arm as he pushed a path for them through the people. He, conscious perhaps of his advantage, talked playfully
of other things.

"How on earth did you come to be driving down-town?" he asked. "It is awfully risky."

"I know. Papa told me not to. But there was—there was an important engagement over on the West Side which I had to keep."

"An important engagement with the dress-maker?" he asked.

"No; that is mean. Women sometimes do other things besides see a dress-maker."

"Hats, perhaps?" he asked.

"It was a very — important — engagement," she replied, "which had nothing to do with any part of my costume."

"Then I give it up," he said. "When is a woman not a woman? When she has important engagements which have no reference to dress."

So they talked nonsense until they reached a place where the sidewalks were not crowded. Then she withdrew her arm from his and walked on by his side. Presently he said:

"Now, as I consider myself your keeper for the morning —heigho! that it is only for a morning!—I am going to order you about."

She pursed up her lips and gazed up into his face with an affected air of meek and childish attention, folding her hands in front of her. But he looked as if he were going to kiss her then and there; so she dropped her hands and asked, in her natural tone:

"I beg your lordship's pardon?"

He laughed. "The first thing that I am going to do is to leave you and send you home in a hack. You won't half appreciate the heroism of it; but you must be tired, and you have walked enough."

She was aware now that the strain of the events of the morning had made itself felt; so she offered no protest.

"We will go over this way to the station," he continued, "where we shall find plenty of vehicles of all sorts. We will select the shabbiest possible hack with the most sheep-like horses. And then—and then I will say good-bye."

Arriving within view of the row of carriages which were

drawn up in a single file along the side of the road, he stopped and examined them.

"I think," he said, deliberately, "that those gray things, which may or may not be horses, in the second hack from this end are sufficiently peaceful. They might fall down; but they couldn't do anything more than that."

So they crossed the street, and, after resisting the importunities of a score of other drivers who vociferously volunteered to drive him and "his lady" to "any part of the city for one dollar," he succeeded in installing her in the vehicle in question. He held the door open while the hackman busied himself with ostentatious speed in removing the horses' blankets and lifting the weight to which they were hitched up to the box.

"I am very, very grateful to you," she said, earnestly, as she gave him her hand.

"And do you suppose that I am not very, very happy?" he asked, as he took and held it.

"Where to, sir?" asked the driver.

"To Mr. Holt's, in Jefferson Avenue," replied Blakely, and then, leaning into the carriage, he said, in a voice which was almost a whisper:

"I suppose you will be angry with me, but do you know that you are the sweetest and most beautiful woman that the Almighty has made?"

It was a moment before she could reply.

"You know that I am too grateful to be angry at anything. But that is not fair."

None the less she smiled, and she knew that her eyes said to him that she was glad. He closed the door quietly without taking his eyes from hers, and raised his hat slowly as the carriage pulled out and drove away.

Arriving home, Jessie had barely time to get ready to receive Mrs. Tisserton. At the lunch-table she told the story of the morning's adventure. Miss Willerby received it rather coldly, while Mrs. Tisserton looked at Jessie, and said:

"Take care! Do you remember what I wrote you of Mr. Blakely when you were at Mentone?"

Jessie did remember—"Pity the girl who finds herself in

his power, as doubtless many girls have done before, and probably more will in the future."

But Miss Caley said it was just splendid. She loved those sort of things; they were so romantic.

"Oh, how I wish Mr. Barry would save me!" she sighed. "Can't I take the brougham, Jessie, and tell him where to wait for the catastrophe? But probably he would only run away when the time came. Nothing heroic ever happens to me!" she complained, forlornly. "I have never been rescued by anybody—except when I was about thirteen, and Willie Maxey pulled me out of the ice when I was skating. We made ever so much of that, and it was lots of fun. But we both knew that the water was only two feet deep, and there was no possible danger of anything except a cold—and the fishes. And he didn't even save me from that (the cold, I mean), because I had it horribly—oh, for *weeks* afterwards!"

XIV

AN EVIL GOD

HORACE MARSH, returning to town on the following day, read an account of the incident in the morning paper. The Democratic organ, in the paragraph which it devoted to the affair, made no mention of any hostile demonstration on the part of the strikers as having contributed to the panic of the horses. It appeared that they had simply been alarmed "by the derailed cars and the crowd on the sidewalk." The courage and coolness shown by Mr. Marshal Blakely, "the well-known young society man who is a close friend of the Holt family," were gracefully commented upon; and Horace wondered what courage or coolness was required to help a young woman out of a carriage which was standing still. And why had this good-luck fallen to Blakely of all men in the world? Why could not chance have thrown the opportunity in the way of Horace Marsh himself?

Mr. Holt, receiving a more veracious account of the episode from his daughter, sent Blakely a short note of thanks "for the assistance which you rendered to my daughter—who, I need not say, is very dear to me—at what was undoubtedly a moment of danger. I shall always," he added "—as will Miss Holt — feel under obligations to you for the courage and promptness with which you acted."

Blakely received this letter on his arrival at his office on the following morning. Having read it, and not being over-burdened with business, he swung his chair round to the window, put his feet up on the sill, and set himself to think it over.

Was he in love with Miss Holt? He was making love to her, certainly. That was his habit—a habit from which he

never permitted himself to depart in the case of any woman
who was reasonably young and sufficiently good-looking.
" The chief business in life of the youth of either sex is thinking of the youth of the other sex." The accuracy of this as
a maxim of universal applicability may be debatable; but
with Marshal Blakely certainly no other interest engrossed so
much of his time and abilities as did the making of love. He
was not without other interests, for he was fond of, and as a
rule proficient in, most of the things in which men delight.
He rode well, was a good shot, and a keen fisherman. But
there was no sport which appealed to so many sides of his
nature and gratified him so fully as the pursuit of woman.
There was pleasure undoubtedly in killing a salmon or a deer.
But at best it was not a contest with one's equal. Moreover,
when you killed them they were dead; and there was an
end.

Not that he had ever deliberately reasoned it out with
himself in these terms. He accepted the facts as he found
them, and went where the best sport was.

He was not the typical villain of the novelist, nor the
typical operatic villain; only a young man in ordinary life,
rather better equipped than the majority of his fellows—
firstly, by nature, and, secondly, by practice—for the con-
quest of women. He has his counterparts in every community. In the opera — no matter whether the maiden is
married to the villain with the bass voice or to the gentle
swain with the tenor; no matter whether the ceremony oc-
curs in the village market-place among the pealing of bells
and the pelting of paper flowers, or in the bandit's cave, with
only the banditti for witnesses and an unfrocked friar for
priest—it is always on the wedding ceremony that the curtain falls. In real life there is an "afterwards." And this
was the trouble in regard to Miss Holt.

Blakely had made love to many women, but had never
been formally engaged to be married. Precisely how the
affairs ended was known only to the women and to him.
Some of those to whom he had laid siege had been marriageable; others were not, under a constitution of society
which refuses to recognize polyandry. But Blakely had

never been consciously near to the danger of falling into
wedlock. Some day he might; but why do it yet a while?
In the first place, he had never felt any disposition to become
seriously—or, at least, sufficiently—in love. Not that there
were not admirable women—women in whose society he had
taken much delight for a while—women in whose possession
he professed to consider other men very lucky. There were
beautiful women, witty women, delightful women, intoxicat-
ing women. As Blakely would have put it himself: For a
man who wants a wife, there are plenty of women who will
make wives altogether too good for him. For himself, he
did not want a wife. Pushed to an ultimate analysis of
his feelings, he would probably have confessed that he had
been so accustomed to dissipate his affections over many—
so habituated to the pleasure of pursuit and change—that he
doubted his own ability to concentrate his regard now and
to the end on any one. He had so practised playing with
the deepest emotions, used the solemnest vows so lightly,
had so feigned every form of enslavement and self-abasement
and self-surrender, that he could not imagine himself as
really enslaved—carried away by real emotion and breathing
vows in earnest. How often had he sworn that his whole
life lay in winning one woman's favor! And how soon
afterwards had he yawned and gone elsewhere! Could it
be that the issue would ever arise on which his life was, in
fact, at stake? He could not conceive of himself as being so
absorbed in one woman that forever after all others would
lose their attractions.

He often wondered whether he was an exception in this.
There were happy homes, of course. For that matter, there
were churches. Both were eminently desirable institutions
for the preservation of society. But when you came to look
at particulars and individuals, it was undoubted that devout
church-members sometimes were backsliders. And he knew
married men of his acquaintance, men most happily and
charmingly married, who did not impress him, when out of
the society of their wives, as impervious to the attractions
of other women. And with married women—women who
were apparently model wives—it had not been his experience

that devotion to a husband necessarily excluded the possibility of a second passion. If it were possible to look into the very souls of some of these—say, a hundred carefully selected of the most exemplary husbands and wives—what would be found there? Were they really, in their innermost hearts, happier for the ties which bound them?

Society was happier, of course. But that was not the question. It was incontestably necessary that people in general should marry. But how about the particular person? Was it not only a sacrificing of the individual for the public good? "The individual withers, and the world is more and more."

Supposing a man (himself, for instance), of whom a woman need never be ashamed, to have married a woman as beautiful and charming as you please; supposing them to be well-off in a worldly way, and with all desirable surroundings; supposing, then, the excitement of pursuit and the pride of possession to have passed, what would be their life afterwards? Understanding them, of course, both to have strength enough and sense enough to appear happy, and to respect the conventionalities, what would be their true inward feelings? It was a question which he would have very much liked to have had answered. But, so far, the evidence which he had seen had been confusingly contradictory. The bulk of the evidence, that which appeared on the surface, and which was contained in the professions of married people, was largely on one side. But one-half of this evidence was at best open to a suspicion of being biassed. Such fragmentary testimony as came to him on the other side from his own experiences was sometimes startlingly positive and unprejudiced.

As for Miss Holt, he had set himself, just like the villain in the play, deliberately to win her. He modestly believed that he could succeed—that he had, in fact, succeeded. Luck had been on his side. He had played boldly, and the thing, so far, had gone far more easily than he had anticipated. And what then? Did he wish to marry her? She was rich, certainly; but he had means enough. As her husband he would, from a worldly point of view, hold an eminently desirable position. If not exactly "the sweetest and most beautiful woman that the Almighty had made" (and he wondered how often he had used that particular phrase to various women—a phrase which, he flattered himself, was rather neat, and which he had never yet known a woman to resent), she was certainly a beautiful as well as a very high type of woman. All this he understood. But—? To the bachelor the land beyond the altar is almost as unknown and mysterious as the land beyond the grave; and, for purposes of experiment, marriage has practically the same disadvantage as death of being irrevocable.

And if he did not mean to marry her? On this point he pondered considerably, before his reverie came to an end, as he turned Mr. Holt's letter over and over in his fingers. Oh, well, he would wait, and see how things turned out. It was not a situation that was new to him, and, in the past, circumstances had worked themselves out to various results; but never, so far, with any great disaster to himself. So he would wait. He would not show himself to be in any haste to thrust himself upon her. It would do no harm to let her wonder for a day or two why he did not call. Meanwhile he would send her some flowers, with a polite note hoping that she was none the worse for the excitement of the previous day.

To Mr. Holt also he wrote briefly, thanking him for his letter, which, Blakely said, attached much more importance to the incident than the facts warranted. The service which he had been able to render was very slight.

Jessie received the flowers and the accompanying note on her return from the second visit to Mrs. Silling, which had been made in a hired carriage and by a roundabout route which did not take her through the heart of the city. At the sick woman's bedside she had found Dr. Chinnery, who proved to be a large, hearty man, possessed of that cheery manner which goes so far to inspire courage in a patient. Altogether, Jessie was pleased with and felt confidence in him.

The rooms had undergone a transformation. Lizzie had carried out her orders faithfully, and Jessie saw that the floor and the wood-work had been well scrubbed. The "things" had been recovered from the pawnbroker, including a table and three chairs, a large tub and a stool to set it on, ironing-boards, a wringer, and flat-irons of various sizes. A square of cheap carpet was on the floor between the two rooms, while in the rear one a large mattress with a couple of quilts lay on the floor, whereon evidently the children slept. A number of small articles—a kettle and some pitchers, a dish or two, some plated spoons and forks, as well as the children's shoes, were arranged in their proper places, and Jessie was moved to amazement at the number of things which a pawnbroker requires from the poor and helpless before he will advance eighteen dollars and thirty cents.

Mrs. Silling already showed signs of improvement, turning her head without effort, and being able, and rather too willing, to talk in a weak and husky voice. The doctor laughed at Jessie's suggestion that a trained nurse should be employed to look after the patient.

" Oh, she is just run down," he said, " with overwork and worry. If you were in her condition, Miss Holt (supposing it to be possible for you to bring yourself to it), you would need not only one nurse, but two. As soon as you could be moved I should order you away for a change of air—somewhere in the South. It would take you six months to pull up. But with these people it is different. The mere revolution from hunger and cold to warmth and proper nourishment, from want of care to the feeling of comfort and of being looked after, is change enough in her case. It is more of a change than all the travel or dieting could bring you. She will be at work again inside of two weeks. If we did need a nurse," he added, " we could not have a better one than little Lizzie here."

" I saw in the paper this morning," he said, at another time, " that you had some trouble yesterday with your carriage in the mob, Miss Holt. It was on your way home from here, I suppose ? Well, you can comfort yourself with the knowledge that the trip was worth the risk. Forty-eight hours later—perhaps, even, if you had waited until to-day—it would have been too late."

Jessie did not reply, but her heart was filled with anger against the conditions of society which made it possible that the life of this woman and the lives of her three children should thus be left in the centre of a large city, with wealth and plenty on every side, to the accidental intervention of a stranger like herself. It was by what to her seemed the merest chance that Jessie had heard of the family—a friend of one of the house-maids had heard of their condition from another friend, and the story had been casually repeated till it had reached Miss Holt; just one of those chances, Jessie thought, by which Providence loves to work. But what were the churches doing? Had they really "no use for poor folk?" And what of all the charitable organizations in which Mrs. Flail was so benevolently interested? Was it nobody's business to see that women and children did not die of hunger and cold?

Jessie Holt was no novice in charitable work. Often before had she been filled with bitterness at the apparent powerlessness of organized charity to cope with real distress. But during this last week, since that day when in her father's office she had for the first time heard from another mouth comments, not intended for her ears, on her own extravagance—her carriage and her dresses—the landscape of life had somehow arranged itself in clearer perspective before her eyes. The high lights were sharper and the shadows deeper. Or, rather, it was no longer as on a painted canvas that she looked, but a play, a Passion play, a play of life and death, in which real men and women and little children moved and suffered and died—died trampling on each other, "one-half of mankind against the other half." And of those who trampled she herself was one.

Just as in childhood we have, each of us, to learn our individuality,

> "So rounds he to a separate mind,
> From whence clear memory may begin;
> As thro' the frame that binds him in,
> His isolation grows defined,"

as we find

> ... "I am not what I see,
> And other than the things I touch;"

so there comes to all of us later—all of us, that is, who have
any right to be of mankind at all—a reverse current of discovery, a current "remerging in the general soul." This humanity from which we had thought ourselves distinct—we
are still of it. These men and women around us—they are
but other ourselves. There is no magic circle drawn around
our own small personality. Our part is but a part of the
common life, just as is that of each of them. We are our
brother's keeper, and our sister's and her children's.

Mrs. Silling at least should not die ; and as for Mrs. Flail's
organizations, at the worst here were two recruits for the
kindergarten. So Jessie set herself to unpack the great bundle which she had brought in the carriage with her, and
which the hackman had carried up-stairs — blankets and
sheets for the sick woman's bed, clothes for the children,
and towels and all manner of odds and ends for domestic
uses—while Dr. Chinnery looked on with a broad smile on
his wholesome face, and Lizzie moved quietly about, taking
each article in its turn from Miss Holt's hands, and folding it
up and setting it in order away.

Throughout the morning Lizzie said little, except when she
insisted on rendering a scrupulous account of her expenditures, and offered to return to Jessie the four dollars and
twenty-six cents which remained. When Jessie had arrived
the girl had simply nodded in an indifferently friendly way,
and thereafter remained silent, but watchfully ready to do
whatever was needed of her. A stranger, unaccustomed to
specimens of her class, would have said that she was curiously insensible and ungrateful. But Jessie and the doctor
knew better, and had the former wanted thanks those of the
sick woman, contained more in her looks and the pressure of
her hands than in words, and the wet but demonstrative
kisses of the younger children would have sufficed.

On leaving she could not but see the change which she
had brought to the family, nor help feeling that the work
which she had done was good. On the drive home she was
light-hearted, and looked with eager interest at whatever
caught her attention on the journey. Sombre though the
background of her thoughts might be, there was light and

color in the foreground. As in times of illness the permanent and deep-seated pain may be forgotten in moments of incidental pleasure, so the local happiness overlaid and obscured the sadness which was at her heart. She read Blakely's note, and, taking off her gloves, arranged the flowers that he sent in the same Rookwood vase as had carried Marsh's American Beauties a short time back, humming to herself the while, and bursting into short, glad, unconscious snatches of song. Neither of her guests was at home; so she tripped up the broad staircase, still singing to herself, to her room, and, having taken off her things, and finding still half an hour to spare before luncheon, sat down to write a note to Mrs. Flail, saying that she had two candidates for admission to the kindergarten, and inquiring what formalities of a fiscal or other kind were necessary before they could be accepted.

Meanwhile, Marsh sat in his office in the Metropolitan Block. He had reported to the General on his return, and had given in outline an account of his trip, answering many questions as to the tone of his reception at one place and another, and what this or that prominent Democrat whom Marsh had met had said. In turn Marsh had asked questions about the strike, and about the outlook of the campaign in the city. General Harter was something more than hopeful, and well satisfied with himself and the progress of events. He spoke in unctuous, well-rounded periods, as if already delivering himself from the august elevation of the gubernatorial chair.

This over, Horace set himself conscientiously to pick up the threads of the office work where he had dropped them, distressingly conscious the while of the difficulty of doing justice to a legal practice and a political campaign concurrently. Moreover, he was in no mood for work. He wanted to see Jessie. She haunted him. Her presence was around him, by his desk, as he wrote. He could hear her voice and see her face, and he "named her name to himself silently." After dinner he would call; but till then the day dragged wearily.

At last he was there, standing with Barry (who was a regular caller now) on the door-step of the house. Yes, the ladies

were at home—and Marsh could have blessed Thomas for
saying so. But that functionary seemed to regard the fact
as not at all out of the common, and set himself with his customary archiepiscopal solemnity to relieve the callers of their
hats and coats before leading them to the drawing-room.
Horace was conscious that his heart beat almost audibly as
he entered the apartment, where he saw that there was already one caller sitting with the women—Baldwin, the much
becuffed and becollared young man of flaxen hair.

Miss Holt had known that this meeting must come. The
flowers which she had received and had passed on to Thomas
were a sufficient intimation that Marsh proposed to endeavor
to retain his footing in the household. She had thought at
one time of telling Thomas to say that she was not at home
when Horace called; but she shrank, however much he might
merit it, from making the servants parties to the knowledge
of his disgrace. It was best to face the meeting when it came,
and to let him understand by her manner that she knew of
his treachery and valued him as he deserved.

Her greeting now was entirely courteous. It could not
have been otherwise. Of the others present, Miss Willerby
alone noticed its coldness, and was at a loss to understand the
reason. But to Horace himself, who knew how impulsively
and frankly glad and eager her usual welcome to him was—
especially when he had chanced to be away for some days—
and who had so looked forward to her quick questionings
about his trip, it was as if a sudden blow had struck him.
By the time that he had shaken hands with the others, Miss
Holt had resumed her seat, and, with her back half-turned to
him, was deep in conversation with Mr. Baldwin, while that
callow gentleman, amazed at the unwonted interest which his
hostess showed in him, wondered how he had ever thought
Jessie Holt "stuck up."

It was evident that she did not propose that Horace
should catch her eye. To force himself upon her was out of the
question. Moreover, as Miss Caley and Barry were already
deep in confidences upon the sofa in the corner, Marsh found
himself standing alone with Miss Willerby, to desert whom
would have been impossible. There was nothing for it but to

sit down with her. That experienced young woman saw that
something was wrong, and saw also that Horace was as much
bewildered as pained; and she forgave him when he said
that he had been "very well, thank you," in reply to her
question whether he had been out of town. She strove to
maintain the semblance of an animated chat. She talked of
whatever came to her, and he said "no" and "yes" at ran-
dom; all the while watching Miss Holt and wondering —
wondering—wondering.

What did it mean? That article? Nonsense; that was a
week ago, and his letter to her father had remedied any evil
that could have been done by that. Had the opposition papers been maligning him since he went away? Possibly, but
he would have heard of that from his party associates. Some
so-called "friend," then, had been poisoning her mind? But
who? Blakely? That was scarcely credible; for what could
Blakely say? Turn it which way he would, it was incompre-
hensible, and the only thing to do was to learn the truth from
her. But Pryce, the Englishman, arrived, and, dividing Miss
Holt's attention with Baldwin, only made another barrier
around her, and left Horace paired, as before, with Miss Willerby. Then the Tissertons came, and Baldwin left; and
Horace found himself talking to Mrs. Tisserton, while Miss
Willerby labored with "Jack." Presently that curiously
mannered personage arose unceremoniously, and, deserting
Miss Willerby, went over and annexed Baldwin's vacated
chair—a thing which Horace had longed to do for half an
hour past, and had lacked the courage. Horace now had two
ladies on his hands. Soon Mr. Pryce rose to go. Horace
could stand it no longer. He would take the Englishman's
place, and compel Miss Holt to speak to him at least. But as
he got up from his chair to carry out this resolution, the per-
verse Barry, who until that moment had been oblivious to
everything except Miss Caley's proximity, saw Marsh's sudden
uprising, and, taking it to be the signal for departure, stood up
also.

Miss Holt saw Barry rise, and she walked as far as the door
of the room with the retiring Englishman, and, smiling her
adieux to him, moved to where Barry was standing without

turning her face in Horace's direction—and Horace knew in his heart that she did it purposely.

"What! going so soon?" she asked Barry, sweetly.

"Is it soon?" he said. "I know it *seemed* soon to me; but I had no idea that anybody's company could make time pass as quickly for you as Miss Caley's makes it pass for me."

"Well, I don't wonder that Mary monopolizes you if you say things like that," replied Miss Holt.

She shook hands with Barry, and then turned slowly round, as if unaware that Horace was at her shoulder. As soon as she faced him—

"Good-night, Mr. Marsh," she said, and held out her hand.

"Good-night," he said, slowly. But in answer to his questioning gaze she only looked at him steadily, as if he had been at best but an indifferent acquaintance.

It was a raw, cold night. The Indian summer, it seemed, was breaking, and mist hung low in the streets, so that the houses on either side of them, as they walked, were no more than shapeless masses of solidity, and the electric lights which hung suspended at the crossings of the streets were surrounded with a halo of pearl. Marsh felt the chill of the weather in his bones, and turned up the collar of his coat and thrust his hands into his pockets; but Barry, impervious to climatic influences, whistled aggressively as he walked. He was deplorably destitute of an ear for music, but strove to atone in vigor for lack of melody. As a rule, Barry's whistling rather entertained Marsh, who would amuse himself by guessing whether his friend was rendering an air or only improvising. Now the noise jarred on Marsh's nerves, and he answered briefly to such commonplace remarks as his companion occasionally blurted out between whistles.

When they were settled in their customary places—Barry stretched at full length on the lounge and Horace ensconced in his favorite chair—it was impossible that the latter, after the nights of hard work and of scanty sleep in the forlorn bedrooms of second-class hotels, should be entirely unmoved by the grateful sense of warmth and homelike comfort. The feeling of physical well-being, in spite of his mental wretchedness, prompted him to be the first to break the silence.

"It is an amazing world!" he said.

Barry, being in love, promptly applied the remark to his own circumstances. Whatever he read or heard now bore significance only as it could be traced to a connection with her. The matter in the newspapers—whether it related to politics, business, sport, or crime—had no interest unless it dealt with affairs feminine. A hint at a woman in the heading of an article was enough to commend it to his perusal. Even the price of wheat was meaningless, except in so far as "wheat" rhymed with "sweet," and Mary Caley was that.

"It *is* an amazing world!" he replied. "A month ago—think of it! a month ago—I had never seen her, scarcely knew that she existed; and now— Why, it seems incredible!"

Marsh forbore to make even an allusion to Longfellow.

"Have you seen Miss Holt often lately?" he asked.

"Two or three times a day," replied Barry, calmly.

"She seemed out of sorts in some way to-night," pursued Marsh, craftily. "Has anything particular happened to her?"

"Not that I know of. Maybe the scare of yesterday was too much for her."

"Possibly;" but Marsh knew better. "How has she seemed when you have seen her before during the last week?"

"Oh, I don't know"—the absurdity of supposing that Barry would know!—"about as usual. Of course she hasn't been particularly gay. The strike would account for that." He was abominably obtuse.

"Has that man Blakely been up there much?"

"No; only seen him once, I think."

Evidently nothing was to be gained from this source; so Horace relapsed into his own thoughts. Barry went on talking, but his companion paid no heed to him. What could it be? It was useless conjecturing—conjecture was baffled at the outset. How was he to find out? He could not call—or thought he could not—again. Would it be possible to write—to word a letter so that she would be compelled to answer, without any danger of seeming impertinent and giving offence? He turned the idea over and over in his mind, phrasing a note this way and that. Yes; probably that was the best thing to do. He would write, and in writing would simply ask her the point-blank question, "What have I done?" It was a relief to have come even to this poor resolution, and he would execute it at once; so he rose from his chair.

Barry was still talking. With the sobering responsibility of prospective matrimony upon him, he had worked his way round to a discussion of his financial condition and a bewailment of what he termed his lack of "stick-to-it-ativeness" in business.

"I tell you," he said, "the main thing in this life is advertising. Take up a thing—no matter what—and advertise—advertise—advertise! Keep pounding away at it! It is all bosh to talk about not wanting your name in the papers. Name in the papers means success. Whether you have a church, or a school, or a grog-shop—advertise it! Especially if you are starting out as a young man—advertise! If I had to begin life again in a new place I would commence from the first day to call attention to myself. Wear a green hat; wear your coat inside out; don't wear a necktie—do anything that nobody else does. Wear your hair long or walk with a skip and a jump. That's the stuff. In ten years you'll be famous. When you get into a street-car everybody will tell everybody else 'That's Tompkins.' You will be pointed out in theatres to strangers as 'Tompkins, one of our well-known men.' To be one of our well-known men nowadays is to be half-way on the road to wealth. Reporters know you, and they always mention you as being wheresoever you happen to be. The public gets to know your name, and those who are not acquainted with you think you must be a devil of a fellow. Even those who are acquainted with you come under this influence. They like to be seen with you and associated with you. People want your name on things. Banks give you credit. Why, national reputations have been made in this country by wearing no neckties and going without overcoats."

Horace laughed.

"As usual, in what you say, Barry, it's only one-half idiocy. The public is always mixing up cause and effect. Because big men are notorious, therefore they think that the man who is notorious is big. Because genius is eccentric, eccentricity shows genius. 'To be great is to be alone;' and, therefore, to be alone is to be great. The public has grown so accustomed to miracles in science, to inventions which have created revolutions, and to hearing it said that it is unsafe to say that anything is impossible, that the surface impossibility of the latest and craziest scheme is its surest recommendation. *Credo quia incredibile!*"

"That's what!" Barry exclaimed. "We all expect the unexpected now. If I had made a fool of myself for the public benefit once a week for the past five years, I should be a big man now."

"Six feet two ought to be big enough as it is," Marsh suggested, "and I don't know what you have to growl about. You are as happy just now as a man can be. It is we poor devils who work hard, as hard as we know how, and only look up from our work long enough to see that everything worth having in life is slipping away from us—it is we who suffer."

To this Barry did not reply.

"Well, I have got to write a letter," said Marsh; and he sat himself down at a writing-table in the corner. He hesitated a minute, and then wrote boldly:

"My dear Miss Holt,—You may think this letter an impertinence, but I trust that you will not—at least, please understand that I do not mean it as such.

"It was impossible for me to-night not to see that something had happened to change your attitude towards me—to make you dislike me, which I have hitherto made bold to believe that you did not do. This is no time for me to tell you how much your like or dislike means to me, but I hope you will believe me when I say that I am utterly at a loss to guess what this thing may be. There must, I am sure, be some misunderstanding somewhere.

"Will you let me know what the matter is? If you will tell me when I may call and see you, you know that I shall be only too happy to come at any time.

"Yours, very much in earnest,

"Horace Marsh."

He read it over twice. It was not an ornately worded epistle ; but it told its tale.

"I guess it will do," he thought.

As he was putting it into an envelope, Barry arose and knocked the ashes out of his pipe, and the two separated for the night.

XV

THE next morning it was raining—not an accidental shower, but a steady, gray downpour, telling of a permanent change in the weather. It rained all that day, and the next and the next, which was Sunday. The effect of the change was quickly seen in the course of the strike.

In the sunshine it had been pleasant for the crowds to stand at the street corners and easy to be good-humored. Under the cold, persistent rain, falling in small drops, but fast and thick, loafing in the open air was a different thing. Even around the loop now the number of strikers was small—just a single row of men standing back against the walls; and they watched the cars go by in sullen silence. The majority either stayed at home or at their boarding-places, where time hung heavy on their hands, and they grew morose; or they congregated in certain resorts where beer was accessible, where they quarrelled among themselves, or, encouraging each other's discontent and growing bold in company, talked bitterly against the companies and broached plans of violence. In these places they segregated themselves into groups, according to their nationality—in one, the Irishmen; in another, the Poles; here the Bohemians; there the Huns. Among the mill hands were men of a dozen races, and the great majority spoke but little English. Certain drinking-saloons located in a low quarter of the city, which was known to the newspaper men as "The Pit," were the rendezvous of the Poles and Bohemians, and in each of these once and again during the day the clamor of voices and rapping of beer-mugs on the tables would be stilled as some fluent speaker, red-bearded and fierce-eyed, mounted on his chair and preached to them in their own tongue doctrines of what they knew as "liberty"—the liberty of the bomb and the assassin's knife.

The street-railway company, from the time when it had begun to hire new men, increased its force daily. Taking advantage of the change in the weather which drove the men from the streets, efforts in this direction were redoubled, until by the end of the week the service on all lines in the city was in regular operation with a full force of men. There were those who said, in the streets and in the newspapers, that "the backbone of the strike was broken." But Mr. Holt and his colleagues knew better. The real struggle had not begun.

The effect of their long idleness and of the inflammatory speeches to which they had listened soon began to be seen in the temper of the men; and in place of the open and half-bantering hostility of the street-corner crowds, secret deeds of violence began to be perpetrated. Employés of the company going home from their work at night, if by any chance they were found singly, were assaulted and roughly handled. The wires were cut several times, and in one case the end of the "live" wire, falling to the ground, killed the horse in a passing wagon, while a policeman who endeavored to remove the harmless-looking thing received the current in his body, and his recovery was doubtful. Stones were thrown through the windows of the barns and the power-houses, and men, working their way into the former and eluding the vigilance of the watchmen, tampered with the standing cars. A car on its last trip one night on the Milltown line was attacked, in the neighborhood of the deserted works, and though the conductor escaped, the engineer was beaten and trampled almost to death. An attempt was made on the same night to burn a boarding-house wherein a number of the men were now living, but without serious results. The officers of the company were in daily receipt of threatening letters, warning them that unless the company yielded they would die. Harrington received many such epistles.

Harrington, little by little, had come to be regarded by the strikers as one of their worst enemies. He had not

sought to make himself conspicuous, but notoriety was
thrust upon him.   In the vindictive speeches in the saloons
his name now occurred nearly as often as that of Mr. Holt himself, or those of General Manager Darron and Superintendent Boon.   It has already been seen that he was not liked
by the labor organizations before the trouble began.   Being
the only officer connected with both companies, with the exception of Mr. Holt, he was known to the employés of both.
In the very first hour of the strike, as has been told, he provoked the hostility of the men by taking the place of the
deserting conductor.   Later, under similar circumstances, he
had made almost an entire round trip, handling a car as its
engineer.   In each case it was accident that brought him on
the scene at the moment when his services were needed; but
the two instances together served to give him in the eyes of
the strikers the appearance of peculiar activity in behalf of
the company.   Then as his duties kept him largely confined
to the main power-house and central barns, he was formally
intrusted by the company with the task of protecting these
buildings, a dozen extra men being put under his authority
for the purpose.   It was an exasperating office, for the strikers resorted to all manner of devices for his petty annoyance,
and constant watchfulness was necessary to guard the property against minor injuries.   His men, too, were continually
in small broils and scuffles with individual strikers; and his
name (he was sneeringly spoken of as "Captain Harrington") came to be well known to newspaper readers.   One
day as he was walking through the barns, going in and out
between the idle cars, he came suddenly face to face with
Craft, whose name has already been mentioned as among the
speakers at the meetings in the Labor Temple, and who was
an officer of the local organization of the street-railway employés.   How Craft had managed to smuggle himself into
the barns Harrington could not conjecture, but he knew him
well by sight.   They met in the narrow pathway between the
cars standing on parallel tracks.

"How did you get in here?" asked Harrington, quickly.

"Go to hell and find out!" replied the other.

Before he could speak again Harrington hit him.   The

electrician had learned to spar, and hit both quickly and hard. Almost before he was aware that Harrington intended to strike, the labor leader found himself sprawling upon the floor. Before he was fairly on his feet a second blow struck him. In spite of his bulk and his blustering talk Craft was a coward at heart, and now suffered himself to be pushed almost without resistance to the door of the barns, where Harrington half threw and half kicked him out into the mud and rain, a woful spectacle. A score or more of strikers standing round saw their leader's humiliation, and the incident found its way into the papers the next day.

All these things together contributed to single out Harrington as one of the especial objects of the strikers' hatred, while Wollmer, for his personal dislike's sake, saw to it that the electrician's unpopularity was not suffered to decrease.

Jennie Masson, who was still much alone, and for whom these days were very gloomy, saw how frequently her lover's name was now in print with mingled feelings of fear and pride. She knew that he was right, and would not for worlds have had him be less courageous or less a man; but her heart ached for the peril that he was in. When he called one evening she found that he carried a revolver strapped round his waist; and this evidence that, in spite of the laughing way in which he talked, he was conscious of his own danger deepened her forebodings.

At last, as the strikers grew bolder and the deeds of violence more frequent, Mr. Holt, in behalf of the street-railway company, applied to the mayor of the city for protection for the company's property and the lives of the employés. He enclosed the mayor a list of the individual acts by which his company had already suffered damage, and represented that the situation demanded especial precautions. The step was taken less with the hope of obtaining the assistance asked for than with a view to placing himself and the company on record as having sought protection in abundance of time, and throwing on the municipal authorities the responsibility for whatever might follow.

His honor replied that he could see no reason as yet for any extraordinary measures of protection. The public peace

was not threatened, and he (the mayor) had an abiding faith
in the orderliness and love of law of his fellow - citizens.
He ignored the list with which Mr. Holt had furnished him,
and said that the official reports of the chief of the police
department showed no remarkable increase in crime — certainly no more than was reasonably to be expected when so
many men were out of work. The regular police-force of
the city was fully occupied with its present duties; nor was
there at the disposal of the city any fund which, as the
mayor was advised by the City Attorney, he would be justified
in using, in the present condition of affairs, for any such purposes as the president of the street - railway company re-
quested.

Mr. Holt replied that he was well aware that his own
sources of information as to the prevalence of crime must be
vastly inferior to those at the disposal of the mayor and the
chief of the police department. None the less, his personal
belief was that the situation was threatening in the extreme,
and that there was danger at any moment of concerted action on the part of the men now unfortunately unemployed,
which might result not only in considerable damage to private property, but in grave disturbance of the public peace.
The mayor would doubtless understand that he (as well as
the other officers of the street-railway company) was anxious
to take every possible precaution to protect the interests of
the stockholders of the company, which were intrusted to his
charge. As the mayor had suggested that the police-force of
the city was inadequate to meet emergencies which might
arise, and in view of what the mayor had said as to the lack
of funds in the city treasury, the street-railway company was
willing to provide any number of men that might be thought
sufficient, at the company's own expense, to give the needed
protection, if the city government would assume control of
them, and would invest them with the proper authority as
special officers.

The mayor answered that the city was not yet in such
straits that it was necessary for it to throw itself on the
generosity of private citizens or corporations for assistance
in the conduct of public affairs. When the city government

needed men to enforce the laws he had no fear that enough would not be forthcoming from the residents of the city at large in answer to any call which might be made upon them. It would be time enough, the mayor said, to consider the means by which riot or disorder should be repressed when riot or disorder showed itself.

Mr. Holt informed the mayor that he was much gratified to know that his honor felt so little uneasiness as to the outlook. The street-railway company had no doubt of the ability of the city government to protect the lives and property of the citizens, but the mayor would doubtless pardon Mr. Holt's natural anxiety in behalf of the large interests which were in his care. Mr. Holt further begged to officially notify the mayor that the street-railway company would be compelled to hold the city responsible for any danger to its property or the lives of its employés which it might suffer from the acts of violence of other parties, against whom the company had tendered the city all possible assistance in securing protection, which tender had been refused in his honor's recent communication.

This correspondence was published in full in the press, and the party organs attacked the president of the street-railway company bitterly for his "aspersions on the intentions of the strikers," and his "attempt to sow uneasiness and apprehension in the public mind." Mayor Bonderson was correspondingly applauded for his patriotism, his confidence in his fellow-citizens, and his refusal to place the city under a "reign of terror, by establishing a condition of affairs which would have bordered upon martial law."

The more thoughtful of the citizens, however, looked on at the course which things were taking with alarm, as from day to day crimes of all sorts grew more frequent. The employés of the street-railway company did not dare to go to or from their work except in bands of ten or more. An epidemic of burglary broke out in the city. Inoffensive citizens walking alone were held up and robbed. Attempts were made on two successive evenings to set fire to the iron-and-steel company's plant, and a large force of watchmen was kept constantly on duty there. The guerrilla warfare against the street-railway company was continued, and small injuries were done to its property in every conceivable way. Not only were the wires cut (or, rather, shot in two; for the strikers found a charge from a shot-gun to be the easiest and surest way of parting the cable overhead), but at night groups of men would set silently to work at remote points on the various lines and tear up the tracks, sometimes for a space of fifty yards at one place, and, carrying the rails away, hide them in ditches and out-of-the-way corners. Switches and frogs were battered and broken so that cars could not pass without derailment. Employés on the cars were attacked with missiles of every sort. Out of the darkness in the night figures would suddenly appear beside a moving car, and hurl huge stones and clubs at the engineers and conductors. Not infrequently the weapons thrown broke through the window, and showered splinters of glass over passengers within.

Occasionally offenders would be arrested, not by the energy of the police, but captured first by employés of the street-railway company, and handed to the police afterwards. When brought before a justice, they were either discharged or let off with a small fine, for which the money was readily forthcoming.

As in all troubles between a railway company and its employés, no matter whether it be a street-railway company or a larger steam road, the chief sufferer was the public. No individual member of the community suffered as largely as did the company, but in the aggregate the loss to the people was incomparably larger than to either of the immediate parties to the fight. This is always so. The direct and indirect injury to the public interests by the railway strikes of the last decade in the United States has amounted to many hundreds of millions of dollars. But the American people are most patient. In the individual controversy their sympathy at the outset is invariably on the side of the employés. It is only as the strike progresses—as crime and disorder become prevalent—as the worst side of the system of labor organizations is turned outward to the public view—as the lawless element, which will always ultimately control the mass of the unemployed, begins to tyrannize over the public, that the people rebel, and their sympathy is alienated from the side of the men.

As each successive strike begins, however, the public continues to give the same ungrudging support to the men that it has given before. But out of the many particular disappointments it appears that the public is slowly and unwillingly coming to learn the general lesson — the lesson that it is no disinterested spectator of the conflict, but that if it suffers the trouble to continue, itself will infallibly be the chief loser, whichever side wins. There is a natural instinct in all men, when two parties of evenly matched strength are fighting, to stand aside and let them fight till the best man is victorious. But the case is different when the arena which the contestants have selected for their struggle happens to be in the centre of one's own flower-bed. And no matter where the ring may be pitched for any struggle between a railway company and its men, it must always be the public property that will be trampled under foot.

Moreover, in spite of the talk of labor leaders about "peaceful strikes" and "lawful and constitutional warfare," the public is having forced upon it the knowledge of the fact that a peaceful strike, carried through without infraction of the laws, is, at least in the case of such quasi-public institutions as the railways, an impossibility. The labor leaders know when they embark upon a strike that they cannot carry it through to success without violation of the law. If they simply call their men out, and make no further move to prevent the employer continuing operations with new men, the strike is necessarily a failure. The essence of the modern strike is that the employer should be prevented from continuing with new men; and this cannot be done without violence. In the case of a railway, the mere attempt to do it (apart from any individual acts of violence) is a violation of the law of the nation and an insurrection against the government. The regulation of commerce is a function of the State, and to interrupt that commerce by violence is rebellion. Under the modern labor doctrines of the solidarity of all labor organizations, the public is coming slowly to an understanding of how serious such a rebellion may become.

In this controversy between the street-railway company and the labor organizations, the public men of both parties, owing to the nearness of the elections, were more than ordinarily loath to take the initiative in coming forward to interfere. After much delay, however, a mass-meeting of citizens was called by a number of leading men, irrespective of party, "to consider," as the call said, "the condition of affairs now existing in our city, and to endeavor to derive means for harmonizing the conflicting interests of the two parties to the struggle now in progress, which struggle is so seriously detrimental to the welfare of the public in general."

At this meeting a committee of well-known men was appointed to confer with the officers of the companies and the leaders of the men, as well as, in case of failure to arrange a compromise between them, with the mayor of the city. The committee did its best; but that best was futile.

Mr. Holt assured the committee that he and all other officers of the street-railway company were as anxious to see crime suppressed and order restored in the town as any other citizen could be. But as for the company itself, Mr. Holt could not see what it was able to do. It had no quarrel with its employés or anybody else. It was operating its road, and had all the men that it needed. These men appeared to be entirely contented, and the feeling between them and the company was excellent. As for the former employés who were now out of work, the company had no quarrel with them — no relations with them of any kind. The company only desired to let them alone and be let alone. As for discharging the present hands and re-employing the old men, such an injustice was not to be thought of. As for the labor organizations, the company had no members of any in its employment, and there was no more reason why it should have any dealings with them than with the Unitarian Society, or the Bimetallic League, or the Woman's Christian Temperance Union.

On behalf of the iron-and-steel company, Mr. Holt said that the company had simply shut down and gone out of business indefinitely. There was nothing in the condition of trade to warrant a reopening. He did not think that there

13

would be for twelve months to come. The men had left of
their own accord, and had not applied for re-employment. If
they did apply, even unanimously agreeing to come back on
the company's own terms, it was improbable that the company could consider a resumption of business. It would need
a fund of from a million to a million and a half of dollars to
justify the company in starting now, with the certainty of
operating for some months at least at a loss. The company
could raise no such sum. Mr. Holt did not think that the
men could, or that the citizens would be willing to.

From the labor leaders the committee derived even less
comfort. Wollmer, who spoke for the strikers, said that
they had nothing to do with the crimes which were being
committed. They were done by others, chiefly by emissaries
of the street-railway company, who injured the company's
own property for the purpose of discrediting the strikers
and exciting public prejudice against them. The strikers
themselves, Wollmer said, were a peaceable, law-abiding set
of men, who proposed to continue to keep the peace. But
they would never give in. As for the crimes—that was a
matter for the police.

So the committee went to the mayor, and Timothy Sullivan assisted, as a silent partner, at the interview. His honor
took much the same ground as he had occupied in his correspondence with Mr. Holt. He himself saw no especial
necessity for extraordinary measures for the public protection. But if the committee insisted—"mind," he repeated,
"if you, as representatives of the citizens, *insist* upon it "—
why, of course, he would instruct the chief of the police department to make a large increase in the force, and otherwise to take all possible precautions to prevent crime and
suppress disorder. The mayor warned the committee,
however, that the expense would be great, and that the
city treasury was in no condition to stand any additional
drain.

After some consultation, the committee decided that it was
best that the mayor should "go ahead" and do whatever was
necessary. Anything was preferable to a continuance of existing conditions.

So the mayor sent for the chief of police, who approached and listened attentively while the mayor said:

"These gentlemen here, as representatives of the citizens by whom they were appointed as a committee, when in mass-meeting assembled, have instructed me to spare no expense in maintaining peace and a respect for the law in this city. They insist on as large an increase in the police-force as may be necessary, and on the taking of any other measures that we can devise for the proper protection of the lives and property of the public. I want you, if you please, to draw up a scheme, showing how many additional men you will need for the thorough patrolling of the city, and making any suggestions that you can which will assist in carrying out the wishes of the committee." The chief of police bowed.

"I think, gentlemen," continued the mayor, turning to the committee, "that those instructions fairly represent what you require of me. Of course, it is unnecessary for me to say that if any question as to the wisdom of these expenditures should come up hereafter, I shall expect you to relieve the present administration of all responsibility for them."

The committee signified its understanding of these conditions, and after some desultory questions with a view to ascertaining what the expense was likely to be — questions to which the mayor found it impossible to even hazard an answer without further consideration and consultation — withdrew. As soon as the committee had left, the chief said:

"What shall I do?"

"Nothing," replied the mayor. "Better put on a few new men and talk a good deal about the enormous increase in the force."

The chief winked at Sullivan and retired. Then that worthy arose and stretched himself:

"Talk of rollin' off a log!" said he, and he too strolled out of the office.

Thenceforward the Democratic papers talked much of the extraordinary expenditures which were made necessary by the large additions to the police-force which had been made, and the "other measures" (which were not specified) which

Mayor Bonderson, with the able assistance of Chief Winley, was taking for the prevention of crime.

But there were citizens who had the temerity to say that they saw little difference either in the number of policemen on the streets or in the amount of crime committed.

Even Timothy Sullivan indeed seemed to think that there was too much crime, judging from his remarks at a stormy interview which took place two days later in General Harter's office. The parties to the conversation were the usual triumvirate.

"They must stop it, I tell ye," said the Irishman, violently, bringing his fist down on the baize-covered table with a bang which made the inkstands jump. "There's no use o' palaverin', they must just stop it! The public may be a dom fool up to a certain point—it always is; but beyond that point ye'd best not monkey with it. I've been there before, an' I tell ye they must stop it. We can blow all we plaze in the papers about the amazin' ingenuity of his honor an' that goat Winley in arrestin' criminals, an' we can swear till we're green that ther' isn't a striker who'd descend to violence, but it's the public that knows best when it's held up an' robbed an' hit with clubs. Talk of the ingenuity of the administration don't go when a man's been sand-bagged."

"What do you want me to do?" asked Wollmer. "Do you think three thousand men, and out of work at that, can be given rag-dolls and bottles and kept in a nursery?"

"I don't care a dom what ye do," replied Sullivan; "only stop it! When ye first came to the Gineral and mesilf here in this same office and said as ye could have the men strike if we willed, ye also said ye could hould 'em till after election. We took ye at yer word, an' in two weeks ye've received from the sacred funds of the municipality just one hundred thousand dollars, for the which, next to the Almighty, ye're indebted to the dom fool of a committee. How much money ye may have got beyond that from the assessments of the orders is none of my business, an' I guess that the other friends who are in wid ye need all that. But ye've had yer price so far, an' we can pay ye (thanks to the same committee agin) for four weeks to come, which is the elec-

tions. But it isn't for the sake of yer swate face as we're
payin' ye, nor for any other consideration whatsoever beyond
that ye should kape these men quiet an' hould public sympathy wid them an' against the Republicans."

There was silence for some seconds, and then Sullivan continued:

"If ye can't hould them, thin we must; and if we hev to
employ the extry men in airnest as we're philanderin' about
now, there'll be no more money comin' from the city for Wollmer. An' if riot breaks out an' the militia come in, there'll
be more votes lost to the Dimicratic parrty than all the
dom labor element in the State can give it. An' mark ye
further," said the Irishman, rising, "if there's any such
trouble occurrin' as that comes too, I'll hould the red head of
ye in that same stove there till yer own mother won't know
the face of ye from the side of a baked apple."

XVI

A TALK AT THE CLUB

THE letter which Horace had written he sent by messenger on the following morning. If she were at home and replied at once, he ought to receive the answer by noon. As the morning wore away he looked up anxiously every time that the office door opened, thinking that it was a letter from her. By one o'clock no answer had arrived, and he went out to luncheon, telling himself that she could not have been at home when his message arrived. Through the afternoon he waited in vain, uneasily at first, but comforting himself with the assurance that she had doubtless preferred to write to him at some length, and would send the letter by mail that evening.

The following morning he was at the office early, and picked up his mail without waiting to lay aside his hat and umbrella. He ran the envelopes over quickly. There was nothing in her handwriting. Once more he looked at them. No; there was nothing.

"Franklin, is this all the mail there was for me?" he called to the outer office.

"Yes, sir. General Harter's mail is on his desk."

The General was out of town, speaking at outside points, and Horace, thinking that perhaps the clerks had made a mistake, went into his office and looked through the pile of envelopes lying on his partner's desk. No; there was nothing for him. Could it be that she had posted the letter too late for the first morning delivery? Possibly; outside of the business centre of the town, in localities such as that wherein Mr. Holt lived, the collections from the mail-boxes were few. She might have written to him in the afternoon, and sent Thomas out to the mail-box after dinner. In that case the letter might well fail to arrive the first thing in the morning. It would come by a later delivery.

Once more, however, the morning dragged along without a word from her. Lunch - time arrived, and Marsh took his way to the club through the rain and mud, wondering what could have happened. There had been a miscarriage somewhere. The idea that she would not reply to his letter—that the misunderstanding which had arisen between them was of a permanent nature, or anything so serious as to make her refuse to have anything more to say to him—did not occur to him. But this delay was inexplicable. Moreover, this was Saturday. If he did not hear that afternoon, the whole gulf of Sunday would intervene before there could be any communication between them. How in the world would he manage to get through the long Sunday if he could not call on her? He had counted on spending much of the day in her company.

Arriving at the club, he put his wet umbrella in the stand by the door, and handed his hat and overcoat to the boy in the cloak-room. He was still standing by the door in the cloak-room, turning down the bottom of his trousers, which had been rolled up as he came through the wet, when Judge Jessel and Major Bartop issued together from the reading-room opposite.

"Ah-ha!" said the judge, on seeing Horace, "here is the very man we are looking for. Marsh, Bartop and I have entered into a conspiracy to get you to lunch with us. Have you anything else to do?"

"No; I shall be delighted." And Horace shook hands with the two friends.

"That's good. It's Saturday, and you need not rush back to your office, so we can have a long talk," said the judge, heartily. Turning to the broad shelf which ran out from the wall, and on which were arranged the luncheon-cards and order-blanks, he picked up one of the small pencils tied by a string to a ring in the wood, and set himself to the serious task of ordering a meal.

"What will you fellows eat?" he asked. "What do you crave? Blue Points, anyway, to begin with,

"'For blue is the sweetest color that's worn'

—or eaten," he hummed. "Blue-fish, blue-winged teal, blue-berries—everything blue is good. I never ate a blue shark or a blue-faced baboon, but if I did I know they would be better than other sharks and baboons." The judge was noted for the austerity of his bearing upon the bench, but his wife always said that he was only a great big boy.

> "'Though the brilliant black eye may in triumph let fly
> All its darts without caring who feels them,
> Yet the soft eye of blue, though it scatters wounds too,
> Is much better pleased when it heals them,'"

quoted the major.

"That's bosh!" said the judge. "Mrs. Jessel's eyes are black. Blue noses are bad, too. But luncheon! Here, why don't you fellows help me? If you don't make suggestions, I will feed you on tripe and ginger ale. Bartop, I know, insists on a baked apple to wind up with, but we must have things between; Blue Points and baked apple won't do. Here, help me! *Consommé royal*," he murmured; "that means with an egg in it, though I have no idea what eggs have to do with royalty—except that they are brittle and smell foully when they are bad. Do you men like eggs in your soup? Well, I do, anyway. *Consommé royal*—one portion and a half. If you won't eat the eggs, I will take all three—

> "'There is a happy land, far, far away,
> Where they have soup and eggs three times a day.'"

"I don't think you need help," said Horace, laughingly. "Anyway, if you do, the major can give it. Too many cooks spoil the lunch—especially in ordering it; and I am going to wash my hands."

"If you do, you shall have nothing but vinegar to drink. 'Wilt drink up Eisel?'"

"I will drink anything," said Horace, as he made his way to the lavatory. Contact with reasonable fellow-beings was doing him good, and he was surprised to find himself almost light-hearted as he joined his companions in the reading-room, where they had ensconced themselves in two large arm-chairs, a third being drawn up close to them for Horace. As he approached they had their heads together in deep consultation, but they broke off as Marsh joined them. He felt that they were talking of him, but judged from their cordiality that they had said nothing bad.

Ten minutes later a servant informed the judge that his luncheon was served, and the party ascended to the diningroom. As soon as they were seated at their table the judge spoke.

"Now, Marsh, we told you that this was a deliberate conspiracy. We wanted you to lunch with us because we want to talk to you—talk politics."

"I am willing," Marsh replied, as he dropped Tabasco sauce on his slice of lemon, preparatory to administering the dilution to the oysters.

"I hope you will stay willing, because we are going to try and convert you. This is an organized attack for the purpose of seducing you from your party."

"To make a Republican of me?" Horace asked. "How are you going to abet any such scheme as that, major?"

"It is not to make a Republican of you," Major Bartop said, "but to draw you away from your present crowd. This campaign is not a conflict between Democrats and Republicans; even the fight of two years ago was not, though it pretended to be. The Populists are not Democrats any more than they are Republicans. In some states and localities they are fused with the Republicans to-day. They are simply the accumulation of the malecontents and dissidents from both parties. In every country which is under party government the people first divide themselves on some large question into two more or less equal parties. From these great bodies in the process of daily friction fragments are constantly being rubbed off, and this detritus goes on accumulating until it amounts to enough to make a third party. So, on some one issue or a jumble of issues, it finally coheres and starts out as an independent entity, and generally sells its support to whichever of the other two bodies is able to pay most for it at the time. In this State two years ago, as you know, the Democrats bought it. Perhaps I know more than you do of the inside of the deal.

The judge doubtless knows what price the Republicans could have had it for; but they declined the offer. What the Democrats got when they made the purchase was a certain number of votes. What they paid was a certain number of offices. The persons who cast the votes were the offscourings of both parties in the State—all the cranks and theorists, demagogues, anarchists, ignoramuses, and others, who were too good or too bad to be Democrats or Republicans, or did not know enough of the English language to be either. When the heterogeneous mass was dumped, neck and crop, into the Democratic camp, there were a good many of us who shook our heads and fought shy of our new comrades. Putting myself out of the question, I think I may say that they were the best men in the party. Two years of experience of the allied forces in power has only strengthened our aversion. The present campaign started out on a basis of the Democratic party *minus* its best element, but *plus* the Populist offscouring, *versus* the Republican party. The best element of Democracy held aloof. As time has passed, and especially since the strike began, the neutral Democrats have one by one gone over to the Republican camp. I myself shall vote a straight Republican ticket this fall. More than that, a great many more Democrats who managed to stomach the Populists two years ago are throwing them up now, and within the last week or two so much has been going on quietly that I believe that one-half the regular, old-time Democrats will be Republicans in this election. It is no longer a question of Democrat against Republican; it's a question of law and order and decency against mob-rule and anarchy and crime."

" What we want to know," said the judge, as Major Bartop ceased, " is, what common ground or sympathy you can possibly have with this latter party ?"

" You gentlemen," said Marsh, after a short deliberation, " are of course very much better posted than I am in the details of politics. You are considerably older than I am, and much more experienced both in politics and life. At the same time, I do not think your statement of the case, major, is entirely fair. Much of what you say as to the miscellaneous character of the Populist contingent is justifiable ; but not all.

In large measure they are the offscourings and the dissidents
from both parties. They represent in detail all manner of
queer beliefs and impossible theories. They lack any unity of
principle. But they have one thing in common, which is the
capacity to be led. The mere fact of their incongruity and
aimlessness—or, rather, the diversity of their aims—makes
them, as a party, open to conviction. They have now no single
common cause. Give them one, and they can be solidified and
concentrated upon it. So far they may have been misled and
used chiefly for evil. They can be led rightly and used for
good—for great good. As with any other force, it is only a
question of the direction in which it is turned whether it becomes a beneficent or a maleficent power—whether it works
for ruin or for salvation."

" What do you hope to be able to make the Populist party
do that is good? What evidence have you that you can lead
them at all? Wherein are they now without leaders?"

" I understood you yourself to say that they were leaderless,
at Mr. Holt's dinner-table, not very long ago."

" As a national party, yes. As Bartop pointed out, looking at the whole country, they have no political unity, no
consistency. In some places they are allied with one party,
and in some with the other. That is not a phenomenon peculiar to this particular party in this particular crisis. It is a
necessity for all new third parties; the most that they can
hope for for a while is the balance of power. The present
situation in this country has had its counterpart in every country and in all ages. The words ' Democrat ' and ' Republican '
are only symbols—localizations of eternal facts. What we are
saying now was doubtless said over and over again in ancient
Athens and Rome. It has certainly been said within the century—almost within the decade—in England and France and
Germany and Italy." Marsh nodded his acquiescence, and the
judge continued : " This human detritus, as the major calls
it, accumulates until it includes enough individuals to make
it in itself a political factor. At this point, if the right leader appears, it may be converted from an inert mass into a
fighting-machine—from a mere negative protest against the existing parties into a formidable opponent of them. This has

been done again and again in history. In this country now
the process of detrition has been at work for a quarter of a
century—since the war; and it looks as if the neutrals, the
Adullamites—the unannexed—were numerous enough to form
a third party of considerable bulk. In human nature it could
not be otherwise. But "—and the judge emphasized the word
with a rap of his wineglass on the table — " we are not now
considering an abstract historical proposition, nor have we to
deal with this new party as a national fact. We are talking
practically of municipal affairs — at most, of a State campaign—and we have to consider that distinct section of the
general detritus which has accumulated around our own locality. It may be a good thing that snow should fall on the prai-
ries and the farms. In due course it will melt, and moisten
the soil, and be led into its proper channels in the river-beds.
Let it fall, then, and lie there, by all means. But shall we not
shovel off that which has drifted on our own front door-
steps?"

" You mean that the Populist party here, because it happens
to be opposed to you, must be beaten down and smothered?"
Marsh asked. "And if this is done in each separate locality,
what becomes of the great mass in the country at large as a
possible power for good?"

"I mean that while the great mass may be no worse
than neutral, and may contain the potentiality of good, the
local portion of that mass with which we have to deal is
working for harm—desperate harm. If you will pardon me,
here is your fallacy. The party as a whole is leaderless;
therefore you assume that in its several parts it is unled.
The snow falls evenly over the plains and lies there; but are
we to ignore the local eddy which swirls it round the street-
corner into our faces and chokes up our halls? What are
Sullivan and the City Hall crowd—Wollmer and the labor
chiefs — Bailey and the Democratic Central Committee — if
they are not leaders? And what are they working for?
What will be the result if they are victorious at the polls
next month?"

" With similar victories in other parts of the country,
which I believe will occur," said Marsh, "it will help to im-

press upon the people the fact that the new force is a force
which must be reckoned with. It will—for nothing succeeds
like success—give the party itself more strength and courage. It will help to unify it. It may call out the leaders
who are destined to mould it—the men who will temper it,
and harmonize it, and show it the straight path to the work
which it has to do. And when that work is done, it will be
found that the shadow of revolution now hanging over the
country will have passed away."

"And locally?" asked the major.

"Locally? Well, locally—in the State and in the city—I
believe that the Democracy is as capable of giving a reasonably good government as is the Republican party."

"But there is the trouble," broke in the judge; "it is no
question of Republican or Democrat. Supposing that this
conglomeration had been joined to the Republican party two
years ago, I should be a Democrat at this election, Bartop
would be the party's candidate for governor, and you would
work with us to have him elected. There is little difference
enough between the two parties, and little enough between
the men who compose them. Neither is inspired; nor is
either entirely diabolical. In the past the Democracy has
shown itself capable of the worst abuses in municipal affairs,
and the Republican party has produced the greatest national
scandals, which is only a result of the fact that the Democrats have been chiefly in control in our large cities, and
the Republicans most in power in federal affairs. Each has
sinned in proportion to its opportunity. Had the positions
been reversed, the burden of offence would have to be exchanged. But here comes in a new factor — neither Republican nor Democratic, but composed of all the bad and
dangerous and disaffected elements, which happens tempora-
rily to be tacked on to the tail of the Democracy. They have
not one good aim. There is no one man who is trying to
lead them aright, with the exception of yourself. They have
alienated the good-will of the decent men of their own party,
and have attracted to them the scum of the other. And you
are working with them—why?"

"How comes there to be this large element of the disaf-

fected ?" asked Marsh, in his turn. " What is the ground of
their discontent ?"

" Ignorance chiefly," replied the major, shortly—"ignorance and false teaching."

" That is a large question," Judge Jessel said, more deliberately. " In the main the third party consists of two distinct
classes — the labor element and the granger element. They
are the counterpart of each other, and at bottom, in spite of
surface differences, it is a mistake to say that their alliance
is not legitimate and natural. They are the two halves of
the one portion of mankind, each modified according to its
environment : in the one case the environment of city life,
and in the other the environment of the farm. The labor
element (and mind that a sharp distinction must be drawn
between the labor element and the working-men — the labor
element as a political factor, a public entity, is no more
coextensive with the working-man than is the Prohibition
party, politically, coextensive with that mass of the people
who do not drink—the labor element, as we speak of it, is
a small portion of the working-class—a portion which has a
certain fanaticism and love of notoriety—united to a large
number of men who ought to be working but will not)—the
labor element, I was saying, if, individually, it had gone to
farming, would be grangers. The members of the Farmers'
Alliance, had they happened to stay in cities, would be the labor politicians. *Cœlum, non animum*— It is the surroundings,
not the nature, which makes one one and the other the other."

" But how has either come to be where it is ?" asked
Marsh. " There never was in history a case of popular discontent without a legitimate popular grievance at the bottom
of it. It is only the smoke from the fire."

" There never was in history a case where a large part
of any people did not consider themselves to be ill-used,"
replied the judge. " As a mass, these people all believe that
society as it is now constituted is in conspiracy against
them. You and I know very well that individually a great
majority of them are incapable of maintaining themselves
decently in any condition of society. If we had a dividing
up and a new start, so that

'Distribution should undo excess,
And each man have enough,'

it would not be ten years—not two—before they wanted another division. Even the Chinese plan (or is it Japanese?) of wiping off all debts with the new year, so that every man begins
even, would be no good. No one would trust them after the
first year, and their last state would be worse than their first.
I admire the American farmer as a whole, and have great
sympathy with him. We all must have. He is a great part
of our country's strength. But, again, we are considering him
in the mass. Take him as an individual, and I grant his stur-
diness and intelligence, and even, from a common-school point
of view (in the rudiments of ordinary learning as it is taught
in schools), I grant his education. But when it comes to political and economic teaching, he is either as ignorant as a
child or helplessly ill-taught. The ability to spell and 'figure' does not equip a man to use his political judgment.
The bane of the farmer (of course I mean the Western farmer) has been and is his inaccessibility. In his scattered, iso-
lated situation he is not reached through the ordinary channels of information by which the educated, thinking man in
the city is instructed. Literature does not reach him. He
is not lectured to. He is not in contact with current thought;
it does not circulate in his atmosphere. The difficulty of arriving at and arguing with him in the mass is so great that,
in each locality, he has been left to the instruction of his local
prophets—usually one of himself, a farmer like himself, who
has no advantage over him except a certain fluency of speech,
and who is shrewd enough to see that politics offers an easier
career than farming. This man is as thoroughly unfit to teach
as a man could be—mentally unfit, and, what is more, morally unfit, because he has no larger ends to serve than his
own advancement. The farmers, as a whole, are having hard
times, and vaguely think that they are ill-used and need a
change—no matter what. The prophet arises and promises
them a change — if they will send him to the legislature.
Generally he attacks the nearest railway company, because
that happens to be the most tangible manifestation near at

hand of the concentrated wealth and power of society. On
it he unloads all the burden of the farmers' ills—makes it responsible for poor (or too plentiful) crops, and for the foreign competition which affects prices in European grain-mar-
kets. The farmer has no other teaching, and believes him.
And there's where the trouble begins. This has been going
on all over the West now for some decades. Those who
ought to have been the farmers' right teachers have let them
alone—left them to the local demagogue. The result is the
Populist party. And it has not only been with the farmers
proper, but with all Western communities—farming, mining,
and, on a small scale, even industrial. The President of Harvard College, a short time ago, made a speech somewhere—
in St. Louis, I think—in which he said that the chief danger
to the country lay in the 'uninformed public opinion' of the
West. He was badly abused for it; but I thought it was the
best thing that had been said on our public affairs for a long
time. It is not only uninformed, it is *mis*-informed public
opinion. The farmer not only needs teaching, he needs *un*-
teaching. He has been neglected for so long and left only
to bad influences that the undoing of what has been done
wrongfully will be a tremendous task. But it will have to
be done. What is needed first is schools—schools—schools.
But they are not enough. The rising generation will come
out of its schools, and, exposed to the same influences, will
go as its fathers went. It is the later instruction, post-graduate teaching in the rudiments of sociology and economics
that is needed. And it must be given, if the country is to be
saved from chaos and catastrophe."

"It is something of that kind of teaching," said Marsh,
"which we are now trying to give."

There was silence for a while.

"Suppose we adjourn down-stairs for our coffee?" suggested the major, and the party rose and moved to the wine-
room, where cigars were permitted, much to the disappointment of the waiter, who, notwithstanding his well-trained
rigidity of attitude and his imperturbable countenance, was
something of a politician himself, and was interested in the
discussion.

When they were seated around the small table in the wine-room the conversation was resumed, but in more desultory and less formal fashion.

"I know," said the judge to Marsh—"I know that, as you say, you are trying to teach these men rightly, and I honor you for it. I wish there were more doing the same. But, if you will pardon me, my young friend"—and he laid his hand on Horace's shoulder—"I am afraid that, in your enthusiasm for your work and your high ambitions for the party as a whole, you are in danger of failing to see the particular direction in which the party locally is travelling."

Marsh was silent.

"Nor do we want you to misunderstand us," said Major Bartop. "Men are at work, of course, all day long and every day—men of both parties—trying to win over men from the other parties. You will not think that we—the judge and myself—have any narrow or merely partisan objects to serve. You know us better. Next year probably Jessel and I will be enemies again. Just now it seems that all good men are uniting—except you. And we want you with us."

"No," said Marsh; "of course I understand all that, and I am flattered that you think me worth working with."

"We do, frankly," interrupted the judge; "you are the one man on the Democratic side just now who is worth working with—the one public man; which is to say that you are, in our opinion, a good deal the best man in your party."

Marsh bowed his head in acknowledgment.

"Well, with all my thanks," he said, "I do not think there is much chance of my changing sides in this campaign. There may be personal reasons—in regard to General Harter, you understand—which would make it particularly difficult for me to change. But, apart from that, I believe in the cause. I believe in the possibilities of the party. I believe in human nature — it is part of me to do it. I think you underestimate the goodness of the motives of some of the Democratic leaders, and overestimate the danger which the party's success would mean to the city and the State. I don't think you will find that the country will be ruined if the allied parties do remain in power a while longer."

14

" Well," said the judge, rising, "a man's convictions would not be worth holding if they could be changed by one talk over a luncheon-table ; but we wanted to have the talk, and I hope you will think over it, and look, if you can, more clearly into the local situation, and the direction in which the teaching of your friends is trending."

" If you do ever find it necessary to change," said the major, "you know now that we shall welcome you."

The party separated at the cloak - room, and Horace hastened back to his office. It was impossible that the talk should not have made an impression on him ; but as soon as he had separated from his friends the eagerness to receive Jessie's answer reasserted itself.

As he left the club an incident occurred which he remembered afterwards. On the door-step two men were standing, both members of the club—Blakely and Carrington, the latter the husband of Mrs. Carrington, of whom we have already caught a glimpse. The two seemed to be engaged in an altercation of some kind, and barely recognized Horace as he passed. He could not help, however, hearing some words spoken by Carrington.

" I have not asked you any questions, sir," he said, " nor do I wish to discuss the matter with you. I simply inform you that I do not wish you to come again."

And Horace, hurrying to his office, pondered over the scene.

" A messenger brought a note for you a few minutes ago, sir," said Franklin, as Horace entered, "and said the lady wanted an answer. I told him you would send one as soon as you came in. The note is on your desk."

With a beating heart Marsh tore open the envelope. It contained a short but gushing epistle from Mrs. Carrington, asking if Mr. Marsh would join them at dinner that evening, and if he would promise not to be offended at being asked at the eleventh hour.

" Is this the only thing that has come for me ?" he asked.

" Yes, sir."

And Horace sat down and gazed blankly out of the window, wondering what the silence could mean.

XVII

BETWEEN THE CUP AND THE LIP

WHEN Miss Holt received Marsh's note she glanced over it, and threw it into the fire. The feeling that it excited was chiefly one of contempt of his pretended innocence. It was a shallow trick, at best. How could he imagine that she would for a moment believe that he did not thoroughly understand what it was that had given the offence? How could he believe that she would for an instant consent to argue the matter with him? He trusted, doubtless, to his own glib tongue, if an opportunity was given him, to persuade her that he was impelled in his treachery only by the highest motives. He counted upon her simplicity and lack of knowledge of the world. But she would not give him the opportunity, for she would take no notice of his letter.

But though she affected to dismiss the matter lightly, and turned away to her household duties with a song upon her lips, as she tossed the note into the fire her heart ached within her. It has been said that if Jessie had met Horace as a character in a novel, she would have admired him unreservedly, and have thought him worthy to win the best woman that lived — the Horace, that is, of the old days—Horace before he fell. Under any circumstances, his cleanliness and earnestness of character, his quiet, unobtrusive manliness must have appealed to her. In the crisis through which she was now passing, when the cruelest realities of life had for the first time been laid open before her, and when her whole being shuddered at the new knowledge that had come to her, it was precisely he—or such a man as she had imagined him to be—that she needed. She was so alone in the darkness! Out of the abyss her soul cried for some human comfort.

Not content with threatening the lives of Mr. Holt and the other officers of the two companies directly, the strikers had begun to send anonymous letters even to her. She had already received two in different handwritings, but couched in almost the same words: if she did not wish her father to be killed she had better use her influence to make him yield. She had not mentioned them to any one, but had asked her father whether he had received any threats against his life.

"Oh yes; some," he answered, lightly.

Every moment that he was away from the house now was a moment of torture for her. From the time that he left in the morning until his return in the evening she awaited in terror the news of some calamity. Every ring at the telephone, every messenger who arrived at the door, made her heart stand still. Her friends, meaning it well, united to increase this fear.

"I should think you would be very anxious lest something should happen to Mr. Holt," they would say.

"Oh no," she would reply, calmly. "He has no fear that they will attack him personally."

But every day her wretchedness grew more nearly insupportable, and Miss Willerby saw, with secret misgivings, her listlessness during the day and the heaviness of the eyes, which told of sleepless nights; and she did what she could to comfort her. But it was not a woman's comfort that Jessie needed, but that of a man with knowledge of the world—one who was accustomed to look the real things of life in the face; to whom she could unburden her heart of its load, and appeal for guidance and consolation.

It was unavoidable that her thoughts should now turn to the Marsh who had been. He was no longer part of her life. No relation existed between him and her heart to prejudice her judgment of him. She could see him now, as it were, impersonally and dispassionately. He was not even a character in fiction, except in the fiction of her own imagination. He had never existed; but oh! if he had— If only such a man were to come to her now, how gladly she would confide in him and trust him, placing her heart and her mind in his

care. As a young girl dreams of the prince with his sword
and his plume who is some day coming to seek her, so Jessie
now longed for the prince of her imagining — a latter-day
prince, armed only with his courage and the purity of his
ambition, who would pass his arm round her and support her
while they faced this danger of life together—a prince with
just such a face and manner as Marsh had had in the former
days.

As is often the case with better men than he, Blakely suffered by the hold which this ideal had upon her mind. Many
a lover has failed because the heart that he would win was
already in possession of a rival who had no existence outside
of the heart, and who might be an entirely impossible character. Daughters of men still walk with the sons of God in
their fancies, and for their sakes the sons of men are rejected.
In the loneliness of her desolation, Jessie never dreamed of
casting Blakely for the part of the fairy prince—withal that
his face might better fit the rôle than Horace's. Without
reasoning it out with herself, she knew that it was to another
side of her nature that Blakely spoke. He might fascinate
and dazzle her so that she would forget the hunger; but
satisfy the craving, never! A drug, however potent and in-
toxicating, will not feed the starving, though it may dull the
pain and give happiness till the waking come.

"What a splendid lover Mr. Blakely would make!" Miss
Caley had exclaimed one day.

"And what a terrible husband!" Miss Willerby had added.

Jessie, as she sat on the other side of the room, apparently
immersed in her book, had heard the conversation; and in
her heart she recognized the truth of Miss Willerby's rejoin-
der. But when the pain is at its worst, the temptation to
seize the relief which the drug will bring may be beyond resisting, and the solace of it for a while unutterably sweet.

Blakely, meanwhile, was constant in his attentions without
being obtrusively persistent. Almost every day he sent her
flowers—bouquets that were daintily chosen, a few choice
blossoms and a frond of fern, perhaps, or a single perfect
spray of orchids—on which she could not but see that he
had expended some thought, instead of leaving the selection

of his gift to the taste of the florist.   Once she received a
book from him—the book which she had been reading that
day, and which he wished her to read.   It was what is known
to-day as an old-fashioned romance, wherein the heroine, following the dictates of her own heart, fled with and wedded
the reckless, dashing, prodigal son, whom the worldly parents
scorned in favor of a commonplace and objectionably worthy
suitor of a dull and workaday kind.   On the very day of the
wedding the prodigal son fell heir to the colossal fortune of
an East Indian uncle, and the volume closed in an atmosphere heavy with the scent of orange blossoms, and with just
a glimpse of vistas of ideal and golden happiness ahead of
the wisely wayward girl.

Blakely thought that the moral of the tale—that a young
heart is better than old heads—might be useful to him.   But
he had miscalculated somewhat.   He had not looked into her
mind and seen with what a glory the workaday suitor was
invested there.   He could not guess how, in passing through
the prism of her thoughts, the ordinary white light of day
was broken into glorified tints of emerald and amethyst
and rose.   She only thought the tale dull and "washy"—as
it was.

The evening that Marsh spent with the Carringtons (for
he had accepted the tardy invitation, in the hope that he
might meet *her* there) Blakely spent at Jessie's house.   Though
Marsh did not know it, it was Blakely's place that he was
filling—the latter having found it advisable, for reasons which
have already been hinted at, to send his regrets that very
morning.   Jessie had passed a terribly anxious day, for the
attitude of the strikers grew constantly more bitter and threatening, and she welcomed Blakely gladly when he came.   He
in his turn was frank and outspoken now in his admiration
of her, saying to her things, such as he had said when he
parted from her at the carriage on the day of the rescue, of
a kind which no man had dared to say to her before.   It was
always adroitly done, and with such an air of impulsiveness
that it was impossible to be offended.   Indeed, if it were
most ardent love-making, there was nothing at which offence
could be taken.

As she shook hands with him that evening he had said, in low tones:

"I wish you knew how hard it is for me to let your hand go when you give it to me. I want to crush it, and fall down on my knees and worship it. I would rather you would cut off one of mine than take yours away."

And when, later on in the evening, she had thrown a light lace scarf over her shoulders, he had exclaimed:

"What a shame! My eyes cannot spare an inch of you. But"—as he leaned forward and, making pretence of adjusting the lace, let his fingers brush her neck—"at least it gives me the privilege of touching you."

That evening he had asked her to take a walk with him on the following Sunday afternoon, and she consented to do so "if it were fine." It was fine for an hour or two, and he called for her. As they were starting she stopped for a moment before a large mirror in the hall to adjust her hat.

"Don't touch it," he said; "you are too unutterably beautiful as you are."

Then he had stepped into the sitting-room, and, taking one of his own lavender orchids from a vase, had handed it to her, saying:

"Please put it on, there"—indicating her bosom by touching himself on the chest. "Let me dream that it is I who am touching you there, if only at second-hand."

And she had put on the flower as he wished. During the walk he was very devoted, seizing every pretext of an unevenness in the footway to touch her arm as if to support her. There was no need of assistance, but he wished to convey to her the idea that he longed to touch her. More than once he half stopped as they walked, and, stretching out his arms before him as if in ecstasy, said:

"Oh, how blissful it is!"

She was conscious that there was a certain prematureness in all this—a bold assumption of relations which did not exist. The passionate outbursts were rather those of an accepted suitor than of a lover who had still the heart to win. It was no such desperate love that the ideal Marsh would have made, but—well, the drug was sweet.

But she was rapidly reaching the point when drugs of another kind would be needed. The mental distress, the anxiety and sleeplessness were having their effect. She was seldom ill, unused to giving way to little ailments, and a doctor rarely visited the house in a professional capacity. Had she been of the type of woman that takes pleasure in being sick, and welcomes an opportunity to play the invalid, she would have been confined to her bed before this. As it was, it needed effort each morning to face the duties of the day; and when there was none to see, she would sometimes sit for an hour together, thoroughly exhausted, in some easy-chair; her arms hanging down, looking blankly into space, and wondering, only wondering, where her father was, and what would be the end of it all.

At last there came an evening when it was necessary to go to a reception given by Major and Mrs. Bartop. For her own sake, Jessie dreaded going; for she knew that she was not equal to it. Mrs. Bartop's receptions were formidable functions, extremely starched, and, as Mrs. Bartop flattered herself, very free from anything approaching Western unconventionality. There would be a great crush, with little chance to sit down, much smirking and exchanging of social platitudes, and some lemonade. The thought of it unnerved her, but Jessie knew that for the sake of her two friends—or, rather, of one of them (for she would not have hesitated to disappoint Miss Willerby), it was necessary to go. So she braced herself for the effort and went.

Blakely was there also. He arrived late, according to his custom, and told his coachman to wait—he would not be more than half an hour or so. The invariable brevity of his stay at such entertainments was partly owing to the fact that they really bored him (in which he was not peculiar), but still more because he knew that this line of conduct was socially effective. He did not propose to surfeit society of his company. Doled out in small doses, it would always be in demand.

He soon discovered Jessie, and was struck by her pallor. Indeed, she was feeling miserable. She was struggling to sustain her share in a conversation of nothingness among the group of people of both sexes by whom she was surrounded;

but the room swam round her, and she longed for air. The
unceasing clamor of the tongues about her seemed to jar her
brain, and she yearned to be away from it in the silence.
She welcomed Blakely's arrival as opening a possible chance
of escape, and connived readily at his scheme to draw her
away by himself. He led her from the room (which was on
the second floor of the house), and they went down-stairs.
But half-way down it seemed as if the stairs in front of her
heaved upward, and she was compelled to clutch at the baluster
for support.

"You are ill," he said, with eager tenderness. "I saw
how pale you were when I came in."

"No," she said, wearily, "I am not ill, but I am not well.
I feel as if I were going to faint. I ought never to have
come this evening."

She had never fainted, and had all a woman's horror of
making a "scene" in company.

"Well, you must not stay," he said; "you must go home."

"How can I? The carriage will not be here for an hour
and a half yet, and I cannot leave the girls."

"Yes, you can. My coupe is here—I always keep it waiting. You can go home in that, and I will tell Miss Willerby
and Miss Caley, and see that they get back safely."

She hesitated; but the stairs still swam around her, and
she felt that her knees would give way.

"Perhaps I had better," she said, faintly.

Without waiting for more, Blakely led her back to the
floor above, where the ladies' dressing-room was, and left her
there. When she came out, he too had on his overcoat, and
his hat was in his hand.

"Come this way," he said, and took her down by a rear
flight of stairs where they would meet no one. His carriage
was quickly called, and he handed her in, told the coachman
to drive to Mr. Holt's house, and stepped in beside her. She
sank back into her corner of the coupe without a word, too
weak and sick to speak. He laid his hand once gently on
hers, saying:

"Let me know if I can do anything," and relapsed into
silence by her side.

Once in the course of the drive she aroused herself enough to say :

"It is very silly of me, and I am sorry for troubling you."

"Do you think it is trouble ?" he asked ; and the drive was completed in silence.

Arriving at the house, he rang the bell and handed her carefully out of the carriage. When the door opened—

"You will come in ?" she said, interrogatively.

"I will if I can be of any use," he replied, and he helped, almost supported, her into the house.

"Are you any better ?" he asked, so that Thomas might understand that this unexpected return was owing to her illness.

"I think I am. I know that I should have fainted if I had not got away from the crowd and the noise. Is Mr. Holt in ?" she asked of the butler.

"No, miss."

Blakely slipped off his overcoat quickly, handed it with his hat to Thomas, and followed her into the drawing-room. She walked languidly, threw her wrap over a chair as she passed, and advanced to the fireplace, where, placing her hands upon the mantel, she leaned her forehead upon the cool marble between them. The room was lighted only by the doubtful flicker of the flames in the hearth and the glow which came from the tall lamp by the piano, with the rose-colored shade. He also approached the fireplace, and stood with his hands on the mantel. The house was very still, and they were alone in the semi-darkness. Was she, he wondered, as acutely conscious of it as he ?

For some minutes he waited, hoping that some word or movement on her part would give him his cue. Meanwhile, the very silence, with their proximity and isolation, was on his side. But she did not move or speak.

He raised his left hand, and gently, quietly laid it on hers. She did not resist, and he let his fingers slowly close upon it with the faintest pressure. He moved nearer to her, and laid his lips upon her hand as with a lingering caress. Still she did not resist (he wondered how far she was conscious of what he did), but a moment later she drew her hand away, and, turning, moved listlessly towards a sofa. He followed, with his arm lightly encircling her waist. As she reached the sofa she fell, rather than sat herself down, upon it, throwing her head back into the piled cushions with her eyes closed.

Was she about to faint? He did not know ; but at least the possibility of it was a sufficient excuse for anything. So, sinking on one knee, with his left hand he raised her feet on to the lounge, and with his right pulled away one of the cushions, so that her head sank lower.

She had not fainted, for she opened her eyes, and looked at him with a long, slow gaze, and then closed them again. She was conscious that she was lying at full length before him and that he was leaning over her ; but conscious of it in a curiously far-away manner, and oh ! she was too weak and too ill to resist.

He felt his heart beat almost stiflingly as he kneeled by her side. How white and clear her face was in the dim light, with the black lashes of the closed eyes and the curved lips— the beautiful lips which were now at his mercy. He did not put his own to them at once, however, but approached her by almost imperceptible degrees. Silently he placed his left arm over and around her, pressing the hand between the yielding sofa and her back. Leaning very slowly over her, he passed his right hand, palm upward, beneath her head. Still her eyes did not open, and he let his face draw nearer to hers, straining her body gently to him as he leaned. Their lips were but a few inches apart. He felt her breath upon his cheeks, and knew that she must feel his.

"My darling," he whispered — "my sweet and beautiful darling !" And her eyes opened slowly, but at first they did not seem to be looking into his. He waited until his gaze could entangle hers before taking the first long kiss. But even as he held his breath for the meeting of the lips her expression changed—almost imperceptibly ; but the look in the eyes as at last they met his fairly was not one of passion or of love. Her right hand, which had lain stretched upward against the wall, moved between her lips and his.

"Let me get up," she said, faintly ; but he did not move.

"No, my darling, don't !" he whispered.

"Let me get up," she said again, more firmly; and he knew that he must do it.

Slowly he arose and helped her to her feet. She sat for a moment, dazed, before rising, and passed her hand languidly over her eyes.

"I beg your pardon," she said, as at last she stood up. "I am not myself to-night, Mr. Blakely. Please imagine it was some other girl. I can hardly see now. I think I must be ill." And she sat down again on the sofa, and buried her face in her hands.

To him, as he saw her slipping away from him, it seemed as if the whole world was as nothing compared to the winning of her. He had felt so in somewhat similar circumstances before; but for the moment he was in earnest. All the other women of earth did not count in comparison to this one sweet, dark-eyed girl, who but a moment before, he had believed, was his, and who was already beyond his reach.

"Pardon me," he said, and he dropped on his knees at her side—"pardon me ! But, oh ! I do love you so !"

"No, Mr. Blakely," she said, quietly, as she drew away the hand which he had taken and rose to her feet again; "it was all a mistake. I cannot say that I was unconscious; I was not. But I did not know. It seemed to be somebody else that was here — not I. My own mind — my own conscience—was not in my body. It was a mistake, and other things have been mistakes. I have been too wretched, I think, in these days to know what I have been doing or what you have been saying. But I understand now. Please believe me—it was all a mistake."

She spoke quietly but very firmly, and moved away towards the fireplace again. He felt that it was all over; but no game is lost until it is won, and in critical moments the bold play is always the best.

"It was not a mistake," he said, ardently. "Nothing can be a mistake which makes any one as madly, deliriously happy as I have been. I love you utterly, Miss Holt. It seemed to me as if Providence had given you to me this evening, and I will not believe that you are to be taken from me again."

She only shook her head and smiled wearily into the fire. He came and stood by her, so close that his arm touched hers, but there was no response to the contact, no evidence that it affected her.

"The passion of his life," he said, "is not given to a man by a mistake. I have longed by day and dreamed by night of making you mine—of possessing you. Just now you *were* mine. You were in my hands, and it seemed as if all heaven was given to me." He paused, but she did not reply, and he added, between his clinched teeth, "I wish I had let my lips touch yours before I did. You would not, then, so easily have thrown me aside."

But she only shook her head in silence, and he dropped to a more matter-of-fact tone.

"Now you say the past has been a mistake. To-morrow you may see that you are mistaken now." Then, passionately, again : "You must be mine! Why did you draw away from me? Why did you not give yourself to me for just one minute more? I do love you so! I could take you in my arms now and crush you, and—" And as if he were unable to end his sentence for passion, he reached out his hands as if to take her.

But she moved away from him again.

"No," she said, simply, "I am not mistaken now. Out of my sickness has come sanity. Your words break by me now without touching me. I do not feel them."

"You are ill," said he, shifting his ground, "and I would give all the world to help you."

"Thank you." But it was coldly and indifferently spoken. So he changed his tone, and, laughing lightly, said :

"But the way to help a woman when she is sick is certainly not to bother her and thrust one's self upon her. I will leave you, Miss Holt. The two poor girls at the Bartops' will be wondering where you are, and I must go and tell them."

She rose to say good-bye to him, and gave him her hand at parting. He pressed it long and tenderly as he said :

"It was not a mistake. I am not for one instant going to

assume that it was. I have been too near to the happiness of my life to let it go so lightly. At worst, I am only where I was before I met you this evening—and that, I think, was at least somewhere on the road to heaven."

As he left the house, however, he knew in his heart that this was not so. He was farther away than he had been from her since the first night in the theatre, when they had not even spoken. He might renew the attack—he would, of course; but he knew that, barring some desperate stroke of luck, it was a forlorn and hopeless outlook. He threw himself back into the corner—*her* corner, he thought, cynically—and lit a cigarette, and set himself calmly to think it over. Had he made any mistakes? he wondered. He must have; because when a man misses a woman, he told himself, it was always by his own mistake. The individual characters made no difference. It was just a question of the man's skill. Up to that evening he could not think that he had made any error. The way had been straight and he had progressed rapidly. And that evening? Had he been foolish in not pushing her more ardently? Suppose that he had made passionate love to her in the coupé? He could have done it well, and he pictured to himself what he might have done and said. He might have established a different footing between them before they had reached the house, and would have had less way to make up afterwards. Then, in the house, too, he had wasted his opportunities. He ought not to have waited so long and given her time to recover herself. But how in the world was he to know that she would do it, and at the very moment when it seemed as if the last chance was gone? If he had lost, it was by the narrowest margin. And his thoughts slipped back into reminiscences.

When he reached his destination he was thinking of other women.

Miss Willerby, whom he found without difficulty, received him coldly. She had seen Miss Holt and him go down the stairs together the first time, but had not seen them return to the cloak-room or leave the house. For some time she had supposed that Blakely had led Jessie to some out-of-the-way corner of the house, where they were sitting. At length she had grown uneasy, and had started with a companion to look for them. It was only a minute or two before Blakely's return that she had learned from the maid in the cloak-room that Miss Holt had left.

As Blakely told his tale she looked at him scrutinizingly, and wondered within herself what might have happened on the drive home and at the house. Though he was gay and smiling, he had not, she decided, the air of a conqueror, and was much comforted thereat. She declined his offer of his coupe to take her and Miss Willerby home, as the Holt carriage must be there by this time. She declined, also, his offer to go and find Miss Caley for her; she was much obliged, but she would do it herself. And she left him feeling rather uncomfortable—as if, in some way, he had been seen through and found out.

Jessie had waited, standing where he had left her, until she heard Blakely's carriage drive away, and until Thomas had disappeared again to the lower regions. Then suddenly her knees gave way, and she flung herself, kneeling, on the floor, burying her face in a chair, and burst into passionate sobbing. They were tears partly of shame and humiliation, but in the flood all the pent-up wretchedness of the past weeks found vent. Thank Heaven that he had not kissed her! That was her only consolation. Thank Heaven that she had recovered her senses in time for that! But that she herself should ever have been so weak, even for a minute, no matter how ill she was! Knowing herself as she did, but being unable to measure the strain which she had been under, it seemed to her to be almost incredible. But she did thank Heaven, prostrating herself on her knees, and praying with all the fervor of her overwrought nature that she might be made stronger against peril in the future; that she might be shown her path more clearly; and that the burden of these days might pass from her father and herself.

To those who have faith prayer never fails to bring solace and peace. By degrees her paroxysms subsided, and she rose from her feet with her mind cleared, feeling less shame for what she had suffered than gratitude that her eyes had been opened in time.

She went to her room and bathed her face, endeavoring to remove the traces of tears before her friends arrived. So far as Miss Caley was concerned she need have felt no concern, for that young lady was plunged in an abyss of woe. Something evidently had gone amiss between her and Barry that evening, and she was too deeply engrossed in the task of bearing herself with the properly tragic air to notice others.

But Miss Willerby, though Jessie strove to keep herself in the shadow and away from the light, saw that there had been weeping, and felt misgivings. So she was very tender to her hostess, very solicitous as to the sickness which had taken her away from the reception, and very affectionate in her parting for the night.

Miss Caley did not say good-night. Such trivialities were beneath the dignity of her grief. She wrapped herself in her sorrow as in a robe of state, and stalked haughtily to her room. Ten minutes after the door was locked, however, she was stretched in luxurious dishabille, ecstatically absorbed in the latest and flimsiest novel.

XVIII

On leaving Major Bartop's house Blakely drove to the club. The night was fine, though dark and moonless, with occasional savage gusts of wind. The club was but a short distance from his chambers, so he dismissed his carriage with the intention of walking home.

Strolling into the wine-room, he had just ordered some brandy and soda when a friend entered.

"Don't you want to beat me at a game at billiards, Blakely ?" he asked.

"Yes; I'm willing. Boy "—to the retiring waiter—" bring my drink up to the billiard-room."

The events of the evening certainly had not impaired the steadiness of Blakely's nerves. He played a dashing game, and defeated his antagonist comfortably.

"Oh, you're too good for me," said the latter, as he put up his cue.

"I'm a bit above my form to-night," remarked Blakely, as he leaned over the table to knock the balls around in a final stroke. Then he dropped his cue on the table, and dusted the chalk off his fingers with his handkerchief.

Fifteen minutes later he left the club. It was now just after midnight. As he descended the club steps he saw that the sky had grown blacker, and a fierce burst of wind which came swirling up the street made him turn his back to it and pull his hat more firmly on his head. He turned up the bottoms of his trousers, thrust his hands into his overcoat-pockets, and set his face homeward. Between the gusts the night was very still, but at each corner the wind, as if it had lain in wait for his coming, jumped out upon him bois-

15

terously, compelling him to turn sideways to it, and to hold his hat on his head with one hand. The swinging signs over the sidewalk creaked and rattled, and from the house-tops came sudden noises of loose tiles and chimney-tops swaying. In the shelter of the next block of buildings the stillness would settle down again.

Few people were abroad, and Blakely was surprised when about half-way between two cross-streets he met a woman. She walked fast, with some kind of a dark shawl thrown over her head, and keeping her face averted from him in passing. Not the type of a woman that interested Blakely— a house-servant probably, out later than she ought to be, and hastening home in fear of her mistress's disapproval.

At the next turning—perhaps a hundred feet farther on— was a large dry-goods store, with broad plate-glass windows and a deeply recessed entrance fronting diagonally on the corner. As Blakely reached this point his eyes happened to fall upon what he supposed to be a dog lying in the shelter of the doorway. Moved by some idle curiosity, he stepped towards it. No, it was not a dog; it was a cat. No, it was not a cat. And he leaned over it to see what it might be. It was a bundle of some sort. He stretched out his hand to it. Inside the wrappings was something firm and warm. Suddenly it flashed upon him. It was a child— a baby.

Then he remembered the woman. Stepping quickly out to the sidewalk again, he looked in the direction in which she had been going. She was standing at the next corner, where he could see her dark figure, motionless, against the street lights beyond. A second later she disappeared round the corner. Evidently she had waited to see if he would notice the child.

Blakely started to run with all his speed towards her. When he reached the corner she was nowhere in sight; but she could not have reached the next turning. She must be somewhere close at hand. He hurried down the street, looking on every hand. In the rear of the first clump of buildings a narrow alley ran off the main street to the right. She must have gone up that, he thought. A gas-lamp stood at the mouth of the alley, but its light pierced the darkness only for a few yards, beyond which all was black. Blakely walked cautiously up the narrow passage. Everything was still. On one side was a deep, brick-arched doorway—the rear entrance to one of the stores which faced on the other street. Was there something black in the shadow of the arch there, or was there not? Blakely stepped up closer. Yes; here she was, pressing herself back in the corner of the doorway, her shawl pulled close over her face. Blakely raised his hat instinctively.

"Excuse me, but is that your child?" he asked.

There was no reply.

"I beg your pardon," he said again. "There is a child in a doorway on the next street. Did you leave it there?"

Still there was no reply. He waited a moment, and then, reaching out, took her gently by the arm and drew her from her hiding-place. As he did so the light of the gas-lamp fell upon her face. He let go of her arm suddenly.

"My God!" he exclaimed, "Annie!"

For answer the woman buried her face in her hands and sobbed. It was some seconds before he could speak again.

"And—and the child?" he asked, almost timidly.

"Oh yes! yes!" and she fell on her knees before him, sobbing passionately. "Oh, you do not know what I have suffered!"

"But why did you not tell me in time?" he asked.

"I could not—I was ashamed to—I was afraid. So I waited and waited, and then I went away."

"I thought you went to your aunt?"

"No; I pretended to. And I wrote home a lie about my having got off accidentally at the wrong place."

She was still kneeling in the dirt of the alley, her face leaning on her hands, which clung to his coat, her shoulders convulsed with sobs. He felt the situation to be extremely embarrassing. He ought to show some tenderness for her, he knew; but somehow he could not frame the words. His chief feeling was one of intense annoyance.

"Well," he said, at last, "we cannot leave the baby there while we talk. You wait here, and I will go and fetch it."

He helped her to her feet and handed her back to the
shadow of the doorway, then retraced his steps to where the
child lay.   If any one had passed in the interval, evidently
the bundle had not been noticed.   He picked it up, feeling
curiously awkward and fearful of breaking it, not knowing
which end was which.   His child!   He ought, he told himself, to feel some love for it—some strange yearning towards
its helplessness.   But he did not; he felt only dislike and
bitterness against it for thrusting itself upon him.   He
hoped it would not cry; and it did not, but lay still and
peacefully in his arms.   Why had she not done differently?   How impossibly foolish women were in times of crisis!
And by what mad freak and caprice of chance had it been
ordained that he, of all men in the world, should be the one
to come along at just that moment?   Yet perhaps it was as
well, he thought.   Suppose that some one else had been in
his place—had found the child, and then, as he, had followed and captured her!   Suppose that it had been a policeman!

Rejoining her, he handed her the child, and she took it
eagerly and, with the quick, instinctive movements of mater-
nity, cuddled it to her under the shawl.

He stood back beside her in the shadow.   A gust of wind
burst up the alley, making the dim light of the lamp to flicker, and rattling a loose sign on the wall near by.

"And now what are you going to do?" he asked, when
the gust had passed.

She told him.   She was expected to arrive home the next
morning at eleven o'clock.   She had taken an earlier train
which had reached the city at nine o'clock that evening, and
had left the car with the child at Brooklyn — a poor suburb
of the town, some four miles away.   From there she had
come in by the electric road.   She had planned to abandon
the child, as he had seen.   There was a train leaving the
Union station at half-past one that morning—in three-quarters of an hour from that time—by which she could go to
Jackson, reaching there at six o'clock, and meeting the in-
coming train on which she was expected to arrive, which left
Jackson at six fifteen.   She would return on that train, and

nobody would know that she had not come all the way from Indiana. She had thought the plan out carefully, with a prescience which surprised Blakely, having even left the train when it waited a few minutes at Jackson and bought a ticket from there to the city, so that it would be unnecessary to show herself to the ticket-agent that morning, or to spend time which might be valuable in getting the ticket now.

"When I throw off the shawl," she said, "no one will ever recognize me for the same woman as got off at Brooklyn with the baby."

As he turned it over in his mind, it seemed to Blakely that this was the best plan that could be followed, and he was immensely relieved that he was not to have the responsibility of finding a hiding-place for her that night.

"Have you money?" he asked.

"Oh yes; plenty," she answered.

"Then give me the baby. I will take it to the police-station and say I found it—which I did."

"They won't hurt her, will they?" she asked, anxiously, as she handed the child to him, and then lightly moved a corner of the cloak in which it was wrapped for a last look at the little face.

"Oh no; they will advertise it. And if no one claims it, it will go to one of the institutions and be well cared for."

"Can I find out where she goes?" she asked, eagerly.

"Yes, I can find out for you," he said. "Now," he continued, when he had bestowed the child upon his arm as carefully as he could, "you have half an hour to catch your train. We must not leave here together. I will go this way — to the right. You wait until I have turned the corner; then you start to the left, and go straight to the station. Good-bye, and be careful," and he prepared to leave.

"Kiss me, Marshal!" she said, appealingly. "I love you so, dear, and oh! I have suffered so much!"

There had been a time when he had sought her kisses eagerly, but now something in him shrank from her. He kissed her, and tried to make the caress seem loving and tender. But it was difficult, and he stepped quickly away into the darkness.

It was but a short distance to the police-station. As Blakely entered, an officer lolled, half asleep, on the long wooden bench which ran along the wall. The lieutenant sat at his desk on the raised dais, separated from the rest of the room by a wooden railing. As the door opened, the man on the bench woke up. Blakely advanced to the lieutenant.

"I have got a present for you," he said, resting the bundle on the railing.

The lieutenant dropped his pen, and, leaning over, lifted the shawl from the child's face.

"Jiggered if it ain't another baby!" said the man, as he rose from the bench and came across the room, treading heavily on the wooden floor. "In these hard times, seems as if it rained babies. That's the third this week."

"You're Mr. Blakely, aren't you?" asked the lieutenant.

"Yes."

"Where did you find it?"

"In the doorway of that dry-goods store at the corner of Sixth and Quincy—what is its name?—that place with the large windows and big door opening on the corner."

"Griesheim's?" suggested the lieutenant.

"Griesheim's; that's it," said Blakely.

"Mike found one in the same place about a year ago," remarked the man. "Seems a popular locality. I remember Griesheim gave it a whole outfit of baby things, advertised it in the papers, and worked it for all it was worth. Pretty smart old man, Griesheim. Don't let nothin' slip by him—even babies."

"Seems to be healthy and sleeping like a good un," remarked the lieutenant, who was still examining the baby. "Looks something like my youngest did — same kind of mouth." Then he replaced the shawl with the tenderness of a father, and, pulling a big book towards him, he took a pen and began to write in it.

"Marshal Blakely, isn't it—your name?" he asked, after writing a line or two.

"Marshal Blakely," said the other.

"Now go ahead and tell your story," said the lieutenant; "only give me time to write it. Found it in Griesheim's doorway—Sixth and Quincy—about what? One o'clock?" as he glanced at the clock.

"No; it was earlier than that. I've been looking for the mother," Blakely explained.

"Where had you been and where were you going to?"

"At about nine o'clock this evening," Blakely began, "I went to a reception at Major Bartop's, on Adams Avenue. I left there at about nine thirty, and drove Miss Holt, who was ill, home to her father's house—Lawrence Holt's, on Jefferson —and got back to Major Bartop's about ten thirty. I left there at ten fifty or eleven o'clock, and went to the Union League Club, and played a game of billiards there with Arthur Calderly. I don't know what time it was when I left. It struck twelve while we were playing — may have been twenty minutes or half-past when I came away and started to walk to my rooms—"

"They are over here on Eighth Street, are they not?"

"Yes; Eighth, between Madison and Douglas. As I came along Sixth, just the other side of Griesheim's, a woman passed me. I—"

"What kind of a woman? Best description you can give."

Blakely thought a moment. Annie was dressed all in dark clothes, and was slender and blonde.

"Well, I couldn't see well. She was rather large — tall and, I should say, stout. She had on some kind of a lightish dress—sort of striped print or something, and a black jacket, short. Her hair was dark, as nearly as I can guess. It is a pretty black night, and I did not notice very much."

"Dark — stout—lightish dress—jacket," murmured the lieutenant as he wrote. "Any hat?"

"Let me see," pondered Blakely. "I am almost afraid to say. It seems to me she had a largish dark hat, but I would hate to swear to it."

"Largish dark hat — uncertain about hat," murmured the lieutenant. "All right. Go on."

"Then I found this," said Blakely. "At first I thought it was a dog, and I don't know what made me stop. Then it looked like a cat. It wasn't till I touched it that I saw what it was."

"How about the woman?" asked the lieutenant.

"As soon as I saw it was a baby, I started to look for her. I ran back to the corner, but she had a good start of me. I went along Sixth to Harrison, and up an alley there; poked around in the dark; then came back along Sixth to Quincy; stood around for a bit, and wandered up to Seventh; looked into alleys and doorways and things, but she had disappeared. I went back to the baby, and stood there for ten or fifteen minutes, thinking she might show herself if I stayed quiet. But she didn't. Then I came on here."

The story was plausible, and had been given in a straightforward, consecutive way. The lieutenant read it over, and asked a few questions, in the hope of locating the time more exactly. They finally decided that twelve thirty-five or twelve forty was about as near as they could get. Could Mr. Blakely give any better description of the woman — anything peculiar in her walk, or anything else? No; Mr. Blakely's recollection was drained dry.

"Tell Charlie to come in here," said the lieutenant to the other man. The latter disappeared through a door, and presently returned with another officer.

"Baby's been found in the doorway of Griesheim's store by Mr. Blakely here," said the lieutenant to the new-comer. "Just before finding it he passed a woman—about an hour ago now—tall, stoutish, light dress, black jacket, dark hair. Just go and hang around there, and see if you run against anybody like her. Tell the other men in that neighborhood —Greeley and Mark."

The man called Charlie repeated the description of the woman as given to him, and went out into the street.

"Telephone to the other stations, Maxey," said the lieutenant to the first officer, and that individual disappeared into the closet where the telephone was located.

The lieutenant read his notes over to Blakely.

"That all right?" he asked.

"Yes."

"Anything more you can think of?"

"No; nothing else."

"Just sign your name there, if you will, please," indicat-

ing the place on the open page of the book where the notes
had been made, and handing Blakely a pen. "And now
about the baby."

He leaned over and moved the shawl aside again, and, putting his rough forefinger under the baby's hand, raised the
soft, limp little fingers.

"It's a pretty child," he said; "look at those fingers!
They are the best part of a baby, I think. About two weeks
old—a girl, I guess." And Blakely only just checked himself from saying "Yes, she said so."

"You don't want to adopt her?" looking up at Blakely.

"No," said the latter, surprised. "Why?"

"The finder has the right to do so—provided, of course,
the parents do not turn up. Finder has first chance."

Blakely laughed.

"No. I confess I have not felt any yawning need of an
infant yet."

"Wonder if she has ever had a bottle?" remarked the
lieutenant. Again Blakely found himself on the point of
venturing an opinion. This second narrow escape warned
him that he must be on his guard, and the safest course was
to speak as seldom as possible.

Maxey now returned from the telephone.

"Just go back and call up the 'Foundling'" (as the institution was called among the police), said the lieutenant, "and
ask Mrs. White if she can take a baby-girl two weeks old.
No message with it."

Maxey disappeared again. The door opened, and another
officer entered.

"Jinks!" he exclaimed; "more 'lost or stolens'?" and he
looked inquiringly first at Blakely and then at the lieutenant. The former kept silence, so the latter explained to the
new-comer where and how the little thing had been picked up.
The two men leaned together over the child, while Blakely
marvelled at the interest which they showed in every crease
in the fat fingers, and the tenderness with which they lifted
the shawl by inches away from the small crumpled face.

"She says ' all right,' " said Maxey, returning.

" Well, you'd better take it up right away," said the lieu-

tenant. "I guess there is no message with it; they usually
pin them on the outside. Have Mrs. White undress it at
once, and bring the clothes back here. Make her look at
them first, and see if there is anything about them that we
would not notice—in the style of sewing, and so forth—that
would be likely to help."

The lieutenant folded the shawl again over the child, and
Maxey lifted it in his hands. The other officer opened the
door, and Blakely drew a long breath as it closed again
behind the departing policeman. Once more he told himself that he ought to feel more deeply. It was his own
child that was being taken through the black and windy night
to an institution of public charity. Surely he ought to feel
stirred in some way. But he did not; only immensely relieved—as if a great burden were lifted from him.

"Well," he said, addressing the lieutenant, "it is nearly two
o'clock. If I can be of no more use, I will be off to bed."

"No; that's all, I guess," replied the other. "If we need
you in any way — for identification or anything — we can
always find you, I suppose. You are going to be around
town for a while?"

"As far as I know."

Blakely buttoned up his coat and prepared to go.

"I am very much obliged to you," he said. "I suppose it
is all in the line of your duty—an every-day thing with you;
but I confess I feel as if you had taken a load from me. I
did not know what the devil to do when I first found it."

The lieutenant laughed.

"It isn't quite the same as finding a silver dollar, is it?"

At this moment the door opened, and a man entered whom
Blakely guessed to be a reporter.

"Anything new?" asked the representative of the press.

"If you had been here a few minutes ago you might have
seen a baby," remarked the lieutenant.

"Can see all I want at home," remarked the reporter, lacon-
ically. "But what was it?"

"This gentleman found it. Mr. Blakely, let me introduce
to you Mr. Gale, of the *World*. Mr. Gale is an old friend of
mine, and we hope to have him in jail yet."

" Pleased to meet you, Mr. Blakely," said the reporter. " I know your name well enough—Marshal Blakely, is it not ?"

Blakely bowed. The reporter turned to the lieutenant.

" Having quite a lively time to-night, aren't you ?" he asked, playfully, " what with murders and babies—' births, deaths, marriages, and all uncharitableness,' fifty cents a line for each insertion. Let us have the baby story "—and he took out his note-book and pencil—" and make it short, for I can only run in a stickful or so now. Why don't babies come earlier ?"

Blakely was anxious to get away to avoid further questioning, but he felt that something was necessary from him. So he asked the reporter, casually :

" Has there been a murder to-night?"

" We don't know," Gale replied; " but it looks like it—an old woman on Fourth Street called Masson."

" Called *what ?*" cried Blakely, in a tone which made both the others stare at him.

" Masson — Mrs. William Masson, a widow, 317 South Fourth Street. Do you know her ?"

" Yes—or, rather, no," stammered Blakely. " I know one of her daughters slightly."

" Which one?" asked Gale.

" The younger—Annie."

" She's away in the country now somewhere — down in Indiana ; expected back to-morrow, isn't she ?"

" I believe so."

" Pretty tough home-coming for a girl," suggested the reporter. " But she's only a step-daughter. Did you ever meet the mother at all ?"

Blakely saw that the reporter was making a note in his book.

" No," he said ; " please don't quote me. I never spoke to the mother in my life ; I never spoke to the other daughter, and only know the girl Annie very slightly."

" The trouble is," mused the reporter, " that we need some more stuff about it badly. Two other fellows have been working on it, but it only came in late. It's pretty hard to find any one who knows the Massons. This Captain Harrington, of the street-railway company, is engaged to one girl, and he cannot be got at. A printer called Weatherfield is engaged to the other, and he lives five miles out in the country. Wollmer, the labor man, boards in the house, and he is the only one who has given us anything. He'll talk all night. He thinks Harrington did it. Do you take any stock in that?" he asked, addressing the lieutenant.

"Not knowing, can't say," said that cautious gentleman.

"Anyway, Wollmer would fix it on Harrington if he could, naturally, because of the labor matters," said the reporter. Then, turning to Blakely again: "I wish you would tell me whatever you know."

"I don't know a thing, and I really must protest against my name being mentioned. I shall have to appear in connection with the baby. That is enough for one day. I appeal to you, lieutenant; don't you think I am right?"

"I guess you had better let Mr. Blakely go, Gale," said the lieutenant, slowly. "You can see him to-morrow if you want to. As he says, he has given you one story to-night. Let it go at that."

The reporter hesitated a minute.

"Well," he said, at last, "if you will promise not to talk to any other paper, but will give me to-morrow whatever you have to say, and if the lieutenant here will promise not to mention your name in connection with it to any of the other boys, why, I will leave you out altogether."

"I promise," said Blakely, and the lieutenant nodded.

"And now I'm going," Blakely continued. "It's time to be in bed. He," nodding towards the lieutenant, "can tell you all about what you call the 'baby story.'"

"I guess so," said the lieutenant.

So Blakely said "good-night," and left. As the door closed behind him, the reporter remarked, quietly:

"Seemed awfully anxious not to have his name appear, didn't he?"

"Young fellows usually are," replied the lieutenant, "when they know one daughter of a family, and have never spoken to the mother or other daughter."

Blakely was glad when at last he had escaped from the police-station and was out in the street again. It was an unpleasant job, well over. Annie, he thought to himself, was

now some three-quarters of an hour out of town, on her way
to Jackson. There was little danger to be apprehended from
that quarter, and he wondered again at the sagacity and fore-
thought which she had shown in laying her plans.

When he arrived at his rooms it was after two, but he felt
in no mood for sleep; so he stirred the fire, lit a cigar, and
sat down to think it over.

His were not cheerful thoughts. He was chagrined at the
outcome of the meeting with Jessie. Then there was this
confounded child, and the murder coming in to complicate
matters. In another affair, also, things had taken a rather
unpleasant turn. Altogether, luck seemed to be running
against him. He had been in perplexing predicaments and had
experienced narrow escapes enough before. But this seemed
to be a superfluous accumulation of untoward events. The
more he looked at the situation the less it contented him. He
even wondered, in a vague way, whether the game that he
was playing was worth the candle, and was tempted to make
a resolution to be less reckless—not more good, but only less
reckless—in future. But he knew himself too well. He
had made resolutions of that kind before; and they had been
scattered to the winds when the next opportunity offered.
"Adventures are to the adventurous"—a motto which he
was fond of repeating, and which had stuck in his mind ever
since he had run across it in reading Disraeli's works when a
boy. Adventure had its dangers certainly. Everything that
was worth doing had. There were times when the dangers
seemed to outweigh the pleasure; and this was one of them.
But the clouds would pass, as they always had before; and
the next chase would be just as irresistible as the last. The
risk was never very clearly visible when an enterprise offered.
It was only when you were over the hurdle—either well in
mid-air or safely on the other side—that you saw the width of
the ditch beyond. If his horse's hind-legs did get in once
in a while, Blakely, so far, had always managed to pull out
somehow, and he would again.

XIX

A HOME-COMING

On the evening of the Bartop reception Harrington had taken the first holiday which he had allowed himself for many a day. The strikers had not abandoned their plan of warfare. There was no material relaxation of the system of petty annoyances and minor outrages to which the street-railway company, and incidentally the public, was subjected. The assaults on employés, the cutting of wires and injuring of equipment, the holding up of inoffensive citizens—all these things continued. But at least the men had not yet proceeded to any concerted and violent action. The company, more-over, was acquiring knowledge by experience. For more than a week it had maintained what was practically its full ser-vice of cars in operation, and each day the new employés became more familiar with their duties, and they and the company grew to have more confidence in each other. The company's property was better protected at all points, and damages, when they occurred, were more quickly repaired.

About the barns and the power - house especially, where Harrington was in command, the situation seemed to have quieted down. The young electrician had shown himself equal to the charge which was laid upon him. His guards were as well drilled as a military garrison. Their number had been increased, and, by weeding out from time to time any who showed sign of lack of courage or promptitude of action in moments of emergency, he had gradually collected a small force of men on whom he felt that he could thor-oughly rely, and who in turn had perfect confidence in him. The strikers appeared to have reached the conclusion that his little command was unsafe to tamper with. This seem-

ing quietude, however, he believed to be only a temporary
respite. The strikers, he reasoned, hoped to lull him into a
false sense of security, and then, thinking him off his guard,
would seize an occasion for some more formidable attack
than had yet been attempted. What form this attack would
take he was at a loss to conjecture. So many things were
possible. Of this only he was convinced: that the men had
by no means given up the fight, and that they would not forever remain content with their present desultory and inef-
fective methods. "Something," he told himself, "will drop"
—and that before very long.

Meanwhile there was no reason why he should not take
one evening for himself — and Jennie. A certain famous
Eastern orchestra, in the course of one of its Western tours,
was to give a concert in town. Both Jennie and he loved
music, and this was a treat not to be missed; so, on the evening in question, after a final tour of inspection and assuring
himself that everything was running smoothly, he jumped on
a car that left the barns about seven o'clock, and took his way
to his sweetheart's house.

They started for the opera-house where the concert was to
take place with all the light-heartedness of two children es-
caping from school.

"I suppose it will be midnight before you get back," grumbled Mrs. Masson.

"Oh no, mother," Jennie answered, gayly; "the concert
will be over before eleven o'clock."

At the door they met Wollmer coming in. It was an unusual time for him to be returning to the house, and as he
passed them he said something to Jennie about papers which
he had forgotten.

"Confound the fellow!" remarked Harrington. "He knows
now that I am not on duty to-night, and may take advantage
of it to make trouble."

In their present mood, however, the incident could not
worry them for long, and Wollmer was soon forgotten in the
half-loverlike, half-childish nonsense which they talked on their
way to the entertainment. The concert was excellent, and
they were in a frame of mind to enjoy every note of it. For

both it was one of those ideal evenings which, however peaceful, live in the memory long after the most passionate crises are forgotten.

In one of the intervals of the music Harrington had told Jennie that on leaving the opera-house he must go to a telephone and assure himself that all was right at the barns. At the conclusion he left her in the foyer while he did so. When he returned it was with an air of calamity.

"Jen, girl," he said, wofully, "I'm afraid I must go right up there. They've been having more or less trouble all the evening, and there is a big crowd of strikers collected now. It is that man Wollmer's fault, as I feared; and there's nothing for me to do but to leave you and get there as quickly as I can."

"That's all right, dear," she said, bravely. "That is where you ought to be, of course. I need not say that I hate to have you go, but if you have been as happy as I to-night it ought to last us for quite a while."

So he kissed her under the shadow of a doorway and then saw her safely to a car that would take her home, and himself boarded another car that was bound for the barns.

As Harrington had said, there had been trouble all the evening, not only about the central barns, but all over the city. It seemed as if the strikers had decided that the time had come for more vigorous action.

The car on which Jennie Masson was travelling had made, perhaps, about half the distance to her house when suddenly the lights in the car flickered, jumped up again, and went out. At the same moment the car began to slacken speed and stopped. Jennie saw the conductor in the dim light leaning backward over the railing of the platform looking at the wire overhead, while he pulled at the dangling rope, as if endeavoring to replace the trolley. A minute later he walked silently through the car to join the engineer. As he returned, one of the passengers asked what was the matter.

"No current, replied the conductor."

"What does that mean?"

"Well, we will wait a few minutes and see if it comes on again. If it don't, it means the wires are cut, and you had better get out and walk. It will take an hour or two before they get it repaired."

For some minutes the passengers sat in the darkness, with an occasional grumble from one direction and desultory witticisms from another, chiefly having reference to the location of Moses when the light went out, or being in the nature of speculations as to how long it would take to get there at that pace. Finally the conductor threw open the door.

"I guess there ain't no uset in waitin'," he said.

And one by one the passengers arose and stepped off into the darkness.

Jennie did not fear the walk, black and gusty though the night was, but rather enjoyed it. Arriving home with her cheeks in a glow and panting from the struggle with the wind, she was astonished to find the front door wide open. The light in the hall was turned low, and flickered in the wind which whistled in from the street. The door of the front room was shut, and Jennie passed on, wondering at the silence and the deserted aspect of the house, to the dining-room. Here also the light was turned down, but as she entered she saw that in the front room the gas blazed brightly. She passed through the open folding-doors between the apartments, and then her heart stood still.

Stretched at full length on the floor before her lay her mother, her feet towards her, and her head almost in the fireplace. For a minute it seemed to Jennie that she herself was paralyzed. She opened her mouth as if to scream, but no sound came. She tried to lift her arm, and it would not obey her. She endeavored to walk, and her legs trembled. How still the body was!

Slowly the blood and the power seemed to come back to the girl's limbs, and she stepped forward, walking on tiptoe round the thing as it lay. She passed by the feet and up to the woman's farther side. Then the face came into view, upturned to the full glare of the light and ghastly white. From under the head the blood had oozed and trickled over the tiles of the fireplace, where it lay in filmed and stagnant pools.

Jennie's first impulse was to scream. It seemed as if her whole being screamed—as if every nerve and every drop of

16

the blood that had been frozen in her body found relief and united in the scream. As she stood with her hands pressed against her cheeks, which were almost as white as those of the face upon the floor, shriek after shriek rang through the deserted house and passed out to mingle with the sob of the wind in the street. As suddenly as she had begun to scream she ceased, and, dropping on her knees beside the body, burst into tears.

Recovering herself, she at last ventured to touch the face of the woman before her. It was warm. Jennie tore open the waist of her mother's dress, and laid her hand upon the heart. She fancied that it beat. For a moment she looked wildly round the room, as if with some idea of lifting the body to a chair or the sofa. Then, rising, she ran out into the hall, flung open the front door, which she had closed on entering, and screamed again out into the night. The letters of the photographer's sign across the way glittered in the electric light, and, scarce knowing what she did, she screamed, "Mr. Eldred! Mr. Eldred! Help!" She had never met or spoken to the photographer. A window in No. 319 was thrown up, and a woman's voice called, "Is it fire?" A front door across the way opened, and a man's figure stood in the doorway. "What's the matter?" he called.

"Help! Help! Murder!" she screamed. "It's murder!"

The man came hurrying across the road, and from both directions along the street Jennie was vaguely conscious of people running in her direction. Turning into the house again, she went through the dining-room into the kitchen. When the first-comer entered the sitting-room she was on her knees wiping her mother's face with a towel dipped in water which stood in a pitcher on the floor by her side.

"Oh, get a doctor! get a doctor!" she said, without looking over her shoulder; "she is not dead."

Men were now crowding into the house, and the hall was filled with the shuffling of feet and whispered inquiries from those behind. A heavy hand was laid upon her shoulder as she kneeled, and a voice asked:

"What is it?"

Looking up, she saw a policeman.

"Oh, it's my mother! She has been killed!"

"Who by?"

"I don't know! I don't know!" But she set herself to bathing the white face again, and chafing the thin, wrinkled hands.

The policeman turned to the crowd.

"Come, you must get out of here!" he said, and, pushing with his baton, he thrust the reluctant spectators back into the hall.

"Has anybody gone for a doctor?" Jennie said, wildly.

"Yes," a voice answered, "minutes ago."

The policeman stooped over the body and laid his hand on the heart.

"How did it happen?" he asked.

"I don't know. I only just came in and found her here."

"Anybody else in the house?"

"No. I left her alone when I went out, and the front door was open when I came back."

"Who do you suppose can have done it?"

"Nobody! Oh, I don't know!"

Presently another policeman arrived. The two held a short consultation, in which Jennie caught something about telephoning. The later arrival went out again, and she heard him talking to the men in the hall as he pushed them out of the house. The other policeman followed him, and Jennie was alone with her mother; but she heard the murmur of voices without, and knew that one of the officers was keeping guard at the street door.

Soon the doctor came—a bustling little man, who set to work in a business-like way to feel Mrs. Masson's pulse. He lifted the eyelids and laid his hand on her breast. Then, raising her head slightly, he began to feel among the blood-clotted hair with his fingers.

"Is she killed?" asked Jennie.

"I don't know," he said.

"What did it?" asked one of the policemen who had re-entered the room; "a blow?"

"Can't tell," said the doctor. "May have been a blow or a fall. It is over the left ear here; cut the temporal artery. That is where the blood comes from."

As he spoke, the doctor had been looking up and down the fireplace. Then he leaned over and touched a sharp angle about eighteen inches from the ground, where the marble was bevelled.

"May have been that," he said, and, wiping the marble with his thumb, looked to see if any blood came off. But there was nothing.

"Be able to tell later on," he said. "We must get her on a bed. Have you a cot in the house?" turning to Jennie.

"Yes; up-stairs."

"Better bring it down here. Bedrooms are all up-stairs, I suppose. No use in carrying her up."

Jennie left the room to fetch the cot. One of the policemen met her at the foot of the stairs on her return, and helped to carry the bedding into the room, where Jennie found two other men in addition to the doctor and the policemen. One of the two she saw by his uniform was a superior officer of the police-force. It was, as a matter of fact, Chief Winley himself. The other, she soon gathered, was a detective. These two looked at her keenly as she entered, and continued the examination of the apartment in which they had been engaged. They walked round the walls, examining the paper and the wainscoting, to see if there were any marks of blood. They scrutinized the floor; passed into the adjoining room, and subjected that to the same careful investigation. The detective leaned over the woman on the floor, and looked at her hands, her dress, her shoes. Nowhere was there any sign or clew; no evidence of a struggle, nor any indication as to who, if any one, had been with Mrs. Masson at the time of the catastrophe.

Meanwhile the others had moved chairs aside, and set up the cot in the middle of the room. The doctor and two policemen lifted the stricken woman carefully and laid her upon it. The doctor asked for a basin of water, a sponge, and a towel, which Jennie brought. As she returned, Winley stepped up to the doctor and asked him if he needed Jennie for a few minutes.

"I guess not," replied the other. Then to Jennie: "Have you any other woman in the house?"

"No; my sister will return from the country to-morrow." And her voice broke, and tears burst forth anew as she thought of the shock that it would be to Annie.

"We want some one here to-night. Miss Parley, who helps me in my office, lives close by here, and she might be able to come. Could any of your men go and fetch her?" he asked of the chief.

The latter nodded to one of the officers.

"You go, Williams," he said.

The doctor took a tablet of prescription-blanks and a pencil from his pocket, and wrote his messages, which he folded up, addressed, and handed to the man named Williams.

"That is for Miss Parley," he said, as the officer took one of the notes. "There is the address—327 Fifth Street—just round the corner. She will probably be in bed; please wait for an answer and find out if she can come. Then I wish you would take that to the nearest drug-store and have them send me the things I ask for here right away — some antiseptic gauze, absorbent cotton, and roller bandages. Then I wish you would telephone yourself, or have them telephone (better do it yourself), to Dr. Garcelon, who lives on Eighth Street, and say that Dr. Butler wants him to come round at once for a consultation in emergency. A physician prefers to share the responsibility in a case of this sort," he explained to Miss Masson, who stood silently listening. "Two heads, you know."

Williams departed, and the chief of police addressed Jennie:

"May we ask you to step into the other room a minute?"

Jennie led the way into the dining-room, followed by the detective and Chief Winley. They seated themselves about the table, and the detective began his examination. In reply to his inquiries Jennie told of her departure for the theatre with Harrington—yes, "Captain" Harrington, of the street-railway company, she explained. She recollected the meeting with Wollmer at the door, and told of that.

"What terms was your step-mother on with Wollmer?" asked the detective.

Jennie said that they were very friendly, dwelling on Mrs.

Masson's sympathy with the strikers, and mentioning incidentally her curious ideas as to the benefit which she was to derive from General Harter's election, and her disapproval of her daughter's *fiancé*, Harrington. No; her mother never had any sum of money in the house, nor were there any valuables in the place worth stealing. Resuming the thread of her narrative, she told of her parting from Harrington. Could she give the exact time of that? asked the detective. Yes, it was just twenty minutes to eleven. Had she come straight home? As straight as she could; and she described the interruption of the trip by the cutting of the wires and her walk home. In all, she presumed, it had taken her half an hour—perhaps forty minutes—to reach the house from the time she left the opera-house.

"It would have been possible, then, for any one leaving the opera-house at the same time as you to have come straight here, say, in a carriage, and have had fifteen or twenty minutes to spare before you arrived?"

Jennie understood the object of their questions, but she replied calmly that it would have been — provided that the person could have foreseen the delay to herself. She answered many inquiries as to Wollmer and Harrington, Tom Weatherfield and her sister Annie. She could think of no reason which any one could have for wishing to kill her mother. Mrs. Masson had not been a woman who made friends; but there was nobody who had sufficient ground for hatred of her or interest enough in her death to wish her out of the way.

"You said that you thought that it must have occurred," said the detective, addressing the doctor, on their return to the front room, "not later than ten o'clock. Can you be sure of that?"

"We can be sure of nothing," replied Dr. Butler; "all indications go to show that she had been injured at least one hour and a half or two hours before I arrived."

"Could it possibly have been done at, say, eleven o'clock —within one hour of your arrival?"

"Anything is possible. My opinion is, however, that it must have been done at least one hour earlier."

Jennie was informed that a reporter from the *World* was in the hall and wished to see her.

" Cannot some one else see him ?" she asked, looking round the company.

" I will go," volunteered the chief of police, and he left the room.

Miss Parley arrived—a spare, prim-faced woman of perhaps thirty years of age—and, with just a nod to Jennie, set to work in a business-like way to remove her wrap and gloves and hat, and, depositing in a corner of the room a small valise which she carried, placed herself at the doctor's disposal, and was soon busy holding bottles and towels, handing him bits of cotton, and tossing blood-stained locks of hair, which he severed with his scissors, into the grate.

" May I go up-stairs, over the rest of the house ?" asked the detective.

" Certainly," Jennie answered. "You will find it untidy, probably. On the next floor are Mr. Wollmer's room and my mother's. The third room is vacant. My room and my sister's are on the floor above. Her door is locked. You will find the key on the mirror on my dressing-table."

The detective went out, and she heard him ascending the stairs. A few minutes later Dr. Garcelon arrived—a large, forceful man, with a red face and a bristling mustache, whom Jennie already knew by sight. The two medical men exchanged brief greetings, and the new-comer leaned over the cot, while Dr. Butler showed him the wound on the woman's head, and the two carried on a desultory colloquy in undertones.

" I think it is safer to wait a while—say until noon to-morrow," said Dr. Garcelon, straightening himself up.

" That is what I think," rejoined Dr. Butler.

" What is it ?" Jennie asked, anxiously.

" There is a fracture of the skull," Dr. Butler explained, " though the outer fracture is not very serious. The blood has come from the severing of the temporal artery. The inner table of the skull, however, appears to be broken also— what we call a depressed fracture—and a portion of the bone seems to be pressing upon the brain. That is probably what is the matter. It is that which produces the state of coma in which she is now lying. Dr. Garcelon here and I have been considering the advisability of what is known as trephining. But it does not seem to either of us that the patient's condition at present warrants it."

" You mean that she could not stand it ?"

" We mean that it is always a dangerous and critical operation. The patient has lost a great deal of blood, and she is old, and not very strong, I should say, naturally. It may be that she will come out of the coma without our intervention in the next twelve or fifteen hours. If she does not, it will be necessary for us to consider the advisability of an operation again."

" At present we can do nothing ?"

" Nothing but watch her. Have you any ice in the house ?"

" Yes."

" Crack a little, then, and do it up in a bag, and keep it applied to the base of the brain—there. I will leave you now, and on my way home I will send some medicine from the drug-store—just an arterial sedative, which Miss Parley will show you how to administer. You can stay here to-night ?" he asked of that young lady.

" Yes."

" Well, you and Miss Masson can relieve each other as you think best. I will leave the thermometer with you. If there is any marked rise in temperature, you had better let me know. Otherwise, go on as you have heard me say."

The policemen had all gone, and now the physician and the surgeon withdrew together, and the two women began their long vigil in the silent house beside the sick-bed.

There were few interruptions during the night. Once Miss Parley went to answer a ring at the bell. It was another reporter, who was quickly dismissed and told to go elsewhere for his information. Miss Parley saw that a policeman stood on guard at the foot of the steps.

About two o'clock Wollmer came in, full of professions of sympathy, but Jennie thought his face had never borne a more vindictive expression, and she loathed him even more than she had done before. Finding that his offers to share their watch

with the two women were not cordially received, he retired to
his room.

Soon after six o'clock Weatherfield, who was an early riser
and had seen the news in the morning paper, arrived. When
Jennie went to the door, she found that there was already
a small crowd of idlers collected in the street watching the
house. The printer's distress was transparently sincere if
awkward. He was willing to do anything he could (if it
would have done Jennie any good to have him lie down that
she might trample on him, he would have submitted gladly),
but very much at a loss to put his sympathy into words. His
woe-begone air, as of a dog that has been beaten, was scarcely
more pathetic than ludicrous. With all possible desire to be
of use, he felt that he was only in the way—as if he were
somehow too large and his feet too clumsy for that silent
house. Jennie was grateful to him, but felt none the less relieved when he left, promising to look in again before he went
to meet Annie at the station.

At that moment Annie was waiting on the platform at Jackson. Her train was ten minutes late, and she was nervously
uneasy. At last it arrived, and with half a dozen other early
passengers she stepped on board and made her way through
the train to the sleeping-car, where the atmosphere at that
time in the morning was foul and stifling. She explained
to the porter that she wished to pay for a berth from there
to her destination, and, after retiring to the ladies' dressing-
room for a while, settled down in a vacant section which had
not been occupied on the preceding night.

Soon the other passengers began to appear from their berths,
looking uninvitingly untidy and unwashed as they made their
respective ways to the dressing-rooms, whence each returned
much improved in appearance. Among them Annie saw
Horace Marsh, who had been speaking the night before in
a distant part of the State, and had boarded the train in the
early hours of the morning. Harrington had pointed him
out to her, and she was afraid lest Marsh should know her by
sight; but he did not.

At an intermediate station a boy came in with the morning
papers. Annie did not buy one. She rarely read the papers,

and it did not occur to her that the finding of her baby might have already made its way into the news of the day. Marsh took one, however, and was shocked to read of the calamity in the Masson household. He thought of the distress that it would cause to his friend Harrington, but little guessed that the pale-faced girl who sat across the aisle of the car and gazed so wistfully out of the window would be so much more deeply interested in the news than he. Then he saw the account of the finding of the baby—only a short paragraph—and the sight of Blakely's name sent his thoughts back into the melancholy channel which now they so rarely left.

Breakfast was announced by a wide-mouthed colored waiter with a white apron, who called it "bwck-fuss," and said that it was now ready in the "dahnin' cyar." Annie was surprised to find that she was hungry, and a cup of hot coffee and a chop made her feel better. She delivered the check for her trunk, which had arrived the evening before, to the transfer company's agent who boarded the train at Brooklyn, submitted to the ostentatious dusting of the car-porter, and then sat down to await the arrival at the station. Issuing from the car, she found Weatherfield awaiting her. She assumed an air of as much gayety as possible, and prepared to make excuses for her thinness and pallor.

But Weatherfield was too preoccupied with the tidings which he had to tell her to give much thought to her appearance. He noticed, indeed, that she was pale, and wondered whether she had already learned the news through the morning paper. She, seeing his solemnity, feared lest somehow he had heard of the thing that haunted her, and she could scarcely nerve herself to greet him.

"Have you heard?" was his first question. And her heart sickened as she replied.

"No; what?"

"Have you heard about your mother?"

She shook her head. Her lips were dry, and she could not speak.

"She is very badly hurt."

Did he mean hurt in her pride and her feelings at the news

of her daughter's shame? But she could only look at him blankly, white and trembling.

"Come here, and I will tell you." And he drew her gently aside from the stream of passengers that flowed along the platform, and, with many falterings and hesitations, he told her all that he knew. She listened in silence, but gradually the blood came back to her face, and in her heart she knew that the tidings which she heard brought more relief than sorrow. At least, as yet her secret was not known, and, she could not help telling herself, this new calamity would serve in some manner to distract attention from herself.

Weatherfield was surprised at the bravery with which she bore the shock, and in his simple mind remembered that the girls had not, after all, much cause for tenderness towards their step-mother, nor reason to feel deeply grieved at her loss.

In the course of the drive from the station he made one or two efforts at conversation on different topics, venturing inquiries as to how she had spent her time in the country. But Annie was unresponsive. As the carriage turned into Fourth Street they could see from the distance of a square away that there was a large crowd gathered about the house, in spite of the cold which had succeeded the winds of the night before. On the sidewalk immediately in front of the door two policemen kept a passageway, but in the road and on the opposite side of the street stood some two hundred people, men and boys for the most part, but with not a few women sprinkled through the throng. As the crowd stood and stared at the front of the house, watching every arrival at and departure from the door with morbid interest, so on every door-step and at almost every window on both sides of the street stood other men and women staring at the crowd.

The coachman had difficulty in making his way to the house, and when at last the spectators realized that the occupants of the carriage were bound for the fateful domicile itself, Annie felt that every eye was fixed upon her.

"That's the other daughter," she heard a voice say, and the news was passed back from mouth to mouth.

In the hall Jennie and Harrington were waiting. As the

two sisters met they reached out their hands to each other, and fell sobbing on each other's shoulder. The two men stood awkwardly by, exchanging now and then a word in undertones. At last Harrington laid his hand on Jennie's shoulder.

"I don't believe that we can be of any use," he said. "You know that Tom and I will do anything in the world we can. We will stay all day if you wish, but at present I think we are only in the way."

Jennie, drying her eyes with her handkerchief, tried to smile at him, but could not speak.

"Is there anything we can do?" asked Harrington again.

"Nothing at all, dear; thanks. You are awfully sweet!" And Harrington kissed her for thanks.

"How is she?" asked Annie, in a low voice.

"She is alive," her sister said. "The doctors are in there now"—pointing to the closed door. "We will go in this way, by the dining-room."

The two men left without another word, and the girls passed arm in arm into the sick-room.

All through the long night and the morning the stricken woman had lain in the darkened room without movement or sign of returning consciousness. The doctors, now in consultation, decided that it would be unsafe to wait much longer. They agreed to return at four o'clock that afternoon, prepared to operate if no change had taken place, and if the patient's general condition, as indicated by her pulse, seemed to justify it.

At four o'clock no change had come, so Dr. Garcelon began the operation with Dr. Butler's assistance. For nearly an hour they worked in silence, while the two girls stood by with hands clinched and nerves tense awaiting the result. They were aware of another figure entering the room, and, turning, saw Wollmer standing in the folding-doors between the apartments.

A minute later there was a movement on the cot. The patient's feet stirred. The doctors straightened themselves up and waited in silence. The patient's eyes were open, and

they roamed aimlessly around the room. She tried to raise
herself in bed, but Dr. Garcelon held her gently down. Lifting her head slightly from the pillow, she looked blankly from
one to another, and clutched at the sides of the cot with her
thin fingers. She made an effort to speak, but her voice
would not come. Again she tried, and a harsh, cracked
whisper went through the room.

"Where is he?" she asked. "Has Harrington gone?
What made him come here like that? I will never give
them to him. After all these years—"

Her voice ceased. For an instant her lips moved, and then
it was as if her body collapsed. Dr. Garcelon let her head
rest on the pillow. Each of the doctors took one of the
yellow hands and placed their fingers on the pulse. Then
one laid the hand gently down and the other did the same.

"She is dead," said Dr. Butler, solemnly.

XX

WHEN the first shock had passed, and the girls came to talk the sad scene over, they had some difficulty in deciding upon the exact words that the dying woman had used. What did the reference to Harrington mean? Jennie put it down to delirium. Annie, after questioning her sister, wondered whether Harrington could possibly have made his way to the house by some short cut from the theatre, and done this thing before his sweetheart arrived. She could not believe it, and yet—

Wollmer alone had no doubt as to what Mrs. Masson's last sentences were. Five minutes after she was dead he was on his way to police headquarters, where he found the chief of police closeted with Sullivan. The labor leader hardly waited to exchange greetings with the two men before blurting out his news—the news that Mrs. Masson was dead, and that the last words that she had said were that Harrington had murdered her.

The announcement elicited no enthusiasm from his auditors. On the contrary, in the silence with which his information was received Wollmer read incredulity and distrust of himself. His temper rose, and he insisted vehemently on Harrington's immediate arrest. The chief remained silent.

"Ye can't do it," said Sullivan, dogmatically. "It would look like parsecutin' him. The public 's none too friendly to us an' yer dom strikers now."

"Persecuting him! Isn't there ground for suspicion enough?"

"I doubt it," said the chief. "If he was a tramp or a vagabond, yes; we should have to arrest him to prevent his leaving town. But with a man like Harrington it is different."

"And suppose he does leave town," Wollmer said.

The chief shook his head.

"Not he," he said. "If he is guilty—which, mind you, I doubt—he has too good a chance of making out an alibi at the trial to be scared now—enough scared to proclaim his guilt by running away. Guilty or not, he will stay."

"There'll have to be an inquest," remarked Sullivan.

"And it will be time enough," added Winley, "to do the arresting then according to the evidence."

"But don't you hold men on suspicion?" Wollmer protested.

"Yes; when I suspect," said the chief, dryly.

"And you mean that you don't suspect Harrington?"

"I mean that there is no use in making mistakes from being in too great a hurry. He will be just as easy to reach to-morrow as to-day. As Sullivan says, it would look bad if we jumped on him too quickly — especially on information coming from you, Mr. Wollmer."

Wollmer bit his lips and rose to go.

"Well, I've done my duty. I have put you on the man's trail. If you decline to arrest him to-day, and he escapes, the responsibility is on you."

"An' if the chief is afraid of the responsibility, I'll take it meself," said the Irishman, quietly.

It was nearly six o'clock when Wollmer left the City Hall and directed his steps to a certain notorious saloon and restaurant where the strikers congregated, and where Wollmer proposed to get some supper. Here in the half a hundred men who were assembled he found a more sympathetic audience than that which he had left. He did not hesitate to spread the news, and on his lips the words of the dying woman became more and more sensational and explicit. It appeared that she had said distinctly that Harrington came there to murder her, and that he had done it. "He knew I would never give in to him," she had said (so Wollmer declared), and that referred both to her consent to his marriage with her daughter, and also to the advocacy of the striker's claims,

which he had endeavored to make her abandon. Nor did
Wollmer spare the chief of police and Sullivan for their refusal to act on his suggestion. Secretly he hated Sullivan—
hated him for his strength, and because he knew that the
Irishman despised him. Indeed, Sullivan had never been at
any pains to conceal his contempt for the labor leader. But
for Sullivan, Wollmer asserted, Harrington would even then
be under lock and key. Winley would have done his duty
but that he was afraid of the Irishman; and Wollmer let it
be understood that he had something more than a suspicion of Sullivan's political honesty. He could tell things,
if he pleased, about the Irishman's relations with some of
the Republican leaders that would make interesting matter if
they were published.

Wollmer had smarted under the consciousness of the other's contempt. He had been restrained from saying or doing anything which would lead to an open rupture between
them partly by an undefined physical fear of Sullivan's huge
frame and forceful character, and still more by the fact that
it was through Sullivan that he received the funds from the
city treasury, so large a part of which went into his own
pocket. But, after all, was it not on him—Wollmer—and the
labor vote which he controlled that Sullivan and the whole
Democratic ticket had to rely for their success at the polls?
What right had the Irishman, then, to treat him as he did?

Now, in his chagrin at the rebuff which he had received,
embittered by the postponement of the gratification of his
personal hatred of Harrington, he grew reckless. All his
pent-up hostility against Sullivan broke out, and in the con-
genial atmosphere of the assembled strikers he let his spite
have vent.

An hour and a half later, when he left the saloon to go to
the strikers' headquarters, he was accompanied by nearly all
those who had been listening to him. At the headquarters
some thirty or forty of the ringleaders of the strike were collected, and here Wollmer told his tale again, and it increased
in circumstantiality of detail and in bitterness at each repeating. In his hands the figure of Mrs. Masson grew to an he-

roic stature. She was a Joan of Arc, a fair champion of their own cause, and had given her life for their sake. Harrington was a cowardly assassin, who, playing upon a girl's confiding heart, had stolen into the house, and by her own hearth-side had stricken down the friend of labor simply because she had refused, even to the death, to abjure their cause. By the mercy of Providence it had been granted that she should come back for one minute from the very shadow itself to confound her slayer, who might otherwise have escaped. Even now, by the treachery of Sullivan, it seemed that the murderer was to be suffered to escape, though her voice had issued, as it were, from the very portals of death to accuse him.

Wollmer more than hinted that he had private information of plans which Harrington had laid for leaving the city that evening. There was none among the strikers assembled who had ever seen Mrs. Masson, and the glorified picture of the dead woman which Wollmer drew was accepted without question. The material which the labor leader had to work with was excellent, and he used it cunningly—the two girls, one blinded and betrayed by this man whom they all hated; the other plighted to a sturdy workman like themselves, but smuggled off into the country lest she should interfere with the murderer's well-laid plans. The very evening before this poor girl's return the villain takes her sister out, and, under a flimsy pretence of duty calling him, leaves her and hurries to her home, where she arrives only to find that he has done his work. The next day the other sister returns, and now there is only the blasted hearth, with the two orphans weeping in each other's arms and the dead crying aloud for vengeance —the dead who died in their own cause.

The men in the mass were accustomed to follow Wollmer's leadership. There were his own personal satellites among them, moreover, who took up his theme, and chanted it with repetitions and exaggeration. Fiery speeches were made and demands for the death of the murderer. From the head-quarters the news spread over the city, travelling from one saloon to another, from the crowd at one street corner to the loafers on the next, until all the strikers in the town knew

17

that Harrington had killed Mrs. Masson, and had killed her because she had refused to renounce her sympathy with the strike; that she had told how the deed was committed with her last breath of life; and that, owing to a conspiracy between Sullivan and the friends of the street-railway company, he was to be suffered to escape from the city that night.

Meanwhile Harrington himself was busy, and did not hear of Mrs. Masson's death till some hours after it had occurred.

After leaving Jennie at the opera-house, his trip, like hers, had been interrupted half-way to the barns by the stoppage of the current. He had had farther to walk than she, and had thought it more prudent to go by the less-frequented streets than by the more direct but more travelled thoroughfares. Some fifteen minutes, moreover, had been spent at a telephone, endeavoring to obtain information as to where the trouble had occurred, but without much satisfaction, so that in the neighborhood of an hour had elapsed before he finally reached his destination. Here a large crowd was collected, through which he had succeeded, under cover of the friendly darkness, in shouldering his way without his identity being discovered.

It had been a stormy and eventful evening, as he had been informed. One of his men, he found, had been captured by the mob, and badly beaten and trampled upon before he was rescued, and he was now lying in the barns on a cot, unconscious. About nine o'clock the situation had looked so threatening that an urgent summons had been sent to the police headquarters for additional protection, in response to which Chief Winley had detailed half a dozen officers, with a statement that that was all that could be spared. The presence of these men, though they made but a perfunctory show of opposition to the strikers, had served in some manner to keep the crowd in check. When Harrington arrived, however, there was scarcely a pane of glass in either building unbroken, and stones which were still being thrown at intervals from the rear ranks of the mob made it dangerous for the employés within to show themselves at any of the windows. About a hundred yards from the barns the flames still rose fitfully from the smouldering ruins of a car, which, having stopped at that point when the current gave out, and being deserted by the engineer and conductor, who were compelled to fly for their own safety, had been set fire to and burned.

This same thing had been done in other parts of the city. On all the lines affected by the severance of the wires groups of masked men had passed along the tracks—evidently having been in hiding until the moment arrived—and driven the employés away from the standing cars, which were then entered, and, oil having been poured over the seats and floor, set in flames.

It had not been until towards dawn that Harrington had been able to lie down on a lounge in the office at the barns and snatch a few hours' rest, and it was well on in the forenoon, having had no time on rising to read the paper, that he had heard of Mrs. Masson's injury. He had been at the house at noon when Annie arrived, and then returned to his post of duty. At the time of Mrs. Masson's death he was present at a conference of officers of the street-railway company, at which a formal protest had been drafted for presentation to the mayor, calling upon him to more fully protect the property of the citizens, and demanding that, if the city or county government was unable to maintain order, the governor of the State should be appealed to to call out the militia. A petition was also drawn up to be circulated among the best citizens for signature, in which it was set forth that, the city being practically in a state of riot, and the municipal administration and the officers of the county totally unable to maintain the peace, the signers prayed the governor to exert the powers reposed in him for use in such emergencies.

Between seven and eight o'clock, when Harrington had returned to the barns, he heard of Mrs. Masson's death. His informant gave him no details—only the news that she had died. As soon as he was able Harrington hastened to the house, where he found the two girls sitting with the faithful Weatherfield in the dining-room, while through the open doors was dimly visible in the darkness the outline of the white sheet-covered cot whereon the dead woman lay. For an hour, or as long as he dared to remain away from the barns, Harrington stayed, and they talked in subdued tones of the

dead woman, of the inquest which was to be held, and of the
funeral.   But none of the other three (for the girls had told
Weatherfield) had the heart to mention to Harrington the
dying woman's last reference to himself.

When he left, Jennie accompanied him to the street door,
and they stood together in the hall for many minutes, talking very tenderly, and each feeling that they were closer together now than they had ever been before.

As the door closed behind him and he descended the steps
Harrington saw that even at this hour of the night two figures stood across the way gazing at the now notorious
house.   Somewhere farther up the street he heard the voice
of a newsboy hawking the "special extra" edition of an evening paper.   Harrington tried to catch what he said, but failed,
and wondered what the "special extra" might be about.
Could he have distinguished the syllables, what he would have
heard was : "All about the Fourth Street murder!   The dying woman discloses the name of the assassin !"

But the boy's voice grew fainter, and Harrington, ignorant
of the accusation which hung over him and which was being
thus publicly shouted in the streets, buttoned his coat around
him—for the night was cold—and started for the barns.

He had walked but a few steps when he saw coming round
the corner and advancing along the sidewalk to meet him a
body of men, some twenty or thirty in number.   He knew that
they must be strikers, for no others paraded the city thus in
crowds together.   What he did not know was that they had
just come from the headquarters, where for two hours past they
had listened to Wollmer's fiery harangues and the still more
reckless utterances of his subordinates.   They were coming
full of wrath and fanaticism, as on a pilgrimage, to gaze upon
the house where the deed had been done—where their champion and friend had been murdered for their sakes.

For a moment Harrington meditated crossing the street to
avoid them, but it was too late to do this without attracting
their attention.   It was best to go boldly on, and trust to
passing them without being recognized.

The men advanced in twos and threes, talking loudly as
they came.   Harrington moved to the outer edge of the side-

walk to give them space to pass. Some six or seven went by without a sign of recognition. Suddenly Harrington heard a voice say :

"That's him, boys!"

He caught his name mentioned, and an instant later a blow from a fist, striking him on the ear, sent him staggering from the sidewalk to the road. Before he could recover himself they were around him. He fought as best he could, striking out right and left, but they were too many, and he was quickly overpowered and was held, panting and hatless, while fists were shaken in his face and the air was filled with curses.

"Quiet, boys! Let's take him across the bridge," said a voice as of authority.

The clamor of angry voices ceased, and the men with one accord fell into their places around him, and he found himself being pushed forward at a rapid gait in the direction suggested.

The first settlement of the city had been on the edge of what had at some time been a river of considerable size. It was now shrunken to a narrow and sluggish stream, but the rest of the wide bed of the old torrent was occupied with railway tracks, which found here a broad right of way of nature's making into the heart of the city. As the town grew it had spread northward away from the river-bank, and what had once been the centre of the young community was now a squalid and unfashionable part of the city. The locality where the Massons lived, as has already been said, was in the older portion of the town, and at a distance of only about a quarter of a mile from where Harrington was captured ran the old river-bed, now chiefly filled with the iron highways, and spanned by a long viaduct supported on iron columns. Many efforts had been made by speculators to induce the town to spread over to the south side of the river, but so far without material success. The low land was all owned by the railway companies, who had covered it with tracks and yards wherein the freight-cars stood in rows, with round-houses and other buildings scattered here and there. Beyond the territory occupied by the railways were

a number of houses of the meaner sort, some of the less poor
of which were occupied by railway hands—the majority, however, constituting what was known as "the Diggings," an uninviting settlement composed chiefly of Italians who lived
sordid and lawless lives, and made their bread by the pursuit
of all those miscellaneous and seemingly precarious avoca-
tions to which the members of that nationality chiefly devote
themselves in our American cities. Beyond the Diggings
again rose what were called the Bluffs — high ground on
which was located a charitable institution or two, but which
was chiefly wild and rocky, sparsely clothed with patches of
scrub-oak and sumach, as the white men had first found it.

If once his captors had him in the desolate regions across
the river, Harrington knew that his case would be desperate.
The mere fact that they set themselves thus resolutely to
take him there showed that they meditated some more deliberate and formidable vengeance than the hap-hazard beating which they could easily have inflicted in the street where
they met him. What form this vengeance might take Harrington did not care to think. The immediate business in
hand was to prevent, if possible, their carrying him across the
bridge. But meanwhile they made rapid progress towards
it, and he, in the centre of the solid squad of men, was power-
less to resist or seriously to retard their march.

He hoped that they might meet a policeman; but with
every rod that they covered the chance of that grew less.
At one crossing Harrington saw a man passing some yards
ahead and he called to him for help. But a fist struck him
in the mouth, and the stranger evidently thought that it was
not his duty to interfere in so unpromising an affair.

At length they reached the bridge, and as their feet left
the silence of the solid road for the resonant structure of
the viaduct Harrington's heart sank in him. The men, too,
seemed to think that the beginning of the end had come,
and, more certain of their prey, walked in looser ranks, while
only one man retained a hold on the prisoner's shoulder.
There was one last hope, and only one. For the first two
hundred yards of the viaduct there were railway tracks beneath. Then came the shrunken river, some fifty yards in

width, and then more tracks. The viaduct was nowhere at any great elevation—not more than thirty-five feet in the centre; but to leap from it to the tracks would be certain death. Where the river ran, with some two or three feet of water to break the fall, it would be less dangerous. His guards had apparently little fear now of any attempt to escape, and there was, he told himself, just a chance that by a rush he might, when the water was reached, succeed in getting to the side of the viaduct and jumping into the stream below—at least, it was worth trying. So, looking out of the corners of his eyes, he watched between the files of men on either side for a glimpse of the water in the darkness. The one hand which still held him was on his left shoulder. He would make his dash, therefore, to the right. At last dimly through the night he caught a gleam of the water not far ahead. Forty paces more, he said, and the time would have come. And he counted the paces stealthily. Thirty-seven—thirty-eight—thirty-nine—forty! As his left foot struck the road at the fortieth pace he sprang to the right, dashed between the lines of his captors, and, before they realized what had happened, gained the side of the viaduct. Holding to the edge of the parapet with his hands he flung his feet over, landing on a narrow ledge on the outer side.

Even as he was in the air, however, he saw to his dismay that it was not water beneath him. At two points in the width of the river the columns supporting the viaduct rose out of the water. Around the base of each was a pile of rock, to which the water was constantly making additions of stones and pieces of timber. It was immediately over one of these columns that Harrington found himself, and directly below, instead of the friendly river, was a forbidding surface of hard and jagged stone, stretching some ten or twelve feet on either side of the base of the column, and perhaps twice as far down the stream. He could not let himself drop, as he had intended, straight down, but must leap to one side or the other. The moment's hesitation made necessary by this discovery, when he was deciding which way to jump, was enough for the strikers to collect their thoughts, and already they were around him again. Even as he bent his knees for the spring, hands reached over the parapet and clutched him by the arm and shoulder. Wrenching his right side free, he faced his enemies, and, using his right hand as a club, endeavored to break their hold of his left arm. He struck with the fury of despair. As soon as a hand was knocked off, it found a new hold; but at last came a moment when he was free. He snatched his arm away and leaned backward, already too far gone to recover his balance if he wished to, still fending off the hands that reached after him.

At this moment one of the strikers thrust his foot through the railing of the parapet. The heavy boot struck Harrington's ankles, forcing both his feet off the narrow ledge. The spring which was to have sent him clear of the rocks below spent itself helplessly in the air; and with one sharp cry he dropped—dropped straight down.

The men above leaned over and peered into the darkness. They heard him strike heavily, with a grinding of the stones below, and as if, with nothing to break the fall, his whole body had met the rocks at once. Dimly they could see the black mass where he lay close by the water's edge, motionless. For a minute they stood and gazed, and then turned and made their way back in silence cityward.

XXI

IN THE VALLEY OF SHADOW

To the most zealous and earnest reformers, it may be presumed, there are times when their beloved cause seems colorless and futile. We know that to the holiest of old there came at some point in their careers seasons of sore temptation, when the powers of darkness appeared, transmogrified, and by all cunning wiles that they could muster sought to lure virtue from its path—on a high mountain, or under the sacred Bodhi-tree, or in the study at Wittenberg. In these latter days the imps come not incarnate, but chiefly in subjective forms, disguised as toothache and indigestion and catarrh, whereby the world looks jaundiced; or, perhaps, a loved one ceases to smile, and the rose-color dies out of even the cause itself; or, bitterest of all, the reformer finds treason among his own disciples and fellow-workers and those who dip in the dish with him. Then it is that the lean devil of desolation and despair sits by the heart which aches, feeling itself alone in a world of fraud.

Something of all these malign influences combined to harass Horace Marsh on that morning when he arrived by the same train as brought Annie Masson home. He was not well. The strain of constant travelling, irregular hours, poor food, and of speaking three or four times a week, was telling upon him. The work—any work—was light and easy so long as it was done both for its own sake and for hers. Then all effort was doubly inspired. But now that Jessie's face was turned from him—since that bitter evening and her failure to reply to his note—one, and he wondered if it were not the chief, incentive to labor was withdrawn. He still believed in the work which he was doing—or, rather, in the need of such work; but many things, little things individually, but mighty in the mass, had on this last trip come to him to make him feel terribly alone in his ministry.

Perhaps the echoes of what Judge Jessel and Major Bartop had said disquieted him—as to the present campaign not being one on party lines, but only a conflict of the good against the bad; of law and order on the one side against anarchy and crime on the other. Certain it was that even in the small towns in which he had been speaking he had been struck by the fact that it was not that portion of the population whom he would have chosen for his fellow-workers that came to hear him speak and to meet him at the hotels. The feeling of which he had been so keenly conscious when standing in the lobby of the Boston House at Jackson, the sense of an essential lack of sympathy between himself and the men who gathered round him, came to him now again and again. He had grown to expect it, to regard it as necessary. His audiences, indeed, listened to him attentively. They were carried away by the fervor of his oratory, and while he talked stood with him on his level. But he could not but discover that it was he, and not any force within themselves, that uplifted them. They did not of their own prompting seek the higher altitudes, but, as soon as the spell of his influence was removed, dropped back into a less rarefied atmosphere—an air thick with the clammy vapors of petty partisan politics and small local issues. Their very congratulations were awkward, as when one totally ignorant of music seeks to compliment a master on the excellence of his execution, and fears lest he should blunder into misnomers. Their praise halted, not from insincerity so much as diffidence, and they hastened to take refuge on the more familiar ground of the local and the concrete, burrowing into the labyrinthine darknesses of party intrigue, in which Marsh himself was lost. Above all, they spoke of labor questions and the strike with an assumption of his sympathy with the strikers which perpetually affronted him. More than once on such occasions he had replied sharply, in a strain which called forth surprised rejoinders from his auditors, to the effect that they had supposed that the cause of the strike was the cause of the party, or that they thought that, being a Democrat, he was, of course, an enemy of corporate capital.

The news in the paper that morning seemed to be particularly distasteful. It was evident that the strikers were growing daily more bitter. In spite of the attempt of the party organ to make light of the outrages of the preceding evening, the list of acts of violence perpetrated was a long and unpleasant one. Sandwiched in between other paragraphs relating to the strike appeared an interview with General Harter, in which he expressed himself, without attempting to condone individual crimes, as an ardent sympathizer with the men. Then the sight of Blakely's name, in connection with the baby, for some reason irritated Horace. Finally, there was the news of the calamity in the Masson household, with its bearing upon his friend, and Marsh's blood boiled when he read the long interview with Wollmer on the subject (the reporter had said that Wollmer would " talk all night "), filled with covert innuendoes against Harrington. Without venturing to accuse him directly, the labor leader had laid great stress upon the ill-feeling which had existed between Mrs. Masson and the electrician, and had recurred to the subject again and again in the course of his talk.

On arriving at his office the first thing that Marsh did was to go to the telephone and inquire for Harrington at the street-railway company's barns. The electrician, however, was, as we have already seen, at that moment at the Fourth Street house awaiting Annie's home-coming. Determining to endeavor to catch Harrington again later in the day to express his sympathy with him, Marsh repaired to his partner's office, as was his custom, to render an account of his trip.

The General received him with grandiose cordiality, and Marsh did his best to bear himself with good grace. From conversation about Horace's experiences they drifted to talking of the political outlook in general, and thence to the strike.

" I see an interview with you in the paper this morning," Horace remarked. " I don't know whether you said all that is ascribed to you, but, if so, I am afraid I can't agree with you."

" Well," the other replied, cautiously, " an interviewer never gets things quite as one would like them, you know. But you mean that you do not agree with me in my general attitude on the strike ?"

" Yes," said Horace, decisively. " I do not think the men are right. They deserve to be beaten."

" Well, in these cases "—and the General assumed his senatorial air—" one must look at general principles rather than at details of a particular controversy. There may be *minutiæ* in which the action of the men has been open to criticism ; but in the long run, and on abstract grounds, the cause of the men is the cause of the right. I have not in mind so much Mr. Holt and the street-railway company, or of Wollmer and his men—the question of a few cents an hour or of an individual labor organization is immaterial. It is the broad principle which we in public life must consider. Undoubtedly the right position for myself and for the party is one of advocacy of the masses ; not only on grounds of policy, but on grounds of conviction, and for the sake of eternal truth and justice. There is no one who feels that more deeply than yourself, Marsh."

" That may be," he replied ; " but the names of Truth and Justice, and of every eternal principle of right, can easily be, and constantly are, used to cloak individual and incidental wrongs. The cause of the masses is not going to be advanced by the advocacy of the strikers' present claims, if those claims are wrong."

" When we descend to the particular," rejoined the General, pompously, " it is difficult, as in this present quarrel, for outsiders like you and myself to decide which party is right and which is wrong. There are many influences to be considered. A seeming temporary wrong may be only one facet, as it were, of a permanent right, as we should discover if we could see all sides of it. The best we can do, it seems to me, is to take a stand in line with our general convictions —of course within certain limits," he added.

" And it seems to me that those limits have pretty nearly been reached," remarked Horace, " when it comes to cutting wires and beating men nearly to death."

The General did not reply, and Horace retired to his own room, where he was glad to find Barry awaiting him. From him he might learn some news of Miss Holt.

The two friends shook hands cordially.

" I guessed you'd be in about now," Barry said, " and came round to ask if you had seen about Mrs. Masson in the paper, and your friend Harrington."

" Yes, I have. It's pretty hard on the girl, isn't it ?"

" Did you read what that man Wollmer said ? What do you think of it ?"

" Wollmer is a cur," Horace replied. " But how are your affairs going ? How's Miss Caley ?"

" Oh, she's all right," replied Barry, but in a tone which implied that that lady's condition was a matter of entire indifference to him.

" Why, what's the matter ?" Horace asked in surprise, responding to the manner rather than the matter of his friend's words.

" Well "— and Barry hesitated — " I don't much like to talk about it, but she isn't quite the girl that I took her to be. There's a fellow called Jones—Fred, she calls him— whom she knew at home in Chicago. I opened a locket of hers last night and found his portrait in it—wearing it round her neck, you know. And she got mad and said—oh ! she said all sorts of things. It appears that she gets letters from him every day. Damn Jones !" he added, moodily.

" I'm sorry," said Marsh. He felt that the words were inadequate ; but it was not a situation wherein sympathy was easy to offer. And, after all, it was difficult to take Barry's love affairs quite seriously. " How's Miss Holt ?" he asked, after a pause, to change the subject.

" She was sick last night up at the Bartops' "—and Barry spoke spitefully, as if he took pleasure in yielding bad news in his present mood. " Blakely took her home."

" Was she seriously ill ?"

" Oh, I don't know — fainted or something. Anyway, Blakely hustled her into his carriage and took her home— did it as if he owned her," he added, wickedly. As a matter of fact, Barry's knowledge of the method of Miss Holt's departure was of the slenderest. He felt that he was unfair and repented. "But I don't think it was anything much. Blakely came back again soon afterwards."

On the whole, Barry's visit did not contribute appreciably to the cheerfulness of the day for Horace. All things seemed to conspire to make him miserable. Chief, perhaps, among the matters which gave him uneasiness — more persistently present even than the estrangement with Jessie — was an undefined dissatisfaction, which he could not ignore, with the political outlook. He was glad that he had but little more speaking to do—three more nights only, and all three in town. The committee might, of course, call upon him to fill a vacancy or two; but he resolved if the vacancy was in some outside place to do his best to evade it. The next evening he was to speak in Columbus Hall, where he would probably have the largest audience that had listened to him yet. After four days of respite he was to appear twice more on successive evenings in different parts of town. Those were all his "dates" until election.

On this day he had to be much out of the office, in consultation with a fellow-lawyer. Returning late in the afternoon to the Metropolitan Block, he met Sullivan just leaving General Harter.

"Hey there!" cried the Irishman. "It's back again ye are, flittin' into the middle o' these troublous times like that onaisy pelican a-ridin' into the heart o' the storm. The plot thickens, me boy, an' there is quare times ahead of us. An' the Gineral tells me this Mrs. Masson was a friend of yours."

"Hardly that," said Marsh. "I know her daughter slightly. Harrington, you know, is one of my best friends, and he is engaged to her."

"An' I gather by the papers that there's no love lost between Harrington and Mr. Wollmer"—the Irishman always put a "Mr." before the labor leader's name.

"Oh! that whelp Wollmer—" began Horace, hotly; but Sullivan interrupted him.

"Aisy, me lad, aisy!" he said; "that same Mr. Wollmer is one o' the pillars o' the parrty — an' will be till election.

Wait two weeks, me boy, an' then maybe there are some others that 'll be wid ye."

Horace liked the Irishman. His code of political ethics might be peculiar, but, at least, he made no pretensions to be other than he was. In the ordinary way of politics, and to advance the interests of " the party " (which Sullivan always spoke of, as it were, with a capital " P "), he would lie unhesitatingly, bribe without scruple, and make use, in fact, of whatever weapons the corruptness or gullibility of human nature might put in his hands. In party matters he did not shrink from doing " evil that good may come." But in a personal affair Marsh would have trusted him implicitly. He would never, according to his own light, be dishonorably dishonest. Open-handed he was and generous without stint, and loyal to his friends. The mere blunt strength of his nature, coarse and brutal though it might seem, had its attraction.

It was of Sullivan that Horace was chiefly thinking when, as he sat disconsolate in his room that evening, he said to Barry :

" It is a good deal easier, after all, for a man to be respected in the churches than it is to be respected in the saloons. I do not mean to say, of course, that the best men are not in the churches, or to deny that the crowd around the saloons is, as a whole, the worst element in our population. But to stand well with that element a man must possess certain good qualities which he need not have to hold high place in a church. There is a certain type of man—the worst, in my opinion, that God makes — slinking, hypocritical, and cowardly, who can come to be a church-warden and to have the handling of parish funds, yet who could never get credit for fifteen cents' worth at a bar.

" ' He wa'n't no saint, but at judgment I'd take my chance with Jim
Along o' some pious gentlemen who wouldn't shake hands with him !'

There's a good deal in that. It is pretty hard to put one's self outside the moral environment — the ' climate of opinion ' — of one's own immediate day and community ; but if one could look at men with the eye of eternal Truth, I

wonder how far his judgment would coincide with the con-
ventions and convictions of the times.   In other stages of
society the recklessness and animal courage—the brutality,
even — which are the chief characteristics of the saloon element to-day, were high virtues.   They went a long way towards the making of a knight ; for I suspect that the chivalry
and courtesy which we ascribe to those gentlemen—the man-
ners which were

> " ' . . . The fruit
> Of loyal nature and of noble mind '

are chiefly the additions of the romancers and scribes of a
later day.   The average knight was a pretty coarse beast—
according to our ideas.   And according to his ideas, and the
ideas of the world of his day, the qualities which make a
man 'respectable' with us caused him then to be buffeted
and spat upon and spanked with the flat of a sword.   There
is still lurking in the bottom of the hearts of all of us a certain sympathy with those ideas.   Is that sympathy only a
relic of the brute in us, not quite civilized away, or is it a
smouldering spark of a higher than human nature, a fragment
of omniscience, which has not altogether been stifled ?   Is it
better or worse than our current code of morality ?   After all,
' respectability ' is only a negation—a lack of certain attributes.   Are those attributes inherently evil, or is it only that
society — a most ephemeral society — says that they are evil
in its cowardice ?   Is it better—better, I mean, in the view of
all time—to have wine mixed in one's veins and chew tobacco
and attend prize-fights, or to be a man whose 'blood is very
snow-broth '—and to take an interest in Sunday-schools ?"

"I give it up," said Barry.   "But I think I rather like a
thorough-going 'tough.'   I know that there are respectable
members of society whom I would willingly hit with a brick—
but for the police."

It was the first evening for a long time which Barry had
not spent in Miss Caley's society, and cynicism and misan-
thropy suited him.   So the two sat and croaked at each other,
in forlorn antiphony, like two birds of evil omen, far into the
night.

Horace, hungering for tidings of Miss Holt, and not daring to go and seek them for himself, had endeavored to persuade Barry that he ought to call on Miss Caley that evening, but he had exhausted his powers of sophistry in vain. It rested with her, Barry said, to make the first advances; for that matter, he didn't care whether they ever came together or not. Which was palpably disingenuous. The best that Horace could do with his obstinacy was to wring from him a half-promise that, if no news came from Miss Caley on the morrow and there were no tidings of Miss Holt, he would call on the following evening—merely as a matter of common courtesy to inquire after Jessie's health, Marsh said. On that evening Horace himself would be holding forth at Columbus Hall.

During the conversation Marsh opened his heart rather unreservedly. His love for Miss Holt had never before been openly talked over between them, but, as we have seen on a former occasion, Barry was not blind to the situation. Now he listened while Marsh told him of Jessie's behavior on that occasion when Barry had been so absorbed with Miss Caley on the sofa; and Barry vowed that he had seen nothing of it, and opined that his friend was a victim of his own imagination. But Horace told him of the note which had not been answered; and the best that Barry could offer in the way of comfort was a banal suggestion that the letter had miscarried. Horace spoke of the article about his speech at Jackson and of his note to her father; but to all of that he attached little importance. It was more likely that some common acquaintance had poisoned her mind against him. And so they united in abuse of Blakely. But whenever Barry spoke of Blakely, he meant Fred Jones.

18

XXII

It was not until late in the afternoon of the following day that Marsh heard of what had befallen Harrington.

For some hours after striking the rocks the latter had lain stunned and insensible. The first sensation which came with returning consciousness was that of intense cold. He must, he thought, have left a window too wide open, and the bedclothes had fallen from him in his sleep. When he realized that he lay in the open air, the discovery puzzled him. Moving his right hand, he felt the jagged edge of a large stone, and then his fingers dipped into the water. The sudden movement, as he withdrew his hand from the cold contact, sent an excruciating pain through his sides, so that he caught his breath quickly. And all at once memory returned.

He lay partly on his left side, his face turned eastward towards the viaduct, under and beyond the black shadow of which the sky already showed the greenish-gray tinge of approaching dawn. Behind him the water lapped to within a foot of his back. Turning his head slightly, he looked straight upward to where the edge of the viaduct was sharply outlined against the sky—darker here than towards the east—and seeming in this dim light to be lower and scarcely twenty feet above him. How seriously was he injured? he wondered, and endeavored to move; but the pain in his sides and back was acute, and his legs refused to obey him. How much of the pain and numbness was due to injuries and how much to the cold and the roughness of his couch he could not guess. And still the most prominent sensation was that of chill. Another and more determined effort to raise himself from his position resulted in such agony that he sank back again, faint and half-swooning.

For some time he lay so, dimly conscious of external things as the day grew and noises came to him from far away — the barking of dogs, the rumble of an early market-wagon driving overhead, the clanking and banging of railway-cars from where trains were being made up in the distant yards. And it was very cold. Once or twice he tried to shout in answer to some noise which sounded near, but his voice was thin and weak. Small details of his surroundings thrust themselves upon him. He noticed that the paint was cracking off the iron column of the bridge close by him, and thought that the city engineering department ought to discover it and give the metal a new coating. He heard the ripple of the water against the stones, and wondered why, when the flow of the stream was even, the ripple at times should be so much louder than others—almost as if some live thing moved in the water. He had noticed just such inequalities—eddies, presumably—in electric currents.

All at once he became aware of the head and shoulders of a man protruding over the parapet above him and clearly outlined against the sky. It was a policeman, stopping in his deliberate march across the viaduct to lean over and look at the slow water and the dim outlines of the mists below. Harrington could see that it was a policeman by the form of his helmet, and he tried to call. At first his voice would not rise above a whisper, and the head above disappeared. A second or two later it reappeared a few paces farther on. Summoning all his strength, Harrington called again and yet again. The figure above remained motionless. At length a voice answered:

" Who's that, and where are you ?"

" Down here by the water—help !"

" How did you get there ?"

" I fell. Help! Help !"

His voice died, and he was unconscious again. Some time after—how long he could not tell—he heard the same voice again calling, this time from somewhere on his own level. For a long while Harrington heard him call, and vaguely thought that it was very curious that a man should go on shouting like that. Suddenly he grasped the fact that the voice was calling to him, and he answered, but very feebly.

" What's that?" called the voice.

" Help!" Harrington cried. " I'm cold."

" We can't hear you," replied the voice.

How can I help that? thought Harrington, hopelessly. Why did they not come to him, instead of standing over there and asking questions? But it did not matter, and he ceased to attempt to answer them.

The next thing that he was aware of was the splash of oars in the water and men's voices close at hand; then the bumping and crunching of a boat against the loose stones. A moment later two men, policemen both, were leaning over him.

" How did you come here?" asked one.

" I fell over and they pushed me," Harrington said, wearily.

" Who pushed you?"

" Oh, I don't know. I'm cold."

One of the men passed his hands under his shoulders and began to raise him. Harrington felt other hands lifting his legs. But the pain was horrible—intolerable; and, mercifully, he became unconscious once more. He was dimly aware later of renewed pains as he was lifted from the boat, and then recognized mistily that he was in some sort of a wheeled vehicle being driven somewhere.

When next he came to himself it seemed to be mid-day. He was in a room — a large room, very white, with several other beds like that in which he lay — evidently a hospital. He was no longer cold but most delightfully warm, though intense pain was shooting up his legs, and it hurt him to breathe. As he lay the figure of a nurse came silently to his bedside. He smiled at her, and whispered, irrelevantly:

" Thank you so much!"

" Hush!" she said, and laid a soft, cool hand on his forehead. It was very pleasant, and the room grew misty and faded away from him.

When his eyes opened again there were other figures around him. The nurse still stood at his left, and on his right were two men. One held his hand, and Harrington saw, after a while, that it was Superintendent Boon, of the street-railway company.

" How are you, old man ?" Boon asked, cheerily. " Dr. Garcelon here says you will soon be about again."

Harrington could only smile in reply.

"Tell me how it happened," said Boon.

" But don't exert yourself to speak too much," added Dr.
Garcelon.

For some minutes Harrington lay silent while he collected
his thoughts. Then in a voice which was little more than a
whisper, he said:

" They got hold of me—about twenty of 'em—and called me
names.—' Take him across the bridge,' said some one, and they
did.—Nobody came.—Pushed me along till bridge.—Then I
broke away—meant to jump into water—wasn't any water—
so I fought, and then I fell—and somebody pushed my feet and
I went down.—Then policeman came, and it was awfully cold."

He told the tale with difficulty, and with many pauses between sentences; but his auditors understood him.

" Who were they ?" asked the superintendent.

" Just men—strikers."

" Did you know any of them ?"

Harrington shook his head.

" Could you recognize them again ?"

" Perhaps—some—dark," said Harrington, wearily.

" Where was it ?"

" Fourth Street—just leaving Jennie's house."

" Whose house ?"

" Jennie's — Miss Masson, you know — Mrs. Masson's dead,
too."

" That will do," said Dr. Garcelon. " No more talking."

" Just a minute," replied Boon. " Listen here, Harrington,
and see if I have got it straight. Don't speak if I have.
About twenty men, strikers, got hold of you on Fourth Street,
just as you were leaving Miss Masson's house; they abused
you, and some one suggested that they take you across the
bridge. They did so, pushing you along among them. When
you were in the middle of the bridge you broke away and
tried to jump into the water. There was a fight, and some
one shoved your feet from under you and you fell, not into
the water, but on the rocks. Is that right ?"

Harrington nodded.

" What time was it ?"

" About ten o'clock."

Boon and the doctor talked together in low tones for a while, and the former turned to go.

" Good-bye, old man," he said ; " keep your courage up, and you will soon be all right again. The strikers are not going to get away with you." Harrington smiled, and the superintendent continued : " Who would you like to have me tell to come and see you ?"

"Jennie," said the injured man, feebly.

" Miss Masson ?"

Harrington nodded ; and the other went away, bidding him again to keep his courage up.

Then Dr. Garcelon set himself to make further examination of the injuries, during which Harrington was again unconscious. The surgeon found a fracture of one rib, but what internal injuries there might be he could not guess. The right leg was broken above the knee, and the left ankle badly sprained and swollen, as also was his left wrist. Many minor bruises were scattered over his body, and one ugly scalp-wound ran down over his forehead above the left eye. It had been a terrible fall, and even if there were no other injuries than those which appeared on the surface, recovery would at best be a long and tedious process.

Leaving the hospital, the superintendent went at once to the office of the president of the company, and told Mr. Holt the story as he had heard it from Harrington. It was decided that the newspapers had better be informed, and messages were telephoned to the offices of both the afternoon papers, asking them to send reporters up to Mr. Holt's office, as there was interesting news in regard to Harrington.

The fact of Harrington's injury and his present location at the hospital was already known. An outline of the facts—of his having been found by Officer Gleason, and so forth—had been given at the coroner's inquest on Mrs. Masson, which had been in progress for a great part of the day. The announcement had created a decided sensation, and two widely different theories were afloat as to the origin of the accident. According to the theory of Harrington's friends, he had been captured by the strikers, badly hurt, and then thrown insensible from the viaduct. The sympathizers with the men believed that he had himself leaped from the bridge, intending to commit suicide, probably by drowning, to avoid the disgrace of conviction of the murder of Mrs. Masson.

There were a number of witnesses at the inquest whose testimony was listened to eagerly by as many people as could gain admittance. On the general questions as to the manner of Mrs. Masson's death, both Dr. Butler and Dr. Garcelon inclined to the belief that it was accidental, caused probably by a fall in which her head had struck against some sharp, hard substance—perhaps the jutting angle of the mantel, in close proximity to which she was found lying. Against the theory of accident, however, were, firstly, the fact of the open front door, and, secondly, the deceased's last words, with their direct reference to Harrington.

In regard to the exact form of those words the testimony was divergent. Wollmer was confident that she had distinctly said: "Why did he come here to murder me?" He was positive that he was not mistaken. He told, at considerable length, of the unfriendly relations which had existed between Harrington and the dead woman, and cited various instances from his recollection of conversations which he had had with her, in which Mrs. Masson had confidentially expressed not only dislike, but bodily fear, of the electrician.

Annie Masson's testimony was given nervously and in tears. She did not believe that Harrington was guilty, but, pressed for a reason, only said that he *could* not do it. She spoke reluctantly of the ill-will existing between him and her mother, but her evidence was only the more convincing by reason of her apparent reluctance in giving it. Her memory of Mrs. Masson's last words was confused and vague. She could not swear that Wollmer's version of them was not accurate.

Jennie was cool and collected, though very white. She was sure that Harrington could never have made his way to Fourth Street and left again before she arrived. She described her parting from him, her trip to the house, and her discovery of the body. Much time was spent in the endeavor to arrive at the exact number of minutes which it had taken her, after leaving the opera-house, to reach her home. Her recollection of those accusatory words was clearer than her sister's. She swore positively that there was no mention of "murder," or any word like it. Her mother, she was aware, had never liked Harrington, but she did not believe that he had ever entertained the smallest ill-will towards her. She recalled various scraps of conversation with him, in which Mrs. Masson had been discussed — among others, that which had taken place before her portrait, when Harrington had laughingly suggested the possibility of Mrs. Masson's taking Wollmer for a third husband. As she related the incident she looked at Wollmer, who flushed angrily. She told of her step-mother's growing eccentricity, as shown particularly in her mysterious references to the good which was to come to them from General Harter's election. The sympathy of the audience seemed to be with her while she spoke; but then she was in love with Harrington, and could hardly be expected to see things dispassionately.

Tom Weatherfield was called, and expressed a clumsy but earnest conviction in Harrington's innocence.

On the subject of the wording of Mrs. Masson's dying sentences, both the medical men were disposed to support Jennie's testimony, but, with professional caution, each declined to swear that the words could not have been as Wollmer said. They were both strongly inclined to believe that the word "murder" had not been used. Dr. Butler reiterated his opinion that the injury must have been caused not later than ten o'clock; but he could not swear that he might not be mistaken.

The engineer and conductor of the car on which Harrington had started from the opera-house testified as to the time of the stoppage of the current, and to his leaving the car to walk.

One of the men from the barns gave evidence as to the time of his arrival there.

The clerk at the drug-store from which Harrington telephoned was on hand, and told of that incident.

The policeman, Williams, described his arrival at the house, having heard Miss Masson's screams when he was on the beat in the next street; and the detective spoke at length of the position of the body and the appearance of the room, with the entire absence of any indication of a struggle or of the presence of any other person in the house at the time that the injury was inflicted.

It was nearly six o'clock in the evening before the jury returned its verdict. Some members of the body, sympathizers with the strike, were in favor of simply saying that the deceased came to her death by a blow or blows given with an instrument unknown in the hands of Charles Harrington. Others did not believe Harrington guilty. Finally a compromise was effected. The verdict set forth that the testimony as to the manner of death was inconclusive, and the jury was at a loss to decide whether it was the result of accident or of an act of violence. The leading points in the evidence were gone over, and it was pointed out that there was much to support a suspicion that Charles Harrington was the cause of death. Meanwhile, however, as there was great uncertainty as to the possibility of Harrington being present at the house at the time when the injury appeared to have been inflicted, and inasmuch, further, as the said Harrington was at that time understood to be himself suffering from bodily injuries of such a nature as would keep him in the hospital for at least some weeks, so that there was no danger of said Harrington evading the arm of justice when he was needed, the jury deemed it best to declare that the deceased came to her death from causes unknown. The police department was urged to use its best efforts to obtain further evidence upon the subject, which, together with the testimony given at this inquest, should at the proper time be laid before the prosecuting attorney, who would then use his judgment as to the course to be pursued.

Altogether, the verdict was as reasonable as such documents commonly are, and no more clumsy than many which are on record.

Long before the inquest was concluded Jennie had left, and was at Harrington's bedside. He had lain unconscious through nearly the whole afternoon. Once only he opened his eyes, and seeing who it was who held his hand in hers, smiled contentedly, and passed again into insensibility.

During the afternoon Marsh had sat in his office. Having been unable on the preceding day to obtain connection with Harrington over the telephone, he had written him a note of condolence and sympathy, placing his services at his friend's disposal if there was any way in which he could be of use. From the morning papers he had learned of Mrs. Masson's death and of her dying words, which appeared as Wollmer had rendered them. Horace knew that there was a mistake somewhere; Harrington was incapable of such an action. But he waited anxiously for news from the inquest, which was in progress. When the carrier came into his office and tossed the afternoon paper on his desk, he took it eagerly, and spread it before him to read the report of the inquest.

The first words which caught his eye were in large black type at the head of a column: "Harrington Hurt. The Captain has a mysterious fall off the Seventh Street viaduct." Reading on, Marsh learned of his friend's accident, not only as it had been reported at the inquest, but in the words in which Superintendent Boon had given Harrington's own account of it in Mr. Holt's office.

From that he turned to the account of the inquest, which was still unfinished when the paper had gone to press. But he read no further than Wollmer's testimony. "The hound!" he said to himself, between his clinched teeth, "to dare to talk so of such a man as Harrington!" when Harrington himself was lying bruised and mutilated — killed, perhaps — by Wollmer's own lawless followers.

He looked at his watch. It was half-past five. He was due at Columbus Hall at eight. There would be time enough to drive out to the hospital and back, if he hurried with his dinner and his dressing. So, sending one of his clerks out for a cab, he hastily put away his papers and left the office.

Jennie was at Harrington's side when Marsh arrived, and rose quietly to greet him. They had only met once before, but their common interest in the injured man made them friends.

"He is unconscious?" Horace asked. She nodded. "He has only opened his eyes once since I came."

"Do you know what the prospect is?"

"He is very badly hurt—one leg broken and one rib. The doctor does not know if there are any serious internal injuries. If not, he thinks he will get well again." Tears welled from her eyes as she spoke.

"Do you know how it happened?"

"The nurse told me something."

Horace had the evening paper in the pocket of his overcoat. He took it out, and handed it to her, with his finger on Boon's account of the accident.

"Have you seen that?"

She had not. The nurse had given her the substance of what Harrington had told the superintendent; with that exception, Jennie knew nothing but what had been contained in the brief announcement at the inquest. She took the paper and moved away from the bed to read it, while Marsh leaned over the injured man and touched his hair caressingly. Having read the article, Jennie handed back the paper, the tears running down her cheeks.

"You came here from the inquest?" Marsh whispered. She nodded.

"Does he know anything about it—about the suspicions?"

"I think not," she replied. "He was at the house just before this happened, and we did not tell him anything of what mother had said. Unless these men told him something, I don't suppose he knows."

"All the better," Horace said. "Of course it will be kept from him."

Before leaving, Horace assured Jennie of his sympathy, and of his desire to be of any service that he could, in words which made her very grateful. Here was at least one friend who assumed her lover to be innocent of the crime with which he was charged without stopping to question or to weigh the evidence. Horace explained that he was obliged to leave now, as he had to speak that evening; but he would return in the morning, and also call at her house to offer his services to her. She thanked him. Mr. Weatherfield, she said, was very kind in helping them with all the necessary arrangements for her mother's funeral; but she would let Horace know if he could do anything.

It was nearly seven o'clock when Horace entered his cab again at the hospital door, telling the driver to go to a restaurant which lay on the way to his rooms. Here Marsh ate a hasty meal, which could scarcely be dignified with the name of dinner, and hurried home to dress.

All the way from the hospital his thoughts were of his injured friend and of the double outrage to which he had been subjected—the bodily assault which had brought the physical injuries under which he was suffering, and the greater cruelty of the suspicions which Wollmer had caused to be directed towards him. Horace's heart was filled with indignation against the labor leader and the lawlessness of the men. That afternoon in his office Marsh had signed the petition to the governor of the State, though General Harter had refused to do so, and now, under the spur of these new evidences of the malignancy and blood-thirstiness of Wollmer and his followers, his sense of justice cried shame upon the city government that suffered such things to be. Ugly threats, moreover, were being made by the strikers that the members of other labor organizations would be "called out"—organizations which had no connection either with the steel works or the street-railway company, and whose members had no grievance against their respective employers. The injustice of the tyranny which could compel men who were working peacefully and contentedly to throw up their positions and resign the means of livelihood of themselves and their families outraged Marsh's sense of right. A quarrel between a certain number of employés under one employer and that employer might be legitimate; but when the quarrel was taken up by "sympathy" by other classes of employés, and it became a fight against society, this was at least a conspiracy in restraint of trade, and came measurably near to insurrection.

He hoped that the governor would be compelled to respond to the petition of the citizens. He almost hoped that if the troops were called out their presence would, as the strikers predicted, precipitate open riots, that the lawless element of the city might be taught a lesson which they would not soon forget.

There might be a superficial inconsistency between these

feelings and his public attitude as a champion of the masses.
But behind this inconsistency lay truth. As he had told
General Harter that morning, the cause of the masses or of
labor was not to be advanced by encouraging men to do wrong.

These thoughts boiled within him as he dressed, and he
thanked Heaven that he had not at the outset made the mistake of professing any sympathy with the strike. He gave
little thought now to the speech which he was to make that
evening. With experience he had gained courage. Above
all, that night at Jackson had taught him that he need have no
fear, however ill-prepared he might be, of finding lack of words
to express his thoughts when the moment came. His theme,
indeed, was usually the same, but each time that he took it up
he shaped it into new forms and clothed it in fresh phrases.
Some accidental collocation of words in one of his own sentences would suggest to his mind new imagery, in presenting
which to his audience he found himself led into untried paths
which he illuminated as he trod them with illustration and
metaphor.

Columbus Hall was situated but a short distance from the
rooms where Marsh and Barry lived, and when Horace was
dressed he found that there remained abundance of time. He
was on the point of leaving when Barry entered, returning
from dining at the club. Marsh asked him if he remembered
his promise to call that evening upon Miss Holt.

"I am going right up there," said Barry. "This is to be a
call of state, so I am going early."

Horace was anxious not to appear selfish, but he implored
his friend to remember his errand.

"If she will not talk to me," he said, "at least make her
tell you what is the matter. You may be able to help in
some way, and I know you will if you can. I can hardly tell
you how much it means to me, old fellow. It seems that
everything else in life is so black just now. I doubt if I
should keep sane in this condition much longer. Remember
that I shall be thinking of you all the evening. No matter
what I may be saying to those men, my thoughts are with
you and her. I am going to believe that you are succeeding,
and I shall talk fifty times better for it."

"I will succeed if I can," Barry said ; "but I wish I could be there and hear you talk.   I may get in later, in time to hear you perorate."

Twenty minutes later Marsh was bowing before an audience which filled every seat, above and below, in the great hall.

XXIII

HORACE PUTS HIMSELF ON RECORD

BARRY had been accustomed of late to inquire for "the ladies" when calling at the Holt mansion. On this occasion he asked with dignity if Miss Holt was at home. Whatever surprise Thomas may have felt at the unusual formula, no evidence of it was visible in his imperturbable face as he replied that she was.

Entering the sitting-room, the visitor found Miss Holt and Miss Willerby only. Neither by word nor manner did he imply that the existence of any third person was of the smallest importance to him.

"Miss Caley is not well," said Miss Holt, as soon as the party was seated; "she had a headache, and was not able to come down to dinner."

"I'm sorry," said Barry, in a tone of supreme indifference; "but how are you yourself, Miss Holt? You were not well the evening before last. Has it all passed?"

"Oh yes, thank you! It was nothing—only feminine foolishness, I suspect," she replied.

There had, in truth, been no return of the indisposition of that evening. Perhaps the violent counter-irritation of the scene with Blakely had operated favorably upon her system— just as there are cases of apparent authenticity wherein officers have left their beds when seriously ill to lead their troops into battle, and have found themselves at the end of the hard-fought day cured. Thoroughly worn out, moreover, she had slept that night as she had not slept for weeks. Scarcely awaking to drink a cup of tea and eat a piece of toast at breakfast-time, she had slept on dreamlessly till noon. It was rest—rest both of mind and body—that she had needed, and the twelve good hours of slumber were excellent medicine.

Some flowers and a note, short and carefully worded but
ardent, were brought to her from Blakely at the luncheon-
table. The note did not affect her, and the flowers she handed
in the open box to Miss Willerby, with the indifferent comment:

"Pretty, aren't they?"

They were pretty—pretty enough to rave over. But when
Miss Willerby returned the box, Jessie merely passed it to
Thomas, saying:

"Just put them in water somewhere, please."

Sitting after luncheon in the drawing-room listlessly, with a
book which she was not reading in her lap, she let her thoughts
go back over that passionate scene which had occurred in this
same room the evening before. It seemed much longer ago;
and she looked curiously at the mantel on which they had been
leaning and at the lounge. In her present healthier condition
she could study the episode critically. What was it, she wondered, that had brought her to her senses at that moment?
With the mood which had preceded the awakening, in which
she had permitted so much, she believed, looking back upon
it now, that she could honestly tell herself that Blakely's personality had little or nothing to do. If it had been any one
else? she asked herself. But there was no one else whom it
could conceivably have been; so the question was fruitless.
To the extent that he had known so well how to handle himself so as not to break in upon the spell which held her, to that
extent it was he—the individual he—to whom she had yielded.
But the spell itself was not of his own weaving, but of her own
sickness. If she had not recovered when she did, had he had
but a little more time, how far his power would have asserted
itself and held her — that was another question. He himself
had said: "You would not then have thrown me off so easily." But it was a question which she preferred not to consider.

And what was it that had come to her rescue? Sitting there
in the dreamy languor of the silent afternoon and seeming to
see again, not without some stirring of her blood, his eyes as
he had leaned over her, she knew what it was. Something in
those eyes as they met hers had, vaguely through the mist,

recalled to her mind the words of Mrs. Tisserton : " He is like
some sort of an evil god ;" and also the words which followed :
" I pity the girl who ever finds herself in his power, as many
doubtless have done in the past and more will do in the future."
It had dawned upon her gradually that she was one of those
girls—a girl to be pitied—in his power.   And, almost without
her own volition, she had put her hand up between their faces
and had made him let her rise.

It was with a comfortable sense of relief and of escape that
she sat with all her muscles relaxed and her head thrown back
upon the soft cushions of the chair.   She was sitting so when
Mrs. Tisserton herself was announced.

" I wanted to come and ask how you were this morning,
dear," she said, in her even voice ; " but I had so many million useless things to do that it was impossible.   But how are
you ?"

" Oh, I am really well," Jessie answered.   " I was miserable
last night, and came dreadfully near creating a scene.   But
it was nothing, after all ; and I am not sure that I am not disappointed.   I slept most prosaically last night, and I am perfectly well — only awfully drowsy," and she raised one of her
hands, and let it fall lifelessly again on the arm of the chair to
illustrate her heaviness.

" And how did your escort conduct himself ?" asked Mrs.
Tisserton.

" Oh, about as you would expect him to," Jessie answered.

" I am sorry to hear that," said the other, dryly, " because
under such circumstances I should expect him to behave very
badly—about as badly as he could."

" Well, perhaps he did not behave very well," Jessie said,
lightly ; " but then you know you warned me long ago, and I
am proof."

" Yes, I did—and I meant it."

There was silence for some seconds, during which Jessie
could see that her friend was trying to say something which
she did not quite know how to approach.   So she waited
patiently.

" I really did mean it," Mrs. Tisserton said at last, " and I
mean it now.   You know me too well to think that I am

19

meddling, don't you, Jessie, dear? You know that I love you
too well to be really impertinent, even if I seem so?" Jessie
smiled and held out her hand, which the other squeezed and
went on : "Well, I don't know how to say it, but oh! Jessie,
don't let Mr. Blakely take you in! Don't, please, let yourself
care for him—don't, even a little bit! I know the type of
man so well, Jessie! I am married, you know—and then my
wicked appearance brings them all to me. You will never
know as much of men as I do—they will never dare to say the
things to you that they do to me; and until after you are married you won't know a quarter of what I do. But, please take
my word for it, Jessie, don't have anything to do with him.
Do you know, darling, that before the reception broke up
everybody in that room last night knew that he had taken you
home. I heard it a dozen times, and, oh! it made me just
burn !"

Jessie, too, felt herself burning a little, and she said, rather
weakly :

"Do you mean that people talked about us?"

"Oh, I don't know—not quite that; but yes! they weren't
exactly nice. It was their manner, you know, more than anything that they said."

Mrs. Tisserton had been speaking with unusual vehemence
for her—not at all like her ordinarily placid self. It occurred
to Jessie that there must be some reason to account for her
friend's warmth more than a mere instinctive distrust of
Blakely; she must have some positive knowledge of things to
his discredit.

"Did he ever say or do anything to you?" she asked.

"Oh, he approached me, of course, at first—sounded me, as
it were. But that is nothing. Either I was not encouraging
enough or he found me too commonplace. At all events, I
have not had anything to complain of from him; but "—and
she hesitated before proceeding diffidently—" you know that I
don't tell tales and carry scandal, don't you, dear? Well, there
is a dreadful story going round about him and one of our
friends. Jack told me, and says that it's true. I am not
going to tell you about it, dear; but it's horrid. And, oh!
please, Jessie, don't have anything to do with him."

"Do not be afraid, dear; there is no danger."

Mrs. Tisserton looked at her doubtfully a minute; then leaning forward and placing her hands on Jessie's knees, she looked into her face.

"Honestly, darling, there is no danger at all of there ever being anything between you and Marshal Blakely?"

"Honestly, there is no danger at all!" and there was a ring in the words which so satisfied Mrs. Tisserton that she got up impulsively from her chair and kissed Jessie warmly twice.

For the rest of that day Jessie was better and more light-hearted than she had been for a long time, so that Miss Willerby wondered at her gayety. There was still cause enough for anxiety in the aspect of the strike, and the news of the injury to Mrs. Masson touched Jessie deeply. She had met Harrington, and of course knew his name well. Of late she had felt most grateful to him for his faithfulness to her father and the company. Jessie wondered whether it would be out of place for her to call on Jennie Masson and tell her of her sympathy. It would probably, she decided, be in better taste to wait for a few days. The next morning came the news of Mrs. Masson's death, and in the afternoon the account of the inquest and the report of the calamity which had befallen Harrington. Jessie read the paper with scarcely less indignation than Horace had felt. When her father came home to dinner she ran to him eagerly, and asked if there was any possibility of Harrington's guilt.

"None at all, my child," said Mr. Holt, confidently. "It is much more likely that Wollmer did it himself."

The assault upon Harrington, showing the increasing boldness of the strikers, naturally made her more uneasy in regard to her father. He was obliged to go down-town that evening, and Jessie was anxious and nervously restless. It was difficult for her to settle down quietly.

"I wish there was somewhere to go to-night," she had been saying when Barry was announced. "Why isn't there a theatre-party or something—something where one can forget one's self for a while?"

With her nervousness and Barry's preoccupation the conversation did not flourish. They talked flaccidly of various mat-

ters—the Bartop reception, the Harrington-Masson complica-
tions, and the strike generally; and all the while Barry was
fearful lest other callers should arrive, and wondered how he
was to find an opportunity to broach the cause of Marsh. He
had taken a seat close to Miss Holt, Miss Willerby being on the
farther side of the fireplace. It was not long before that
young lady, conscious of the restraint in the conversation and
long accustomed to finding herself the superfluous third person
at conversations which ought to be tête-à-tête, began to suspect
that Barry had something to say to their hostess in private.
So, under pretence of going up-stairs " to see how Mary is,"
she escaped from the room, leaving those two together. As
soon as Barry had resumed his seat he nerved himself for a
plunge.

" I have something very particular to talk to you about," he
said, in solemn tones.

" Really? How delightful! I want some excitement to-
night."

" I want to talk about Horace Marsh."

Her lip curled slightly as she asked:

" Did he send you here to talk to me?"

" Hardly that. He knew I was coming, and implored me
to speak to you for him."

" That was very condescending of him, but a little hard on
you and me; don't you think so?"

" No; I think he is a good enough topic of conversation for
anybody. What is the matter between you and him?"

" He need not have sent you to me to ask that," she said,
contemptuously. " Why did he not tell you himself?"

" Because he does not know."

" Because he chooses to pretend not to know," she said.

" No, you are mistaken," Barry replied, earnestly; " he
really does not know. He knows that you came as near cutting him as a lady could in her own house the other evening,
and he knows that you do not answer his letters—"

" I have had only one," she interrupted.

" Well, his letter, then. But the reason of it all he does not
know."

Miss Holt remained silent, so Barry said again:

"What is the matter? Surely it is nothing so dreadful that it cannot be spoken of?"

"It is dreadful enough; but it is ridiculous for him to pretend not to know. If I tell you now, it is *you* I am telling and not him. When a man turns traitor, and, after pretending to be your friend and calling at your house, attacks you bitterly—not behind your back, but in public speeches, so that it is all published in the papers and the whole town knows of it—what is the use of his pretending to wonder why you no longer like him? What is the need of explanation?"

Barry began to think that he saw light.

"I believe you do Horace Marsh an injustice, Miss Holt."

"Possibly, according to the views of politicians. Men say things, I believe, in the way of politics and business which they would not dream of saying to each other at the club or in private life, without either meaning or giving offence. But, for my part, I cannot understand how a man can be one thing on the platform and another at the dinner-table. Perhaps it is only woman's ignorance; perhaps I am prudish. But the fact remains that I cannot and will not tolerate as a friend and a visitor at this house a man who attacks my father in public and takes part with his enemies."

"And when did Horace do this?" asked Barry.

"I am not keeping a record of his public utterances. I suppose that he does it every time that he makes one of his precious speeches—at least, he did it once, and that was enough."

"I think I can name that one occasion," said Barry.

"Possibly you can. It was disgraceful enough for any one to remember it."

"If I am not mistaken," he continued, "the speech you refer to was one that he made at Jackson nearly a month ago—just when the strike was beginning."

"Perhaps it was. But what does that matter?"

"I think you heard of it through the Democratic paper, the *World?*"

"And what if I did?"

"Did you ever speak to Mr. Holt about that speech?"

Jessie hesitated. "No, I think not. Why should I?" she asked.

"Did you ever hear that he received a letter from Horace on the subject?"

"No; of course not. Mr. Marsh seems to be fond of writing letters." But even as she spoke her heart was beating violently, and dimly it dawned upon her that possibly there had been a mistake somewhere.

"Miss Holt," Barry began, slowly, "you are, let me say again, doing Horace Marsh a great injustice. He did deliver a speech at Jackson; but he never said one word of what was imputed to him."

"It is very easy to say that now. How can I prove to the contrary? And how did it get into the paper, then?"

"He is not saying that only now. He said it at the time. He was angrier that day when he returned to town and read that article than I have ever seen him, I think, in my life. He told me of it that evening. He wrote to your father that day. He would have written to the paper to contradict it, but he was dissuaded by his partner, General Harter, and other leaders of the Democratic party."

"Do you expect me to believe all that? Do you believe it yourself?" But her heart misgave her as she spoke.

"Certainly I do. Ask your father; ask General Harter— he would probably tell the truth."

"And how would such a thing get into the paper at all, I should like to know?" she asked, defiantly.

"That was a trick of what is called party journalism. The strike was practically decided upon that day. The Democratic leaders wanted the labor vote, and the Democratic organs prepared to bid for the support of the strikers at once, before there was a possibility of the other fellows getting ahead of them. Horace happened to be the only party leader who was making a speech that evening. They took his speech and tacked on to it a lot of stuff as a text on which to preach. Horace, as I have said, was furious when he read it. He was dissuaded from contradicting it publicly by the arguments of his friends, who appealed to him not to make a split in the party ranks at such a critical moment. Have you read any of the reports of his later speeches?" Barry asked.

"No. That one was enough."

"That is a pity. If you had, you would have known by this time that Horace has never once, in all this campaign, referred to the labor question from the platform."

"I suppose he thinks that he has expressed himself once, and that is enough. He cannot be accused of not being friendly to the strikers; there is that speech to prove his friendship. And now he hopes to keep the good-will of the other side—my good-will and my father's—by keeping silent, and in private disowning the one thing that he has said. That, I suppose, is clever politics."

"You are uncharitable, Miss Holt. Such things are not worthy of your lips."

"And what interest has Mr. Barry in helping him in his deception? Is it his gratitude or mine that you hope to gain?" She spoke hotly, and knowing that she was wrong. Something within her told her that Barry spoke the truth, and in her anger against herself she spoke blindly and unthinkingly.

"Pardon me," said Barry, quietly, "but that is even less worthy of you than the other."

In the silence which followed an idea occurred to Barry, and he acted upon it at once.

"Miss Holt," he began, "I am going to make a proposition to you which I should not think of making to a lesser woman. It may sound absurd at first, but I believe your real sense of justice will tell you to act upon it. Horace is speaking to-night at Columbus Hall. I tell you that you have wronged him bitterly. You think you have not. You were wishing, a short time since, that there was somewhere to go this evening. Come and hear him. Come and listen with your own ears to the doctrines which he teaches, and let your own judgment decide for you whether he is a traitor or not. Come!"

Jessie hesitated.

"Will there be any women there?"

"Oh yes; plenty. We can stay back near the door somewhere, where we shall not be seen. It is now nearly nine o'clock; we can get there by a quarter past, and he will still have nearly an hour to talk. Come!"

Again she hesitated. At last she rose hastily from her chair.

"I will, if Grace will come."

"I will telephone for a carriage," said Barry, as she left the room to seek Miss Willerby, whom she found, to her astonishment, sitting reading peacefully in her own room.

Twenty minutes later, when the three arrived at the hall, it was so crowded that they had difficulty in obtaining admission. Way was made for the women, however, and two seats at the very back of the hall were surrendered to them by the occupants, who stood thereafter with Barry and other men in the aisle.

Long before she was seated Jessie was already absorbed in what the speaker was saying. At first she had said to herself, "This is not he." There was a strength and a ring to the voice which filled the vast auditorium which she could not reconcile with the subdued accents that she was accustomed to hear from him. He looked of larger frame, too, there in front of the stage alone, and the vigor and manliness of the few gestures that he used differed so widely from the quiet movements which he employed in the drawing-room. By degrees, however, the more familiar undertones of the voice reached her, and she settled in her seat breathlessly to listen.

"I tell you," Marsh was saying, "and not only I, but all the voice of history tells you—all the accumulated evidence of the ages, all the daily experience of each one of you in your walk of life tells you—that there is no other way. Whether it be an individual or a party or a nation, there lies no path to honor but the path which conscience points. There is no man so powerful, not though he be 'born in the porphyry chamber' with 'queens by his cradle,' that he can outrage his conscience and live happy and die in honor. The outward husk of public honor may be given to him; but nothing can 'save his secret soul from nightly fears' and the curses and the tears of those whom he has wronged. There is no party, though it be lifted into power by the unanimous voice of a victorious people, that can hold that people's suffrages if it be untrue to itself. There is no nation that can do wrong and live. These sound like platitudes," he said, dropping his voice, "and perhaps they are. You hear the same things weekly from the pulpit and daily from the press; you say them to each other every hour. And how many of you act upon them? I am speaking now as a politician, not as a clergyman. I do not ask you of your private lives and business morals—those are your affairs. But in affairs political, how many of you will hesitate to gain a party advantage or to help some friendly candidate by tampering with the truth, or playing upon the weaknesses of human nature? Believe me, that when you do that you are doing your party and your friend the unkindest wrong. I have to-night—a thing I seldom do—arraigned the Republican party or some of its leaders for what I take to be the conscious dishonesty of those leaders on certain questions connected with the tariff. I do not do this for the sake of attacking them, of hurting them, or of pulling them down. There is no need of that. The wrong itself injures them far more than anything which we can do or say. The rot within destroys far more surely than the winds without. The ungodly never yet digged a pit but they fell into the midst of it themselves. A nation may stand unshaken against the united armies of the world, and crumble by the vice that is within itself. A party may have recourse to party tricks and may cater to the support of unworthy men, and gain thereby the votes which will win it a given election. It may rise to power more quickly, and it will fall as quickly as it rose. There can be no monopoly of fraud and falsehood, for they are many-sided, and the tricks of one party at one election will be matched by the tricks of the other at the next. But truth is one, and there is no weapon in all the armory of falsehood which can be used against the party which possesses it. The party which rises solely by the use of truth may rise more slowly, but once in power not all the thunders of national adversity nor all the lightning of partisan abuse can shake or scathe it."

Barry, as he stood, glanced from time to time at Miss Holt, and saw that she sat leaning eagerly forward in her chair, listening with parted lips and glowing face to every word that fell from Marsh's lips.

The speaker had dropped his voice to a conversational tone to tell an anecdote. He did it well, and a laugh ran over the audience. Then he rose to speak in a strain of triumphant

confidence of the certainty of success which lay before the
party—a success which need never end or weaken if the party
was but true to itself; and the hall shook to thunderous applause.   In closing Marsh made a lofty plea in behalf of the
high principles of the Constitution of the United States, the
Constitution which, he said, when it was framed, was but an
embodiment of an ideal—a hopeless and wild ideal, as it
seemed then to all the world but those few patriotic souls who
framed it.   It was common to believe and say that ideals had
no place in politics to-day; but it was only by virtue of the
spark of the divine in it, the high inspiration that lifted it
above the level of all other governments of earth, that the
United States Constitution had lived.   But how far, he asked,
had the government, based upon the Constitution, fallen from
the first ideal and lost sight of the inspiration which illumined
it?   Oh! for a party which would go before the nation with
no platform but the Constitution of the United States, and
would live up to the spirit of it!   The party which took this
government and placed it once again on those pure principles,
and held it there, might live forever.   And this was the task
which lay before this party now—a task the accomplishment
of which would lift the party even above the level of those who
first had welded that noble instrument—a task more sure to
hold the honor of the ages than any deed which had been done
by man.

He ceased, bowing acknowledgment of the applause.   The
chairman of the evening advanced to the front of the stage
and raised his hand for silence.   Before he could begin to
speak, a voice issued from under the side gallery, in close proximity to the stage.   The speaker himself was not visible,
though the whole audience turned in his direction; but his
words reached amply to all corners of the hall.   "Mr. Chairman," said the voice, "I should like to ask Mr. Marsh one
question, if I may."

The chairman turned to Horace, who came forward, and by
a bow in the direction from which the voice came signified his
readiness to answer.

"I wish," resumed the voice, "to ask you a question which
I know will interest everybody here.   I have listened to you

to-night and on former occasions with great pleasure. I believe in what you say and admire the way you say it. But neither in the speeches to which I have listened, nor in those of which I have read abstracts in the daily papers, have I known you to express an opinion on a question in which we are all profoundly interested, and which is likely to have great influence upon the party in the coming election. I wish to ask you for your opinion on the merits of the strike now in progress in the city."

As the voice ceased a murmur ran through the audience, and scattered cries of "Hear!" were heard. Barry glanced at Jessie, and saw her start and her color heighten as she edged herself still farther forward on her seat. All eyes were now on Marsh. He hesitated a moment, and then said:

"The gentleman is quite right. I never have referred to the strike in any of my public utterances. I have not done so because it seems to me that the subject is entirely irrelevant. The strike is not a party question. It is not a national issue. It is not a State issue. It is a question with which Democrat and Republican, *as* Democrat and Republican, have nothing to do. I am speaking, when I speak in public, as a member of the party, and neither the party, nor I as a member of it, have any concern, publicly, with the difference between these companies and their men."

"But would you mind telling us," asked the voice, "what your personal opinions are?"

"Not in the least"—and Horace spoke very distinctly—"provided that it is clearly understood that I am not speaking for my party, nor as a member of any party; I represent nobody's opinions on this matter but my own. I speak as a private individual, for whose utterances no party or man outside of myself is responsible."

"We understand," said the voice; and a cry came from the back of the hall: "Let us hear."

"Well," said Marsh, coming nearer to the footlights, "speaking for myself and myself alone, I beg to say that I consider that the strikers are wrong! They were wrong when they struck, and have grown more wrong every day." A murmur of indignation arose from the back of the audience, but it was quieted by the shouts of " Sit still !" " Let him speak !" which came from all quarters.   " I say," Marsh continued, " that the men in the mass were grievously misled, and that the men who misled them were wickedly to blame."   As he spoke the thought of Harrington, lying ill in the hospital, came to him, and he thought of Jessie and her anxiety, and his voice rang clearer as he went on.   " I say, moreover, that those men will suffer for it; in what way, I know not—whether by the law or by their own consciences, or by the public contempt which in the end will be visited upon them ; but they will suffer, each man of them, in the measure of all the accumulated suffering which they have brought upon this city and upon the men whom they led astray—in the measure of all the hardships and crimes and cruelties which have been inflicted and perpetrated since the strike began. They will suffer, and they will deserve it !"

Whether he would have said more is uncertain.   At this point the storm which had been gathering at the rear of the hall, where a number of strikers were collected, broke in a hurricane of hisses and shrieks and groans.   Here and there cheers arose, but they were few, and were completely drowned in the clamor of wrath which seemed to swell louder every second. Amid the din words could now and then be caught : " Scab !" " Scab !" " Kill him !" " Turn him out !" and the like.   Jessie clutched the back of the chair before her, deadly white.   On the stage Marsh stood unmoved, also very pale, for it was the first time that he had faced a hostile audience, but waiting quietly for the tumult to subside.   By his side the chairman was waving for silence.   At length the uproar sank sufficiently for the latter to make himself partially audible.

" Gentlemen," he cried, " please remember that this has nothing to do with the object for which we are assembled!" Gradually the noise decreased until he could be easily heard. " Bear in mind what Mr. Marsh said when he told us that he was not speaking as a politician or a public man or a leader of his party.   Many of us—most of us, I think—differ entirely from his private sentiments as just expressed."   A burst of applause interrupted him, and it was some minutes before he could continue.   " But whether we differ from him or not as an individual, we are all in hearty accord with what he said when speaking for the party. It is that which I now ask you to bear in mind — the magnificent and patriotic oration to which we have all listened—forgetting entirely his later and personal words, and, in recognition of that oration, I now move that this meeting does by acclamation render to Mr. Horace Marsh its unanimous thanks for the pleasure which he has given us, and the noble way in which he voiced the sentiments and set forth the principles of the united Democratic party!"

From the rear of the hall came cries, of "No! no!" but the better instincts of the greater part of the audience responded to the appeal, and, beginning with a scattered cheer here and there, there gradually arose a roar of approval which, if less loud than the former storm of antagonism, was not without enthusiasm.

Marsh bowed in acknowledgment, but with downcast eyes and a smile upon his lips. As he backed towards the rear of the stage the committee upon the platform rose from their seats, and from among them Sullivan came forward to meet Horace. Laying his hand upon the young man's shoulder, he said:

"Holy Moses, me lad! but if it were not that ye can spare the party better than the party can spare ye, it would be readin' yersilf out of the Dimocracy entoirely ye 'ld be by sintiments like them."

Horace turned to face the Irishman; looking him in the eyes, and with his color rising, he said, simply:

"And if the Democratic party wants any other sentiments from me, the Democratic party can go straight to hell!"

And he turned quickly on his heel and disappeared in the wings.

Meanwhile the audience was dispersing noisily and amid a sputtering of hisses and groans, which still continued to be heard from various directions. On Barry's suggestion, the ladies waited until the hall was nearly empty before attempting to leave their seats. On the way home Miss Holt said nothing, while Barry and Miss Willerby exchanged commonplace remarks across the carriage about the size of the audience and the character of Marsh's voice and style of speaking.

When they arrived at the house, Miss Holt asked Barry if he would come in.

"No, I think not," he said. Waiting until Miss Willerby had passed out of ear-shot, he continued, "And what may I tell him? Shall I say that he may come and call?"

Jessie hesitated a moment.

"No; tell him that I will reply to his note, which has remained too long unanswered. I will write to him." As she gave Barry her hand she added, "I may not write at once; he may not hear to-morrow. But he will hear. Good-night!"

When Barry reached their rooms he found Horace awaiting him.

"Well?" said the latter, eagerly.

"Well?" Barry replied, with unconcern.

"Did you see her?"

"Who?"

"Why, Miss Holt, you wretch!"

"Oh!"—as if he had forgotten—"yes. Oh—yes, I saw her all right!"—and he disappeared into his room to change his coat.

"Look here," said Marsh, as he came out again, "don't be a mule! What did she say?"

"Well"—and Barry filled his pipe deliberately—"before I say a thing, I want you to promise that you will not ask a single question, but will take just what I choose to give you."

"I promise. Go ahead!"

"She said—let me see, what did she say?"

"Oh, go ahead!"

"Well, she said that she would write to you."

"When?"

"That's a question. You promised not to ask questions. However, I'll answer it. Perhaps not to-morrow—not at once. But she will write to you. Your note has remained too long unanswered."

And Barry threw himself on his favorite lounge, and proceeded to smoke in silence. Marsh waited patiently for a while, until he could bear it no longer. Then he came over to where his friend lay, and, kneeling on the floor at his side, said:

"Tell me one thing more, old man—only one! Is it well? Just tell me that."

And Barry puffed at his pipe, and said, sententiously:
"It is well."

As Marsh went back to his seat, the hypocrite on the lounge rolled over and said, deliberately:

"And now tell me how the meeting went?"

XXIV

THE WHIRLIGIG OF TIME

THE influence which had prompted Miss Holt to tell Barry that she might not write to Horace at once was a sudden and prophetic prompting of a feeling which did not attain its full development until the following day. For that night the conflict and turmoil of her emotions forbade any close analysis of her sensations. She knew only that a wellspring of gladness had bubbled up in her heart. It was filled as with music, as of bird-song and of rippling water when winter breaks suddenly—not with happiness itself, but with the hope and promise of the summer days in store.

Horace had not been the traitor that she had supposed. She had wronged him. He had never spoken the words ascribed to him. She even strove to assure herself that in her secret heart she had known all the time that he was true.

So the Horace whom she had believed to be the real Horace had been only a thing of her imagination. Conversely the Horace of her imagining, the ideal Horace, was real. How she had wished—then, when it was impossible—that it might be so! How gladly, so she said to herself, she would give her trust and—yes, her love—to such a man! But lo! here he was! The prince was at the door.

And that made a difference.

To exchange vows with a fairy prince of one's own creation was as easy as telling confidences to the moon. But when Romeo was listening beneath the balcony—

> "I should have been more strange, I must confess,
> But that thou over-heard'st, ere I was ware,
> My true love's passion. Therefore, pardon me!"

And now — she knew it — this Prince Romeo was sitting fidgeting in his office, only a mile or so away, waiting for the word which she had bound herself to send him. It must be she who must call him to her. The thought was intolerable! She could never write that letter — never, never! At all events, thank goodness, she had given herself one day's respite. So she busied herself with her household duties, and sang as she did them.

. It would have comforted her much could she have known with what discretion Barry had carried her message to the prince. But that she did not know. Doubtless they had discussed it at length ; Barry had put him in possession of all the details of the evening's events—including, she fancied, clothing Barry with a gift of insight which he did not possess, many details which had never escaped from her own breast. They had doubtless talked it over and laughed—yes, positively laughed !—with the accompaniments of brandy-and-soda and tobacco smoke. Her cheeks burned as she thought of it.

Meanwhile the world was glad. Even the sun shone, with a last, false gleam of the dying Indian-summer. Miss Holt could not be sad, even in sympathy with Mary Caley's statuesque desolation. That young lady was bitterly provoked with herself for having gone to bed when Barry was about to call—or, rather, with Barry, for having called when she had retired. He must have known that she had retired. It was evident, at least, that he had been glad not to see her, and did not care a bit about her, or he would have sent some message. Even Miss Willerby's charitable fib to the effect that he had seemed " awfully distressed " when he had heard that Miss Caley was indisposed was contemptuously received. If he had been so distressed, how had he invited them to go out with him so gayly ? And no doubt he had flirted with one or other — probably both — of them atrociously. They had talked her, Miss Caley, all over ; she knew it. If they had not wanted to talk her over, why had they stolen off in that way, leaving her alone ? Why had they not come and asked her to go with them ? It would not have taken her three minutes to dress, and she would have dearly loved to go. It

20

was just what she needed, and would have done her headache worlds of good. Those things always did. Besides, they knew how she longed to hear Mr. Marsh talk and see him sway people. She just adored that kind of thing.

Altogether she had been abominably ill-used. It had been a conspiracy—a cold, perfidious cabal—between those three from beginning to end. Barry had probably been waiting on the very door-step when they had smuggled her off to bed, and then they had stolen away. And she stalked rigidly about the house, clutching in her hands a bundle of letters, understood to be those of Fred Jones, which she seated herself at intervals in forlorn corners to read ostentatiously and with evident emotion.

Jessie tried once in a while to pet and console her; but her own heart was too full of her own affairs to admit of maintaining a sustained strain of sympathy. Besides, she was well aware that Miss Caley would "come round" all right if left to herself.

In the afternoon Mrs. Jessel called for a friendly chat, and Jessie longed to unburden herself on the other's good motherly bosom. As it was, Miss Holt was so transparently lighthearted that the kindly Mrs. Jessel was perplexed, and even ventured some remote references to Mr. Blakely. Of all of which Jessie understood the drift thoroughly, but she only laughed elusively, and the older woman was more puzzled than before. It was like conversing with a will-o'-the-wisp.

Horace that morning took his way to his office, in eager hope that possibly some word from Jessie might have already arrived. An hour later he went to the hospital to see Harrington, whom he found lying uneasily in his bandages, but conscious and able to talk. Horace sat with him for an hour, and was glad to learn, by cautious questioning, that the injured man had no knowledge of the suspicion which hung over him.

Mrs. Masson was to be buried that afternoon, and from the hospital Horace went to the house in Fourth Street. Here, however, he found that Weatherfield had taken everything in hand, and that he could be of little use. So he returned to his office to hope against hope that word would come from Jessie that day.

The papers that morning naturally had much to say about the dramatic episode at Columbus Hall. The Republican organs belauded Marsh's courage, and assured him that a cordial welcome was awaiting him within that party whenever he chose to accept it. The *World* spoke with some bitterness of the incident—the bitterness being directed, however, less against Horace, who, the paper was convinced, would soon see cause to regret and change what it could not help regarding as the inconsistency of his opinions in the matter of the strike, than against the unknown individual—an emissary, doubtless, of the Republican party—who, by his ill-timed inquiries, had precipitated the catastrophe. In all other matters Mr. Marsh, the paper knew, was a good Democrat, and the party could afford to forgive him this one obliquity.

Marsh had read the editorial lucubrations with mingled amusement and indifference. To the many acquaintances who spoke to him on the street and at his office on the subject he treated it lightly. His partner even had taken the matter more good-humoredly than Marsh anticipated. Perhaps General Harter had spoken to Sullivan, and had imbibed the Irishman's idea that Marsh could spare the party better than the party could spare Marsh. At all events, he talked to Horace in a tolerant, fatherly way, as to a young man who had committed an indiscretion; but a venial one—one, perhaps, not entirely without some element of credit in it. The General had been in the hall—though declining, as he was Marsh's partner, to occupy a seat upon the platform—and he generously complimented Horace upon what he was pleased to call the dignity of his bearing during those trying minutes.

Altogether the incident did not seriously worry our friend. It was trivial, everything was trivial, compared to the fact that Jessie was going to write to him—perhaps already had written to him, and the message might even now be on its way to him. He was still waiting for the feet of him who brought the glad tidings when the clerk informed him that "the two Mr. Pawsons" were in the outer office, and wished to see both him and General Harter. By "the two Mr. Pawsons" Horace knew that Franklin meant the editor, Quintus L. Pawson, and his brother, Marius C. Pawson, the lawyer.

With the latter Horace was already well acquainted, while the editor he had met but once, and that formally.

The lawyer entered first—a brusque man of decided movements, rather squarely built, with a ruddy complexion, and heavy black eyebrows and side-whiskers. The editor, who followed, was, though the younger, some inches taller than his brother, thinner and paler of face, and with stooping shoulders, telling of years of drudgery at the night desk on a daily newspaper. The same heavy black eyebrows and a certain similarity of the line of the hair as it grew from the forehead gave the two brothers the reputation of resembling each other; though here, when they stood side by side, they appeared but little alike.

"You know my brother Quintus, I think, Marsh?" asked Marius, the lawyer.

"I have had the pleasure of meeting him only once, I think," said Horace, as he rose to shake hands with his visitors.

As soon as they were seated the lawyer opened the conversation, but with evident embarrassment.

"We have come on a rather remarkable errand, Marsh," he said. "It is really—er—my errand to General Harter. But it happens to be in connection—er—with a matter to which—er—my brother was an accidental witness, so I asked him to accompany me. We want now—er—another witness to be present with us to-day, a witness who is—er—a friend of the General, and who—er—knows him well, as well as being a Democrat. We decided that you were the man that—er—we wanted. Would you—er—mind coming in with us to the General's office, and—er—being present at what may follow?"

Marsh was puzzled. There was an air of formality about the proceeding which was in itself sufficient to provoke curiosity, while the hesitation of the ordinarily fluent, not to say reckless-spoken, lawyer signified that the matter in hand was of something more than common moment.

"Why, certainly," Horace said, in tones which showed his surprise. "I shall be delighted to be of any use that I can. I ought to be only too glad to be invited into such good company."

At the suggestion of the lawyer Pawson, Marsh went into his partner's room, and informed him that the brothers wished to see him.

" Bring them right in !" said the General.   So, returning to the door, Horace signalled to the others to enter, which they did.

The General was as genial as usual, but it seemed to Horace that the brothers responded but glumly to the cordiality of his greeting, and bore an air of solemnity, as if they were bearers of bad news, and he grew uneasy.

" Well, gentlemen and brethren," said the General, with a certain magnificent way which he had of making small jokes, and which was very effective with country audiences, " what can I do for you ?"

The General sat in his revolving-chair at his desk.   As he spoke he looked alternately at the lawyer and the editor, who were seated directly in front of him.   Marsh had taken a chair beside the big table, some paces farther away, to the General's right.

" General," began the lawyer Pawson, " I want to ask you a very unusual question.   Would you mind answering it ?"

" Not if I am able to," said the General, affably.

" Well, I want to know exactly what it was that killed Mrs. Masson ?"

The question was so absurdly irrelevant, addressed to General Harter, that Horace's first impression was that it must be intended for a recondite witticism.   A glance at his partner's face, however, dispelled that idea, and Horace gazed in amazement.   As the lawyer's words reached General Harter's ears it was as if a spectre had suddenly appeared before him. The blood fled from his face, leaving it flaccid and wrinkled. His figure seemed to shrink within itself in his chair.   He had grown in a second older by twenty years.   When he opened his mouth to speak there came only a strange noise— half sigh and half hiss.   The hands which rested on the arms of his chair twitched violently.   He moved them and clasped them together in his lap as if trying to keep them still, but they continued to jerk spasmodically, when folded, with a motion like that of St.-Vitus's-dance.

However irrelevant and absurd the question might seem to Horace, it was evident that to his partner it bore a terrible significance. What was it?

Seconds—oppressive seconds—passed before at length the General gathered strength enough to speak.

"What—what do you mean?" he gasped.

"I only mean just what I ask," replied Pawson. "How did Mrs. Masson die? You will have to tell us, General—er —*Harrington!*"

The wrong name was used with evident and deliberate intention. The emphasis with which the lawyer spoke it could not have been accidental, and Marsh saw, with mingled amazement and horror, his partner bow his face upon his hands. His questioner—or accuser, rather — waited patiently. Suddenly the General raised his head, and, reaching out his hands appealingly with a gesture which included all his auditors, said, vehemently:

"I did not kill her! Before God, I swear I did not kill her!"

"Tell us about it," said the lawyer, quietly.

"She was angry, and she stepped suddenly towards me," said the General, earnestly. "I do not know whether it was a sudden fit that seized her or whether she tripped. But she fell. She did not say a word, but simply fell backward. Her head struck the mantel. I went to help her up, and I saw the blood trickling over the tiles. And then—then I left the house." His voice broke, and he hid his face once more. Then burst out again: "What could I do? I might have saved her, perhaps, by calling help at once. But how could I be found there? What was I doing at her house? My whole secret would have been discovered."

It was inexpressibly pathetic to Marsh to see this man whom he had honored bowing his gray head, overwhelmed with grief and shame. That in the brief story which he had just told, not without some dramatic gesture, he spoke the truth, Horace had no doubt. General Harter was not guilty of murder. But what did it all mean? What was this secret? Why had he been at Mrs. Masson's house? And why did Pawson call him "Harrington"?

Pawson meanwhile drew from the inside pocket of his overcoat a large envelope.

"You may," he said, "wish to know how I came to learn so much. It was quite by accident." Removing the outer envelope from the package in his hand, he held a small bundle of letters, frayed and discolored, tied up crosswise with a piece of red twine — evidently their older fastening — and again held together with a rubber band, which had presumably been more recently added.

"'Not to be opened until I am dead'—signed 'Honoria Masson,'" he read from some writing which was on a strip of paper which encircled the bundle. Removing this slip, with the string and the band which enclosed it, he read from a loose half-sheet of note-paper which lay folded on the top of the letters: "'General William Harter will pay five hundred dollars apiece for these letters.'"

Marsh looked again at his partner, and saw a tear ooze through the fingers in which his face was hidden.

"These letters," said the lawyer, "were brought to my office by Mrs. Masson one day some months ago, when it happened that my brother was present. She came to me because I happened to have been the attorney in settling up her last husband's affairs. She told me not to open the package until she was dead. I had no idea what the package contained, and put it away in my vault, scarcely giving it another thought. Once again she came in and undid the package in my presence, and added another letter—this one," touching the top one with his finger—"to those which I now for the first time saw that the bundle contained. I do not think the matter entered my mind again until I read of her death. Last night I took the package home with me to read at night, so as not to waste time during the day. I had very little idea of the surprise that was in store for me."

The lawyer paused, and, running over the letters with his fingers, selected one which looked very old and worn. "This letter," Pawson continued, as he opened it and read the date-line, "was written nearly twenty years ago. At that time she was a widow—Mrs. Brady. You call her only 'Honoria.' I did not know that you had ever lived in Freehold, New Jer-

sey, General; but that is where this letter, as were most of
the others, was written. Mrs. Brady lived there also. You
sign yourself here ' William Harrington.' There are a dozen
or more letters signed that way — all within the space of a
few months. Then comes a break of a year, and the next
letter is written from Detroit — still to her at Freehold. But
you sign yourself " — Pawson had been turning over the
papers as he spoke, as if looking for one in particular; finding it, he turned to the signature—" simply ' W. H.' There
are three letters from Detroit. I read them all last night.
In the last you say that you do not like the place, and are
going West. Between that and the next letter," and he
opened another, is " a gap of seventeen years. That brings
us to less than two years ago, when, of course, you were
living here. There are two letters since that one—one written only six weeks ago, after your nomination for the governorship, to which you refer in the letter. These last letters, like those from Detroit, are signed ' W. H.' "

Gradually an outline of the facts was dawning upon Marsh.
Evidently his partner's name had once been Harrington, and
Horace now remembered how little he or any one else knew
of the General's early life. Evidently the General and Mrs.
Masson had known each other well in the old days, and Horace recollected that in the report of the inquest there had
been a mention made in somebody's testimony (was it not
Miss Masson's?) of a picture of Mrs. Masson taken years ago,
in which she was shown to have been a beautiful woman.
And suddenly, thinking of the inquest, those last words of
the dead woman, about which so much had been said and
conjectured, came to his mind : " Where is he? Has Harrington gone?" In her last delirious moments her memory
had taken up again the name by which she had known him
well in the old days.

" Yes," said the General, rousing himself, as if to face the
worst, " the story is all there in those dates and signatures.
I am William Harrington. Your friend, Marsh — the one
who is now in the hospital — must be some sort of a cousin
or nephew of mine. I come from your part of the country,
in Massachusetts. That was one of the things which drew

me to you, I think. I have never dared to go back there, not for twenty years, lest some one should recognize me. But I have so often longed to ask you about old people and places there! I left there when I was eighteen and went to Boston, where I only stayed for three years. For the next five I wandered a good deal, chiefly in New England, and finally drifted to New York, and thence to Freehold. I lived there for nearly four years. It was in my last year that I met Mrs. Brady, and fell in love with her. I trust you will believe, gentlemen, that there was nothing wrong in our relations. There was not. I intended to marry her. We were then both about thirty years of age; and if I could have afforded it I would have married at once. But I was poor, and had hard times to get along. It was out of my poverty that grew the thing which ruined me. I was honest, or meant to be, but I was in debt, and the debt grew larger every month. My practice was small, and I am by nature incapable of economy. Finally I owed everybody in town money—small amounts. The whole of my obligations did not reach seven hundred dollars. But I saw no way to pay even that; and I was being dunned—dunned for humiliating sums—until at last I grew wild and—disappeared! It was a hopeless mistake. I ought to have lived on there, and fought it through somehow—at least, if I went, I should have gone openly, and with my creditors' consent. But I was inexperienced in business. I had not the courage to face the music, and I fled—just ran away. I always intended to pay every cent as soon as I had the money; but I thought if I stopped to tell my creditors so that they would make trouble. So I just left everything and struck West."

He ceased speaking, and sat drumming on the desk with his fingers, while his mind wandered back over those old, thorny paths.

"Changing my name," he resumed — "that was another bad mistake. My idea at the time was only to lose my identity for a while until in some way I could make enough to pay my debts and go back to Freehold. But I had hard work to earn a living. In Detroit I failed to get a footing, and wandered on to the Pacific slope, and thence drifted

back here.   Meanwhile I was making acquaintances, and
making them under my new name.   Then I took to politics.
The rubbing against people of all classes and different sections of the country gave me a certain facility in making
friends—taught me how to get along in any company in
which I found myself.   That helped me to come to the
front in politics; but it did not bring me money.   I am not
over-scrupulous, perhaps, in some ways, and am willing to
wink at other men's dishonesty for the party's sake; but I
am afraid that I have always been too honest—or too cowardly, it may be, when it came to making money for myself—
to get rich.   Not until the last two or three years could I
ever at one time have commanded seven hundred dollars of
spare money.   I am incapable of living within my means.
Moreover, in ten and fifteen and twenty years the conscience
rusts.   The old debts in Freehold troubled me more rarely
as time went on, and there stood always in the way of my
paying them some uncertainty how to do it without disclos-
ing my identity.   I always meant to pay; but after so many
years what especial hurry was there?   And how could I put
into the hands of my enemies a clew to my past?   Once the
debts were paid, there would really have been little enough
to be ashamed of.   But of a politician in my position, who
will believe that he had changed his name and lived for
twenty years a life of deception without some good reason?
The discovery would have damned me forever.   So time went
on, and William Harrington, I believed, was dead forever.
Then this woman recognized me.   What chance brought her
here to live I do not know, but she saw me on the streets and
wrote to me.   I had changed, it seemed, in appearance less
than I had supposed — certainly less than she had, for I
should never have recognized her.   She wrote to me, and I
went to see her.   She had kept my letters—for love, she
said; but now she used them only as a means for extorting
money.   She had me in her power.   My election to the governorship promised me relief.   Then I would be able to buy
those miserable documents from her, and, as she has written
there, I was to do so at the rate of five hundred dollars a letter.   For ten thousand dollars I was to have them all.   I

have only seen her to speak to three times since she came to the city — that time when I received her first letter, once again some months ago, and then the other night. I went there to make one last effort to get those things. I have had any number of letters from her—of late very many, and they seemed to me hardly to be the productions of a sane person. I think she was mad that night. There had been hanging over me for weeks a constant terror lest in some frenzy she should make the secret public before Election Day. At last the load grew intolerable, and I went to endeavor to persuade her to give me the documents in exchange for notes —notes which I had already arranged with a third party, who was willing to trust me without my telling him for what the notes were needed, to make out in his favor and have him indorse. But she would not listen. She would hardly permit me to talk, but raved with the ravings of a maniac. It was hopeless, I saw, and was about to leave. I was already walking to the door when she took those steps forward—I can see her now with her wrinkled face (to think that that face was the face of Honoria Brady!) and her eyes glowing, her two clinched hands, raised on either side of her head, shaking with her wrath, while her shrill voice rang so loud that it seemed that passers-by on the street must hear. Suddenly she stopped in the middle of a sentence — I think the intensity of her anger choked her—and she fell."

When the General finished his story, for a while no one spoke. Marius Pawson began deliberately tying the fatal documents together again with the scrap of red string. He snapped the rubber band around them, and replaced them in their envelope. Then the General, with a new sound of hope in his voice, asked :

" Can I have them now ?"

" I am afraid not," replied the other. " You see that they are part of the estate of the deceased, and were confided to me. She regarded them as a valuable asset ; they are the property of her heirs now. I can only turn them over to her step-daughters."

" But now that the secret is known only to you three, and she, the only person to whom it was of importance, is dead ?"

"That does not matter. It may be that now you would not buy these letters; it may be that you would. But whether they have any real value or not is not for me to judge. They are in my hands in trust, and I must give them to the heirs. You know that yourself."

Again there was silence, until Marius Pawson rose, and, clasping his hands behind his back, set himself to pacing up and down the room.

"You see, General," he said, as he walked, "the trouble is here: This other Harrington, who is in the hospital, is suspected of having murdered her. On the evidence now before the public there is a very good chance of his being convicted and hanged. But whether he would be convicted or not is immaterial. The suspicion must be removed from him. The facts must be known. My brother and I have twisted it every way, and there is no way to clear him and do right except by telling the whole story."

"And my candidacy?" faltered the General.

It was the editor who replied to this question.

"You must withdraw," he said. "There is no other way. As Marius says, we have turned the situation every way, and the facts must come out. The idea of your remaining the candidate for governor is out of the question. It would kill the party, as well as yourself, forever."

"And are all these years that I have lived here—all these twenty years, in which I have lived blamelessly among you, and in which I have worked so hard for everything that I have won—are they going to count for nothing?"

"They will count for much," replied the editor.

"Would you have me go elsewhere and start life again—now?" the General asked, piteously. "Shall I take another name?"

"You have done that once," said the editor, "and say yourself that it was a fatal mistake. Stay right here—here, where you have the twenty years of blameless living to your credit. Live it down. You may never be candidate for governor again, but the story will soon be forgotten, and a year from now, though conspicuous public office may be impossible for you, you will find that you are as much respected as you are to-day."

"My brother is right," said the elder Pawson. "The frank, straight way is the only one worth taking. Resume your name of Harrington if you will—or comply with the legal formalities to make Harter your real name. But let the story be told clearly, and then go on living as you have done. You will find in a few months that you have lifted a terrible weight from your life and from your conscience. You will be happier than you have been for twenty years."

"The plan that we had outlined," resumed the editor, "is that you should write your resignation at once—to-night, if possible. There are only a few days to election, and justice to the party demands that we should have our new man in the field at once. Justice to this other Harrington is not so urgent. While he is in the hospital and ignorant, as I understand he is, of the suspicion which hangs over him, the suspicion will do no especial harm. But that is a matter for your choice—you can tell your story at once or you can tell it later, after election. When you do tell it, you can place it before the people in such a way as you please. We three in this room are good enough friends to you to keep secret what has passed here to-day. As for the newspapers, I can answer for them—for others besides my own. The press will be generous enough to you when you are no longer an object of partisan hostility. You will be telling the tale from the spontaneous promptings of your own conscience. It need not be said that you were discovered. It was your own innate sense of justice which made you, to save an innocent man, throw away your brilliant prospects, abandon your career, and voluntarily expose the secret of your life to the public eye. It will be almost heroic. You will find that you will get only eulogy for your unselfishness from the press and only praise from your friends. It will show a high sense of honor in you, and, as a private citizen, it will do you good in everybody's estimation."

The General leaned his head upon his hands and remained sunk in thought.

"It is bitter," he said, at length—"very bitter. At least, let me have until to-morrow. I am in no frame to write my letter of withdrawal to-night."

"But to-morrow," said Marius, "it must be. Between now

and then you can go over the matter in your own mind, and I know you will reach the same conclusion as we have come to. There is no other way."

The editor rose and buttoned up his coat, standing beside his brother. Marsh also got up. The three stood for a minute and looked in pity at the old man with his gray head bent upon his hands. Then the two brothers silently withdrew. Horace advanced and placed his hand upon his partner's shoulder.

"I am sorry, General," he said, softly—"more sorry than I can say. I will help you in any way I can."

The shoulder on which his hand rested shook with a sudden convulsive sob. Horace pressed it gently, and, treading stealthily, left the room, closing the door carefully behind him.

In his own office the brothers were awaiting him, and the three stood and gazed out of the window in silence, as men may who come out of the presence of death. From beyond the closed door the sound of sobbing came to them, and broken groans as of a man in mortal agony.

"We are obliged to you for coming, Marsh," said the elder Pawson. "It seemed to us both that you were the right man."

"I suppose I was," Marsh answered, wistfully.

The brothers prepared to go. With an air of forced gayety, the editor spoke:

"Well, I am glad to have met you again, Mr. Marsh. It is needless to say that I am familiar enough with your doings and sayings."

"Yes," Horace said, "and that reminds me that I have a bone to pick with you."

"Is it a large bone?"

"It seemed large at the time," Horace answered. "I made a speech at Jackson a few weeks ago, and you, in your paper, misrepresented me atrociously. Not only was the report of the speech erroneous, but you published a long editorial that was incomparably worse than any inaccuracies in the report—an editorial in which you imputed to me all manner of sentiments on the subject of the strike, which I not only never

expressed, but which were totally different from any which I
have ever entertained." Marsh spoke hotly, as the recollection of the wrong revived in him and smarted. "It happens
that I was compelled last night to say some things which
have put my record straight, I suppose. But it was an unwarrantable thing of you, or the *World,* to do at the time."

The editor hesitated for a moment, and then asked, in a
curious tone :

"Do you know who wrote that article?"

"I always supposed that you did."

"General Harter wrote it," said Pawson, very slowly and
distinctly.

"Who?"

"I beg his pardon, General Harrington," Pawson replied,
calmly.

"There is some mistake here," said Marsh. "We are speaking of different articles. The article that I mean I called to
the General's attention when I returned home myself next
day, and we had quite a talk about it. He had hardly noticed
it before."

"That is quite interesting," remarked Pawson.

"The article that I mean," resumed Horace, "was in reference to a speech which I delivered at Jackson on—let me
see—the 3d of last month. There was an idiot called Dallas—you know him, 'Poker Dallas'—who was chairman of
the meeting. When I had finished he made some remarks,
and his remarks did bear upon the strike. In your report
you got his remarks and mine mixed, and in your editorial
you spoke of the scathing way in which I had denounced
the street-railway company—and all manner of trash, which
I never said."

"That's the same article," said Pawson. "General Harter,
as he was then, wrote that."

"You are joking."

"No, I am not. Ask Sullivan !"

"Ask whom?"

"Sullivan—Timothy Sullivan—'Holy Moses' Sullivan."

"Why, I did. I talked it over with Sullivan that same afternoon. I discussed the propriety of writing to you about it—"

" And he stopped you!" asked Pawson

" Yes, he did. Why, he said he would speak to you about it. Didn't he do it?"

" Yes. He said that the lad—that was you—didn't like it. You did not mind it for once, when it was necessary for the sake of the party; but that in future I must be very careful to let the public know that you did not speak about the strike. I'll tell you, Mr. Marsh," and the editor sat down to speak, " I had my compunctions at the time. But it was all cut and dried in advance. The strike, you know, was practically decided upon that day, and the party leaders determined that it was to be an issue in the campaign—*the* issue. The position had to be taken at once. So Dallas was telegraphed to that afternoon, and told what he was to say. That article must have been written before your speech was delivered. The General brought it up to me early in the evening. He came in again with Sullivan about twelve o'clock, and read it over to us aloud from the proof. Sullivan suggested some changes—put in an epithet or two. Can't you recognize Sullivan's epithets? I can. If there was only one in a column, I could pick it out. Well, as I say, I had scruples at the time, and asked them how you would take it. I did not know you and they did, and when they told me that you would not mind, why, I took their word for it."

Horace pondered, and he remembered the General's manner when Horace had called his attention to the article. He remembered what Sullivan had said, and how plausibly he had argued on the exigencies of the party's welfare. He remembered what the Irishman had told him of his own impressions on reading the article that morning, and how Pawson could not appreciate him—Horace Marsh.

" I think," Horace said at last, " that this is even more amazing than what has been going on in there," indicating his partner's room. " Sullivan said that you were a blathering idiot for having written that."

" Quite possibly," said Pawson. " Sullivan is, I think, the best liar that we have in the party. He is by all odds the best politician."

XXV

A TRIP TO THE CEMETERY

In making the arrangements for Mrs. Masson's funeral, the detail which Weatherfield found most troublesome was the handling of Wollmer. The labor leader was officious to obtrusiveness. Weatherfield could not well reject bluntly the services of the man who, besides having been the only male inmate of Mrs. Masson's household for many months, had undeniably been the dead woman's closest friend during the last days of her life. On the other hand, Weatherfield himself disliked Wollmer, and Jennie frankly expressed her wish that the labor leader should have no voice in the arrangements. The printer did his best to listen to the other's numerous suggestions with patience, and to decline his offers of assistance without giving offence. But, with all his slowness to anger, even Weatherfield's forbearance was sorely tried when Wollmer unfolded a project for making the funeral procession an excuse for a public demonstration in behalf of the cause of labor. On this subject words ran high between them. Finally, Wollmer, apparently consenting to abandon his original plan for a grand marshalling of all the allied forces of the strikers on the road to the cemetery, promised to confine the deputation to participate in the ceremony to the officers of the several unions only. With this concession Weatherfield deemed it best to seem content.

The services at the home on Fourth Street were brief; but while they were in progress a large crowd of idlers assembled in the street, bent on catching a glimpse of the casket containing the body of the woman the manner of whose death had become so notorious. When the cortege started on the long march to the cemetery, which lay in the northwestern part of

21

the city, it consisted of five vehicles only in addition to the
hearse.   The two sisters occupied one carriage, and Weatherfield and the minister another, the remaining three containing
the officers of the labor organizations.

In their carriage, over the windows of which the shades were
drawn close, the girls sat in silence, each too sadly preoccupied
to give thought to anything that might be passing without.
From the next carriage Weatherfield looked listlessly at the
people standing on the sidewalk to see the funeral pass; but
they had gone but a short distance when he saw that which
filled him with bitterness against Wollmer.

A large body of men stood in orderly ranks, drawn up by
the sidewalk.   They waited with bared heads as the hearse
and the carriages containing the mourners passed, and a minute later Weatherfield heard the word of command given, and,
looking through the small oval window in the back of the carriage, saw the company falling in to join in the march. A little
farther on the same thing was repeated, and again and again at
other points along the route.   The companies, composed evidently of strikers, varied in size from bodies of fifty to those of
three hundred or four hundred men.   As his carriage turned
a corner, still a mile away from the cemetery, Weatherfield,
looking backward, could see a solid column of figures stretching
almost as far as his eye could reach.

At the cemetery the girls left their carriage and walked with
downcast eyes across the grass to the side of the newly made
grave.   It was not until, when the coffin had been lowered and
the last words said, they turned to go back to the carriage that
they became aware of the crowd, numbering over two thousand
men, which had followed them.   Sidling up to Weatherfield,
Wollmer said, in a low voice:

"I could not help it.   I told them not to come."

But Weatherfield only shut his lips and walked on.

The men did not return with the carriages to the city.   On
the contrary, the three last vehicles, which had each held four
men on the outward journey, contained now but two apiece,
the others having stayed with the strikers at the cemetery.   Almost before the carriages were out of sight, Wollmer's lieutenant, Henderson, had mounted one of the small seats which were

scattered through the cemetery and was addressing the assembled throng. Nothing was said inciting directly to acts of violence; nor was there any demonstration which could be called unseemly in those solemn precincts. Rehearsing again the circumstances of Mrs. Masson's death, as the strikers understood them, Henderson paid a tribute in not ill-chosen words to the faithfulness and courage of their dead champion. When weak women, he said, enfeebled with age and with no self-interest nor any motive but their own love of justice to bind them to the cause, could thus face death for its sake, it was not likely that they—strong men whose living and the livelihood of whose families depended on their success—would weaken or prove recreant. In his closing words he spoke bitterly of the tyranny of capital and of the wrongs of labor; but only in generality, and with a certain soberness and self-restraint. The men listened in silence, and refrained from any applause as he ceased speaking. Then, falling again into their ranks, each detachment under command of its appointed leader, they started in resolute sullenness on the march towards the city.

They did not take the same route as they had followed coming out, and which the carriages had again chosen on going home; but, striking eastward, they came in less than a mile to where the deserted works of the iron-and-steel company stood silent and forbidding.

As they drew away from the cemetery the sobering influence of the presence of the dead wore off, and the army grew less orderly and more demonstrative. The men shouted and laughed one to another, and bandied jokes with passers-by upon the sidewalks. Flasks and bottles, which had hitherto been concealed in pockets, made their appearance and passed from hand to hand. About half-way to the iron-and-steel company's plant the procession halted in front of a clump of saloons and beer-halls until every man had had something to drink and the flasks and bottles had been replenished. When the works were reached the men howled and shouted curses at the frowning buildings.

"Pull down the fence!" cried a voice, and immediately a thousand men had left the roadway and were grappling with the gray, weather-stained boards, some five feet high, which encircled the iron-and-steel company's property. The barrier swayed and wavered under the weight of the bodies of the men against it. There was a sharp report as it yielded, first at a point near the centre, and a second later, amid the sound of splintering wood and the mingled cheers and hoots of the men, the entire stretch of some two hundred yards of fence lay flat upon the ground. Here and there a post, more deeply rooted than its fellows, stood defiantly alone. Each of these was quickly seized by a dozen men who, swaying their bodies in unison, loosened it in its socket until one after another the last remnants of the fence were pulled up, amid triumphant shoutings, and thrown upon the boards already lying upon the grass.

For a minute the crowd stood undecided whether to advance upon the works themselves, which stood a hundred feet back from the highway ; but cries of " Fall in !" arose, and slowly the long column reformed itself in the road. At the command to march it moved forward towards the city, but it was no longer a disciplined army advancing in even ranks, but a dishevelled mob, crowding upon itself and filling the road from one side to the other. The effect of the liquor which still circulated freely from man to man was intensified by the excitement of the successful attack upon the fence. It was as the first taste of blood to a wild beast. Many had armed themselves with splinters of the broken boards, to the ends of which they knotted handkerchiefs and waved them aloft. The air was filled with a babel of shouts and cries and laughter, while from various sections of the line voices—perhaps a dozen or a score —rising together, made themselves heard above the din, singing in desultory fashion scraps of marching songs—"John Brown's Body " and " Marching Through Georgia."

They advanced towards town by the road which Harrington had taken on the day when the strike began. It was not long before an electric car met them. The column parted to make way for it. The engineer, seeing his only chance of safety, put on full speed and dashed at the approaching army at a rate of twenty or twenty-five miles an hour. A roar of wrath arose from two thousand throats, and with the pieces of the fence or whatever they held in their hands the men struck at the engineer and the car as it flew past. Cowering back against the door, the engineer escaped serious injury. The conductor had entered the car, and with the solitary passenger within crouched upon the floor, while splinters of glass and wood showered around them. Before the car was clear of the crowd it had not a hand's-breadth of unbroken glass in any of its windows.

What would happen when the next car was met? Evidently the question occurred to some one of cooler head who was leading the column in its progress, for at the next corner the army swung to the right until a street on which there was no railway was reached, and then the course cityward was resumed. With every minute the march waxed more disorderly and more clamorous. Whenever a drinking-saloon was reached men, without waiting for order to halt, fell out singly or in small parties, falling in again farther to the rear, wiping their lips or carrying bottles in their hands. The army was now no more than a rabble, advancing with hats and handkerchiefs and empty bottles brandished in the air, and coarse jokes and laughter of hoarse and half-intoxicated voices. At its approach other pedestrians escaped into doorways, and scared faces peered from windows on either hand. The drivers of vehicles stopped when they came in sight of the mob, and, wheeling round, turned up side-streets. And as every one fled before it and made way, the insolent consciousness of its power grew upon the mob.

Without communication in words, the men knew that possession by right of might was theirs, and that the city was at their mercy. With this knowledge came also the unspoken sense of defiance of the law and of the people.

Imperceptibly but rapidly their attitude changed towards the individual citizens. Harmless, frightened faces looking from windows saw fists shaken at them. The wooden figures standing at the doors of cigar-stores were seized upon and broken, barbers' poles were pulled down, and occasional show-cases upon the sidewalk were wrecked. When the men entered a saloon it was not to buy, but to plunder. It was no longer a demonstration of strikers against the companies with which they were at war, but a riotous mob beyond the pale of the law, and whose enemy was the public peace.

As the traveller in Africa crossing a patch of the sensitive-plant sees the gray-green life shrink and recoil from him on every side as if his presence exhaled death, so human life fled at the approach of the mob, leaving it to sweep unresisted along deserted streets.   The occasional policeman stood sullenly back against the walls of buildings, and looked angrily at the men who jeered and hooted as they went by.

The first united halt was made at the City Hall, in front of which the crowd massed itself and raised, first, cheers for the mayor and then groans for Sullivan.   Word of the coming of the crowd had preceded it, and if any of the city officials were still within the building, for it was late in the afternoon now, they did not show themselves.   The faces of clerks appeared now and again at windows, and, being greeted with cries and hisses, vanished.   For perhaps a quarter of an hour the men hung about the public building, shouting aimlessly with an undefined expectation that something would happen, until, tiring of this, they moved on again towards the strikers' headquarters.

Here Wollmer, standing at an open window (the headquarters were situated on the first floor above the street), was waiting.   He signalled for silence, and as the men gathered into a solid mass below he spoke to them, arguing in behalf of peace.

"We are no lawless rioters," he said, "but peaceful citizens, who have no enemy except the tyrant corporations which are trampling on our rights and destroying our manhood.   I implore you to keep the peace.   If this demonstration ends now it will have served only to show the people our strength.   They will respect us for not using that strength, as we might so easily do, for ends of violence; and with the respect and sympathy of the people victory will soon be ours.   But we must not give our enemies the chance to say that we are breaking the laws."

Much more he said, and what he said was good.   There was reason enough why he should wish the laws to be observed.   But though he spoke vehemently, the audience received his utterances with apathy.   Inflamed with liquor and their taste of lawlessness, they were in no mood to listen to the voice of reason. When Wollmer ceased, another figure arose, standing on a door-step and waving its arms above its head.

"Let them remember," shrieked the new speaker, "that they shed the first blood! We have buried her to-day. They murdered her, and what may follow is on their heads."

That was all. But as the voice ceased and the figure stepped down into the crowd again, a roar of approval arose.

Wollmer had retreated from the window above, and for a while the mob stood irresolute in the gathering dusk. Some, the cooler headed probably, began to make their way through the door and up the stairway to the headquarters rooms. The great mass, however, waited in the street; but from this mass now parties began to break away. It did not disintegrate into individuals, but parted on the old natural lines of cleavage between the different nationalities. The Poles were the first to leave, led by the man who had spoken after Wollmer. They formed a company of some three hundred strong, and they disentangled themselves from the main body of the crowd, with much shouting from one to another of the name of their favorite drinking-place as their point of destination.

Other groups followed them until the army had separated into some eight or ten lesser corps, each formidable enough for mischief in itself, and only a sprinkling of men was left in front of the headquarters.

An hour or so later Marsh, walking moodily home from his office, brooding upon the strange disclosures of the afternoon, fell in with one of these detachments of the mob. At a corner he found his way suddenly barred by the passage of a body of some three hundred men—a ragged, uninviting regiment passing noisily under the electric light, amid the waving of sticks, fence-posts, barber-poles, stray signs stolen from over doorways, and other miscellaneous trophies picked up on the march. It was led by a tall man who had twisted a bright red handkerchief around his hat, and who thumped irregularly as he walked a broken drum. Marsh had heard nothing of what had been going on, and was at a loss to understand the demonstration. He stood on the curb for the procession to pass, looking at it in idle curiosity. Some one in the crowd, resenting perhaps the young lawyer's good clothes and appear-

ance of prosperity, threw a piece of kindling-wood at him, striking him on the shoulder, but without sufficient force to hurt
him, while the rest of the mob cheered and hooted.

Meeting Barry at his rooms, Marsh learned in outline the
events of the day. The municipal authorities, it appeared,
were at last seriously alarmed at the outlook. The street-railway company, after the first collision, which has already been
narrated, between a car and the strikers, had stopped the service all over the city, and had succeeded in getting all cars to
the barns before the army had reached the City Hall, at which
point they would, under ordinary circumstances, have found
cars passing in one direction or the other almost every minute.
Barry himself was considerably excited, intending, if occasion
arose, to offer his services that evening as a deputy-marshal,
or in whatever capacity he could make himself of use. For
Marsh, knowing the manner of Mrs. Masson's death, and understanding the absurdity of the strikers' canonization of the
dead woman, it was difficult to regard the situation as really
serious. But he remembered the old Greek maxim that though
revolutions may have deep underlying causes, they are usually
precipitated on the most trivial occasions.

On their way to the club the two friends bought copies of
an extra edition of an evening paper, from which, and from the
members of the club, they learned how threatening the outlook was. The paper spoke of the city as being already in a
state of anarchy and at the mercy of the mob. There had
been conferences of the city and county officials, and it was
evident that in spite of an effort to use brave language, all alike
were seriously apprehensive of what the night might bring
forth. A preliminary message had already been sent to the
governor of the State by the sheriff, informing him of the situation, and requesting him to issue orders to the militia to
hold themselves in readiness, in case the civil authorities proved
unable to maintain the peace. The atmosphere of the club
was charged with excitement. In the smoking and dining
rooms there was only one topic of conversation. While Marsh
and Barry were at dinner a detachment of the mob passed the
club-house, and, regarding it as an emblem of the party of
wealth and aristocracy, stopped for a minute to hoot and jeer

at it.   It was dark outside, and the blinds were drawn, and, peering under raised corners, the members within could make out but little of what was passing without.   It seemed for a time as if the mob proposed to make an assault upon the building; but they presently passed away with shouts and cheers, confining the active expression of their hostility to a bestowal of a dead cat upon the much-scrubbed club door-step. As soon as the crowd had gone a liveried servant picked up the desecrating thing and bore it delicately by the extreme tip of its tail through the hallway, between lines of gazing members, for disposal somewhere in the rear.

Marsh took little part in the conversation among the members.   At the dinner-table he suffered Barry to talk uninterruptedly, and afterwards, when three or four other men forgathered with them in the wine-room over the coffee and cigars, Horace was absent-minded and silent.   He knew so much about Mrs. Masson and Harrington, about events which, during the next day or two, must have so large a bearing upon the political situation, which these men did not know, that much of what they said seemed childish and absurd.   And he could not enlighten them.   Moreover, he was burning with the sense of his own wrongs — of the deception which had been practised upon him, and the way in which he had been used as a tool by his friends and counsellors.   Above all, he had not yet heard from Jessie, and he was oppressed with undefined fear of danger which the present outbreak might contain to her and to her father.   So he soon withdrew from the convivial circle, and, under pretence of reading a newspaper, seated himself in a corner of the reading-room, and chewed the cud of his thoughts alone.

Why had she not sent him the promised message, so that he might go to her this evening?   And the more he pondered the more uneasy and restless he grew.   At length it became intolerable, and, jumping quickly from his seat, he tossed his unread paper on a table, and walked hastily to the telephone closet, shutting the door carefully behind him.

"Hello!   No. 914, please."

"Hello!   Is that Mr. Holt's residence? . . . Is Miss Holt at home? . . . Would you ask her if Mr. Horace Marsh can have the pleasure of speaking to her for a minute at the telephone?"

As he waited his heart beat so loudly that the receiver which he held to his ear vibrated to it. He wondered whether he could hear her voice when she spoke. But as soon as the clear accent came to him his heart was still. It seemed as if all the world was hushed and silent while somewhere from far away, as if it came over endless stretches of level land and evening mist, came this fairy voice. Only the one word—"Hello!"—but he felt his left hand involuntarily grip the receiver tightly, and for a moment his head swam. He had not considered what he would say to her in the headlong impetuosity of his action.

"Hello! How do you do, Miss Holt? . . . This is Mr. Marsh. . . . I had understood — or, rather, hoped — that I might have a message from you."

"Yes. I had intended writing to you to-night," and over the telephone Horace could hear that there was hesitation and diffidence in the voice which spoke; and it gave him courage.

"But how can I wait?" he asked. "The message would have been to tell me that I might call and see you, would it not?"

"Perhaps."

"Then may I not call to-night? Let this do instead of a written message. Let me call to-night?"

There was a long pause before she answered.

"Yes, certainly, if you wish."

"I do wish very much."

"Well, we shall be very pleased to see you. Miss Willerby is here, but Miss Caley is not very well. Miss Willerby and I will be very glad to see you."

Horace longed to ask her to say that she would be even more glad than Miss Willerby; but he dared not frame the words.

"In, say, three-quarters of an hour from now, then?"

"Yes."

"Very well, and many, many thanks! Good-bye till then."

It was done! He would see her again! He came out of the little closet into the blazing light of the club hallway with his face aglow and every fibre of his being tingling. He clinched his hands and hardened his muscles, and could have shrieked aloud in triumph. Under pretext of lighting a cigar, he stopped to let the boisterous tumult in his veins subside before he rejoined the party in the wine-room. Then he plunged into the conversation, laughing and bubbling with anecdote and comment. It was another man from the morose being who had left that same table half an hour before so silently and moodily. It was as if he had drunk heavily — drunk of an elixir of intoxication and joy.

XXVI

MY FRIENDS THE ENEMY

HALF an hour later Marsh was in a cab, on his way to her house. In the neighborhood of the strikers' headquarters the street was so crowded that the driver was compelled to turn aside and go by by-ways. At another corner Marsh caught, in passing, a glimpse of a black mass of moving figures blocking the road, and he heard their shouts and laughter above the rattling of the cab. But he felt no ill-will towards the men. What did it affect him? Was he not going to her?

Suddenly from somewhere far away came the dull roar of an explosion. From which direction the sound reached him it was impossible to say. He wondered, indifferently, what it might be—an explosion of gas, probably, or perhaps it was only some blasting going on somewhere. It did not matter. He was going to her.

As the cab struck into the avenue on which Mr. Holt's residence was situated, two men crossed the street in the darkness under the horse's very nose, running in the same direction as he was travelling. Passing the Carrington house, Horace saw a knot of figures, men and women, coming down the driveway. Reaching the sidewalk, they too turned northward. At the next corner another figure appeared, running. Others could now be seen on either side of the street, all going the same way.

At first Horace was interested and perplexed. Then perplexity gave way to uneasiness, and uneasiness grew to sickening fear. Could it have been at her house that the explosion had occurred? Was it possible that the strikers would do such a thing?

Looking anxiously ahead, he could see that the number of

people on the sidewalks increased as he approached his destination. Was there not a dark mass as of a crowd of people there, about where the house stood? Before the horse had stopped, Horace had thrown open the door of the hansom and jumped to the ground. The crowd was not large in front of the house, but round on the south side of the building he could see that the lawn was covered with people. He pushed his way, as with authority, through the throng, and ran up the steps. Thomas stood in the doorway to bar the way to chance comers, but moved aside for Horace.

"Is any one hurt, Thomas?" Horace asked, breathlessly.

"No, sir; Mr. Holt had just stepped out of his study when the explosion occurred. It wrecked his desk, and the whole room is in ruins."

"And Miss Holt?"

"She is well, sir."

"What was it—dynamite?"

"We think so, sir."

Horace pushed on into the house. The air within was full of a white dust, through which the lights shone as in a dense smoke. The atmosphere was chill and damp, with a cloistral smell as of moist earth. In the centre of the broad hall a mass of white plaster lay upon the dark rugs, where it had fallen from the ceiling. Upon Marsh's right hand as he entered was the drawing-room, and next to that the less formal family sitting-room. Mr. Holt's study was situated in the rear of this last apartment. But all was blackness there. As he approached, Marsh could see that in place of the study doorway gaped a ragged chasm in the wall, and beyond — there seemed to be no room at all. An indistinguishable pile of broken furniture and débris lay upon what had been the floor, and behind that was nothing but the night. The outer wall of the study was completely gone, and in its place was only the open air, with the lights of the adjoining house shining through the darkness.

From behind a closed door somewhere Mr. Holt's voice could be heard as he spoke at the telephone. Horace, peering through the broken wall into the night, was startled by a sudden sob at his back, and, turning, saw two figures—Miss

Caley, barefooted and in a night-robe, with a shawl thrown over her shoulders, sobbing with her face buried in her hands, being led gently by Miss Willerby, who had one arm passed round the other's waist. Miss Willerby saw Horace and nodded in friendlywise as she helped her charge to the staircase, and the two figures ascended slowly.

Marsh retraced his steps towards the hall-door, looking now into the rooms on the other side—into the dining-room first, where gas-jets burned dimly, but which was empty, and then into the library. Here he found her. She was standing by the fireplace in a favorite attitude of hers, with a foot on the fender and her forehead bowed upon the hand which rested on the mantel.

" Miss Holt!"

At his voice she raised her face and looked at him. She was very pale, and her eyes shone intensely black and brilliant. As he came towards her she drew back. Then standing erect to face him, and throwing out her two hands rigidly with the palms upward, she said, in a strange, tense voice, as between her clinched teeth:

" See what your friends have done!"

" My friends!"

Horace stopped and looked at her in amazement; and as he saw how pale she was and how large and dark were her eyes, the amazement gave way to pity and great tenderness. And as he met and held her gaze he saw the hardness and defiance melt out of her eyes, and in its place came an appealing, helpless look that was all womanly. For some seconds she steeled herself to face him, until came the moment when her nerves would obey her will no longer, and, as instantaneously as the snapping of a violin string, her whole body broke and yielded; and, with a quick catching of her breath, she sank with her face in her hands into a chair. Immediately he was on his knees at her side.

" Miss Holt! Jessie!"

But she only sobbed.

" Jessie, my darling!"

And slowly moving one hand from her face with one of his, and placing the other beneath her chin and gently raising her face, he kissed her. And as if at last she had found the rest-ing-place for which, without knowing it, she had longed through all the weeks of wretchedness, she let her head rest upon his shoulder and gave way to her tears.

But the door of the apartment was open, and any one of the people who were moving in the hall might step into the room and see them. So, tenderly pushing her from him, he said, laughingly:

"I think they must have been my friends, after all."

She looked at him as she sat up and smiled through her tears—smiled, as it seemed to him, in happiness—and gave him her two hands to take. He held them, and raised each in turn lightly to his lips before rising from his knees.

"I must see if I can be of any use," he said. "You stay here."

In the hall he met Mr. Holt, seemingly as self-controlled as ever.

"It is an absurd time for congratulations, Mr. Holt," Horace said, as he shook hands; "but I understand that you had a narrow escape."

"Yes, luck was on my side," replied the other.

At that moment, from the rear of the house, amid a confused noise of slamming doors and hurrying feet, arose a frightened cry of "Fire!" Stepping back towards the study, the two men saw a thin, yellow flame flickering up from the pile of wreck-age. A man-servant hurried from the dining-room with a pitcher of ice-water in his hands, and dashed the contents on the blaze. Apparently it was extinguished, but only for a min-ute; and again it appeared, rather stronger than before. Other servants came with buckets and pitchers, which were emptied one after another upon the flames, which again smouldered down and seemed to die out for good.

"The fire department will be here in a minute," said Mr. Holt. "I have already telephoned for them on the chance. They are good people to have around at such times."

Even as he was speaking the angry clangor of the gong of an approaching engine was heard outside, and the house shook to the sound of the heavy wheels. Close upon the first engine came another, and immediately it seemed as if they were arriv-

ing from all sides at once. The shouts of authority were heard
without amid the panting of the engines and the din of gongs
and trampling horses, and within the hall was filled with hatted
and belted men tramping heavily in their large boots as they
dragged the long, snake-like line of hose behind them from the
front door back to the ruined study.

There is no martial law, no dictatorship or despotism, so
complete as the authority of the fire department when it takes
possession of a threatened building. In their rugged, silent
presence, so intent are they on the work which lies before them
—the work which is the supreme work of the moment—the
ordinary man, in the cowardly costume of common life, feels
himself grow suddenly impotent. His mere existence becomes
an impertinence. Horace, conscious of his uselessness, turned
again to seek Miss Holt. She was standing in the doorway of
the library, and he could not resist taking her hands once more
for just an instant. As their hands met she smiled with a smile
which awoke in him an irrational longing to roll upon the floor
at her feet.

" There is no danger, is there ?" she asked.

" None at all, I fancy."

" Do you know where the girls are ?"

" I saw Miss Willerby taking Miss Caley up-stairs when I
first came in.   Probably Miss Caley is dressing."

" What a dear, good girl Grace is," said Jessie.   " She is a
thousand times braver than I."

" She has not had a thousandth part of what you have had
to bear," said Horace.

Seeing the chief of the fire department passing in the hall,
Horace signalled to him.

" Is there any danger of fire ?"

" None at all, Mr. Marsh."

" Any reason why the ladies up-stairs should be told to get
their things together, and prepare to escape ?"

" None at all. See that thieves don't get their jewels, that
is all."   And the chief shouldered his way out into the night.

As Horace turned to Jessie again Marshall Blakely entered,
apparently the only man not a fireman or a member of the police-force whom the watchful Thomas had allowed to pass into

the house since Marsh had arrived. Horace, in his new happiness, felt forgiveness in his heart, and greeted Blakely cordially; but Jessie met him with a formal bow. Perhaps there was that in Horace's manner or a something in the atmosphere which told Blakely of his defeat; for he seemed unwontedly ill at ease.

"I am so delighted to hear that no one is hurt," he said to Miss Holt. "But can I be of any sort of service?"

"I know of nothing, thank you," said Jessie. "The policemen and firemen seem to have taken everything into their hands."

"As they ought to do. But you are not going to stay here to-night? Can I do anything in the way of going to the hotel and arranging for quarters for you?"

"No, thank you. I have not spoken to my father yet, and I don't know what he will do."

"Am I allowed to go back and see the damage?" he asked.

"I think so, if you can get through the firemen."

So Blakely bowed, seeming glad to get away, and passed on along the hall.

"Come and sit down, and tell me about it," said Horace, as soon as the other had gone.

"There is nothing to tell," she said, as soon as they were seated on a sofa which was out of range of eyesight from the door. "I was sitting looking at the fire, and perhaps—only perhaps, mind!—wondering if it were not nearly time for you to arrive, and what I should say to you when you did come. Grace was at the piano. Mary was up-stairs. Father came into the room to ask a question about Wilson's wife, who has been ill, and was just going back to his study when the thing happened. It threw father against the door-post, but did not hurt him. There was a smashing of glass, and the house shook so that things fell off the mantel-piece, and some of the pictures dropped from the walls. The noise was dreadful, but not as loud, I think, as I should have expected, and it was slow. For a moment I thought the whole house was coming down, and for a minute afterwards we could hear things falling and breaking everywhere. Then we heard Mary screaming, and thought she was hurt; but it was only fright. We have no idea how it

22

was done; probably they crept up to the house from outside and placed a bomb or something on the ledge of the study window. Just think if father had not happened to come out just at that moment!" And her voice broke as she added, "But it did not only 'happen.'"

Horace raised her hand to his lips.

"I heard the noise in my cab on the way up, and wondered what it was. To think of my not guessing! I supposed it was the gas-works or something."

Miss Willerby came in.

"How do you do?" she said, shaking hands with Horace. "I had not time to speak to you before." And by the light in her eyes and the clasp of her hand Horace saw that, by some mysterious process of feminine divination, she had guessed what had passed. And when she leaned over to kiss Miss Holt, Jessie also knew that she understood.

"Where is Mary?" Miss Holt inquired.

"She is talking to Mr. Barry in the drawing-room."

"Is Barry here?" asked Horace.

"He just arrived as we came down-stairs."

"Have you seen father?" Jessie asked.

"Yes; he is in the dining-room with some men—reporters, I suppose." And she leaned over Jessie again with a caress which bespoke congratulations, and, with another glad smile to Horace, turned to leave the room. As she did so Barry thrust his head into the doorway, and, without formality of greeting, called:

"Do you people know that the steel-works are burning?"

Miss Willerby hurried to one of the windows facing north, followed by Miss Holt and Horace. A dull red glare was visible in the sky in the direction in which the works lay, but the trees and buildings shut out the view.

"Let us go to the third story," suggested Jessie; "from the balcony there we can see."

The three started together and made their way through the hall, stepping over hose and skirting piles of fallen plaster, while the firemen stood back to let them pass. At the dining-room door Jessie stopped and called to Mr. Holt, who was seated at the table with three other men.

"Do you know the steel-works are on fire, father?" she asked.

"Yes, dear. But we cannot help by going there."

The three hastened on.

"I feel somehow as if I ought to be able to do something," Horace said to Jessie. "But what can I do? Anyway," he added, in a low tone, "I am too happy to care much whether I do my duty or not."

On the second floor Miss Willerby turned into her bedroom.

"You go on," she said; "I will join you in a minute," and Horace blessed her in his heart.

The third floor was in darkness except for one light burning in the hall. Jessie led the way across the hard, polished floor of the dancing-room to where a wide French window opened on a small balcony. Horace fumbled for the fastening, and finally succeeded in pushing the window open. Stepping out, they could see how completely the flames had fastened upon the great buildings. Of the main shop itself the roof had apparently already fallen in, and the walls, very black against the yellow background, contained nothing but one huge furnace, from which the flames licked high into the heavens. Other of the buildings were burning either at one side or from the roof. The whole quarter of the sky was lit up to a brilliant orange fading to crimson at the horizon, while black scarves and wreaths of smoke rolled upward and drifted away northward before the breeze. Now and again falling rafters or the ruin of a wall would for a moment smother the raging fire, and the smoke rose in denser columns. But an instant later—as if it were some huge beast which devoured whatever was thrown to it, and only raged for food the more fiercely it was fed—the flame leaped again, and seemed to throw off masses of itself, which floated for an instant detached in the air.

At this distance of about a mile the roar of the conflagration came to them like the muffled thunder of a heavy waterfall. The light fell upon their faces and tipped the half-bare branches of the trees with crimson, and flashed upon the walls and roofs of neighboring houses.

Jessie drew a long breath.

"It is terrible," she said; "but, oh, it is grand!"

"It is wicked—wicked—wicked!" said Horace.

They stood side by side and watched in silence. Then Horace turned his face to her, and found that with the glow of the flames on the high forehead and the rounded cheeks she was pleasant to look upon. Presently under his gaze she turned her eyes to his.

"Tell me," he said, faltering; "down-stairs, just now, you meant everything, did you not? You have given yourself to me?"

She did not answer, but in her eyes he read that which emboldened him to take her hands in his and draw her to him, and, holding her closely, to kiss her again.

"My darling!" he murmured; "and to think that only yesterday— Do you know what I have lived through during these last few weeks? Have you any idea of the blackness of life?"

"I am sorry," she said, "and I have wanted you, too. I misunderstood—and yet my heart did not believe it. I know now that my heart never could have believed such things of you. I knew it last night, at the meeting, the instant I heard your voice—"

"At what meeting?"

"Why, at Columbus Hall. Did not Mr. Barry tell you we were there?"

"No. You heard me speak last night? You were in the hall? And he— The wretch!"

"Don't call him names. He persuaded me to go; and if I had not gone and heard you, we should not be here to-night together."

"He is not a wretch; he is a god! And I too," he added, after a pause, "am a god to-night. If I was mortal this happiness would kill me."

> "'She raised a mortal to the skies,
> He drew an angel down.'

Pardon me. I must talk nonsense." As he pondered, the full sense of Barry's duplicity came to him. "If you could have heard that villain—I mean that god—asking me ques-

tions about the meeting, and the simple, childish interest which
he showed in my account of it, and the way he affected to dis-
believe—! He deserves to be smothered—with kindness, bless
him!"

Meanwhile in the distance a fierce fight was raging. The
great shop was still but a huge devil's caldron of flames which
did not seem to abate. Where a smaller building on the
south had been burning when they first came out was now
only blackness, the firemen evidently having mastered the fire
at that point; but from another building beyond the machine-
shop, and only partly visible behind it, a sheet of flame was
rising which was a conflagration in itself. Against the yellow
the watchers could see the dark lines of the streams of water
playing; and the uncertain volume of the blaze and the in-
termingling eddies of steam and smoke told how hard a fight
was being waged. Then, as they looked, the whole of one
wall of the great machine-shop fell inward, the roar and crash
of the catastrophe reaching their ears long after the wall had
gone. At first it seemed that the flames had been overwhelmed
in the avalanche, and only a dull red swirl of luminous smoke
filled the space where the blaze had been. But, first at one
end and then from the centre, the fire leaped up again, angrier
only and hungrier than before.

"It is wicked—wicked—wicked!" said Horace.

They were still watching when Miss Willerby stepped from
the darkness behind out to the balcony.

"There is a little girl down-stairs, Jessie," she said, "who
wants to see you."

"What kind of a little girl?"

"A *very* little girl—thin and old-looking. She will not give
her name, but insists on seeing Miss Holt."

Jessie, followed by the other two, went down-stairs.

"She is in the library," said Miss Willerby.

The party entered that room, and there, standing very stiffly in the middle of the floor, as if seeking to place herself as
far from every article of furniture as possible, stood Lizzie
Silling.

"Why, Lizzie," Jessie exclaimed, "how do you do?"

"Quite well, thank you," said Lizzie.

Jessie settled herself in a chair and drew the child to her. "And how is your mother?"

"She's quite well. She got Mrs. Balderson's washing yesterday. She's been tryin' to get it for a year."

"I'm glad to hear that."

Miss Holt waited for Lizzie to explain her sudden appearance, but Lizzie kept silence.

"Did you want to tell me something?" Miss Holt asked at last.

"Yes," the child replied, simply, looking first at Miss Willerby and then at Horace.

"Do not mind these two," said Jessie. "These are my two best friends in all the world, next to my father." As she said it she looked at Horace, who felt his heart leap; and Miss Willerby discreetly kept her eyes on Lizzie and smiled. "This is Miss Willerby and this is Mr. Marsh," continued Miss Holt, introducing them. "This is Lizzie Silling."

"I wanted to tell you something," Lizzie began, hesitatingly—"I wanted to tell you what they was goin' to do tonight, but I come as fast as I could. I couldn't come no quicker."

"What do you mean?" Jessie asked. "How did you know what they were going to do?"

"I heard 'em talkin'," said the child.

"Whom did you hear talking, and when?"

"To-night. Bart and another man. I was sittin' on the bottom step goin' up to our place, inside the door, an' it was all dark; and Bart and him come in from the street an' stood inside the passage, an' I heard 'em talk. They didn't see me."

"What did they say?"

"They said as Bony said as it would go off about half-past eight. Bart was tellin' the other fellow, an' it was near half-past eight then."

"Who is Bart?"

"He's an Italian what keeps a fruit-stand."

"And Bony?"

"He's another Italian. He used to work for the steel company, an' was fired 'cos he got drunk. He's a tough, Bony is. So's Bart. It was Bony as come nigh killin' Dutch Sam' cos Sam sassed 'im. Oh, he's bad."

" What did Bart say Bony told him ?"

The child pondered a minute.

" He said as Bony said it would go off about half-past eight, when Mr. Holt was in his room writin'. He said as Bony said as there was enough of it to kill the whole family."

" And what did you do ?"

" Jest sat still. I waited till they'd gone, an' that was quite a while. They was waitin' fer it to go off, but they got tired. An' soon as they went I come here. But it's quite a ways, an' I couldn't get here no sooner. I hadn't hardly started before I heard it go off."

" Did you walk all the way ?"

" No, I run."

" You good girl ! But now I want you to tell this all over to somebody else."

" Not to the police ?"

" No ; to my father now, but perhaps to the police, too. Why not ?"

" 'Cos I'm scared."

" Oh no, you are not," said Jessie ; " and if I want you to, I know you will."

" I will go and find Mr. Holt," said Horace.

He found him still in the dining-room in consultation with the chief of police and a detective. The reporters had gone. Horace drew Mr. Holt aside, and told him the situation briefly.

" If you will excuse me a minute, gentlemen," Mr. Holt said, addressing the other two. " I learn from Mr. Marsh that there is somebody waiting to see me whose evidence may be of value to us. If you will wait here, I will be back in a few minutes."

Lizzie told her story again to Mr. Holt, and yet a third time in the presence of Chief Winley and the detective, more diffidently, but none the less producing, under their skilful questioning, many queer odds and ends of information of greater or less collateral value. It was nearly midnight before the policemen said that she could go home, and Jessie asked her how she would go. The child looked puzzled.

" How will you get home ? Will you walk and go alone ?"

" Yes," said Lizzie, wonderingly ; " mother ain't here."

" But you can't walk all that way alone at night."

Evidently the child was bewildered.

"Let me take her home in a cab," suggested Horace.

"I guess not," was all she said.

"Better just let her go," said the detective. "She is used to it, and it would never do for any one to be seen with her. They 'ld kill her."

So Jessie reluctantly let the little one go off into the darkness alone, with three long miles of walk ahead of her. She kissed her many times and sent messages to her mother, all of which the girl received with perfect stolidity, and then slipped sideways out of the front door and down the steps into the night, and was swallowed up.

"And I suppose that I must go," said Horace, as he and Jessie stood side by side on the door-step. "You will be safe here now; but I do not any the less hate to leave you.

"And I may call again to-morrow afternoon ?" he asked, after a pause.

"If you wish."

"And to-morrow evening ?"

"If you wish."

"And may I see Mr. Holt to-morrow evening and tell him ?"

"If you wish."

"And do you know that I am the most insanely happy man in America to-night ?" he said. "And I ought to be. It isn't only a lover's prejudice. I honestly believe that you are the sweetest, truest, dearest, loveliest, best girl living. I know you are. And you are to be *mine*—mine—my wife ! Oh, my darling !"

XXVII

THAT night the city lay under a reign of terror. At a dozen different points fire broke out, but, with the exception of the destruction of the steel-works, with little serious damage. The street-railway company had massed men enough around its barns and power-houses to protect them, and the strikers, having all the city for their prey, made no attempt to carry any of those buildings by storm. But the windows of the company's offices were wrecked, and through the town the drunken mobs roamed unresisted, plundering and rifling where they would.

In the gray of the morning special trains arrived, bringing companies of militia from various points, and the local companies, assembling at their armories, marched through the streets in the dawning light. Early risers after the uneasy night heard the level words of command and the regular tramp of marching feet, and peered from beneath their window-shades to see the blue uniforms go by.

Horace, returning to his rooms, sat down to write to her. Barry, arriving an hour later, found him still writing. But Barry appeared downcast and uncommunicative, and retired. And Horace still wrote. He had nothing to say but the one same thing, and he said it again and again—told how he had known for months that only in one way could his life ever be happy, and how unutterably bitter the world had been for the last few weeks. He tried to put into the words with which he told her of his happiness something of the fervor and triumph of the swirl that was in his veins; and in page after page he told her of her own goodness and how good God was to him. And when he had written far into the morning he

rose and sank into his favorite arm-chair and lit his pipe.
More than once during the night the howls and laughter of
the mobs in the street reached his ears, and before he went to
bed he heard the roll of drums, and the air without was light.

It was late when he reached his office. The door to his
partner's room was closed, and in his happiness Horace's
heart ached for the grief and the shame that lay beyond it.
Work was out of the question, and he sat and gazed, dreaming,
out of the window.

His dreams were interrupted by the opening of his partner's
door. Horace swung round in his chair and prepared to rise,
but instead of the General it was Sullivan who issued from the
adjoining room, closing the door carefully behind him.

"Whist!" said he, in a low voice; "but it's a sad and amazin' pecurious situation; and not the least part of the sadness
is that we'll be losin' yersilf from the party, me lad."

The sight of the Irishman brought back to Horace's mind
the recollection of the trick that had been played upon himself. He rose, and, facing the other, said, very calmly:

"I think so. It is not so much the party that is at fault
as some of the blackguards who lead it and lie to it." He
paused for a moment, and continued:

"Did it ever occur to you, Mr. Sullivan, that in the long-
run falsehood and trickery and blackguardism are sure to lose
you more friends than they will make? Did it never occur
to you—setting the ethical question aside—that it might pay
you to try and be a gentleman?"

Sullivan stood patiently and heard him through.

"Aisy, me lad," said he, when Horace ceased; "there are
not many men as could talk to Tim Sullivan that ways, an' I
think ye'll be afther doin' me the coortesy to believe that if I
don't resent it, it isn't because I'm afraid of ye. It's because
I like the nerve of ye, me young bantam, an' because ye're in
the right."

The Irishman seated himself deliberately.

"Sit down, me lad," he said, and Horace obeyed. Sullivan placed a hand upon his knee. "I like the nerve of ye, I
says, and I like yersilf. Ye'll lave the party, av coorse, an'
maybe ye'll jine the inimy for a while. But ye can't stay

with thim, for ye'll find they're as rotten as us. Thin maybe
ye'll jine a new party that's yet to be formed—an' formed it
will be; but whatever party ye goes to, me lad, ye'll be a
leader of it, an' ye've got a great career ahead of ye. Ye'll go
straight, that I know. An' the man who goes straight goes
far."

Horace's lips curled, and the Irishman saw it.

"I know what ye're thinkin' to yersilf—that Tim Sullivan's
a quare man to be preachin'! An' maybe he is, an' maybe he
isn't. We learn more by our mistakes than by our successes,
an' it may be that Tim Sullivan knows better what he has missed
than the wurrld gives him credit for. Ye think I'm a success?
So I am. I have made me way. But do ye think I never lie
awake o' nights thinkin' what I might have been? I had me
choice, to go right or wrong—to take the long road or the short
one. An' I went wrong. I was young then, and didn't know
what I know now—that I had success in me—an', looked at
frontways, the long road seemed the short one. It's different
looked at from behind. It isn't brains that makes a man govern
men, nor education, nor money—it's the *man* of him." Horace
was still silent, and again the other went on. "I had the man
in me, but I took the wrong road. Ye've taken the right one.
Had I chosen as ye have when I was yer age, I'd be handlin'
the national government at Washington to-day as aisy as I play
with the City Hall. An' ye can have the career that I missed
an' more—ye can git what I couldn't have touched. Ye'll pass
maybe from one party to another, but ye'll never be in the same
party as me. We'll be agin one anither to the end hereafter;
but mind this, me lad, ye'll rise, an' I honor ye, an'—barrin' politics—if ye iver need a friend in life, Tim Sullivan's always where
ye can find him."

The Irishman had risen and buttoned his coat. Marsh too
stood up, and the two faced each other in silence. Then, by a
sudden impulse, Horace held out his hand, and the other took it
with a grip that made Horace's fingers crack; then turned upon
his heel and rolled ponderously away.

"The man of him"—the Irishman was nearly right; nor
was Horace sure that the Irishman's estimate of his poten-
tialities was exaggerated. It was a new side of him which

Horace had just seen—a side which was probably exhibited to few.

As for Horace himself—yes, he must leave the party. He had already recognized it without definitely formulating the fact to himself. It was the end of a dream which had been very bright; the crumbling of castles that he had loved to live in. But not the end of the dream, perhaps. The material that he had been working with, and believed to be good and clean, was worthless. The smooth clay under his fingers had turned to dust and refuse. But was there not good clay somewhere? *Amphora cœpit institui* — and not so much as a wretched pitcher had come of it. But would the shapely vase never be turned? Somewhere, though it slumbered deep, the American people must have a conscience. Somehow it could—and would—be touched. They did not understand as yet; they did not see. They were too busy with other things. But if there is one lesson which is writ large in the history of the nation it is that when once the people are awakened and see and understand, they will have right. Had all the manhood and truth left the race in the course of one generation? Under the lash of the labor union, had the working-classes indeed become but this mob of rioting, drunken fools whom Wollmer juggled with? Had the iron of the ward machine so eaten into the soul of all classes that the whole people were no more than these puppets that Sullivan made to dance? It could not be. When the trumpet had called before, the nation had answered. And somewhere the same stern fibre was in the people—the people whose fathers and great-grandfathers had followed Washington and Grant.

Meanwhile, Horace had yet two speeches to make, according to the programme of the campaign; and he took his pen and wrote to the chairman of the committee, expressing his regret that he would be unable to fill the engagements. He wrote briefly, assigning no reason for his failure, and was addressing the envelope when there reached him from his partner's room a sound which made his pulse stand still.

Springing from his chair, he hurried to the door communicating between the rooms. Franklin, in the outer office, had heard the sound also, and was close at Horace's shoulder. Horace knocked, but no answer came. He pushed open the door and entered. The shades of the three windows had been lowered, and through the semi-opaque fabric the light came thick and yellow. The form of the General, seated at his desk, stood out in profile silhouette against the nearest window. He was leaning back in his chair with his head sunk upon his breast and his arms hanging listlessly on either side, as if he had fallen asleep at his work.

"General!" Horace called, and hurried to his side. But there was no response. Close by the fingers of the right hand, where it had slipped upon the floor, lay a pistol. From the closed lips of the drooping head blood oozed, clotting the tufted beard and trickling across the white expanse of shirtfront.

"Call Dr. Lawton and notify the police," Horace said, and Franklin left the room.

Marsh took his partner's wrist to feel the pulse, but he could not find it. He shifted his fingers and held his breath, and still there was no throb. Again and again he tried, but not a flutter or beat of life was there. Horace gently let the arm down to hang as it had done before. He raised the head slightly, and tucked his handkerchief beneath the chin.

Poor gray head! Horace looked down upon it, and thought that he might have known that this would happen. The man who, twenty-five years ago, had lacked courage to face his petty creditors in the small New Jersey town could not have stood against the larger shame which threatened him to-day. It was "the man of him" that was wanting. "Unstable as water, thou shalt not excel." But Horace knew the kindness of his heart and loved him. Weak he had been—too weak to bear the burden of his own mistakes—too weak to resist being moulded by stronger fingers to whatever form of good or ill they pleased. But to Horace he had been all gentleness and consideration. In the matter of the newspaper article Horace knew that it was not his partner who had planned and done the wrong. In everything else the dead man had been to his young partner lovable and full of kindly thought; and Horace felt that many a stronger and even better man could have been more easily spared.

On the General's desk lay a sheet of paper on which there was writing. It was signed with the General's name, and Horace leaned over and glanced at it. It was addressed to "The Democratic State Central Committee and the Members of the Democratic Party" — a brief and dignified letter, announcing his withdrawal from the candidacy for the governorship of the State.

Franklin re-entered the room.

"Did you get the doctor?" Horace asked. The other nodded.

"Is he dead?" he whispered.

Horace bowed his head.

In a few minutes the doctor arrived. Death, he said, had been practically instantaneous. The General had placed the muzzle of the pistol in his mouth, and the bullet had passed upward into the brain.

An officer of the police-force came, but there was no need of an inquest, and the doctor called the undertaker over the telephone.

"Had General Harter any relatives?" asked the policeman.

"None in the city, I believe," Horace said. "But he may have some at his home in Massachusetts. It would be best to communicate with the chief of police there, and I will telegraph to my father, who lives there too. But "— and Horace hesitated — "the General's name was not Harter." He had drawn the officer aside, and spoke in a low voice. "It is not generally known, and I only learned it yesterday. Please say nothing about it until the proper announcement has been made by Mr. Pawson, the attorney. It will probably be made to-day. Meanwhile treat my information as confidential, to be used only in your telegram to the Massachusetts police. His name was Harrington—William Harrington. He was born at Lowell, and lived there till he was twenty. Then he moved to Boston, to New York, and then to Freehold, New Jersey, where he lived for some years—until he came West. Perhaps with this information you can find his relatives. It is possible that there may be further clews among his papers; but I doubt it, for he had buried his old life deep. The only person in these parts who knew anything of his past is dead — died a week ago."

Over the telephone Horace told Pawson what had happened, and made an appointment to meet at the other's office at once and decide on the right course to be taken in regard to the public announcement which would have to be made.

The undertaker came and bore the body away. Horace wrote a short note to Jessie, telling her of the calamity, and saying that he might be later than he had hoped to be in seeing her that afternoon. Then he repaired to the office of the firm of Pawson & Burt.

There was not need of much deliberation. To Pawson, the attorney, was intrusted the work of preparing a formal statement of the facts, which would be given to the press for publication on the following morning, Horace charging himself with the office of breaking the news to Jennie Masson and her sister. Calling a cab, he drove at once to the house in Fourth Street, but learned that the sisters were both away from home, the elder being at the hospital. This was well; for Horace had intended to see Harrington, and it would be better if the story could be told to the two together.

Twenty minutes later he was at the hospital, where Jennie was sitting by her lover's bedside. The patient was doing well, and the doctor had promised that he should be about again in six or seven weeks. Harrington greeted his friend cordially, and Horace took a chair on the opposite side of the bed to that on which Jennie was sitting, and began at once to tell his story.

He told of his partner's death, and the other two expressed their sympathy. Then with difficulty Horace narrated the events of the preceding day. When he mentioned the dead man's real name, Jennie started as if to speak; but she checked herself, remembering that Charlie as yet knew nothing of the mention of the name of Harrington in the woman's dying words, or of the suspicion which it had brought upon himself. But Horace saw that her eyes danced with gladness, and tears, which he knew were tears of joy, stole down her cheeks. Harrington lay and listened in silence until, turning suddenly to Jennie, he said:

"That's what she used to mean by 'the other Harrington fellow.' How queer! You remember, don't you?"

And Jennie pressed his hand for an answer.

Then Horace went on to tell of where the General and Mrs. Masson had first met, and gave the details of the General's life as he himself had told them—how he, too, had lived in Lowell in his early days, and how he drifted away and wandered till he reached Freehold.

"Freehold!" gasped Harrington, quickly. "Why, it can't be—but it must! He was my uncle Will! I have heard my father speak of him fifty times. I remember seeing him as a child. He was my father's youngest brother. He wandered off to make his fortune, and the family lost all track of him at Freehold. My uncle Will!"

The others listened in silence.

"Will you telegraph to my father?" he said to Marsh. "Tell him the facts, and ask if the body shall be sent home. They will probably wish it."

"And how amazingly small the world is," he continued, turning to Jennie, "or how wonderfully Providence works. My father's brother and your father's wife—you and I! But we shall be luckier and happier than they. They are dead now, but—well, I think I am stronger than he was, and I know you are better than she."

Horace soon left them to send the telegram to his friend's father, and then, it being now after two o'clock, stopped to take some lunch. His meal finished, he repaired again to Pawson's office, and found that the attorney had already drafted the statement for the press. The two went over it together, and Horace found nothing to criticise. Between them they added a paragraph containing the news of the dead man's relationship to the victim of the strikers—a detail of collateral evidence which completed the identification of the deceased.

"As for the moral to be drawn from it and the exoneration of the younger Harrington," Pawson said, "we need not trouble ourselves. I have seen my brother, and he will take this article up to Mallitt, of the *Republican*, himself, and talk it over with him, so that Mallitt will get the situation in all its bearings. My brother, I think, is at work on his article now. But what a preposterous outcome it is! This woman whom the strikers have canonized—this martyr to their cause—died only of her own passion for greed, because she would not forfeit the chance of blackmailing a man whom she professed to have loved!"

"It is about as near the truth as some of our ideals come," said Horace.

"Have you heard," asked Horace, later, "whether there has been any collision yet between the troops and the strikers? I have been too busy to think of it."

"I believe not. The strikers seem to have disappeared. Whether they have made up their mind to keep out of the way of the troops, or whether they are only sleeping off their liquor, I don't know. I suspect that it is the latter, and that there will be trouble to-night."

At his office an hour later Horace found a message from the elder Harrington, asking that the body of his brother be sent on to Lowell for burial. He enclosed the telegram in a note to Harrington at the hospital, and sent word to the undertaker. Then at last he found himself free to go to Jessie. Reporters of the afternoon papers, he was informed, had been looking for him all day; but he was glad to have escaped them, and again entering a cab, he started to drive to Mr. Holt's residence.

He was still a mile from his destination when he saw the familiar, square-set figure of Judge Jessel. Bidding the driver draw up to the sidewalk, Horace asked the judge whither he was bound, and learning that his goal was the same as his own, made room for him in the cab.

Judge Jessel had already learned of General Harter's death, and he expressed his condolences. Horace received them in silence.

"But the greater part of the news," he said, "you have yet to hear. I cannot tell it, but you will learn it from the papers in the morning."

"That's one of the meanest things I know," said the judge— " to hint at a story and withhold it. I would say it was femininely mean, if it was not that I should insult Mrs. Jessel by suggesting that she could do such a thing. She is almost the only woman I know who does not. But I am not sure that the authority of this court would not extend to making you divulge."

They talked for a while of the outrage against Mr. Holt, and

23

Horace felt that there was other and yet greater news that he longed to tell.

At last the judge broached the subject of politics.

"Have you thought at all," said he, "of what we were talking of at the club the other day? Has the course of the strike made any impression on you?"

"Some, perhaps," Horace answered, reluctantly; "but other things have made more. I shall probably vote with you next week—at least, I shall not vote with the Democrats and Populists."

"That is good; then you must vote with us. We are not Republicans this year; we are only against the other fellows. And if you will not help them, then you must help us. Not voting at all would be helping them."

"You may be right, but I am not quite certain yet." And the judge thought it better to let the subject drop.

Outside the house, as they arrived, Horace and the judge found policemen stationed at each gate, to keep away the idlers and the impertinent, who thronged the sidewalks and the street. On the south side, where the explosion had occurred, masons were at work. Before entering, the two friends walked round to the scene of the wreck, and here, in the daylight, even though the débris had been removed, the terrific violence of the shock was seen. The outer wall, from side to side of the study, was entirely gone, and a broad crack ran irregularly upward to several feet above the level of the lower story, where it connected with the window of the floor above. Downward, however, the chief force of the explosive had expended itself. The floor of the study was not, except in a few ragged ends of projecting and splintered boards. The outer wall had been shattered down to the level of the lawn, and for a space of many feet the gravel-walk and the grass beyond were torn up. The floor of the study had been some four feet above the level of the land outside, and through a jagged hole, ten feet across, the basement beneath was laid bare. Here, fortunately, the basement was no more than unoccupied cellarage, for the kitchen and laundry lay on the north side of the house, beneath the dining-room and library.

Within the house other callers were assembled. Mrs. Tisser-

ton was there and Mrs. Flail, with others whom Horace knew
but slightly or was little interested in. Every one who had
the excuse of a calling acquaintance with Miss Holt had been
that day, either to express their real anxiety or gratify their
curiosity.

Jessie's greeting to Horace was very sweet, and the softest
sympathy was in her eyes as she spoke of his partner's death.
She thanked him charmingly for the flowers which he had sent
her that morning with his note, written the night before, and
which were enthroned, as of old, in the great Rookwood vase—
except one large red blossom, which Jessie wore upon her breast.

In the pause which succeeded the greetings, Mrs. Tisserton,
leaning back in her chair, spoke in that evenly distinct voice of
hers, and with a certain frank directness of expression which
she had and which people who did not like her said came very
near at times to being impertinent.

"Do tell us, Mr. Marsh, about General Harter," she said.
"It is so difficult to speak about dead people in the presence
of their relations or friends. One never knows whether they
really liked the deceased or not, and it is so absurd to gush,
when you don't in the least mean it, to people who know
you don't mean it, and have to gush themselves because it is
the seemly thing to do. Please give us the key-note, and tell
us how to pitch our condolences. Did you really care for
General Harter?"

"I cared for him very much," said Horace, gently. "We
worked together in politics, as you know, and as a partner
and a friend he had my deep affection and regard."

Jessie glanced at him gratefully, and Judge Jessel relieved
the silence which threatened to follow by saying:

"He was, on the whole, a good man. He lacked some
strand of manliness which ought to have been twisted into
his being, and had he had it he might have been great—

> "'Had I been two, another and myself,
> Our head would have o'erlooked the world.'

But without it he was still a man to be respected and loved.
His heart was large, and, left to himself, he was anxious to do
and live rightly."

"I am awfully sorry," said Mrs. Tisserton.

The conversation turned to the explosion of the night before, and Jessie answered many questions, until the subject of the strike in general came up, and Mrs. Flail, as it were, took the floor. This good lady seemed to think that in some way the public crisis threw a responsibility upon her—that upon her, in her capacity of general organizer, devolved the duty of restoring public peace. She talked with vigor of what she had done and what she proposed to do. She had hoped to inveigle the strikers into spending their idle hours in the free library, because reading would have opened their minds and been so good for them, she said, and they never had time to read when they were at work; but she regretted to say that, with all her efforts, the attendance at the library had been no greater since the strike began than it had been before. She had striven to arouse their enthusiasm in behalf of a coffee-house which she had established in a poor part of town, and which some day would grow into a people's palace, she hoped; but the men had remained deplorably indifferent to the seductions of coffee. She had hoped that they would accept the invitations, which had been extended to them in the advertising columns of the daily papers, to attend the various classes on artistic and literary subjects; but she had failed so far to identify at any of the meetings so much as a single striker.

"And so much might be done," she said, "if only others would help. I cannot do it all alone. The softening and humanizing influences of art and literature would certainly affect them. I have seen Mr. Wollmer several times, and he thoroughly agrees with me—and yet they do not seem to come."

Horace smiled within himself. Judge Jessel fidgeted impatiently. Perhaps it was owing to the dissimilarity between Mrs. Flail and his beloved wife; but for some reason the judge, as Horace knew, had only an indifferent estimate of Mrs. Flail. There was malice in his voice and a twinkle in his eye as he asked:

"By-the-way, Mrs. Flail, how did the soup-kitchen prosper?"

"It did not prosper," replied that lady, reluctantly. "It

seemed as if these men positively preferred what is known, I believe, as the 'free lunch' at the saloons to a wholesome bowl of soup at the kitchen. A few came at first, but the number decreased every day, and we have converted the kitchen into a moral parlor."

"What was it that they did not like? Did you have any regulations?"

"None at all. They were made to wash, and brush their hair, and wait until all were ready. Then they marched in in two rows to the dining-room, and stood up while prayers were said—just short prayers, you know, only ten or fifteen minutes. Then they were served in turn, and all waited till the last had finished, when prayers were said again."

"What is a moral parlor?"

"It is a place with chairs and tables and good books and papers—not daily papers, you understand, but instructive and edifying publications which will be of benefit to them. Then we permit dominos and spillikens for the men to play with."

"Are they allowed to smoke?"

"Oh no."

"Does anybody come?"

"Very few come, I am sorry to say. It really seems impossible to do anything to help them. If only we could reach them and talk to them and reason with them. The pastors have been very kind. Either Dr. Jones or Dr. Flodder or Dr. Tomkins is at the parlors every evening, prepared to speak to them in an informal, friendly way. But even if there is any one there, they usually go out when the exhortation begins."

"And the men really prefer the saloons?" asked Mrs. Tisserton, as she lay back and looked at Mrs. Flail through half-closed eyes. "They are allowed to smoke there, are they not?"

"I believe so." Then Mrs. Flail made bold to do a thing that she had been longing to attempt for half an hour. "Judge Jessel," she said, "could I induce you to come and speak at our parlor some evening? I think they would listen to you if they will not to the ministers."

"On certain conditions, I would gladly," said the judge.

"If you will take away your edifying publications, and put in their places the daily papers and the comic weeklies; if you will have music instead of preaching in the evenings—with some one to sing a comic song, and let the crowd join in the chorus; if you will let them smoke—give them free tobacco, if possible—you will have a thousand men there every night within two weeks, and then I will gladly come and talk."

But Mrs. Flail shook her head.

"That would be so demoralizing," she said.

"Don't you think," said Jessie, "that it is much easier to get people to do what you want them to do, if you begin by letting them do what they want to do first?"

"But there are things that you cannot let them do."

"Such as smoking and reading the daily papers?" suggested Mrs. Tisserton.

The judge now rose to go, and at the signal others left. One by one they went away, till at last Horace was alone with Jessie.

"Where are Miss Willerby and Miss Caley?" he asked.

"Grace is up-stairs writing letters. Miss Caley has gone home."

"What, back to Chicago! Why?"

"She thought that there was danger in the house here, and—and her mother would not like her staying. She was really awfully frightened, poor girl."

"And Barry?" Horace suggested.

"I think that is all over for good," Jessie answered. "I gathered so from what Mary said."

"Miss Willerby is not going away?"

"Oh no. She refuses to go till I turn her out. She is such a dear girl!"

"Did she guess anything last night?" he asked.

"I am afraid she did," laughed Jessie.

"Did she say anything?"

"She said a great deal."

"And what did you tell her?"

"I told her just what you would have wished me to tell her—very much the same things as you told me on the door-step last night."

Horace could not answer, but only raised her hand silently to his lips, and wondered if this were possible. That he could have won her was wonderful enough—that she should passively consent to be his. But that his love could mean to her the happiness that hers brought to him—that was as yet unbelievable. For Horace Marsh had that clean reverence for womanhood which every pure man has, and which forbids him to believe that a woman can wish for a man as a man wishes for her.

XXVIII

As Pawson had told Horace, no collision occurred between the strikers and the troops during the day. The affairs of the city flowed in the ordinary channels; the electric cars ran unmolested, and outwardly the town was at peace. There were those who said that the governor had acted with unwarrantable haste in responding so promptly to the request of a sheriff who had but lost his head; but the majority of the citizens took comfort in the knowledge that the militia were at hand. The soldiers themselves had gone quietly into camp at two different points in the city — five companies being camped on some vacant ground not far from the central barns of the street-railway company, and the other three companies nearer to the heart of the town, in the railway-yards near the Union station.

It was dusk before news came that the strikers, gathered in their usual haunts, were showing symptoms of reviving turbulence. A car running out to the steel-works was attacked, and the engineer brutally beaten. The street-railway company again suspended the service, and called all cars into the barns. Indefinite rumors of minor outrages, which the police were unable to prevent, came at intervals, and the militia, under arms, stood ready to march at a minute's notice. Then came the definite news that a large body of strikers—estimated at about a thousand men, chiefly Poles and Bohemians — had collected in "The Pit," and, inflamed with liquor, were on their way southward, with the avowed purpose of demolishing the central barns and killing any soldiers who attempted to bar their progress. The mob was advancing by Harrison Avenue, and would presumably follow that thoroughfare till reaching Thirteenth Street.

Silently in the darkness of the early November night three of the companies at the main camp fell in and marched to Thirteenth Street, then swung eastward to meet the advancing mob. At some distance from the junction with Harrison Avenue the noise of the shouting of the rabble came to them on the night air. A square farther on the order was given to halt, and, as they stood, the roar from the east grew louder, till at last, three hundred yards ahead, the front of the mob came round the corner—a black, moving mass, with here and there a waving torch.

They did not at first discover the soldiers, drawn in close ranks across the road, but came howling and laughing and shouting forward. Colonel Gray had advanced some twenty paces ahead of his men, and stood with the sheriff by his side. The mob was less than one hundred yards distant now.

" Halt!" commanded the colonel.

At the same moment it seemed that the strikers became aware of the presence of the militia. The front ranks wavered and stood still, and the shouting died away. In the comparative silence the voice of the sheriff made itself heard, commanding them, in the name of the law, to disperse and keep the peace. But as he spoke, mutterings that swelled to an angry clamor arose from the rear of the mob, who had learned what it was that had caused their van to halt, and in the clamor the sheriff's voice was drowned. The weight of those pushing behind forced the leaders of the mob onward, and bit by bit the space between the two forces lessened.

The streets were dimly illuminated by electric arc lights which hung at every crossing. Under one of these lights stood the two figures of the colonel and the sheriff. The white glare of the next light fell upon the advancing column of the strikers, showing a ragged and uneven line of figures; and among them, in the very front, could be seen the forms of women. In the light the crowd seemed for a moment to halt, but again the weight behind pushed forward until the two figures, standing alone, were almost equidistant from the opposing bodies. On both sides of the street windows were open, and the white faces of men and women and children looked on in silence.

Above the angry uproar of the advancing mob the strong

voice of the colonel, commanding them to halt, rang out, and for a moment there was silence.

"If you continue to advance, I shall be compelled to command my men to fire. I command you—I implore you—to obey the sheriff and the law, and to disperse."

"Stand aside!" cried a woman's voice shrilly. "Stand aside and let us pass. We have a right to parade the streets, and if you don't let us pass we'll sweep your boys aside."

Shouts of approval greeted the speaker, and the colonel and the sheriff strove in vain to make themselves heard. Yard by yard the disorderly front of the strikers drew nearer, and slowly the colonel and the sheriff fell back. At last they were swallowed up in the level, immovable ranks of the waiting soldiers, and there was nothing but the stretch of the street between the forces and the waiting faces of the watchers at the windows on either side.

Silently the front rank of the soldiers dropped upon its knees. There were sick hearts and swimming heads in the ranks, for they were only boys—boys from the bank and the office and the store; but they obeyed the words of command and behaved like men. Already the leaders of the mob were approaching the lamp where, but a few moments before, the colonel and the sheriff had stood, and in the pale light the individual faces and figures could be plainly seen. Stones and other missiles now began to reach the soldiers where they waited. Some struck them, and others fell short or flew overhead. Then from one side of the strikers' line came a flash and the sharp report of a revolver. Another followed, and another; and the soldiers waited in silence.

Suddenly one of the men in the front rank, as the irregular firing from the mob went on, leaped to his feet, spun round, and with a shriek fell full length in the roadway before his comrades.

"Steady, boys!" called the colonel, and a howl went up from the mob, who had seen the poor lad fall. And still the dark mass drew nearer, until at last, reluctantly but firmly, came the command:

"Ready! Aim! Fire!"

In an instant from side to side of the street broke out the

rippling line of flames, and the crash of muskets filled the air.
As the reports died away there arose from the mob in front the
shrieks and screams of the wounded, the cries of the terror-
stricken, and the curses and shouts of wrath. On the ground
in front of the line of the strikers those at the windows could
see dark forms stretched—some struggling, and some still forever. The crowd wavered and yelled, but neither retreated nor
advanced.

"Good God! they will not need another volley!" groaned
the colonel.

But even as he spoke the black mass surged forward, and,
with scarcely twenty paces separating them from the muzzles
of the muskets, the word to fire was given again. Again the
quivering line of fire blazed out, and the crash of the discharge
—so infinitely more terrible here in the confined streets of a
city than on the open fields of war—rang out. And now as
the smoke cleared the ground was covered with writhing forms,
and the colonel, sick at heart, said to himself, "Surely that is
enough!"

And the mob no longer advanced. The shouting and clamor
from the rear grew less as those behind, chilled at last and
panic-stricken, fled—fled by the way they had come, and up
side-streets and into alleys. The dark lines of the soldiers stood
stretched across the street as the minutes passed, until where
the mob had been there was no man standing, but only the
dark masses of the forms upon the ground. Then the word to
advance was given, and at last the soldiers moved forward—
no longer to deal death, but to pass among the dead and the
wounded, and do what they could to help and save.

Already ambulances were arriving, and from every house and
all directions men and women poured, until the militia were
compelled to make a cordon across the street in both directions,
and hold the people back with the bayonets.

In all, at the two volleys, forty of the mob had fallen, and
of these nineteen were dead. And two of the dead were
women.

Horace, driving across town from the hospital—where he had
been again to visit Harrington and consult with him in regard to
the disposition of his uncle's body—to call on Miss Holt, heard

the firing, and, bidding the driver to take him to where it came from, reached the spot while the dead and wounded were being gathered upon the ambulances.

Arriving at Jessie's house, he found that the news had already reached her by telephone, and she met him with tears in her eyes.

"Oh, Horace," she sobbed, "it is so terrible! That they should die is bad enough, but that they should be killed in a quarrel with father! What have we done? How could we help it? Are we to blame? It seems somehow as if we must be; but how? What *could* we do?"

"Nothing, darling—nothing in the world," he said, as he took her in his arms. "There could not be a kinder, juster man than your father, nor a sweeter, tenderer woman than his daughter. I do not know your father's affairs; but I know that he can only have sunk money without return in the steel company, and, I fancy, in the street-railway company as well. He has done everything that a just man could do. The companies have paid good wages so long as they could get the money to pay them; and when they cannot get the money, what are they to do? The men must either take less or cease to work."

"But is there no help for it? I know that the companies could not pay them what they wanted. Father went over it all with me. If he had taken everything he had and turned it over to the company — all his real estate, and stocks, and this house, and everything—it would only have been enough to pay them for another month or six weeks. He could have beggared himself, and it would have done no good. But what is so terrible is that the men should not understand this. When they are unjustly treated, I can see how they might strike; but when it is the impossible that confronts them, is there no way of telling them so? Is there no reason in them? Was there nothing we could have done?"

"Nothing. The blood is not on your father's head — nor yet on the heads of the mass of the men. It is a handful of leaders — it may be only one man or a dozen men — who stand between the employers and the men, and *will* not let them know the truth. These leaders make their living by

the work. They saturate the men with false teachings—
teachings of the tyranny of capital, and making them believe
that the employer is their natural enemy. Many of them,
foreigners who have already drunk in the doctrines of the
bomb in Europe, are only too willing to lend their ear to the
same teachings here. And of the rest, some, hearing no
other side, come in time dully and passively to acquiesce in
what is told them, and the others, conscious of their own individual weakness when opposed to the organization of the
unions, keep their peace, and dare not speak."

"But is there no help? Will there be no end to this? Is
there no way to save these men from breaking themselves
against the wall of the impossible, and giving themselves to
be shot because father, and men such as he, do not do things
which they *cannot* do? Is there no way to teach them? Is
there no punishment for the men who urge them on?"

"Not as yet. Help will come. In time the nation and
the world will recognize that the man who, as a leader of a
labor order, persuades men to strike and to riot is as criminal
in his anarchism as the men who, under the shadow of the
red flag, openly advocate the use of dynamite for the destruction of society. It will come. In another generation the
men who do the things that Wollmer and his friends have
done here during the last two months will be treated as the
most dangerous criminals — far more destructive of society
than the man who commits an individual murder."

"But why is it not so now?"

"Because these same men have votes—all these foreigners
who do not know what the American Constitution means—and
our public men to-day dare not speak the truth. It must be
a slow, slow process; a process of education — education of
these men themselves, after they have so far become assimi-
lated into the American people as to be capable of education
—and still more an education of the larger public, an awakening of its conscience to the foulness of public things and
the cowardice of public men to-day. Then, when the strong
manhood of the American people rises and asserts itself,
when the long patience of the nation is overborne, and the
good men — the great silent mass who at present sit back

and care not—band themselves together to wipe out the corruption that is in high places, and the ignorance and the cruelty that is in the low, and carry the government of our country back to the high principles on which it is said to be founded; when the government of our country is made again in fact what it ought to be, the noblest government of earth, instead of what it is, one of the clumsiest and most corrupt, then—! But you have heard me preach before. You know my dreams."

He stopped, smiling at the wide, earnest eyes which looked into his.

"But they are not dreams," she said, simply. "They will be found true. It is this thing that is the dream — when men lead other men to shed blood and be killed. Forty men wounded! Think of it! Think of their wives and children! Oh, it is too horrible! . . . 'One-half of mankind against the other half!'"

Later in the night, in the temporary study which had been arranged in one of the bedrooms on the second floor, Horace spoke to Mr. Holt. He stated his case very simply, and Jessie's father was equally simple and frank in his reply. He had already learned to have a high regard for young Marsh. This, however, was a matter which he should leave to his daughter. There were certain men whom he should do his utmost to dissuade Jessie from marrying if she had seen fit to choose one of them; but he knew her too well to have had any fear of that. If she loved Horace and if Horace loved her as he ought to love her, he, Mr. Holt, would be satisfied.

Horace's thanks were less coherent than sincere. Had he followed his inclinations he would have danced and shrieked; but as it was he said only the commonplace things, and said them only indifferently well.

But as he walked home that night he pondered how blest above other men he was. The rough political awakening that he had received was bitter—infinitely bitter it would have been but for this new-found happiness. But when she was won, what did other things matter? And was not God good? Had he himself not come to know it? It could not be that somewhere, somehow, the political dawn was not at hand.

And he remembered some words of Judge Jessel: " It is not through Populism that salvation will come. It is more likely to be through the reaction against Populism."

XXIX

ON THE SLEEPING-CAR

THE platitudinist and the preacher love to dwell upon the insignificance of the individual man, and the rapidity with which the place of even the greatest is filled after he has gone and his world adjusts itself to his absence. But never could either have found a better text on which to hang a sermon than the death of General Harter.

The news of his death and the strange story which in connection therewith was given to the public could not, even in the presence of the overshadowing sensation of that night battle, fail to fill men's mouths for a day. But his party was too busy hastening to select his successor to mourn him, and in these last days before the election things moved too rapidly for the public to remember a dead man long.

Horace, reading the *World* in the morning, found a pretty compliment to himself when the editor suggested that, did not his youth forbid his election to the office, there was no man in the party who could probably so surely command the support of all men in the party as Horace Marsh. He being impossible, the logic of the situation would seem, the paper said, to point to Mr. Timothy Sullivan as the natural candidate; and Horace, reading, remembered Sancho Panza's aphorism that "if he knew how to make his Christ-cross it would be enough for a good governor." Mr. Timothy Sullivan, however, it appeared, had already been consulted, and had absolutely declined to permit his name to be used. Under these circumstances, the *World* hoped that the party would prevail on Major Bartop to accept the nomination at the eleventh hour.

The article was evidently written after consultation among

the party leaders—probably chiefly at Sullivan's dictation, and Horace was sure that the Irishman was answerable for the compliment to himself—and was intended to arouse a public sentiment in favor of Major Bartop which the major would be unable to withstand. But Horace knew that the major would refuse to be a candidate; and, courteously but contemptuously, he did.

At length, in despair, the leaders pitched upon one Grierson, an unknown man whose only merits were that he had never been anything but a Democrat, and had not character enough to have made enemies.

It was not Grierson's fault that he was not elected. Out of a forlorn hope of such exceeding forlornness, not even the most consummate soldier could have carved success. The advocacy of the strike, with its damning and bloody outcome, must have ruined any party, even if the party were not shattered on the eve of battle by the death of its standard-bearer.

And if the strike killed the party which had supported it, the strike itself ended with those volleys fired on Thirteenth Street.

For some days the strikers were cowed and terrified. Then, in the rush of election, they found themselves forgotten by the public, and when the election was over they had no longer any friends. No man now had any object to gain by conciliating them, and the outburst of the awakened public indignation was too strong for any man in mere quixotism to offer himself as its victim. So far as the employés of the steel company were concerned, they had no longer anything to strike for. The works were destroyed, and there was no possibility of employment. Even if the company should decide to rebuild, it would be years before any workmen of the class of the strikers could be needed.

Late on the night of the election, as soon as it was evident that all chance of Democratic victory was gone, Wollmer left the city. He had nothing to gain by staying. There would be no more subsidies forthcoming from the public treasury; and possibly there would be investigations, and possibly also —a consideration which would probably weigh more heavily

24

with the labor leader—individual strikers, learning how they had been duped and played with, might seek a more immediate and violent satisfaction than the course of the law would afford.

By the clews furnished by Lizzie Silling, the police were enabled to capture and convict the men who were directly responsible for the outrage on the house of Mr. Holt.   Others of the strikers also who were identified as leaders of the mob in the conflict with the militia were found guilty of the death of the one soldier who died of his wounds—the man from the front rank, who had been the first to fall on that ghastly night—and were sentenced to long terms of imprisonment.

And so, as is the way of strikes, the great mass of men found themselves homeless and workless and hungry, objects of public charity.   A few, perhaps among the most innocent at first, but of weaker nature and more easily influenced, afterwards thrust forward into the position of leaders and made to bear the burden of the bloodshed and the guilt, paid for it by wearing out their lives in jail.   The public suffered, directly by the destruction of property and the temporary disturbance of commerce and public affairs, and ten times more indirectly by the annihilation of the great industry of the steel-works.   The only men who profited were the few leaders—Wollmer chiefly, and doubtless others in their degree—who had sold the men who were credulous enough to believe them, and who escaped with such booty as they had made to enjoy it in such peace as their consciences would permit.

Six months afterwards, when the strike and all that belonged to it had ceased to be talked about except when some wanderers found themselves in the neighborhood of the gaunt ruins of the works or among the deserted portions of Milltown, there was a double wedding.   Horace, who was not to be married for a month yet, was able to keep his promise and act as best man for Harrington, who had recovered from his injuries as satisfactorily as the surgeons had dared to hope; and at the altar at which Jessie Masson became Mrs. Harrington, Weatherfield also took her sister Annie for his wife.

The congregation in the little church — the church where Harrington had first seen Jennie — saw that there was a minute's pause before Weatherfield placed the ring on Annie's finger. They could see also that it was because Annie laid her hand on the bridegroom's arm and asked him some question, to which he replied; but not even the minister caught the words, so low were they spoken.

"Once more, Tom," she had said, "and for the very last time—you are sure? Now that you know everything, you are willing to trust me and take me as I am?"

"I am quite sure," was all he said; and a minute later she was his wife.

The Weatherfields stayed quietly at home after the wedding, and Tom went industriously on with the daily work of the printing-office. Harrington, however, took his wife back to Massachusetts to introduce her to his family. A few nights after their return—they had been away for a month—Horace and Barry called at their cosey little home, and they talked of many things. Suddenly, after a pause, Harrington exclaimed:

"Oh, by-the-way, I forgot all about Blakely. You know we were on the train that night?"

"No," said Horace, "I had forgotten it, if I ever knew it."

"Yes; and it was very queer."

"In what way?" Horace asked. "Nobody saw him fall, did they?"

"I am not quite sure," said Harrington, enigmatically.

His wife had left the room, and, leaning forward, he told the tale so far as he had anything to tell.

"Jennie and I," he said, "were sitting in a section about the middle of the car, sitting facing each other, I with my back to the engine. In the next section on the opposite side of the car—so that they were behind Jennie as she sat, but so that I was facing Mrs. Carrington—were the Carringtons. I happened to be looking at her when I saw her apparently catch the eye of somebody behind me—somebody, as I supposed, who was entering the car. You know the kind of look—a sudden glance of secret recognition and no more. I heard some one coming along the aisle behind me, and I saw Mrs. Carrington

raise her eyes to him again. The man came alongside of me
and passed on, and then I saw it was Blakely. He did
not speak to Mrs. Carrington or she to him; but he went
straight on to the second section on her side, so that he was
directly behind her. Carrington, all this time, had been reading his paper. After a bit, when the train began to move, he
got up to go to the smoking-car, and then he saw Blakely.
He leaned over and said something to his wife, and she
flushed up angrily. Carrington then went out. I suppose—let
me see—it was ten minutes afterwards that Blakely went out
too. This time, in passing, as he came up behind Mrs. Carrington, he stooped slightly, and said a few words to her
in an undertone. She replied, but without looking up, and
Blakely strolled out of the car in the same direction as Carrington had gone.

"I had happened to notice it," said Harrington, resuming,
"but did not think much of it all. I am not sure that I
think anything of it now. But it was an hour and a half or
two hours later—nearly ten o'clock—and we were waiting
while our berths were being made up. Jennie was sitting in
some other section, among a lot of valises and things, and I
was standing in the aisle, leaning against a seat and watching
the porter at work. It was one of those sixteen-section cars,
I think they call them, that they run now on the trains that
have a regular smoking-car—the aisle, you know, goes
straight through at the end out to the vestibule, instead of
kinking round a corner to get by the smoking-compartment,
as it used to do. You can look straight out to the platform,
as you can in a day-coach, from the centre of the car. It
happened that I turned my head to the forward end of the
car, and my eye lighted on the door just as a man came to
the glass and looked in. It was Carrington. He did not
come in, but stayed out on the platform, and I saw him open
the vestibule door.

"Again I don't think I thought anything of it, because I
turned to watch the porter. A few minutes afterwards I
happened to look up again, and Carrington was still out in
the vestibule. I looked back to see if Mrs. Carrington had
retired, and she had. Then the porter finished our section,

and I put Jennie's satchel into the lower berth and said good-night to her. I had the upper berth above her.

"While I was saying good-night I was conscious of hearing angry voices. I was too much occupied with my first good-night to my wife to pay much attention to them, and I know that I had a sort of vague idea that it was the conductor swearing at the brakeman or something. A minute later, as I finished buttoning the curtain of Jennie's berth, the door at the end of the car was opened, and Carrington came in. I sort of squeezed myself against the berth to let him pass me.

"It was not until I got an afternoon paper at Buffalo the next day that I saw the news of Blakely's death. They said that his body was picked up at a point where the train passed at ten five. I know that when I took out my watch to wind it up that night it was ten twenty.

"Now I may be talking about nothing at all, and I should never think of mentioning it to anybody except you two fellows, and I hope you won't talk to any one else. And yet —did you ever hear any gossip about any trouble between those two, either about Carrington's wife or anything else?"

He looked at Marsh as he asked the question, and Marsh shook his head and said "Never!"

Which was true.

THE END

www.ingramcontent.com/pod-product-compliance
Lightning Source LLC
Chambersburg PA
CBHW021708110726
47902CB00005B/1101